Slade sto
over her...

He methodically stripped off his fancy white shirt and his eyes never left hers.

"You're drunk, Jim," she said, forcing herself to sit up.

"Not that drunk, Charlee, not nearly that drunk."

He knelt on the edge of the bed and took her small face between his hands, silencing her protest with a deepening kiss. His lips brushed and caressed hers, until she felt mindless and breathless, as if she were melting into him.

His own breathing became labored and erratic, and his eyes glazed with lust as he stood up to unfasten his breeches.

Through heavy lidded eyes Charlee watched him disrobe, realizing what was about to happen, but too drugged by passion to stir or cry out in protest. *This was what you always wanted, from the first day you ever saw him, wasn't it?* Her eyes drank in his lean, sinewy body. Then he was beside her, his hands and lips luring her into oblivious surrender...

ALSO BY SHIRL HENKE

Golden Lady
Love Unwilling
Capture the Sun
*Moon Flower**
*Night Flower**

Published by
WARNER BOOKS   *forthcoming

Cactus Flower

Shirl Henke

WARNER BOOKS

A Warner Communications Company

WARNER BOOKS EDITION

Copyright © 1988 by Shirl Henke
All rights reserved.

Cover illustration by Max Ginsburg

Warner Books, Inc.
666 Fifth Avenue
New York, N.Y. 10103

A Warner Communications Company

Printed in the United States of America

First Printing: November, 1988

10 9 8 7 6 5 4 3 2 1

For Al and Evelyn Brauer,
who raised us both

Acknowledgment

Cactus Flower is a first for my associate Carol Reynard and me. Carol has helped me with plot problems and research, and edited and typed my handwritten scrawl for all our earlier books. But she never before tried her hand at constructing an entire plot. Jim and Charlee's story, complete with an orange tomcat who is bound for trouble and a villainess who schemes to ensnare our hero, is Carol's creation. When she presented me with the outline, I was initially uncertain. The idea was great, but could I write someone else's story? I dug into Texas history, getting a feel for Sam Houston, San Antonio, and British intrigues in the Republic of 1842, filling in the background around Jim and Charlee's tempestuous romance. With a few changes and additions, *Cactus Flower* came to life, and we proceeded with our usual sparring over characterizations and chronology, just as we had always done. In many ways this book was the most fun yet. Charlee and her cat were perpetually in some sort of a scrape, and Carol's ideas for comic scenes allowed me to try my hand at humor, something I'd been hesitant to do earlier. If you laugh and enjoy *Cactus Flower* half as much as we did, our efforts will be richly rewarded.

Carol and I are indebted to a number of people for technical assistance and personal kindness in rendering it. Hildegard Schnuttgen, head of the reference department at Youngstown State University's Maag Library, secured a number of rare resources for us. Among them was an unpublished master's thesis detailing General Woll's campaign in San Antonio. In addition, Mrs. Schnuttgen requested that the Texas State Archives copy for us in its entirety *The Personal Memoirs of Juan N. Seguin from 1834 to the Retreat of General Woll.* They very kindly obliged.

Mrs. Patty Shehabi has verified and frequently corrected my shaky Spanish idiom, and served as well as a fount of information about Hispanic culture. Mrs. Salle Marple was kind enough to put me in touch with the Rosenberg Library in Galveston, a treasure trove of information on that city's layout and commerce during 1842. Father Daniel Venglarik, Ph.D., has patiently answered numerous questions dealing with spiritual and historical aspects of the Roman Catholic Church in the nineteenth century.

Cactus Flower was the first manuscript Carol produced on her new computer. Mr. Walt Magee was of invaluable assistance in helping her select the most suitable equipment. He also made numerous house calls as her troubleshooter while she mastered her wonderful new machine.

Since our story deals with gunrunners and spies, our list of long arms and short arms was lengthy. Our friend, Dr. Carmine V. Delli Quadri Jr., D.O., weapons collector, filled every request for information with his usual meticulous attention to accuracy and detail.

Author's Note

Although Jim Slade and Charlee McAllister are fictional, the cast of *Cactus Flower* is filled with many historical figures, including such greats as the war hero and president Sam Houston, and the intrepid ranger captain John Coffee Hays. Several more obscure characters are also taken from real life. The British charge d'affaires in 1842 Texas was Charles Elliot, although his ticklish request to President Houston on behalf of William Kennedy was born in my imagination. Kennedy himself was a fascinating figure, author of a two-volume work on the Texas Republic, a wily diplomat with shadowy connections in Lord Aberdeen's Foreign Office. Whether or not he was an agent sent to incite the Comanche against the Texians cannot be proven, but he was undoubtably involved in British intrigues to keep Texas from entering the American union. Vincente Cordova and Antonio Perez were pro-Mexican revolutionaries intent on restoring Texas to Santa Anna; they did deal with the Indians. The French mercenary, General Adrian Woll, was a career soldier of outstanding tactical genius, possessed of considerably more integrity than the dictator whom he so ably served.

During the decade of the Republic, Texas was a nation with a complex and exciting history. In my research, a number of sources proved invaluable, especially General Woll's complete campaign reports, written during the fall of 1842 when he made his incursion into San Antonio. This material is included in the Master's Thesis of Ilma M.

Benavides, University of Texas, 1952, *General Woll's Invasion of San Antonio in 1842*. Also of particular help in fabricating the political machinations of my villain Ashley Markham and his cohorts Cordova and Kennedy was *British Interests and Activities in Texas 1838–1846*, by Ephraim Douglass Adams.

Other standard reference works that gave me excellent background on Texas during this period were John Henry Brown's *History of Texas, Volume II*, T. R. Fehrenbach's *Lone Star: A History of Texas and the Texans*, and Walter Prescott Webb's *The Texas Rangers*. For pictorial excellence as well as a fine introduction to the history of Texas in its formative years, I highly recommend *The Texans*, edited by David Nevin, A Time–Life Book in their superb Old West Series.

The definitive reference work on Sam Houston remains, of course, Marquis James's Pultizer Prize–winning work, *The Raven*. In addition to its droll and wonderful insights, I also found M. K. Wisehart's *Sam Houston: American Giant* to be very useful in bringing the genius and humor of this complex man to life. Sam Houston changed the course of history on the North American continent during the nineteenth century. One of my deepest regrets is that he and his European alter ego, Otto von Bismarck, were not contemporaries. To borrow a phrase from Marquis James, what a "fox-lynx game" Houston could have played with the Prussian! I'd bet on Sam.

prologue

San Jacinto Plain, April 22, 1836

The mud was a foot thick, and his boots felt as if they were being sucked off his feet at every step. He headed toward the general's tent, a haphazard affair set beneath the spreading live oak where Houston had interrogated Santa Anna that afternoon. He wondered absently where they had quartered the defeated "Napoleon of the West," as the Mexican dictator styled himself. At least the rain had stopped, he thought. It had seemed everlasting for the past bleak month of desultory marching. The mud was still with them.

"Drought 'n mud are two sure things in Texas," his pa had always said. *Pa.* He felt a tightening in his throat. As he approached the sentry in front of the graying canvas structure, he said a brief, silent prayer he would not be too late.

"Lieutenant Slade to see General Houston," he said to the lank frontiersman leaning on his rifle in front of the tent. He did not expect the guard to salute him. Militiamen were all volunteers and possessed little or no military discipline. God, how well he had seen the truth of that yesterday afternoon!

The Kentuckian, one of Sid Sherman's men, motioned him inside the dilapidated tent, spitting a casual lob of tobacco juice from one corner of his mouth as he spoke.

"Better talk quick, Slade. Gener'l's takin' some corn likker fer th' pain. I don't 'spect he'll be real alert in a spell."

Nodding, Jim Slade entered the tent. The odd yellow light of a flickering tallow candle cast eerie shadows on the heavy canvas walls. Sam Houston half reclined on a makeshift pallet, his right leg elevated by a pillow. The lower leg was swollen and wrapped in thick bandages. Two Mexican musket balls had shattered the bone in several places just above the ankle.

Houston was working despite the cup of whiskey sitting at his left elbow on the floor of the tent. Papers and books lay scattered in untidy stacks around the sickbed, and he was scribbling with a pencil on damp paper. Without stopping his writing, he raised his shaggy head for only an instant and murmured, "At ease, Lieutenant. Sit down in my humble domicile. I'll be free in a moment."

Slade found a battered wooden stool in one corner and gingerly sat on it.

Houston chuckled. "If it'll hold me, it'll hold you," he said as he went on with his report.

Slade smiled at the comparison. General Sam was six feet six and a bit overweight, although his heavy-boned frame carried it well. Jim Slade was an even six feet and whipcord slim. Yes, the stool would hold him. As he watched Houston work, he could see pain etched on the craggy features. Sweat beaded the older man's brow and upper lip; still, he never ceased writing except to sip now and then from the home-distilled painkiller.

My God, he's in agony with that leg, Slade thought, his own anguish forgotten.

When he had filled a page, the general tossed it onto the pile by his side and fixed Slade with a level, friendly stare. "Now, Jim, what is it you need?" He looked at the youth's haggard face. Lord, he couldn't be more than eighteen or nineteen. What the boy had lived through already would kill most men.

"A couple of days before the battle, sir, a messenger from my father's ranch finally caught up to me. My pa's dying, General. He's had another heart attack. I knew when I left he wasn't well, but I hoped . . ." His voice trailed off.

"You hoped we'd whip Santa Anna and you could go home a lot sooner," Houston supplied gently. "Well, the battle is finally over, and I know personally, Lieutenant, that you've done more than your share. Go home to your pa. I'll issue the necessary papers."

"Thank you, sir." Slade stood up and prepared to take his leave, then stopped. "I would just like to say, sir, that I was proud to serve under you and if you ever need me to fight again, I'll be honored."

"That's a hell of an offer, Lieutenant Slade, especially considering what you saw yesterday," Houston said quietly. "I appreciate it." He grimaced in pain as he shifted his shattered leg on the pillow. "*Vaya con Dios, por ahora.* I just might take you up on that offer someday."

As he walked back to his bedroll, Diego Augusto Slade, son of Teresa Magdalena Sandoval de Slade, mulled over the general's parting words, "Go with God, for now." Slade knew Houston was aware of his Mexican ancestry. Indeed, a good number of men in the revolution were Mexicans—Zavala, Seguin, Navarro. With a man like Sam Houston in control, Mexican Texans need fear nothing from the overwhelming numerical superiority of Anglo Texans. But what would the future bring if the general was not in charge? And what did Houston mean about taking him up on his offer? Slade was certain the remark alluded to more than just military service.

Bluebonnet Ranch, April 26, 1836

"You look like you've been through hell, Jimmy. Sometimes talking about it helps." Will Slade's voice was raspy and thin.

Just hearing it made Jim's heart wrench. His beloved father was so wasted. "It was hell, Pa. I don't mean the fighting, I'm used to that. When you're in the middle of it, with enemy soldiers charging while you duck musket balls and return fire, you don't have time to think or to see what's going on around you. No, I don't remember much about the battle at San Jacinto or any of the other times, even against the Comanche years ago."

His father shook his gray head. Jim had been in the ranging companies, volunteers fighting against Indians and raiders, since he was fifteen. But he had never come home like this. Will Slade waited for the boy to continue.

"We had to fall back again and again, always marching east. The rain never stopped, not since we left Gonzalez. We couldn't feed the horses, so we had to order the men to leave them and walk through the mud. There was always talk of mutiny. The general drilled them and tried to make them into a disciplined army, but by the time we got to the Colorado, it was chaos. Civilians running for their lives, men deserting to go for their families, women and babies walking by the side of the road—all of them heard about the Alamo and Goliad. It was a runaway nightmare. Took two days to cross the river." He shook his head in amazement. "I don't know how Houston held them together as well as he did, but by the time we got to Buffalo Bayou, he told the army we were going to fight. The hard core who stayed on were blood crazy by that time. He couldn't control them— none of the officers could.

"You know how long the battle lasted, Pa? Eighteen minutes by General Sam's own watch! We overran them like sleeping sheep! That's when it happened—the butchery went on until nearly dark, for hours after Santa Anna fled and they surrendered. There were Mexican bodies forming a barricade of human flesh across the bayou. The soldiers trying to get away were trapped by their own dead comrades, hundreds of men who had thrown down their weapons, hacked to pieces." Jim Slade sat very still, his face shuttered and blank; only his voice gave away the emotional turmoil roiling inside his soul.

Gently Will Slade said, "At the Alamo and Goliad it was the other way around, remember? No one walked away, not Travis, nor Bowie, nor Fannin. Santa Anna's still alive."

Without looking at the sick man on the bed, his son replied, "That doesn't mean we have to stoop to the level of a vicious dictator. 'A base, unprincipled, bloody monster,' that's what Stephen Austin called *El Presidente*. God, he was right!"

Trying to pull his son back from the dark abyss threaten-

ing him, Will said, "I bet ole Sam was madder than a
boiled owl when his men broke ranks."

In spite of the horror of his memories, Jim had to join in
the faint humor. "Yep. I never heard a man swear like that,
and I thought Weevils was better than anyone I knew.
Houston has him beat cold. He stayed on horseback in spite
of a shattered leg. He had two horses shot out from under
him, running the length of the plain, beating the men back
and yelling orders to the officers to stop the carnage and
regroup the men. I'm just glad it's over now, Pa. You and I
can go back to what we should have been doing all along—
working the land in peace. We'll—"

"Not me . . . you, son," Will cut him off softly. "I know
Doc has told you how I am. I'd hoped to make it a while
longer before joining your mama. You're still awfully young
to have sole responsibility for a place as big as Bluebonnet,
but that's the way it must be."

"Pa, no! You'll pull through. You did last year." He took
the shrunken, veiny hand in his dark, strong one.

William Emory Slade's body was wasting away, but his
determination was as iron hard as ever. "You can't stop
what's meant to be, son. No, you'll do fine with Bluebonnet. Turn it into the finest ranch between San Antonio and
Nacogdoches. But there is one thing you must promise me
before I die." His clear blue-gray eyes compelled Jim to
return his gaze.

"You know your mother's cousin, Simon Aguilar, who
lives just south of San Antonio. Don Simon has a daughter,
Tomasina Constanzia, who is about your age. She'll be
returning from school in England in a few weeks. She's his
only child, as you are mine."

Jim did not like the direction the conversation was taking.
"Pa, I don't think—"

"I want you to marry her," his father interrupted in a flat,
no-nonsense voice, stronger than it had been since Jim
returned home.

"Has the lady in question been consulted, or have you
and Don Simon already made all the arrangements without
us?" There was a slight edge to his attempt at levity.

"Simon and I have discussed it, and he plans to tell her

as soon as she gets settled at home. At eighteen she's old enough to marry. I'd rather have you wait a few years, son, but after all you've been through growing up on the frontier, well, I know you're man enough for the responsibility of a wife and family."

"That's not true, Pa. Just because I can fight or manage livestock, it doesn't mean I'm ready for a wife."

Will's eyes twinkled. "Sometimes fighting is the only way to manage a wife! And there *are* compensations. I've met the girl, Jimmy. She's a real beauty. In fact, she reminds me a lot of your mama." His eyes became wistful as he remembered a woman dead for nearly a decade now.

"That doesn't change the fact I'm too young to get married, Pa," Jim protested earnestly.

"You too young for Susie Rader, Annabeth Sims, or any of those tarts in San Antonio?" At his son's guilty flush, Will pressed his advantage. "Son, I know you've been sowing wild oats since you were fifteen. I'm just worried about you sowing something else and having to marry some ignorant sod farmer's daughter like that Sims girl. Those loose women aren't for you. They're from inferior bloodlines. I want you to marry quality, someone worthy of you, an educated, genteel lady."

"Like Don Simon's daughter?"

"Yes, like Don Simon's daughter. Her grandfather's served at the royal court of the Spanish kings. She's been educated at the best European schools, and she is downright lovely. Here, look for yourself." He struggled to reach the drawer of his bedside table when a sudden fit of coughing overcame him.

"Lay back, Pa. I'll get it." Jim slid the drawer open and extracted a portrait, an exquisite miniature of a young woman with long black hair and a porcelain-white complexion. Her large dark eyes and haughty aquiline features were arrestingly beautiful. Looking at the worn old man on the bed, he sighed in defeat. "So this is what the future Mrs. Slade looks like. Hello, Tomasina."

St. Genevieve County, Missouri, August 17, 1836

"Miz Charlee! Miz Charlee! Where dat chile be?" Mose

swore to himself as he thrashed through the dense underbrush, searching for his young charge, twelve-year-old Chastity Charlene McAllister. "Done gwine off squirrel huntin' agin, make no mattah Mistah Richard Lee packin' an' Miz Lillian fit ta be tied." The old slave shoved the scratchy ragweed and goosefoot plants aside as he cleared a path toward the sound of a shot echoing from the spring. When he found her, the small child had laid her old musket on the ground and was efficiently skinning a large red fox squirrel. Her brown hair hung in stringy wisps across her face and shoulders where her long pigtail had been torn loose by tree branches and brush. The thin, generously freckled face looked up, a grin splitting it, revealing even, white teeth.

"I bagged me three today, Mose. We'll feast good tonight. That oughta prove ta Richard Lee that I can take care of myself in his big ole Texas!"

"Yore mama be lookin' foah ya. She doin' poorly, Miz Charlee, whut wif Massah Richard Lee goin' off 'n all." The reproof in his voice was softened by the warm light in his eyes as he took the heavy antique firearm from the girl and accompanied her to the farmhouse.

"Your father let that girl run wild for too long, Richard Lee McAllister, tagging along after you and your wastrel friends, hunting, carousing, Lord knows what all." Lillian McAllister's slim, elegant hands rubbed together in nervous agitation as she spoke in her soft, melodious voice.

Richard Lee smiled his crooked, engaging grin and put his arm around her thin shoulders. "Now, Mama, I know I've been a bad influence on Charlee, specially since Dad died. That's just one more good reason for me to leave. You have Mose and Lizzie to handle the chores for you here. I'll get me a land claim. They're giving away over six hundred acres per single man in Texas now! Free! When I send for you and Charlee, I'll be rich!" He regarded his frail, golden-haired mother, reluctantly meeting the anguished plea in her china-blue eyes. At forty-one, after bearing Richard Lee and his sister, and surviving four stillbirths,

Lillian McAllister was like a fragile flower. But she had aged since Micah died, no doubt there.

"Texas is a barren wilderness full of wild savages," she protested.

"It's been settled now by hardy frontiersmen from Kentucky, Tennessee, and Louisiana," Richard Lee countered.

"I rest my case," Lillian replied, arching one delicate golden brow at the youth standing in front of her. The young man looked the way Micah had thirty years ago. Where did all our dreams go? she wondered. The same place Richard Lee's will go someday. "I need your influence with Chastity, Richard Lee. She'll listen to you about school, dressing like a lady, learning to mind her manners."

Just then the subject of their discussion entered the parlor of the small tidy house, dressed in her elder brother's childhood castoffs, baggy homespun trousers and a brown cotton shirt tied in a loose knot at her waist. Her feet were bare and grass stained, and a smudge of blood reddened her nose where she had rubbed it while cleaning the squirrels. Carelessly swinging her fat braid behind her, she sauntered gracefully across the polished wooden planks onto the braided rug where her mother and brother stood.

There was more than a hint of willful rebellion lurking under the surface of her surprisingly husky voice as she said, "Mama, don't keep pesterin' Richard Lee 'bout that manners business for me, please."

"And why shouldn't I? Look at you, Chastity! The poorest colored boy in the county dresses better than you!"

"Smells better, too," teased her brother, catching a whiff of squirrel entrails and riverbottom slime.

"Harumph. That all the thanks I get for bringing in three big squirrels for tonight's dinner, Richard Lee! I knocked one out of the top of that ole cottonwood by the bend of the creek. You shoulda seen that sucker drop! Clean head shot, by damn!"

"Chastity! You know better than to use such language and act so crude! Go to your room and I'll have Lizzie heat your bath water. I've laid out a lovely dress for you to wear."

"I only wanted to show Richard Lee I could make it in

Texas, Mama. I'm sorry." As if heading to her execution, Charlee trudged forlornly toward her room, the bath, and the dress.

Dawn streaked the eastern sky with vivid fuchsias and reds as the sun ascended in a molten ball of fire. Richard Lee finished tying the last of his packs to his brown gelding's saddle. He had just bid farewell to his tearful mother in the house and was eager to be on his way.

"Time to go, little sis. Gonna be a scorcher again today, and I better get me a good start on the heat." Charlee was special to him, and seeing the tears welling up in her big green eyes, he leaned down and planted a kiss on her nose.

"Now, don't take on so. I'll be a big *empresario* down there before you know it, an' we'll all be rich, kitten."

"You can't be an *empresario* now, Richard Lee," Charlee replied in exasperation. "That was only when Texas belonged to Mexico, and they gave big land grants to men who brought in settlers," she said with smug twelve-year-old dignity. Then she added teasingly, "You ain't the onliest one who reads newspapers, big brother."

"Well, Texas is an independent country now, little cat, and the Texian government is still offerin' free land, over six hundred acres for a single man! Why, Sis, you can't imagine how big the place is—it goes on clear to sundown. I'll stake me a claim and get me some of them wild mustangs 'n longhorn cows. We're gonna be rich. Just you wait 'n see!"

"Then why can't I come along *now*? I can ride 'n I can shoot. I'm a hell of a better shot 'n you, admit it, Richard Lee McAllister! I can tan deer hides 'n bake bread, skin out a rabbit or pluck a wild turkey clean in two shakes of a mule's ass. I can—"

"You sound like one of them terrible rivermen, with all your braggin' and swearin', Charlee. You know how much Mama wants you to be a lady. You have to stay here and grow up for her, the way she wants. Dad and I were wrong to take you with us so much, like you was another boy. It ain't fittin' for a girl. Look, I promise to send for you as soon as it's safe, and to show you I mean it . . ." He took her hand and they trudged from the barn down toward the spring-fed creek, where a tall stand of cottonwood trees grew.

The tallest one was their carving tree, gnarled and scarred from the use of their whittling knives. Richard Lee and Charlee had recorded all the triumphs and tragedies of their young lives on it; their birth dates, his first girlfriend's name, her first kitten's name, the date he shot his first deer. Now he gravely took out his knife and attacked a smooth place, carving a large rectangular box on it. Inside the box he carved "G. T. T.," then his initials, "R. L. M.," and the date, August 18, 1836. Just below that line in bold letters he whittled "C. C. M." "As soon as I send for you 'n Mama, you come down here and fill in that date."

"What does 'G. T. T.' mean, Richard Lee?" Her eyes were wide and bright green in the clear morning light.

He let out a whoop and laughed. "Men are carvin' it on their barn doors and fenceposts from Missouri to Maine, kitten, leavin' the past behind an' headin' west. G.T.T. —Gone to Texas!"

chapter
1

Bluebonnet Ranch, 1842

The afternoon sun was hot for so early in spring, its rays warming Richard Lee McAllister mercilessly as he paced by the side of the pond. Sweat ran down his face, soaking his homespun shirt. The water looked cool and inviting, but he had serious business to transact, no time for swimming. In agitation he kicked a pebble from the dry ground toward the slope of the pool, where it bounced into the water with a resounding *plop* and vanished beneath the ripples.

"Damn, where's Markham!" Richard Lee swore and

paced some more. It was just like that arrogant Englishman to keep him waiting. A war of nerves, that's what he thinks he's playing. Well, he told himself, I grew up hunting in the Missouri woods. I know how to wait. Remembering home made him think of Charlee. Lordy, she would be eighteen now, a grown-up young lady. He could scarcely believe it possible. The content of her letters gave little indication of the changes he knew must have taken place in her life. "Soon, Charlee, soon we'll all be back together again. I swear it," he promised her, whispering in the still afternoon heat.

Engrossed in his nervous pacing, the young man never heard the faint rustle of the willows behind him—a careless error for an old squirrel hunter. Then a twig snapped in the still heat, bringing him out of his reverie. He pivoted on one foot, but he was too slow; the blow aimed at the back of his head caught him in the temple instead. Richard Lee dropped to the rocky earth.

As he nudged the still form with his elegantly booted foot, Markham observed absently that McAllister looked taller sprawled full length.

A faint breeze gave welcome relief from the glare of the sun that baked the earth falling in chunks onto the coffin. The large crowd was silent out of respect for the deceased. Jacob Carver had been one of the "Old Three Hundred," an original pioneer who had come to Texas in November of 1821 to settle on Stephen Austin's vast land grant. Like most of the industrious Yankees Austin sponsored, Jake prospered in the wild new land of his adoption. He had arrived in Texas with three cows and two ponies. Now Carver Plantation ran thirty thousand head of cattle over forty thousand acres. Carver had been a county commissioner and a member of the upper chamber of the Republic's congress for the past year, until his untimely death at the age of forty-six.

Jim Slade looked across the clearing, over the gaping wound of the grave that was now being closed, but his attention was not on the burial. For as long as he could remember, his own life had been filled with sudden death; it was a part of life. Rather, his gaze was drawn to the woman standing on the far side of the grave, Jake Carver's young widow, Tomasina.

Damn, he swore to himself as he studied her stoically composed face, she's still the most beautiful woman alive. The passing of six years had only refined the cameo perfection of her features.

Slade's preoccupation with bittersweet memories abruptly ended when his companion, Leandro Velasquez, cleared his throat and said, "Everyone is leaving, Jim. Do you wish to offer your condolences to the widow?" He shifted his weight uncertainly, noting the faraway expression on his boss's face and the way Slade's eyes followed Tomasina Carver as she walked toward the waiting carriage. With a shock, Lee thought, He's still in love with her.

Slade ran his fingers through his hair and donned his hat. He looked at the slim, dark youth and said, "What, Lee? Oh, yes, I suppose it's expected that I call on her, but not today. In the press of this crowd she has too many people to cope with already. Later."

Slade waited and brooded for almost a week, then rode into San Antonio once more and reined in Polvo by the big stone and mortar house on Soledad Street, just off the Main Plaza. When old Don Simon had died, the house had gone to his daughter and her husband. Now the young widow resided in the lovely Spanish mansion, where she had first met Jim Slade.

From her sitting-room window Tomasina watched him dismount with the careless ease of a man born to ride and tether his big buckskin to the rail. "So, Diego, at last you come to me," she breathed low, then gave a soft, exultant laugh.

At Jake's funeral mass, she had watched Jim surreptitiously. He seemed older and more guarded. Well, it had been six years. But his long, lean body with its corded muscles still resembled a young cougar, poised, restless, ready to lash out. Dangerous. Yes, even as an uncertain youth Jim Slade had been dangerous. As a man of twenty-five, he would be a most formidable enemy. Ashley had better take care, she mused.

Tomasina considered her silver-gray dress trimmed with jet beads. She inspected her appearance critically as she smoothed the rustling pale silk. The subdued colors of mourning favored her gleaming black tresses and clear ivory skin. Patting the thick coil of hair at the nape of her neck, she glided to the door.

Tomasina made a grand entry. As she descended the spiral stairs to greet Jim in the foyer, she remembered the night they met. It had been noisy with music and laughter, the joyous sounds of life. Soon it would be so again.

As he watched her float down the winding steps, Jim fought a sudden impulse to spring up and clasp her ethereal beauty in his arms. Get ahold of yourself, Slade—you're not a green boy anymore, he told himself. He stood patiently at the foot of the stairs, his lips twisted cynically into a half smile.

His face was harder than she remembered. A premonition flitted through her mind, but she dismissed it once she felt the warm, callused clasp of his long fingers curving around her small, pale hands.

"Diego. How good of you to come."

He raised her hands to his lips in a brief, brushing salute, then disengaged gently and stood back to look at her. "Mourning becomes you, Tomasina. I'm very sorry about Jake."

Noting with satisfaction that his eyes lingered on her body, Tomasina nodded gravely and ushered Slade into the vast *sala*. "I had a kind and indulgent husband, as we both know, Diego."

"And a rich one," he replied evenly, lifting one thick golden brow.

She smiled serenely, ignoring the barb. "Rich, yes, and much older than I."

"He was a decent man, Sina. I honestly hope you made him a good wife." He ignored her invitation to sit beside her on the settee and went to a small window, where he stared through the iron grillwork.

"And why ever shouldn't I have been a dutiful wife,

Diego?'' Tomasina gave a mock pout, watching his back stiffen as he replied.

''Maybe because you didn't love him.'' He turned to face her now.

''That is not fair, Diego. You presume too much. Just because—''

''Just because we were once engaged,'' he interrupted her. ''I thought you loved me, Sina. But then the senator came along and all that changed.'' He stared harshly at her stricken face.

''Perhaps it did not change, Diego. What would you say to that?'' She heard a small hiss of his breath as he took a step toward her, then stopped himself.

''I guess that's what I really came to find out, Sina, not to offer my condolences. I admired Jake, and I feel like a fox in the chicken coop now. I should have waited longer.'' He began the restless pacing that had always reminded her of a caged cat.

''I'm glad you did not wait, Diego.'' She rose from the settee and walked hesitantly toward him. ''I . . . I saw you at the church and I thought . . . that is, I hoped you would come back here after the burial, but you did not. I need your strength, *querido*.'' She stood in front of him, a vision of beauty as she stared into the harsh, angular planes of his face.

Slade made no move to touch her, but the anguish in his voice betrayed how desperately he fought his own desires. ''Why? Why, Sina! If you loved me, why did you marry Jake?'' He had not asked it then, had sworn he would never ask. But the words were torn from him now.

A hint of unshed tears glistened in her eyes as she replied, ''I was a child, a foolish seventeen-year-old girl, under the sway of my Tia Dolores. Padre favored you, but his sister wished me to marry an older, more stable man. She was my constant companion, Diego, my *dueña* all those years I spent in England. I had not seen Padre since I was thirteen. Everything in Texas was new, unsettling, so foreign.''

''And I had just come back from the conquering army that broke the Mexican yoke and freed Texas,'' he said, scowling at her.

"You have always seemed much more Texian than *Tejano*, for all you are half Sandoval. I was afraid, Diego, afraid of your recklessness, your bold advances"—she colored deeply—"your passions. Tia Dolores gave me no peace after she found us in the courtyard the evening of the *baille*. Oh, *querido*, there was so much I did not understand!" She placed a small, elegant hand on his coat sleeve.

Slade, too, recalled that night, brilliant with stars, warm and languorous. He had brashly taken a delicate, sheltered girl into his embrace and had kissed her with all the fury that a sexually frustrated eighteen-year-old male could muster. He was no novice with women, even then, but from the time he had laid eyes on Tomasina, he had wanted no other. In her innocence, she must have had no way of knowing how she affected him.

"Did I really frighten you so much?" He took one callused fingertip and ran it experimentally down her cheekbone and over her delicate jawline.

"I did not know what I felt. It was all so new, and when Tia came storming out and dragged me away, screaming at me, I had no time to think about it. She hounded me to go to confession that very night. The next day Jacob came to call, right after mass."

"How convenient," he scoffed angrily. For the first time in six years, a great many things were beginning to make sense to him.

"I'm sure he was summoned by Tia Dolores. He was so calm and gentle, making no physical demands, offering me security and respect." She paused and looked into his tawny eyes, taking his hand and pressing it to her cheek. "I have learned, Diego, that respect is a cold, comfortless word and security is merely another name for suffocation. He loved me in his own way, and I tried to be a good wife to him. But what is done, is done. That part of my life is over now. I have seen so little of you in six years. You are changed, Diego."

He took her hands in his and led her slowly back to the settee. "I'm six years older," he said gently.

"And so am I, *querido*. I only hope I have changed as

much for the better as you have." She lowered thick black lashes and sat down beside him.

"You were and always will be perfection, as you well know, Sina. Maybe we've both grown up, though. That's the important thing. I made my father an unwilling promise that I would marry you, sight unseen. But the moment I laid eyes on you, I was lost. I've loved you ever since the first time I walked into this very room and saw you. I still love you, Tomasina." He looked into her eyes, willing her to make the next move, but not forcing the issue, not pulling her into his embrace. She must come to him on her own.

Sensing his control and knowing what he wanted of her, Tomasina responded hesitantly at first, leaning forward, her hands sliding up his arms, her lips joining his in a soft, tentative kiss. She breathed, "And I love you, Diego."

As he rode slowly toward Bluebonnet, Slade relived the scene in the *sala* over and over, recalling her words of love and contrition, her lavender perfume, her soft flesh. Why didn't he feel more exultant? After years of bitterness and regret, he was finally going to get his wish and fulfill his oath to Will at the same time.

He considered the fact that they must wait a decent interval out of respect for Jake's memory. A year was a long time, but after enduring the past six, he knew he could stand one more. Still, it all seemed so easy, so pat, as if Sina had known he would come to her. "Maybe that's what's rankling me," he said aloud to Polvo. "Well, if the lady thinks she'll call the tune with me, I have a few surprises for her. I'm not a doting older man." He chuckled, realizing that he was not the boy Sina remembered, either.

First he must settle the matter of Rosie. He frowned, acknowledging she was another reason for the vague sense of uneasiness that followed his covert engagement to Tomasina. He must bid his mistress farewell. There would be enough gossip when he began to court Jake's widow. He could never keep an engaging saloon doxy living at the ranch at the same time!

Rosalie Parker was a strikingly pretty woman of twenty-seven, with lustrous chestnut hair and bright hazel-green eyes. She had worked in theaters and dance halls from Tallahassee to Galveston. Jim had found her in Houston a little over ten years ago. After several seasons of hard work, he was becoming quite wealthy and could afford to keep a woman in style.

Now he would have to pay her off, but he'd do it in style as well. Rosie had always been as good a sport out of bed as in. He hoped she would continue to be when he made his announcement.

The minute Jim walked in that night, Rosalie knew something was wrong and suspected it pertained to Tomasina Carver. He had never spoken of her, but servants did talk, especially the young vaquero Leandro. He had told her much about the beautiful *Tejana* who had married an older man several years ago and was now widowed. Knowing Jim would explain in his own good time, Rosie did not inquire as they ate dinner in companionable silence.

The green cotton dress she wore complimented her eyes and flattered her ample curves. As Jim finished his coffee, signaling the end of the meal, she rose and came around the back of his chair to place her fingers on his temples, kneading the tension from his brow with soft, deft strokes. Then she planted a trail of soft kisses across his throat and chest where his shirt lay open. He reached up and ran a hand through her hair, feeling the rippling, silky flow of its length.

"Rosie, I have something to tell you. I should have done it at dinner, but—"

She interrupted him with a fierce kiss, then put her fingers on his lips. "I know, but it can wait till later, can't it, darlin'?" *One last time for me, Jim, please,* her eyes pleaded silently. He stood up and drew her into his embrace. They walked slowly to the stairs and climbed them.

She had always occupied a small, sunny bedroom at the rear of the upstairs hall. As she moved past his door and led him toward hers, he pulled her gently back, nuzzling her neck. "My room tonight—the bed's bigger."

With a muffled giggle, she followed him into the dark room. He lit a fat tallow candle on the bedside table and then stood still, watching her undress. She slowly unfastened the tiny green buttons of her basque until her large breasts were covered only by a thin, lacy camisole. With languorous ease she slid one arm, then the other free of her long green sleeves. She dropped the dress to the floor with a twitch of her hips.

"You have a splendid body, Rosie girl, you know that?" He stepped across the floor and pulled her to him, feeling the soft mounds of her breasts pillow against his chest.

"Mmm, so do you, Jimmy boy." She tugged the crisp white shirt from his sun-bronzed torso, while nuzzling the thick golden hair of his chest. He ran his hands around her buttocks and then grabbed them roughly in his palms, cupping her derriere and lifting it to pull her stomach against his aroused groin.

"Get those pants off, lover," she said in mock command as she pushed him toward the bed, pressing her hands against his chest until he fell backward onto the mattress. Quickly, she knelt and tugged his boots and pants off. When he lay naked across the bed, she tossed the last of her scanty underthings on the pile of clothing and slid alongside him. For several minutes they lay side by side, kissing and fondling.

If he was inclined to savor their farewell, she was impatient to feel him buried inside her. Boldly, she caressed his shaft until he moaned in pleasure and rolled her on top of him. "Greedy little Rosie," he gasped out between thrusts, feeling the frantic, joyous working of her hips. His hands grasped her buttocks and slowed her movements.

Slade silenced her murmuring complaint with a searing kiss and let her work her wiles on him. She gradually increased the tempo of their joining until he was as frantic as she. When she arched upward and dug her nails into his biceps, gasping and crying his name, he spilled himself deeply within her. She collapsed onto his chest and he cradled her in his arms while they exchanged soft, affectionate kisses.

After several quiet moments, he reluctantly sat up against the headboard. "I do have to talk to you, Rosie," he said seriously.

Pulling herself up next to him, she covered them both with the sheet and snuggled in his arms. Before he could continue, she said, "You have to tell me you're going to marry your widow lady and I have to go. I understand, Jim." Her voice was low and calm. She was proud of its steadiness.

"How the hell did you know that? I just talked to Sina this afternoon for the first time in six years!" He looked in amazement at her dear face, so strong and composed, so lovely.

She smiled sadly and kissed his neck. "Hired help does gossip, you know, and I was always curious why a stallion like you was still unmarried. Your bein' engaged to Tomasina Aguilar before she married Jake Carver is common knowledge. Now she's a widow, and you come back from visiting her with the weight of the world on your shoulders. Not much to figure, darlin'. I only hope she's got more sense this time than the last."

He let out a small chuckle. "Rosie, my wonderful, honest girl, I do believe you are worth any ten women alive."

"But you're goin' to marry your lady anyway. You'll be a faithful husband to her and raise half a dozen handsome yellow-haired sons, right?"

"I hope so, Rosalie, I hope so. It's what Pa wanted, what Bluebonnet needs. I swore to him I'd marry Sina, even though I didn't want to at first."

"What changed your mind?" She studied his face intently.

"I met the lady in question. Call it love at first sight, I guess," he confessed ruefully.

"And you still feel that way... after all these years?" Rosalie was doubtful.

"Oh, I'm not a starry-eyed, eighteen-year-old boy who'll let her every wish be my command, no. But I do desire her, and she has all the qualities I want in a wife. She says she loves me now that she's old enough to know her own mind and be free of her family. I believe her. The hard part's going to be waiting out the period of mourning for Jake. For decency's sake it should be something over a year."

"A year! Jesus, Jimmy, what's she tryin' to do, kill you to

test your loyalty?'' She sat bolt upright. ''You can't go one week, much less a year!''

He laughed and pulled her back into his arms. ''Well, I'll just have to learn to curb my baser impulses.'' At her skeptical expression and snort of disbelief, he went on. ''I don't mean I'll be celibate for the next year, just that I'll have to be a little more discreet in seeking out my necessary pleasures.''

''And that means no more live-in women, for sure. We've caused enough high-tone noses to be out of joint already, what with my livin' in your house so open. Tomorrow—''

He interrupted her. ''Rosie, I'm not turning you out penniless. There'll be a nice poke sack of gold waiting for you. Where would you like to go?''

Rosalie considered, knowing he'd be generous. She was touched by his concern for her welfare. ''I just might buy me passage west to California. I hear there are lots of big Mexican ranchers and even some rich Yankee sea captains settled out there, just lookin' for a good time. It should be fun, darlin'. Like I was sayin', tomorrow I pack. Tonight...'' Her words trailed off as she ran her hands over his body in devilish ways. ''Ah, Jimmy boy, you're gonna miss me.''

chapter
2

The girl was slight, barely over five feet tall, fine boned, and slim. Her brownish hair was partly tucked into an untidy bun that the sticky Missouri humidity was trying its best to undo. Wisps hung damply on her forehead and neck. She knelt by the fresh graveside and placed a small bouquet of jonquils beneath the rough oaken cross upon which was inscribed simply: Lillian McAllister 1795–1842.

Pushing the hair from her eyes and forcing back burning tears, Charlee rose. "I reckon you'll find peace here, Mama, next to Papa. It's where you always wanted to be buried." Her voice almost broke as she realized how premature Lillian McAllister's death had been. A typhoid epidemic had claimed her while she was nursing the other victims. Now she lay beside Micah, her beloved husband. Charlee was left all alone. But only for the present, she assured herself resolutely, renewing her determination to find her brother, Richard Lee. She had distant kin, her pa's cousins in St. Louis, who said they'd take her in. Even now, Cousin Burt waited for her at the house.

Charlee smoothed her wrinkled black skirt. Lordy, how she hated skirts, so hot in the sticky misery of early spring humidity. Wistfully she thought of her cool, comfortable old shirt and pants, hidden in a satchel upstairs in her bedroom. Mama had forced her to wear ladies' clothes for the past year or so, ever since her figure had begun to show signs of maturing. Charlee viewed her skimpy curves with innate distrust and longed to return to the carefree days of being a tomboy. But that could never be, especially now with Mama dead and Cousin Burt and his prissy wife Maude waiting to take her to St. Louis.

As she walked slowly up the lane, Charlee couldn't help smiling a bit, despite her sorrow. Wouldn't her dour older cousins be in for a surprise when they awakened tomorrow and found her gone! She had it all planned, right down to finding a place for Mose and Lizzie. Her mother had freed them in her will, drawn up the year Micah died. Without her cousin's knowledge, Charlee had sold the small acreage to Cy Forrister, a neighbor and lifelong friend of the McAllister family. He had given his word to her that he would allow Mose and Lizzie to live in their cabin on the farm for the rest of their lives. She was sure that once Cousin Burt found her gone, he would honor the sale.

Charlee had received a fair price for the land, a little nest egg that would enable her to make her escape from Burt and Maude. She would head out to Texas to find Richard Lee.

Texas! The very sound of the word filled her with quivering anticipation, the big, rich, wild, free, uncivilized

Republic of Texas. Imagine going to live in a foreign
country! Well, not really foreign with the former Tennessee
governor Sam Houston as president and a whole host of
Kentucky, Missouri, and Virginia men in the legislature and
cabinet. No, Texas was full of Americans and someday
would be part of the United States. Hadn't Richard Lee said
so?

Thinking of her brother, Charlee felt less alone. Now that
Mama was gone, there was nothing to hold her in Missouri.
Richard Lee had cautioned her to wait until he could send
for her and their mother, but Charlee knew what she must
do. Waiting was no longer acceptable.

Her steamer ticket had been purchased secretly last week
while she had been in town, and her possible sack was
hidden beneath the bed in her room, ready to go. There
remained only one ritual she must complete.

Taking a penknife from her pocket, Charlee headed for
the stand of cottonwoods by the stream. In the fading
afternoon sunlight she read the carvings inside the oblong
patch now grayed with age on the tree trunk. Had it truly
been six years since Richard Lee had made his marks?
Grimly she put the date "3-19-42" and "G. T. T." beneath
her initials. There, she had matched her brother's markings.
In a few years weather would age the new wood until it
looked the same as Richard Lee's carving. Where would she
be when her mark was gray and smooth?

Nervously Charlee scanned the murky depths of the river.
It was the color of blood, rightly named the Red River,
swollen by the dismal, cold rain. It seemed that she had
endured the pulsing vibrations of steamboats forever, first
down the Mississippi, then backtracking northwest across
Louisiana on the Red to reach her first debarkation point on
dry land, Natchitoches. Lordy, it would feel good to sleep
on solid ground once more! Unseasonably heavy spring
rains had raised the river to flood tide and set adrift dangerous debris, uprooted tree trunks, even pieces of boats, and
docks torn from their moorings. After several near colli-
sions, the steamer was docking safe and sound, and none
too soon for Charlee!

In the dim twilight the bleak river settlement looked shabby and forbidding. What to do next? First she must navigate the rickety gangplank and set foot on terra firma once more. After that everything else would be easier. Grimly Charlee resolved never to become a sailor. She hoped the rivers between here and her destination were all small and easily crossed. So intent was she on not looking down at the rushing water that she did not notice the tall, thickset man in her path. No sooner had she stepped onto the dock than he reached for her, grabbing her possible sack and scooping her into his arms.

Whiskey-rancid breath assaulted her nostrils as the reeling welcoming committee of one spoke. "Wal, pretty li'l thang! Yew be all alone and so be I. Yew'n me kin have us a time, I 'spect."

Frantically looking around for help, Charlee squirmed furiously against the greasy girth of her assailant. No assistance was forthcoming; all the other passengers were off the waterfront already. The captain had made it clear to her that a young, single woman traveling alone was no better than she ought to be. He would probably feel she had gotten just what she deserved if this animal raped her right here on the dock! When Captain Morse's attempts to lure Charlee to his cabin had met with a swift, unsubtle rebuff, he had left the girl to fend for herself. Of course, fending for herself had become her long suit ever since her pa died and her brother left home.

"Let me go, ya plug-ugly bastard!" Charlee's elbow connected with the drunk's solar plexus. All the air left his lungs in a *whoosh*. Just as he released her, her kneecap bashed his privy parts with agonizing accuracy. The stench of his breath almost caused her to lose the initiative, but Charlee jumped away as he fell to the ground. Grabbing her possible sack and small portmanteau, she fled up the levee without looking back.

One night's lodging in a cheap hotel was enough to convince her that Natchitoches was no place for a girl alone. Charlee must become Charley. Once more she would be a boy. As she stripped off the skirts and petticoats her mother had lovingly decreed she wear, Charlee looked scornfully at the sign posted in her room.

NO SPITTING ON THE WALLS. The profuse brown stains around and over it indicated the way the injunction was customarily observed.

"In this kinda place, I better be a boy. Sure is a pain in the ass bein' female, that's for certain!" Being a girl was cumbersome and restrictive, and invited all sorts of unwelcome attention, like the drunk's on the riverfront last night. Anyway, who in hell wanted to wear corsets and long hot skirts, curl her hair, and bat her eyes at men? Bah! What a stupid waste of time!

Charlee inspected her appearance after binding her breasts and tucking her shirt loosely into her shabby pants. Not bad, she thought, but she needed to do something with all that hair! Resolutely she braided it into a tight coil, which took some time since it fell well below her waist and was thick and curly. She wadded the braid up and tucked it beneath a weatherbeaten felt hat. Somehow, cutting it would be too much a betrayal of Mama. Now, she'd smear a bit of dirt across her nose and slump like an adolescent boy to hide any hint of bosom—perfect!

With a gamin grin, she picked up her possible sack. The portmanteau had her girl-things in it—dresses, books, and such. She would simply have to leave it behind. She had her cash, some spare shirts and socks, her cooking gear, and a dog-eared daguerreotype of Mama in the sack. As an afterthought, she stuffed in one dress, a loose and comfortable gingham weave. With her possibles slung across her shoulder, "Charley" McAllister slipped from "his" room in the hotel. As a boy, she could sign on one of the settlers' trains leaving Natchitoches. She knew she must have company to cross the Sabine into Texas and follow the long road southwest to the Bluebonnet Ranch, where Richard Lee was foreman.

For about ninety dollars Charlee bought a spavined old nag that would, with luck, get her across Texas. She had little time to find a better deal and so took the horse despite its poor condition. The small wagon train pulling out the next day would take a lone youth only if he provided his own transportation.

In return for passage and food, "Charley" McAllister chopped wood, hitched up oxen and did any other camp chores assigned her. She also displayed her hunting skills by borrowing a musket and bagging squirrels, rabbits, and even an occasional deer for the train cook pots. Game certainly seemed plentiful in western Louisiana, and Texas abounded with every variety, ripe for the shooting. She eagerly looked forward to each day.

Despite the arduous and uncomfortable nature of the trek, Charlee was in love with this new land. Travel was slow and primitive. Roads were nearly imaginary, visible only when so mud rutted as to be impassable during the spring and early summer rains. Mud deep enough to swallow oxen was the rule, and twelve to fifteen miles a day was the most a wagon train could hope to travel. But if the road was long and uncomfortable, it was filled with fascinating glimpses of life in Texas.

This was a rich land, no doubt. Coming from the rocky, poor-soiled lands of southeast Missouri, Charlee thought the rolling plains of east and central Texas were incredibly fertile. Zeb Moser, one of the emigrants for whom she worked on the train, said you could plant ten-penny nails and harvest a crop of iron bolts. Certainly eighty bushels of corn per acre—as one east Texian along the way assured them he produced—set all the farmers among the party agog. One grower bragged of fourteen-foot cotton plants. Although Charlee saw none *that* enormous, the vast acreage set in dense snowy bolls was very impressive to a girl raised on a hardscrabble farm.

Texas was a place of contrasts. She heard stories about alligators and whooping cranes, even exotic spotted wildcats called ocelots, all creatures of storybook fantasy to her. Of course these creatures lived farther south toward the more tropical gulf country. No less exciting to Charlee were the buffalo and wild horses, whose vast, swarming herds were as yet undepleted by the hand of man. The mustangs were wary and kept their distance from the plodding train. Only when she ventured out by herself to hunt did Charlee catch a glimpse of them as they grazed on rich prairie grass. The bison were more placid and easier to approach. The rich, sweet, beef-flavored meat of these shaggy cattle of the plains became a favorite of hers as the train inched its way ever westward.

The vegetation was no less exotic than the animal life. Fields of gently swaying bluebonnets lay beside the spiky outgrowths of yucca plants. Primroses bloomed next to prickly pear. The spring rains, which had engorged the Red River, also had created the spectacular beauty of the flowering countryside. Of all the wild and beautiful flora that abounded in the Republic, the shaggy bronze, yellow, and orange Indian paintbrush was her favorite.

One night as Charlee sat inconspicuously in the shadows of the campfire finishing her dinner of salt pork and cornbread, she listened to Zeb Moser and their scout discuss the remainder of the trip.

The large, heavyset old farmer took a swallow of bitter coffee adulterated with ground roast corn and grimaced. "Supplies are gettin' mighty low, Lon. When you reckon we'll reach San Antonio?"

Lon spat a dollop of tobacco juice, narrowly missing Charlee's boot, as he replied, "Less'n a week if'n nothin' more goes wrong. Keep all yore stock movin' and yew'll be dancin' th' fandango with th' señoritas by Sunday." Lon Farrell, a lean range scout of inderterminate years, laughed and strolled over to squat beside Charlee.

He had gone hunting with her several times, giving her tips on tracking and stalking in the open terrain of central Texas, so different from the dense undergrowth of southeast Missouri. A bond of sorts had sprung up between the seasoned Texian and the masquerading girl. She was uneasy, afraid that he might discover her disguise, but he simply chalked her skittishness up to immaturity.

"Whut yew figger ta do when yew git ta Santone?" Lon looked at the scruffy figure hunched over a tin coffee mug.

"I got me a brother on a big ranch just outside town. He's foreman, practically runs the whole place," she boasted proudly, recalling all the glowing descriptions in Richard Lee's letters. "You ever heard of the Bluebonnet Ranch?"

Lon whistled low. "Thet's one o' th' biggest spreads 'round Santone—th' whole country, fer thet matter. What'd yew say yore brother's name wuz?"

"Richard Lee McAllister," Charlee said with youthful bravado.

"Last I knowed, Asa Ketchum was ramroddin' fer ole Will, but I been gone fer quite a spell. I heered Will Slade up'n died a pretty considerable o' years back, come ta think on it." For the boy's sake, Lon hoped the older brother wasn't spinning yarns. There was a strange vulnerability about the taciturn youth that made the scout feel oddly protective. Despite his scrawny size, the tad did his fair share of the chores. And he could shoot! "Charley" McAllister could bring down a deer at three hundred yards.

Lon had told Charlee a little about San Antonio, or Santone, as the southern-born Texians called it. When she arrived, Charlee understood why the scout had cautioned her that it would be different. During the grueling weeks on the wagon trek across the vast new Republic, Charlee had seen log cabins, corn fields, and people dressed in homespun who spoke English. Texas had seemed American to the Missouri hill girl.

San Antonio was far more Mexican than American, a place where vaqueros flashed knives by night to the music of the fandango and women bathed naked in the warmth of sunlit springs. Black-eyed girls dressed in low-cut white blouses and short brightly colored skirts filled jugs at bubbling fountains. Many even smoked cigarillos in public! Swarthy men, dressed gaudily in tight-fitting pants and jackets studded with silver, rode elegant horses whose saddle trappings were scarcely less ornamented than the clothes of their riders. Everywhere the liquid cadences of Spanish flowed, seeming to keep rhythm with the spilling water of the musical fountains.

Most of the buildings were of adobe and stone, with walls three to four feet thick to keep the blistering sun at bay. Large iron-grilled windows admitted cool breezes. The domes of several large churches were visible, and tall, graceful cypress trees added welcoming shade to the bustling afternoon scene.

Earlier in the day Charlee had said farewell to the Mosers,
who were heading to their land claims north of the town.
Lon was returning to Natchitoches after some recreation in
Santone. In silent amusement he rode beside his young
companion, watching "his" wide-eyed absorption with the
scene in the Main Plaza.

Ox-drawn carts full of watermelons creaked along as a
vaquero swinging a wide reata raced past them, running a
young longhorn to ground. At the side entrance to a fandango hall, two black men unloaded barrels of whiskey. A
balky mule was being beaten and cursed inventively by a
wiry old Texian while several dogs yipped around the
flailing, sharp-hooved critter. A freight caravan pulled off
the main thoroughfare and stopped in front of a frame,
two-story structure of Yankee origin, a large, well-stocked
general store.

Charlee looked to the west at the tall dome of San
Fernando Church, awed by its size and cool, inviting beauty. Across to the east was the clock tower of the old *cabildo*,
once the seat of Spanish government in Texas. It was
three-thirty in the afternoon, and everyone had come alive
after siesta.

"This place is even older than St. Genevieve or St. Louis,
isn't it, Lon?" Her voice held a hint of wonder.

He laughed. "I reckon so, seein's how it was here over a
hunnert years ago, back ta th' 1720s, I think one o' them
padres tole me once't. It was th' capital o' Spanish Texas
way afore th' Mexican gover'ment broke free o' th' mother
country. Now it's gittin' more American ever' time I come
back."

"Yeah. I reckon there are Texians as well as *Tejanos*
living here." Charlee was proud of her newly acquired
vocabulary. "My brother works for a Texian named Slade.
Said he even fought at San Jacinto with President Houston."

Lon quirked a brow. "If'n yew mean Jim Slade, he's
kinda a mix o' Texian an' *Tejano*."

"What do you mean?" she asked, as they dipped their
canteens in the cool spring water of a well.

"His pa was from Virginia, from what I heered, but his
ma was from an ole *Tejano* family right here in Santone.

Lots o' them early adventurers who settled hereabouts married local women. Colonel Bowie hisself had a Mexican wife an' two kids. When they died o' fever, he went plumb loco. Some said thet's why he chose ta stand 'n die at th' Alamo. Yew got yew a lot ta learn.''

Charlee pondered her surroundings. She suddenly felt far from home and very lonely. Don't be stupid, girl, she thought. Richard Lee is all the family you have left and he's here. Together we'll make a home in this wild new land.

On the solitary ride to Bluebonnet, Charlee considered how Richard Lee would react to her unexpected appearance. She could bathe and don her red dress, so he couldn't yell at her. Or she could keep the trail filth and breeches. It would be armor against his inevitable proclamations that a girl couldn't survive on a ranch. However, she saw no place to bathe in security along the way, and even if she had, her only dress was dusty and wrinkled. She decided it was better to remain a grimy male urchin rather than become an ill-groomed white-trash female.

Charlee recalled her brother's letters describing the ranch, the outbuildings, and the three clear creeks that ran through the lush rolling hills of Bluebonnet. The ranch was named for the brilliant wildflowers that covered the countryside each spring. She remembered the descriptions of his place, the foreman's cabin, tucked beneath a stand of live oaks. The small house sported a high chimney and cool dog-run porch between its two rooms. Of course, the Slades' big ranch house was lots fancier, two stories high and built of imported hardwood with all the lumber milled into clean whitewashed boards. But the boss, Mr. Slade, lived there.

Curiously, Charlee tried to imagine what he would look like. In all of her brother's letters describing the lay of the land, the buildings, and the idiosyncrasies of the cowboys, he had mentioned little of Jim Slade except that he was a war hero of sorts, quiet and hard working. Richard Lee had never described the man who had come into such a splendid inheritance, nor mentioned that he was half Mexican. She recalled a man she'd seen in San Antonio, lounging in the doorway of a fandango hall. He'd been short and stocky with a rounded, smiling face and dancing black eyes. Yes, Slade was probably a genial, plump, dark-haired fellow wearing a serape and sandals. She hoped he would not mind his foreman taking in an orphaned kid sister, then assured herself that there was no possible reason he should object. After all, she was a hard worker, a fair country cook, and a superb shot. She could take care of herself and hold her own with the best or worst Texas had to offer.

When she crested the hill and saw the panorama of Bluebonnet before her, Charlee gasped. It was grand, much grander than Richard Lee's letters had been able to convey. The big house was a brilliant white frame building shaded by rustling cottonwoods and gracious live oak trees. A wide veranda stretched across the front of the first and second stories. Large neatly constructed corrals held horses and cattle. The bunkhouse stood nearby, a long, low building beneath more dense shade trees. There was a wash house, a blacksmith shed, and several other structures.

"Lordy, I been in towns with nary so many buildings," she breathed to herself. Then she saw the small house, behind the big bunk house, half hidden by the trees. It was just as her brother described—his place! She quickly kneed her tired old nag and eagerly trotted toward her new home.

It was late afternoon and only a few people were around the corral. Most of the hands would not ride in until dark. Knowing she was filthy, Charlee decided she would rather face her brother alone and not risk embarrassing him in front of his friends. She rode slowly and inconspicuously through a tall stand of grass, avoiding the open road to the complex of buildings and circling to the rear of the foreman's cabin. She slid from the back of the old gray and stealthily crept up to the porch between the cabin rooms. A door stood ajar and Charlee peeked inside. Before her eyes could adjust to the dim light, a fierce, rumbling growl and a sharp tearing sound interrupted her inspection. Then a burning pain lanced through her right buttock. A large black mongrel dog had a singularly uncomfortable hold on her.

"Git, you consarned son of a bitch! Lumpy plug-ugly hound!" As Charlee whirled to kick at the beast, the ripping sound intensified and a sudden draft hit her nether parts.

Feeling gingerly with one hand, she held the sentinel at bay with her booted foot. "Blood! You worthless pile of cow shit, you've gone 'n bit me in the ass! I never!" She wavered between fury over the indignity of being bitten by a miserable cur, and stark terror, for the hound was not backing down. His beady eyes looked hate filled and menacing. If only she could reach her horse and leap into the saddle. But every time she tried to edge off the porch, the growling dog made a vicious snapping lunge, thwarting her plans. Too humiliated to call for help, Charlee seethed and swore.

Just then, a dark orange blur came barreling out of the open door behind her. The creature screeched fiercely as the dog whirled and snapped at its tail. Charlee was forgotten and the chase was on, but only for the distance of a few yards in front of the cabin. There beside a live oak the orange furball took its stand with back arched wickedly. The cat was the most enormous tom Charlee had ever seen, with fangs at least three quarters of an inch long, easily visible in his large, spitting mouth. His dark green eyes glared balefully at the crouching dog. One well-chewed ear lopped over the side of his head. Numerous scars and nicks across his body attested to his valor or foolhardiness, depending on whether one liked cats. Charlee did, and she was not going to stand by while a hundred-and-ten-pound mongrel devoured a twenty-pound cat.

Searching frantically for a weapon, she spied a branch fallen from the canopy of the oak. As the antagonists warily circled each other, emitting low, throaty growls, Charlee edged toward the crude cudgel. Just as she picked it up, a piercing scream erupted, accompanied by a baying howl, both loud enough to peel bark right off a tree. Charlee charged into the churning melee of black and orange fur, flailing wildly with the awkward club. Big spongy chunks of rotted wood flew in all directions, little deterring the combatants, who seemed impervious to her ill-timed blows.

"Leave him be, you low-life cruddy pissant!" She hoped that most of her blows were striking the much larger dog, not the cat, whose yowls went on uninterrupted.

Charlee continued to beat and swear until a sudden deluge of cold water put an abrupt end to the contest. The cat sprang away, back arched and defiant, still spitting and undaunted. The dog let out a whimper and ran around the side of the cabin. In his haste to escape, he knocked Charlee into the newly created mud wallow.

Most of the water had hit the girl, who now lay sodden and hiccuping for breath in the ooze beneath the tree. The cat turned abruptly and began licking his back as if he had not a care in the world.

"I swan ta Jasus, all th' cream in Santone's prob'ly been curdled by thet catterwallin!" The high-pitched yet peculiarly raspy voice belonged to an enormous mountain of a man who dropped a big oak bucket on the ground in front of Charlee. "Who in tarnation are yew? Wall, speak up, boy . . . wait a minute, yore no boy! A gal! Wut 'n hellfire is a gal doin sneakin' 'round Asa's place, settin' Mutt off like thet?"

Horrified, Charlee looked down at her water-soaked person. The bindings around her breasts had slipped down during the hullabaloo, and the thin cotton shirt clearly revealed her sex, clinging transparently to every curve.

"I'm Charlee McAllister, Richard Lee's sister, and I wasn't either sneakin'!" Angrily she struggled to rise, only to take a quick seat in the mud once more when the cool breeze reminded her of her exposed derriere. "Oooh, damblast that hound!"

A strange expression came over the big man's face. "Yer Dick's sister? Seems ta me he did mention havin' a kid sister once't er so, back in Missouri, warn't it? How'd yew git here, a gal all alone?"

Shifting uncomfortably in the slimy mud as her fanny began to ache from the dog bite, Charlee replied peevishly, "I can take care of myself. I hired with a wagon train after takin' the steamer down the Mississippi and up the Red. They're rivers," she added with arrogant defiance, wanting someone else to feel the sting of humiliation.

Before the big stranger in greasy buckskins could reply, another masculine voice spoke. "What in the hell is going on, Weevils? Sina and I heard the screaming and swearing even before we dismounted at the far corral!" As he observed the complacently washing cat and the bedraggled urchin sprawled beneath the tree, Jim Slade's face was a thundercloud. The dog, who had returned from hiding and sneaked behind the fat man called Weevils, began to shake, spraying both men generously with water.

"Get that damn hound out of here before he ruins Mrs. Carver's riding habit," Slade ordered. Weevils nodded and reached for the black beast, who allowed himself to be led away quietly.

While this exchange was going on, Charlee remained on the ground, staring in rapt fascination at the tall, slim man who was the most striking male she had ever seen. He was dressed in form-fitting buckskin pants and a white shirt that was open at the throat, partially revealing a sun-bronzed, gold-furred chest. His hair was that same dark, dazzling gold, dense and straight, falling in one unruly swatch across a high forehead. The planes of his face were chiseled and hard, with a long, straight nose, high cheekbones, and square jaw. The late afternoon light accented his arresting golden eyes beneath thick brows of the same color. Now, as he turned to her, his brows rose and his eyes skewered her. A slowly warming smile spread across his broad mouth, revealing even, white teeth.

"Well, what have we here, scamp? This is hardly the way for a boy to get himself a job," Slade said with mock sternness.

Charlee had pulled the shirt free of her breasts while Weevils and Slade talked. He thought she was a boy! Charlee wanted to dig a hole and crawl into it. She was filthy and bedraggled in front of this fascinating stranger. Never before had she wished to appear feminine and pretty! What was wrong with her?

Charlee scooted toward the nearby tree and carefully got to her feet, her back to the trunk. Her attempt to stand straight only made matters worse, because the wet shirt once more adhered to her breasts, while the loosened layers of the binder thickened her waist so as to give the appearance of a middle-aged spread on an otherwise coltishly slim body.

"I'm no boy, for your information, mister. I'm Charlee McAllister, Richard Lee's sister. He's the foreman here, so you'd better not mess with me," she spat furiously. The amused smile on his face broadened while he eyed her.

Charlee could feel the burning heat of her flushed cheeks and cursed herself for the strange new way this man made her react. She added, "Who in hell do you think you are, insultin' a lady?"

"The only lady present here is Mrs. Carver, and I don't appreciate your swearing in her presence!" Slade indicated the woman who stood a little to one side in obvious dismay at the debacle. She was elegantly dressed in a dark green riding habit and matching plumed hat. Her lustrous black hair was faultlessly coiffed, and she possessed chillingly perfect cameo features.

"Diego, whatever can this all mean?" She stepped daintily up to her handsome escort and placed her slim ivory fingers possessively on his arm.

Never in her eighteen years had Charlee hated another woman with such a sudden burst of intensity.

"This is Mrs. Tomasina Carver, who owns an adjacent ranch. And in answer to your earlier impertinent question, *Miss* McAllister, I'm Jim Slade." Briefly the gold eyes had softened as he gazed at the beautiful woman, then hardened as he returned his attention to Charlee.

"The . . . the owner?" she croaked. "But you're supposed to be Mexican!" The minute the words were out she could have shinnied up the tree. The exposure of her bare backside would be a lesser humiliation than her verbal blunder.

"If by that you mean I should look swarthy and menacing, I'm sorry to disappoint. I take after my pa," he replied glacially.

She thought he did well enough on the menacing part even if he was blond, but she would never give him the satisfaction of saying so. The regal lady by his side was obviously Hispanic. Well, if I scorched her royal ass, I'm glad! Charlee told herself.

Slade said a few hurried words in Spanish to Mrs. Carver, who replied in English, with a mock pout, "You can't be serious, Diego! Why, I do believe she *is* a girl." Sina's earlier annoyance now turned to amusement as she inspected the filthy, shredded remains of Charlee's attire. She was well aware that the slim, high-bosomed frame concealed beneath the mud and rags was female, but hardly one of which to be jealous. Kissing Slade lightly on one cheek, she departed as he had asked, leaving him to deal with the waif.

"Now, Miss McAllister, you and I are going to have a little talk, but first I want you out of those vile-smelling clothes. Weevils!"

The fat ranch cook reappeared instantly from behind the cabin, minus the hound. "She's Dick's sister, Mr. Slade. Whut yew gonna do?"

"I'll handle that, just you see to some bath water and clean clothes. And, Weevils, get that damn cat out of here. He's nothing but trouble!"

The feline in question sauntered toward the woods in back of the foreman's cabin as if he fully comprehended the message but considered it unworthy of his attention. Only a rigidly straight orange tail attested to his pique.

chapter
3

"Richard Lee can't be dead! He just can't!" Charlee's face was chalk-white, her freckles even more pronounced. She jumped up from the chair in Slade's study and nearly leaped across the room at him. "He couldn't have drowned, for God's sake! He taught *me* to swim!"

Slade poured a stiff shot of brandy into a glass and forced the hysterical girl to sit down and take a sip.

She obeyed, sputtering and coughing. "Why that's worse 'n old man Scruggs's corn likker Richard Lee and me used to steal back in St. Genevieve! Oh, Richard Lee!" she sobbed.

"It happens to be good French brandy, but I guess that's

an acquired taste. Look, I'm sorry about your brother, but accidents do happen, even to the best swimmers. It was a hot day and I guess he just took a rest from searching for strays. When he dived in he must have hit his head on a rock. That's what Luke Pile thought. He's the one who found him, Miss McAllister. I was away at the time, in Houston on business, but Asa handled all the details for burial. He wrote you, but I guess you'd already left Missouri by then."

Slade regarded her cynically. How in hell did a girl get all the way from St. Genevieve to San Antonio by herself? he mused. He didn't want to ponder the answer to that question in the least. Why, she was just a kid!

"Asa . . . you mean Mr. Ketchum, your foreman?" It still rankled her that Richard Lee had lied about being foreman of Bluebonnet. No wonder that dog of Ketchum's almost ate her alive. It was his porch she was intruding on, not her poor brother's. Richard Lee had been just an ordinary cowboy. Small wonder he could not afford to send for her and Mama. He may have been a dreamer, even fanciful and weak in some ways, but he damn well could swim, *and* had the sense to look before he dove. Something just didn't add up. As she sat clenching the brandy glass in her fingers, Charlee vowed she would find out exactly what had happened to Richard Lee McAllister.

Slade lounged against his desk, watching the play of emotions across the young waif's face. Now that she had bathed and changed into a dress, albeit a very ill-fitting one, she looked like a girl at least. She was rather scrawny, if the loose folds of the shapeless gingham could reveal anything to his measuring eye. Her face was unnaturally pale and pinched, her eyes red-rimmed from crying. Although her hair was an interesting shade of golden brown, it was drawn back in an unbecoming, hastily pinned knot of braids. All in all no beauty, he judged, but she must have some earthy appeal to have worked her way all this distance to Texas.

The girl had already admitted she had no money. Neither had her charming but lazy brother. What the hell could he do with her? Just then she spoke in a low whispered voice, its husky tenor interrupting his troubled thoughts.

"I'd like to see his grave now, if you don't mind, Mr. Slade." Her voice was raw with pain, but her stiff back was the epitome of resolution.

As he nodded and stood up, Charlee watched. Every move he made was so sinuously graceful. While she followed him down the long hallway and out the back of the house, she found herself blushing as her eyes stared at his long legs and traveled upward to the slim, taut buttocks, narrow waist, and broad shoulders, then down again. What was wrong with her! Sorrowing and alone, her only kin dead, what was she staring at—some strange man's backside! I must be having grief-stricken vapors, she mused. That's the only reason I'd even look twice at a man like him. Why, I don't even like him!

When all the girls her age back home began to have callers, Charlee had been out stalking squirrels. She had always viewed men as hunting companions, never as suitors. She was far more comfortable blaming the sudden attraction on grief than in putting another name to it.

Richard Lee's grave was behind the big house, in the Slade family cemetery, where not only the owner's kin but also his employees were buried. The shady knoll was peaceful and pretty, Charlee thought, taking some solace in that as she knelt and stared at the small stone marker. She let the tears slip down her cheeks freely now while Slade waited some distance away, letting her do her private mourning.

Finally she rose and walked steadily down the knoll to rejoin him. Almost grudgingly she remembered her manners and said, "I thank you for the headstone. Back home we only had wooden crosses for Pa and Ma."

Gruffly he replied, "You're welcome, Miss McAllister. All our markers are made of stone here. Every man deserves that much permanence in this harsh climate."

As they walked slowly to the big house, Slade pondered what to do about his unwanted charge. Rather more brusquely than he intended, he asked, "What do you plan to do now, Miss McAllister? Do you have any family left in St. Genevieve?"

"No. My parents are gone and now so's my only brother." She omitted mentioning the hateful cousins in St. Louis as a plan began to form in her mind. "I got no kin and no money, Mr. Slade." Did he wince just an infinitesimal bit? Grinning to herself, she continued, "I suppose I need a job. If that man Weevils cooks anything as bad as his name sounds, well, I bet a new rifle against a kick in the ass he could use a helper. I can cook, clean, do laundry, even skin a mule. I'm a crack shot—"

"Whoa! I believe you." Slade threw up his hands in mock surrender as he smiled in a dazzling, boyish fashion. "I suppose the kitchen could use a woman's touch. Ever since Etta Tall Tree left us to marry a Cherokee chieftain, Weevils has been filling in as cook. He's all right on the trail as a camp cook for the hands, but when I have guests to dinner, well, he leaves much to be desired. You're hired, Charley. . . is it?" He quirked an eyebrow.

"Yep, Charlee, spelled with two *e*'s," she replied defiantly.

"I never heard of such a name for a girl," he replied dubiously. "What's your real name?"

"I won't tell you er anyone else in Texas my given name. I hate it! Anyway, everyone's always called me Charlee since I was a tadpole. I like it just fine."

"Good enough. Forgive my inquisitiveness, Miss Charlee." His grin was disarming, softening the grim lines of his face, erasing the hardness that he seemed to wear like protective armor most of the time.

She found herself smiling back, hypnotized by those marvelous golden eyes, dazzled by the white slash of teeth.

Slade was surprised. When her face lit up like that, she was almost pretty in a gamin way. She had good straight teeth, clear skin, and delicate features, but these were overwhelmed by the pallor of her complexion and those freckles, not to mention the awful hair style and that atrocious dress! He chuckled to himself; at least Sina couldn't be jealous.

If Tomasina wasn't jealous, Weevils was. When he was told that the muddy urchin who attacked Asa's dog would work in his kitchen, the old man sulked through breakfast. Briskly telling her he was going fishing, he vanished for the day. She decided to win him over later and set out at once to prove her worth to her new boss by cooking a memorable midday meal.

Right after breakfast, she ran down two spry young chickens, wrung their necks, then plucked and cleaned them. While they were slowly roasting with spicy sage dressing, she baked a lady cake for dessert. Fresh snap beans cooked with fatback and light, airy rolls completed the meal. She could not ever remember putting so much effort into lunch. But watching Jim Slade, Asa Ketchum, and Leandro Velasquez devouring every morsel, she knew it was worth the trouble.

"Where did you learn to cook like this, miss?" the courtly old foreman, Asa, inquired as he polished off a second piece of the sweet white cake.

"Our cook Lizzie taught me, mostly. When my pa was alive, he and Richard Lee were always bringing friends home for dinner. I liked helpin' all I could." Charlee remembered her childhood lessons in Mose and Lizzie's comfortable little cabin, where she and her brother ate sweets and listened to old Mose's woods lore. The cleaning and cooking of wild game and fowl seemed a natural accompaniment to hunting. Even Richard Lee had learned the basics of biscuit making and frying breakfast meats and eggs. Thinking of him now made her want to cry, but she quickly forced the thought aside. She vowed, I'll deal with his killer when I find out who he is.

As she cleared the kitchen table, Charlee covertly studied the three men dressed in dusty work clothes. Asa Ketchum was tall, lanky, and gray-haired, with a drooping moustache. His soft speech and careful manners proclaimed him a Virginian, a contemporary of Jim Slade's father who had come to Texas to make his fortune. Asa was the long-time ramrod of Bluebonnet. It seemed unlikely he would have any cause to want her brother dead. Indeed, he spoke fondly of young Dick and offered her his sincere sympathy.

The same was true of the youth Leandro, a boy of seventeen or eighteen, a native-born *Tejano*. The outgoing young man had been taken in by the Slade family when he was orphaned nearly a dozen years earlier. Growing up in the shadow of Jim Slade, Leandro worshiped the older man.

Slimly built, with finely chiseled features and black eyes, he was almost too pretty for a man, but his laughing good humor and whipcord strength kept him from appearing effeminate. Like Asa, Lee, as everyone called him, had made Charlee feel welcome at once, grateful for her help with Weevils's dreadful cooking. Lee shyly teased Charlee, another orphan, and made her feel comfortable. He was a kindred spirit in spite of their different backgrounds. Liking him instantly, Charlee felt certain he had not been involved in Richard Lee's death either. Anyway, her brother was easily forty pounds heavier, so there was slight chance he could have been done in by a mere boy.

That left her most attractive but forbidding employer. As he and Ketchum talked about the calf crop and the early summer weather, Charlee watched Jim Slade. She had learned from Lee that morning that his hero had been a member of the local ranging company since the age of fifteen. Slade had grown up fighting Comanche and other renegade raiders. He had followed General Houston on his long, bitter march across Texas to make the last-ditch, desperate stand at San Jacinto that had won the Republic's independence from Mexico. He was a man with much practice at killing, hardened by the brutality of frontier life.

He was also an enigma, guarded and quiet, possessing a fierce temper when crossed; Lee had told her that, too. Slade was certainly capable of killing Richard Lee, but why should he? Her handsome brother might have been a rival for Slade's beautiful neighbor, Tomasina Carver, but Charlee doubted it. Still, Slade was very protective of the elegant young widow and vague about where he had been when Richard Lee died. Charlee found herself attracted to the Texian in a shocking, physical way, yet she was frightened of him at the same time.

She had been at the ranch for only one day. There was a lot more to learn, and many more people to meet, she decided, before she could solve the mystery of Richard Lee's death.

Jim, Asa, and Lee finished their coffee and left. Slade had given her no specific instructions, so after washing up the dishes, Charlee left the kitchen and began to explore the rest of the house. It had two stories and a large root cellar beneath the north side. The polished oak floorboards left Charlee in awe, as did the smooth mortared walls, elegant carpets, and stained oak woodwork. The white walls and carved furniture bespoke the tastes of the former lady of the house, Teresa Magdalena Sandoval de Slade. It was austere and Hispanic; yet at the same time it was welcoming in a bluff, masculine way attributable to Will and Jim Slade, no doubt.

More recently acquired paintings, cut glass, and carpets indicated how well the house had prospered under the hand of the son. Charlee lovingly touched a beautiful pitcher, admiring the good taste so carefully cultivated even in this wild country. Jim Slade came from educated, aristocratic stock on both sides of his family, and the decor subtly showed it.

"Mama would really approve of these," she murmured to herself as she ran her hands lightly down the heavy lace curtains over the parlor window. Two days a week, a couple of women from San Antonio came and cleaned, she had been informed by Weevils, who could see no use for her at all. He cooked, they cleaned. What was Charlee's job? She realized that she must make an ally out of the crotchety man if her place at Bluebonnet was to be assured.

"I'll just have to learn how—" Her thoughts were suddenly interrupted by a loud volley of inventive oaths, crackling over the still afternoon air in a high-pitched, gravelly voice that piped and broke with fury.

"Hellfire 'n damnation, yew sonofabitchen heathen bastard from th' pit! I'll gut yew 'n use yer innards fer puddin' damn if'n I won't—er new fiddle strings!"

Following the shrieking to the kitchen, Charlee arrived in time to see Weevils attempting to chase an orange blur around the big table in the center of the room. The cat was dragging something, cutting deftly between chairs and table legs, thus far eluding the meat cleaver wielded by the frenzied cook.

When she opened the hall door the cat saw his opportunity to escape with his prize, a long stringer of bullhead catfish. As the cat barreled past her legs, she stamped her foot and held the stringer fast to the floor. Unfortunately, with the momentum of the twenty-pound tomcat and the slipperiness of the catfish, Charlee was unable to keep her balance. She fell in a billow of red gingham, landing on cat and catfish.

"Whoa, you thievin' rascal!" Charlee grabbed the ratty orange fireball expertly by the scruff of his neck, extricating him from the folds of her skirts. She plopped him inelegantly in her lap and began to examine his chewed-up, fish-smeared body. "Phewee, 'n Mama used to say I stank!"

Voice cracking in terror, the cook screeched, "Lookee thar, gal! Thet cat's th' meanest, orneriest bastard ever ta set foot on Bluebonnet, not even barrin' polecats 'n Comanche!" Weevils eyed the tom from a good six feet and gave no indication of coming closer. "He'll take yer laig off clean to th' bone afore yew kin spit!"

The cat fixed his basilisk glare on the obese prophet of doom and then dismissed him with a disdainful flick of his beaver-thick tail. He snuggled up against Charlee's neck and released a volley of loud, rasping purrs. The tom never wasted time where he was not appreciated.

"Why, you are an old lover boy! A little the worse for wear though," she said as she scratched the shredded remains of his left ear. The side of his right eye had been ripped and the resulting scar left a puckering along the seam, giving his face a quizzical expression. The thick, bright orange fur was mottled with burrs, and generous hunks of it had been bitten and clawed away. Charlee laughed and scratched him beneath the chin while he butted his head playfully against her.

"Wal, hellfire 'n damnation! He *likes* you! Thet tom ain't niver liked nobody afore, ever since he wandered in more'n three, four weeks ago. Onliest one who could git near him's Lee, 'n he only lets th' boy put milk down fer him. Niver shoulda encouraged th' sneak thief."

"So, you're a stray, too, just like me, cat. Maybe that's why we hit it off. That 'n the fact I always had me a cat back in Missouri. Sure would admire to have one again, specially a scrappy fellow like you. You need a name. Let me see, what shall we call you?"

"Hellfire! Yew gonna *keep* him, like a pet? He ain't even tame 'nough fer a circus, much less 'round a house." Weevils's indignation caused him to forget himself and move a few steps closer to the cat, who bristled up in Charlee's lap like a lightning-struck porcupine and gave a wicked hiss. "Hellfire! I didn't mean nothin'!" Weevils jumped back, causing the floor to give a reverberating groan under his considerable weight.

"That's it!" Charlee snapped her fingers and then proceeded to soothe the cat, who settled down on her lap with a contented 'murph'. "With all that fiery orange fur, and the way you're always flying around and bristling up, I'll call you Hellfire! Fits your disposition, too, so I hear tell." Laughing, Charlee picked up the large orange bundle and planted a kiss squarely on the battle-scarred face.

"What in hellfire's going on?" Slade stood in the kitchen door, his fierce gaze on the fish-smeared girl and her new friend.

Charlee burst into giggles. Weevils tried to suppress the rumbles of laughter that burbled up from his mammoth belly, but quickly abandoned any pretense and joined her in a hearty roar.

Jim's eyes took in the pile of glossy fish, tails still swishing as they flopped feebly on the stringer, spilled haphazardly across Charlee's dress and the carpet. Hellfire held court from his throne on her lap, one paw proprietarily hooked over a nearby bullhead, daring either of the men to take it away from him.

"It seems every time I see you, you're on the ground covered with muck, and that cat is somewhere nearby. What's so damn funny?" He looked glaringly from the girl to the fat old cook.

"Hellfire," said Charlee idiotically. Then collecting herself and realizing how awful she must look, not to mention smell, she amended, "I mean, I named him Hellfire."

"The cat or his fish?" Slade quirked a golden eyebrow intimidatingly, full well realizing the wily old tom had finally found someone whom he deigned to favor.

"*His* fish! I spent me all day catchin' them fer our dinner tonight," Weevils croaked indignantly. "I'd be obliged,

Charlee, if'n yew'd git thet critter outta here so's I kin pick up *my* fish."

The cat favored the speaker with a fish-eyed look, his claws flexing more deeply into the succulent bullhead, which lay beside Charlee's lap.

"Er, let's have a compromise, Weevils. I know you caught the fish, but Hellfire has to eat, too. Besides, they're really big—Texas-size catfish. We can spare just one for Hellfire, all right?"

She favored the cook with a winsome smile, and once more Slade was startled by how she was nearly pretty, despite her penchant for getting into unladylike predicaments. "Give him the fish, Weevils, but get this damn stinking mess cleaned up before it dries into the carpet. I had it shipped all the way from Boston." With that he took two long-legged steps over Charlee. She watched him go into his office, then gently dislodged the cat, carefully keeping one finger hooked behind the sharp gill fin of the bullhead. Deftly she removed Hellfire's prize from the stringer and then coaxed the cat to the back door, where he claimed his reward and sped off to devour it beneath the bushes.

Wanting to take advantage of her newly won approval from Weevils, Charlee ventured, "I used to be my pa's best fish cleaner back home, 'n bullheads were my specialty. Can I help?"

Never in his life had the seasoned old man seen a female conversant with skinning and gutting catfish. This he would have to see. And see he did, as he and Charlee talked amicably now that he had inadvertently accepted her into the camaraderie of the ranch house. She pinned a catfish to a large wooden block with an ice pick through its head, and with swift, precise strokes she peeled off the skin. Then she removed the entrails and cut away the sharp side fins and oil sacs beneath them. Last of all she cut off the head and tossed the meat into a bucket of cold water, ready to begin the next one.

"Slick as a whistle." Weevils beamed, and Charlee knew her place was assured.

"When we get through with the fish, I'd better put some

vinegar water on that rug, just to be sure no fish smell stays in it. That is, if you don't mind my not helping you with supper right off, Weevils?''

He grinned as he rolled the drained fish in finely ground cornmeal. "Naw, yew git th' rug 'n I'll tend ta supper. Boss man sets right much store by his fancy furniture 'n sech.''

"Where did he learn about fine carpets and lace curtains? I thought he was born and raised here in Texas. I heard his ma was Mexican, but he sure don't look like the men I saw on the trail or in San Antonio.'' Was her curiosity too obvious, Charlee wondered? She kept her eyes averted, intent on the fish cleaning.

Weevils chuckled. "Yew are green from th' states, aintcha? Yep, Mr. Jim's ma was Mexican all right—what Texians call 'white Mexican,' that is. Upper-class, educated folk, with no Injun blood mixed in. Her people was rich 'n high up in th' gover'ment afore th' Texians ever won free o' Mexico. Will Slade come here from Virginie even afore Colonel Austin got here with th' first big bunch o' settlers. Married into th' Sandoval family 'n set out gettin' this spread ta prosper..."

"Then that explains why he doesn't look like the Mexicans in town . . . or even Lee," Charlee said, recalling with a blush her words when she had first found out Slade was the half-Mexican owner of Bluebonnet.

Weevils watched her consternation in amusement. "Yew noticed who he favors, huh? Wal, fact is, them yeller eyes come from th' Sandoval side 'n the yeller har comes from ole Will. Yew kin look all ya want, but—''

Indignantly she cut in, "I wasn't 'looking,' leastways not the way *you* mean it! I was only interested in him because he's my boss 'n was my brother's, too.''

"Uh-huh," Weevils snorted, unconvinced. "Thet's why yew couldn't take yer eyes off'n him whilst he walked down th' hall a few minits back. I seen 'nough females moonin' over Mr. Jim, 'n thet's a fact.'' He paused. "All 'cept fer Miz Sina. She always seems kinda cool. Mebbe cause she's th' onliest one whose sure o' him.''

Charlee almost sliced off a finger at that last remark.

"What do you mean, 'sure of him'? I thought she was newly widowed," she said, still hating the beautiful black-haired woman who had laughed at her.

"She's a widder right 'nough. Ole Jake's been daid nigh onta three months now, I reckon. Hoss throw'd him 'n busted his neck. Right sad, specially considerin' how good a rider he usually was. Anyways, Miz Sina 'n Mr. Jim wuz engaged afore she up 'n married ole Jake. Jim never did git hisself hitched after thet, despite a passel o' females from here ta Houston tryin' their damblastedest ta trap him."

Charlee said sullenly, "You mean he's still in love with her, even after she jilted him for an older man?"

"Somethin' like thet, 'cept now him 'n th' widder lady is fixin' ta git hitched soon as her year o' mournin' is over. It's not supposed ta be fer everbody ta know yet, but I figger yew kin keep yer mouth shut, caintcha?"

Glumly she nodded. Things were increasingly disturbing at Bluebonnet. The beautiful Tomasina had her boss in thrall and they planned to marry. Charlee was shocked at the pang she felt when she envisioned Jim Slade married. Pushing that aside, she had another disquieting thought: Richard Lee wasn't the only man to die an unlikely accidental death recently. If her handsome employer's possible motives for killing her brother were uncertain, they were clear as glass where Jake Carver was concerned.

I hate being gone from the ranch for this long, Slade thought in agitation as he paced in President Houston's outer office. The capital was once more in Houston City, but the public clamored for it to be moved back to the northern outpost of Austin. At least Austin is closer to Bluebonnet than Houston, he considered ruefully, thinking over the past six years and all the traveling he had done for Sam Houston.

Just then the man himself came through the door with his usual flourish, motioning Slade into his office. "Felicitations, Jim-boy. I do appreciate your promptness. Even my loyal Miller is late from his midday repast this afternoon."

"I wondered where your shadow was," Jim said smiling, referring to Sam's indispensable secretary, Washington Miller. "I trust Mrs. Houston is well, sir?"

"Indeed, splendidly so. One of the best things about having the seat of government in this city is having her nearby. Damn that godforsaken pipe dream, Austin!"

He walked briskly to his large, cluttered desk and sat down behind it, while Slade cleared a chair across from it and did likewise. Jim glanced over the strewn correspondence, overflowing wastebasket, and randomly piled books. The president's office had long been the bane of poor Miller, who filed, stacked, indexed, and ordered official business with almost as much dispatch as his chief exerted in creating clerical havoc.

"How are all the good folks at Bluebonnet?" Houston let a shaggy eyebrow droop as he made the overly casual inquiry.

His young protégé quickly picked up on what was left unsaid. "If by 'all the folks' you mean Dick McAllister, he's dead, Sam. He drowned a few months ago. Seems to have been an accident. You must be wrong about him. He was just a Missouri farm boy with dreams of getting rich. Hell, he even had a kid sister who just showed up from St. Genevieve. I guarantee you she's the genuine article, a dirty, illiterate urchin, no Lucretia Borgia for sure! Her brother wasn't our Mexican agent, even if he was known to have a few drinks with that Englishman Kennedy."

"William Kennedy was personally dispatched here last year by Lord Aberdeen himself for the express purpose of spying on the Republic! I'd bet my last gold button on it." The fact that he was dressed in a homespun shirt and buckskin breeches didn't stop the president from making the bet.

Slade's eyes narrowed. "Oh, I'm sure you're right about Mr. Kennedy. He understands the value of our position between the United States and Mexico and wants us unencumbered by alliances to either one."

"He, like all British interests, wants Texas weak and dependent on Britain—as a republic, certainly not as the twenty-seventh star in the American flag," Houston stormed.

"Well, at least we've received diplomatic recognition from the Americans and the French, even de facto recognition from Great Britain herself," Jim said placatingly.

Houston snorted. "De facto is right. It took over two years to get these three damn treaties signed, straightening out trade and naval rights. Now the British finally recognize us, but the sneaky bastards will stoop to any perfidy to keep us from joining the United States. I do not think Great Britain is above inciting another war between Texas and Mexico," Houston pronounced gravely.

"I read the latest reports in the New Orleans newspapers about a six-million-dollar loan from Britain to Mexico," Slade said, watching Houston's face. "Pakenham's always trying to impress the Mexicans with Her Majesty's goodwill."

"Yes. Well, he's one smart son of a bitch. I devoutly wish Aberdeen would replace him as their ambassador to Mexico. I know he's indirectly financing those renegades whipping up the Comanche to butcher settlers on the frontier. But that's not even as serious as the latest news I have."

Slade leaned forward. "Worse than General Vasquez invading Goliad, Victoria, and San Antonio in March? You nearly had a war over that."

"Yes, God save us! A war we have no money to fight. At least Vasquez withdrew and the whole thing blew over when I vetoed the war declaration, but I don't know if I can sit on this, Jim-boy. Two fully armed Mexican warships have been built by British shipyards. The *Guadalupe* just set sail for the Gulf."

Slade let out a long, low whistle. "After all their games as disinterested mediators between us and the Mexicans, this really ends the British charade. A modern battleship in Mexican hands could wreak havoc on all our shipping, blockade us, even mount an invasion of reconquest by sea!"

"You have the picture," Houston said grimly. "And another ship, the *Montezuma*, will sail by early fall. Of course Aberdeen claims the government can't control private shipyard contractors." His tone of voice indicated what he thought of the veracity of that assertion.

"What do you want me to do, Sam?" Slade's voice was calm, belying the agitation he felt. He had been an unofficial agent for the president since Houston's first term of office back in 1837.

"Things are tense all over, Jim, especially since Vasquez's raid in March. Between that and the Indian troubles stirred up by Mexican agents, we're sitting on a powder keg. We can't afford another war with Mexico. I need to know who my friends are and who my enemies are, especially in Bexar."

Slade smiled at the old name for San Antonio, which few except original settlers used.

"I know Kennedy has a contact feeding him information from there. I thought it was your young McAllister. Whether or not he was involved is immaterial now, but someone must be passing along information from there to the British and their Mexican friends. If, mind you, *if* Santa Anna gets brave, he may decide it's time to attempt another serious invasion. The key to land invasion is Bexar."

"In other words, you'll worry about the sea and I'll worry about the land," Slade supplied dryly. "Just one thing, Sam. I know there are some dissident *Tejanos*, but the majority of my friends around San Antonio are as loyal to the Republic as Navarro or Zavala or me, despite Antonio Perez and his cohorts."

Houston's bluntly chiseled features split into a broad grin. "Hell, Diego, I know that. Perez's off south of Laredo last I heard. Let him do his worst. It's San Antonio's defenses I want you to watch." He stood up and walked around the desk, now grinning broadly.

"On a more pleasant note, I understand you're smitten with love for a certain lovely señora from a fine old San Antonio family. And I know she's reputed to be the most beautiful female in south Texas. I am most anxious to meet the lady."

"Not until I've got her safely married to me. If it weren't for your lovely bride, I'd be jealous, Sam." Jim joined Houston's jovial banter.

The older man laughed heartily now. "You flatter me, sir! But I am a very fortunate man, who at the ripe age of forty-seven could induce a twenty-one-year-old woman of wit and beauty to marry me." He sobered, then said, "Have no fear that I harbor mistrust of all *Tejanos* in Bexar. Lord knows, Jim, ever since I assumed command of the army back in thirty-five, I've been stabbed in the back far too often by Anglos.''

Slade's face creased in a frown. ''I heard rumors last night in the saloon when I arrived, talk about plots to assassinate you after you vetoed Congress's war declaration. There are a lot of men eager to become the new Napoleon of the West.''

''Like those paragons of statesmanship Burnet and Lamar?'' Houston queried sarcastically. ''Many of my erstwhile supporters in Congress now nostalgically recall their splendid administrations. What sober, visionary leaders they were!''

Slade let out a sharp Spanish epithet. ''Drunk in a ditch you're worth more than a thousand Burnets or Lamars! You watch your back here in the city, Sam. I wouldn't trust the likes of James Robinson or Albert Sidney Johnston any further than I could toss''—he paused for a moment, to think of a suitable object, then recalled the six-pounder cannons used during the Revolution—''the Twin Sisters!''

Houston replied, with a snort, ''Johnston sent me a challenge to a duel a few months back. I...er...had Miller file it,'' he said, grinning, pointing to the overflowing wastebasket beside his desk.

''At least he was outspoken enough to face you. I worry about lots of others who aren't so open.''

Houston paced over to the window, then turned to face Slade, his massive six-foot-six frame towering over the seated man. ''I've got a bum shoulder and a busted-up ankle. I've been shot and cut, poisoned by sour whiskey and deceived by sweet women. If none of that has yet killed me, I think I am pretty goddamn tough, don't you agree, Jim-boy?''

In mock gravity, Jim Slade concurred. ''I'll watch for any sign of Kennedy or his agent around San Antonio, sir. I don't think McAllister was our spy, but I'll find out who is.''

''What do you know about an English remittance man named Ashley Markham?'' Houston rapped out at his young protégé.

Slade flashed him a surprised look, once more pitying any diplomat who crossed swords with Sam Houston. ''Ashley

Markham, as far as I've been able to find out, first appeared in San Antonio about six years ago, then wandered off to New Orleans and points east. He seems to be a foppish gambler who lives off a modest allowance sent by his English father, a peer of the realm who wants the black sheep far from hearth and home. He's drifted in and out of San Antonio over the years, but never been connected with Kennedy or, as far as I know, anyone in Mexico.''

Houston shook his head. ''Jim-boy, you never cease to amaze me with my own powers of instruction. I took a green boy and made him into a spy who can roll off the life history of every suspicious character between Washington-on-the-Brazos and Washington on the Potomac!''

Slade laughed. ''Now who's flattering who? You obviously think there's more to this remittance man than I've seen.''

''What if I were to tell you someone saw Markham and Kennedy together with Dick McAllister last spring?''

chapter
4

The ride from Houston was long and lonely. Despite several stops at outlying settlements along the way to glean information on Comanche movements, Slade had a good deal of time to think. His meeting with the president had been very unsettling indeed. There was hard evidence linking Dick McAllister to British meddling in the San Antonio area. He would never have credited the fellow with enough intelligence to be a spy, but then again the boy may have been killed for being in over his head with dangerous men like Kennedy and Markham.

Jim gave a mirthless chuckle, realizing ''the boy'' probably had been as old as himself. Richard Lee had been a perpetual boy, a spoiled, lazy dreamer who had charmed

women and drawn sympathy even from the shrewd Asa
Ketchum. Almost every hand on the ranch had covered his
work for him at one time or another, especially Lee. There
was every possibility that someone could have made the
drowning look like an accident when it was something far
more sinister.

To a man like Jim Slade, hardened by facing death from
Comanche and enemy soldiers, even the fierce, unyielding
land itself, McAllister's weakness was even more contempt-
ible than his shiftlessness. Fool, to have died and left a
young sister orphaned and penniless. The poor kid had
probably earned her passage south on her backside, although Slade grudgingly had to admit she did not seem to
share her brother's aversion to good hard work. Still, she
had her own knack for getting into scrapes and creating
havoc. For the time being, he supposed it was best to keep
her on at the ranch. When she filled out a little, he'd find a
respectable settler to marry her, though for some unaccount-
able reason Slade found the thought of Charlee's marriage to
a farmer very disturbing.

He forced the disquieting suggestion from his mind and
considered Ashley Markham. Someone, either another
Englishman or a *Tejano*, must be helping him get information into Mexico. Markham traveled frequently to New
Orleans, but not often enough to be passing on everything
he had learned by that route. Jim hated to think that one of
his friends or casual acquaintances of Mexican ancestry
might be involved with the schemes of British troublemak-
ers. Of course, many good Texians wanted Sam Houston
dead. The *Tejanos* certainly could not corner the market in
treachery.

Despite Houston's bluff scoffing at the assassination threats
and his wife Margaret's brave front, keeping their home
brightly lit and open to guests every night, Slade worried
about the angry warhawks and power-crazy schemers who
might harm his old friend. What a sorry pass things had
come to, he mused. Houston shadowed by assassins and
himself saddled with a ninety-pound urchin and her tomcat.

By the time he arrived in San Antonio later in the
evening, Slade was bone weary and badly in need of a bath.

He toyed with the thought of going to one of several newer, more pleasant hotels in town, but decided on impulse to go to Sina's town house instead. She was probably there, and even in the unlikely event she had returned to Jake's ranch, her servants knew him. Besides, he planned to nose around town a bit to see what he could learn about the current activities of one Ashley Markham.

"Really, Diego, you know it isn't proper for you to stay here alone with me all night, without a member of my family for chaperone," Tomasina scolded, with a ripple of teasing laughter in her voice. She had been embroidering in the *sala* when he arrived, and was the picture of cool Hispanic beauty, dressed in rich navy blue silk that emphasized the blue-black luster of her raven hair.

He had been let in by José, her elderly porter, who vanished immediately thereafter. "Consider the whole house full of servants as more than ample chaperonage, Sina. Now that you're a widowed lady, you aren't expected to have a *dueña* like a schoolgirl. We are old neighbors, you know."

"But everyone in San Antonio knows we were engaged before my marriage to Jacob, Diego. Rumors about us are beginning to circulate." Careful not to soil her gown, she helped him out of his dust-covered buckskin jacket, tossing it on a wooden chair in the hall with a sniff.

"Oh," he said, quirking an eyebrow in that mocking manner she had come to know so well, "and why do you suppose they're talking? Could it be we've gone riding together too often, or sat together at Mass too many Sundays, or even danced too close at the Mendozas' last fandango?"

"Such things, and servants' gossip. You are too forward with displays of affection in public, Diego," she added primly as his hot golden gaze raked her face and figure.

"If I was really as forward as I'd like to be, Sina, I'd grab you right now and kiss you soundly, never mind that I stink of sweat and horses and need a shave," he growled, rubbing the thick golden stubble on his face.

She made a mock pout. "You are too much of a gentleman for that, and I am too much a lady to permit it."

"More's the pity," he sighed. "Lead on to that bathtub."

"I'll ring for José."

After a long, hot soak, a shave, and a change of clothes, Jim felt infinitely refreshed. He would collect that kiss from the maddeningly beautiful woman downstairs.

Tomasina instructed the cook to prepare a simple supper and then waited in agitation for Diego to join her. How fierce and dangerous he had looked, walking casually into the *sala*, filthy from the trail, bearded and armed like a border bandit. Despite her show of coolness, she had felt a surge of primitive attraction. If he had grabbed her and tried to kiss her, would she have resisted? With Jake she always had, but then he was so much older and coarser. With her late husband she had never felt this strange, hypnotic fascination that she did with her future one. The attraction made her distinctly uneasy. She allowed herself to speculate on how he would be as a lover—after they had married. She knew it would be a tactical error to let him lie with her before their wedding night. No, her curiosity would have to be satisfied in nine months, she decided, forcing the disquieting images from her mind.

"Penny for your thoughts, *bella señora*." Slade stood in the doorway, casually but strikingly dressed in a snowy white shirt, tan breeches, and gleaming black boots.

Caught off guard, she flushed, and stood to offer him her hand. He saluted her palm with soft kisses, trailing them up her arm and throat as he pulled her into his embrace.

"Oh, Sina, I've missed you." He kissed her ardently, teasing her lips with his tongue to gain access, pressing her closely to his body. She neither resisted nor responded. After a moment, he regained control of his physical hunger and broke the kiss, loosening his hold on her. "Do we have to wait until next February for the wedding?" he groaned. "I don't know if I can stand it, *amada*."

Breathlessly, she swished out of his grasp and glided over to the liquor cabinet of carved walnut. "You will just have to be patient, *querido*. You know what a scandal it would be if we married now. Perhaps by late fall . . ." She poured a glass of brandy and handed the drink to him.

He took it and planted a light kiss on her neck. "That's still a long time, but not as bad as next year."

"If you were not gone so often, Diego, you might not be so tired or lonely. Why must you always go on these mysterious journeys? Where do you go?" She teased, but her gleaming black eyes watched his face closely.

"Houston, Galveston. It's business, Sina, that's all. Cattle sales, seed and implement buying. What do you do while I'm gone?" he countered, to turn the conversation from the subject of his business.

"Nothing very exciting, I'm afraid. I receive a few callers, walk in the Main Plaza with my women friends, have fittings at the dressmakers, and once in a great while go to a small dinner party. You know all this, Diego."

"In your social travels, have you ever been introduced to an Englishman named Ashley Markham? Medium height, light blond hair, ice blue eyes, rather a fancy dresser." Slade teased her, but he was curious to see how accepted Markham might have become in polite *Tejano* circles. If Sina knew of him, Markham might have contacts in high places indeed.

She cocked her head in consideration. "No, I do not think so. He is a fop, you say, a vulgar man? How unlike the English."

Slade laughed. "You think everything English is wonderful just because you went to school over there. Believe me, Englishmen are like Texians or Americans or anyone else, a mixture of good and bad."

"And this Markham, he is bad, Diego?" she asked softly.

"Poison," he replied emphatically.

Slade had been gone for three weeks. Each day Charlee scanned the horizon in hopes of seeing his big buckskin horse, but she was disappointed.

In an effort to distract herself, she decided to help the two *Tejanas* from town who did the housework. Dressed in her old patched breeches and a large shirt borrowed from Lee, Charlee learned all the intricate details of oiling furniture, polishing silver, waxing floors, and pressing linens. Compared to her simple chores in St. Genevieve, the work here seemed endless.

Gradually as she and the cleaning women got acquainted, they had begun to relax in the company of the strange young *Americana*. They confided stories about the Slade family and others who worked at Bluebonnet.

At first Charlee's mannish attire and unladylike way of speaking had made Lena dislike her, but old Lupe could see a kind heart beneath the rough exterior. After several cleaning days, Charlee's good humor and hard work had won over even the standoffish Lena.

"Why do you love that *gato feo* so, Charlee?" Lena sat at the kitchen table, watching the girl feed Hellfire bits of chicken from her plate.

Charlee's green eyes danced. "Oh, he's not really ugly, just wearing his medals of valor, sort of like President Houston 'n his war wounds, you know. Besides, I always liked cats more than any critters, and this is the smartest one I ever saw. You should watch him hunt gophers sometime."

"Or steal fish," Weevils interjected from the other corner, where he was washing dishes. The two women laughed as the fat old cook went outside with a pan of dirty water.

"Well, it's sure easier to swipe them from you than get his paws wet catching them himself," she called out to the retreating figure as she scratched the fringed orange ear.

"You are a strange one, *muchacha*," Lena said wonderingly. "I must confess, when you first came here and I found you sleeping in *her* room, well, you know, I made a big mistake."

Charlee's attention shifted from the purring cat to her companion. "Whaddya mean, her room?"

"Oh, you did not know! I guess I should not be so surprised after all. Weevils, Lee, or Señor Asa would not tell a *niña* about *el patrón's mujer* . . . his woman . . . you know, his mistress the Texians call it, I think."

Charlee gave a startled croak. "She lived in the room I have now?"

"*Sí*, for nearly two years. Her name was Rosalie Parker, a fair-skinned Anglo woman Don Diego brought back with him from one of his journeys."

"What happened to her?" Charlee asked, already hating the woman she pictured as a golden, lovely Yankee.

"Oh, about two months ago she left suddenly. Right after Jake Carver's funeral. Not long after that *el patrón* began to spend a lot of time with *la Viuda* Carver," Lena said, with a knowing smile.

"I see," said Charlee ominously. "Havin' a vacancy, so to speak, he was real generous to let me sleep in the unused bed. I bet Mrs. Prissybritches made him get rid of his lightskirt, right enough. She sure seems to call the shots with that man."

"You do not like Doña Tomasina? I *cannot* imagine why. She is so kind to all us servants," Lena said maliciously. "It is a shame Don Diego still wants to marry her after all these years."

"You mean all that gossip about them being engaged before she dumped him for Jake Carver? Why would any woman with the sense of half a brick drop a man like Jim Slade for some old geezer?"

Lupe came into the kitchen just in time to hear Charlee's last remark. "*Quien sabe?* Maybe because Señor Carver was rich and had many friends high in the government. Also, you must remember, *niña*, Don Diego was only a boy then, not the man he is now," she chuckled.

"Oh, *sí*, you should have seen the way he worshiped her back then, all clumsy and adoring. I worked in the Aguilars' kitchen and saw much," Lena added conspiratorially. "His papa and her papa wanted the match, but she chose Señor Carver, who her Tia favored."

"Well, Jim Slade's scarcely less adoring now, if you ask me," Charlee said sourly, recalling the warm glances exchanged between the couple on the humiliating first day she arrived at Bluebonnet.

"He has eyes only for her, and you do not like it, *sí*?" Lupe's round face creased in a dozen places as she smiled at the embarrassed girl. "*Chica*, you look like part of Hellfire's dinner—a scraggly bone he did not choose to eat."

At Charlee's sputtered indignation, the older woman placed a motherly hand on her arm. "I do not say it to be unkind but to show you that you must look like a woman, not a boy, if you wish Don Diego to notice you. Why do you wear men's pants and shirts, all baggy and ragged?"

Charlee blushed beet-red and stammered defensively, "They're comfortable to work in, an' besides, I got me only one dress, that red gingham." Thinking of several pretty flowered frocks she had perversely left in Natchitoches, she silently cursed herself for a Missouri mule.

Lena wrinkled her nose. "That dress is big enough to fit you and me at the same time. Anyway, it is *feote . . .* hideous."

"Well, I guess I did kinda favor it back home because I could move freer in it than a good-fitting dress," Charlee confessed ruefully. "Besides, I don't know a thing about fancy duds, even if I was to go to a dressmaker."

"We must find you something to wear that will at least show your shape. You are *pequeña,* but still, you have curves, I think," Lupe said, with a critically appraising eye as she inspected Charlee's slight form. She pulled the bunched shirt and pants close to the girl's body.

"I have it," Lena chimed in, looking from her own slim form to Charlee's. "My clothes . . . a blouse and skirt. They are only cotton, but pretty. We are nearly the same size."

"Oh, Lena, thank you, but I couldn't take your things. You work hard for your money, 'n oughta spend it on yourself," Charlee protested, touched by her friend's kindness.

"Don't be foolish, Charlee," Lupe said sternly. "When Don Diego gives you your wages you can pay her. Anyway, she has many blouses and skirts, and you have none."

It was settled. Charlee received a package the very next day from San Antonio. Taking it secretly up to her room, she unwrapped it and felt the soft cotton of a snow-white blouse with a rounded neckline embroidered with green thread. There was a billowy full skirt of bright, deep green as well. The color suited her, she decided, holding it up to her hips and looking in the mirror. Her skin was tanned now, the pallor of strain and fright gone, the freckles faded into the golden color the Texas sun had given her. Reverently she placed the skirt next to the blouse on her bed, wondering if she would ever have the nerve to wear them, or to follow Lena's advice and let her hair down to flow around her shoulders. Putting it into a tightly knotted braid had always seemed so much easier than having it tangle in the brush back home.

Then she noticed another item in the package, something white like the blouse—a night rail. It was cut in utmost simplicity with a ribbon to close the demure neck. The sleeves were long and it was floor length. It was also sheer. Why, a man could see right through it! Now why did I think *man*, she wondered in agitation as she held the nightgown up to herself. Well, no matter, here in the confines of her room she could sleep in whatever she liked. And she certainly liked this!

At the bottom of the package lay a pair of leather sandals, fashioned for very small feet, made of thin strips of leather. "Huaraches," she said softly, slipping them on to find that they were a perfect fit; the clothing looked to be the same. She would just have to find the courage to wear the blouse and skirt when Jim Slade returned to Bluebonnet.

Slade arrived on Monday with Tomasina Carver riding beside him. She was dressed in a mauve-gray riding habit. Mrs. Carver would stay for refreshments, thank you, Lena reported sourly to Charlee who was out in the backyard beating rugs. Covered with thick reddish-tan dust that stuck to every inch of her sweat-soaked skin, Charlee wiped the perspiration from her eyes and swore aloud.

"Lena, you'll have to serve. I'll run in and get some biscuits and preserves and make lemonade." Quickly she sluiced her arms and face in a bucket of clean water by the well, then dried off as best she could on her shirt, leaving Lupe to pound away with the heavy beating rod.

Once the tray was ready, Charlee called Lena to take it into the *sala* where Jim and Tomasina were waiting. "Wait—I almost forgot the butter," she called to her friend. Reaching to pick up the neat golden round, her hand encountered orange fur. "Hellfire, you git! Honestly, that cat does love cream and butter," she said absently, using her fingers to smooth the scratchy tongue marks from the top of the butter as she placed it on the tray. She licked her fingers, then knelt to let the cat have his turn, but he had suddenly disappeared.

Never one to miss an opportunity, Hellfire had surreptitiously slid through the kitchen door with Lena before either she or Charlee had seen him. Once in the hall, he had followed the heavenly scent of the butter that Lena carried. He slipped behind the long, low sofa in the *sala*, deciding to jump up on its back and spy out the best place from which to get at the butter.

However, once he landed silently on the wide, soft cushions, all thoughts of food instantly fled from his mind. He had a passion for play that sometimes exceeded even his love for food. There, not two feet away, was a long, rakishly curved peacock feather, gently swaying with each graceful movement of Tomasina Carver's head. The grand trophy was attached to a jaunty hat perched on her elaborate coiffure. He crouched low, tail straight out, rear end wiggling furiously, and canted at just the precise angle for the pounce. There, it moved again! So did the stalker. Claws out, he got a good lock on the center stem of the plume and succeeded in ripping it and the hat from Tomasina's hair.

At her shriek of pain and dismay, Jim turned from staring out the window. Tomasina was holding the ruins of her coiffure in one hand while furiously tugging on her hat with her other hand. Her rival in the tug-of-war had one razor-sharp claw firmly imbedded in the thick stem of the large feather. The screaming woman would not let go and the terrified feline could not do so.

Startled by Tomasina's shrieks, Charlee came flying into the *sala*. A loud masculine oath rent the air when Slade's efforts to disentangle Hellfire earned him a stout slash across his knuckles.

Charlee eyed the disheveled, red-faced Tomasina, the kneeling man sucking a bleeding hand, and the cat, cornered with his now unwanted trophy dangling from an upraised paw while he snarled. "What in hellfire's going on?" she asked.

"That's my line, remember?" Slade growled. "Get that refugee from a fiddle-string factory out of here—minus the lady's headgear, if you please!"

As Charlee knelt in front of the frightened cat, Tomasina continued her tirade. "That is a wild animal, a destructive, senseless brute! It should never, never be allowed in a house! You should have it destroyed! I've never been so frightened in—''

"If you want your fancy hat back, quit your yappin' and hand me the butter," Charlee snapped none too gently. She had no patience with blubbery stupid female vapors. Sina Carver was spite-mean to boot!

Tomasina stood rooted to the floor in horror that a servant, this filthy tramp at that, was speaking to her in such a fashion. Jim handed Charlee the butter.

"Now, be quiet. He's scared. All critters are when they're cornered. For your information, he's my cat 'n no one destroys him without answering to me." Charlee spoke in a quiet but firm voice, all the while easing the butter dish toward the twitching cat.

"Now, Hellfire, old lover, just you take a hairball treatment here while I . . .'' Deftly she flexed the paw with one hand and yanked the plume free while the cat's attention was fixed on the butter. Scornfully, she tossed the hat at the black-haired woman, whose fiery, dark eyes radiated hate. Then Charlee rose in one smooth movement, cat under one arm, butter dish in the other hand.

"Take a half pound of butter off my next month's pay," she called defiantly as she sauntered down the hall.

In the next few weeks, Hellfire and his mistress were to become the bane of Slade's existence. It seemed everywhere Jim went, he was either stepping on a screeching feline's tail or encountering a feisty urchin in boy's baggy clothes. Not the least disturbing thing was the way the girl was winning over his whole ranch. Weevils fairly doted on her and Asa was downright fatherly, but the easy camaraderie between Lee and Charlee was particularly irksome to Slade.

The youth who had been Jim's shadow for years now seemed to spend an inordinate amount of time laughing and exchanging confidences with Charlee. Lee had tried to befriend that worthless cat when it had showed up at Bluebonnet and was amazed at how the beast had adopted Charlee.

One day Slade came on them while they were eating

lunch beneath a live oak at the back of the ranch house.
Charlee was laughing at the cat, who was occupied crouching
over a mole hole across the yard, frozen in expectation of
momentary triumph.

"Atta boy, Hellfire, you'll get that varmint sooner or
later," she praised.

Lee let out a good-natured snort. "Later is right, *chica*.
He's been sitting still as a block of wood for at least four
hours."

"Oh, he knows what he's doing, all right. Sometimes it
takes him all day, but he always gets his mole in the end."

"Loco," Lee said teasingly, tapping his head. "Why not
go after a nice fat mouse or a bird?"

"Why bother? To do that he'd have to chase around in the
hot sun or climb a tree. This way, all he has to do is sit still
in the shade. Oops! There, you see?"

The cat made a blurringly fast lunge with lethal claws and
jaws, neatly extracting a mole from its refuge. The animal
had finally made the error of seeing if the coast was clear. It
wasn't.

Lee whistled in amazement as the cat proudly brought his
treasure over to Charlee and dropped it at her feet, waiting
to be praised. With a smirking "I told you so," she lavished
several affectionate thumps on Hellfire, who then reclaimed
his prize and trotted off to the bushes to enjoy his lunch.

"I tried for weeks to get him to come to me and he
wouldn't, even when I put out bowls of milk. How did you
do it, Charlee? He lets you wrastle with him and pound on
him just like he was a big loppy dog."

"Secret," Charlee said, her bright green eyes twinkling.
"Only a body who grew up with cats knows how to tame a
wild one. You have to figure out his name. I mean his real
name that he gave himself, not the one humans gave him."
She looked solemnly at Lee, who stared in amazement for a
minute, then burst out laughing.

"Just like the pony I've been teaching you to ride," he
said in mock cynicism. "I've fed him apples all winter and
you make friends with him instantly, without so much as an
ear of Indian corn in your hand. Tell me, Charlee, what is
his real name? All this time I thought it was Liso."

"I'll never tell," she said, giggling, "but both Hellfire and Liso are right intelligent."

"Why don't you tell him the truth, *niña*? It's not their names, or their dubious intelligence, it's you and your natural way with dumb animals." Slade decided to enter the conversation. "This picnic open to anyone?" he asked, a glass of lemonade in one hand and a chunk of roast beef in the other. He reclined casually across from Charlee and began to eat.

Bristling, she said defensively, "Hellfire and Liso are not dumb animals, 'specially not Hellfire. He really understands people . . . leastways them worth understanding," she added tartly.

"Prickly little thing, isn't she?" Slade said conversationally to Lee. "And it's 'those,' not 'them.' You know decent grammar when you want to use it," he said to Charlee.

"A body can't even speak her piece around here without getting a lecture like she was in school," she fumed.

Lee watched their exchange, not for the first time aware of the way they seemed to antagonize each other. Charlee always got her back up when Jim came around, just like that skittery orange cat, and Jim was always teasing and patronizing her as if she were a child. Lee had been a shrewd observer of human nature since he was a small boy. Could it be these two opposites were attracted to one another? Lord knew, fancying Doña Sina as he did, Jim had a completely different image of what a woman should be.

Charlee certainly wasn't a lady. She wrestled in the mud with Asa's dog Mutt, baited fishhooks with big juicy worms, shot and cleaned squirrels like a real Texian, and even swore like one, too. And for sure she wasn't all curvy and sweet smelling. Still, he and the men on Bluebonnet liked her better than Tomasina Carver. Come to think of it, Lupe and Lena liked her, too. Everyone did. Maybe Jim was smitten and just didn't know it yet. Sitting back with a grin, Lee watched the two of them argue. It was proving to be a very interesting summer.

The next morning dawned hot and bright. Charlee awoke at sunrise as she always did and decided it was a good day to walk down to the creek and knock a few squirrels out of the overhanging trees. She and Mutt had made friends after their unfortunate initial encounter, and he was a first-rate squirrel dog.

Noon found her and the old black mongrel slogging beside the cool rushing water. Three squirrels were already swinging from her belt. "Let's us set a spell, Mutt, 'n give Beulah here a rest." She set the old Springfield musket carefully against a tree and stretched out in the grass beside the water.

Beulah was the antique firearm she had found in the kitchen, an old weapon belonging to Weevils, which he had taken indifferent care of over the years. When she asked if she could clean and repair it, he had gladly given it to her. One of her most difficult decisions upon leaving Missouri had been to give up her beloved hunting musket. It was simply too big and cumbersome to carry on the riverboat. On the wagon train she had borrowed weapons to hunt with. Once repaired, Beulah had become Charlee's pride and joy.

Of course smarty pants Slade had not believed she knew which end of the gun the shot came out of until the day she brought in half a dozen headshot squirrels for dinner. She could still see the amazed expression that he tried unsuccessfully to conceal. Recalling the incident, she laughed gleefully and kicked off her shoes to dangle her small, rather dirty feet in the cool water.

"Ooh, that feels good. Hmm..." Charlee looked over toward a stand of willows across the creek. Beyond the bend in the stream was the pool where Richard Lee had supposedly drowned. Hit his head diving—bunk! It was a hot day, a good day for a swim, and she could scout the lay of the land at the same time. Why not? Instructing the patient dog to stay with her gun and game, she went to the knoll.

Slade took off his wide-brimmed hat and wiped the perspiration from his brow. Damn, it was hot. He had spent the morning with a crew of men running down a nice bunch of wild mustangs. It was hard, scorching work and he had swallowed a barrel of dust. When the men broke for a midday meal, Jim decided to head down to the pond for a fast sluicing. He felt as sweaty and grimy as his big buckskin, *Diablo del Polvo* or Dust Devil, aptly named both for his color and disposition. A cool swim was just what a man needed to soothe his frayed nerves and aching body.

Approaching the meandering creek, Polvo kicked small pebbles in its crystal shallows as Slade guided the big horse toward the pond around the hill. Just then, the buckskin whickered and pricked up his ears, coming to a halt in midstream.

"What is it, Polvo? Oh, you, Mutt," Jim said, spying the black dog half hidden in the shadows of a large live oak. "What are you doing so far from the house? Asa'll skin you. Say, whose gun?" No more was the question asked than it answered itself. He recognized the old weapon Charlee had resurrected from Weevils's junk heap. He also noted the squirrels. But where was the owner of the paraphernalia? Swearing at the independent way such a young girl went off by herself, heedless of danger, Slade dismounted and tied Polvo's reins to a bush. He must search her out and see that she was all right.

The fact that Mutt was so calmly presiding over her trophies indicated to him that she was in no imminent danger, but he pushed that small consolation aside, feeling hot, prickly, and irritated. Just as he was about to yell out her name, a trill of female laughter and a splash drew his attention toward the pond.

Slade silently drew nearer to the sounds of splashing and singing. A sweet, clear soprano voice was rendering a bawdy popular ballad, "Come to the Bower," with surprising innocence. The song triggered memories for Slade. It was the unlikely piece to which the men at San Jacinto had marched against Santa Anna's guns. On Charlee's lips it sounded strangely enticing. Still silent, he drew closer, finally brushing the tall grass aside to see an enchanting and startling picture.

Charlee stood on a large rock overhanging the pool, preparing to dive into the inviting water. If she looked cool, Jim felt distinctly the opposite. That couldn't be Charlee, the grimy, foul-mouthed, homely little urchin he had come to know and be exasperated with so often. The nymph on the rock was delicately curved, slim, and sleek, obviously a woman, not a scrawny girlchild. Her breasts were surprisingly full, firm, and high as she raised her supple arms in preparation to dive. Her waist was tiny, and the subtle flare of her hips tapered to long, delicately formed legs and trim ankles.

He stood frozen to the ground, staring incredulously at the vision, a guilty trespasser unable to take his eyes from her lovely young body. Her face was partially obscured by her hair, now freed to flow in a mass of rippling silk down her back and over one shoulder. It glinted bronze, gold, even a strange silvery tan in the sunlight, the pale honey-brown changing colors with each gentle whisper of the breeze that caressed it. How had so much glorious hair been concealed in one miserable little knot? It fell well below her waist. He felt an unreasoning urge to grab great handfuls of it and bury his face in the gleaming coils.

Before diving Charlee had carefully waded the perimeter of the creek to check for those supposed rocks beneath the surface. Finding none, she had climbed to this warm boulder to plunge into the inviting depths of the pool below. The sun felt glorious on her naked body, beating its insistent summer tattoo on her pale flesh. She stretched her arms up as if worshiping the azure heavens, wondering how it might feel to have the honey kiss of suntan all over her flesh instead of only her face and hands. Such an unseemly pagan idea, she thought with a laugh, breaking forth in another raucous verse of "Come to the Bower." Papa's drinking companions used to sing it in the tavern in St. Genevieve and she had often sneaked to town, sitting outside and absorbing all sorts of information that would have turned a lady's face aflame. But Charlee McAllister was no lady.

Slade watched her sleek little body slice cleanly into the still blue-green depths, half afraid she might fall victim to the same sickening accident as her brother. But before he could take three steps, she broke the surface and began to backstroke artlessly across the pond with her hair fanned out like a glossy bronze skein, floating around her shoulders. Two pointed young breasts sunned themselves impudently as she floated in silence.

Slade swore virulently to himself, trapped now in a hell of his own creation. Why, oh why, hadn't he stayed clear once he had heard her voice and the splashing? He might have known she'd swim mother naked, damn her perverse little soul. Of course, he never would have dreamed she looked like this. Fully aroused and hard, he clenched his fists in a misery of frustration and anger. He had been much too long without a woman, that was the problem. Rosalie was gone, and Sina only tantalized him with what was forbidden. Such trials would make a man succumb to the charms of any female in proximity. The rationalization sounded hollow even to his own ears. No, his little waif was a woman and an amazingly well-made one at that. The fact that she slept next door to him each night took on a completely new significance now as he forced himself to slink back to Polvo.

chapter
5

When he went to the kitchen for a bite of food and a cool drink, Jim overheard Weevils grousing about his diminishing woodpile. He immediately seized the ax and set to chopping wood with a vengeance. Weevils stood agape, watching the boss, who had not performed such a boy's chore in years. For Godsake, what had come over him?

By the dinner hour, the boss was soaking his exhausted muscles in a tub of rapidly cooling water, wondering what he would do when he saw Charlee later. He could not banish the image of her diving into the water. What would he say to her? By the time he had finished bathing he was no nearer to an answer than before.

The bureau drawer stuck. Slamming his palm against the side of it, Slade was rewarded with the cracking of wood and splinters. The broken drawer opened and he extracted a shirt. By the time he had tweezed the oak fragments from his aching hand—already blistered from chopping wood without benefit of gloves—he was in a superb humor. Tripping over Hellfire at the bottom of the stairs was the last straw. The spiteful feline gave a yowl that would have softened Weevils's biscuits and stalked off toward the kitchen. Slade swore virulently, pounded his sore fist against the newel post, and swore once more. It was shaping up to be a terrific evening.

Jim could not have said exactly how he expected Charlee to look at supper that night—changed in some indefinable way, although he was not certain how. When she entered the dining room, carrying a tray laden with fried squirrel, biscuits, and gravy, she looked the way she always had, right down to the patched breeches and Lee's voluminous old shirt. Her hair was back in its grotesque braided bun, with only a few damp tendrils escaping around her temple to evoke the water nymph she had been that afternoon. The same old Charlee. But to Slade she was now paradoxically different. The scrawny urchin's clothes hid a most disturbingly feminine physique. No one but Jim was aware of it, and that made him even more uncomfortable.

All through dinner Charlee could sense his brooding perusal. Damblasted moody sucker, she thought. At first she supposed it had to do with the screech from Hellfire and Jim's resultant oaths of pain, but when Lee made a jesting reference to the enormous pile of firewood Jim had chopped that afternoon, Charlee knew something more than a collision with a tomcat had provoked Slade's black humor.

She was relieved when she could finally clear the table and leave the men to their tobacco and brandy. As she filled a big granite dishpan with warm water and lathered up the rough bar of wash soap, Charlee could still feel the heat of Slade's burning golden gaze. She felt flushed, and swore as she dropped a dish. With clumsy fingers she picked up the broken pieces and assured herself, "It's just the damblasted heat, that's all. Wish I could go for another swim right now. That'd cool me off."

But the next few days cooled neither the tension between

Charlee and Jim nor the weather. Both were blisteringly uncomfortable. One morning when she had asked Weevils if he'd miss her for an hour while she took a quick swim, Slade inexplicably caught his thumb in the mechanism of the rifle he was cleaning and nearly smashed the expensive piece extricating himself. If he was short with Weevils, Lee, and Asa, he was downright hostile to Charlee. One minute he would upbraid her for her use of profanity, the next he would cuss a blue streak himself. He would make a derogatory remark about her lack of personal hygiene, then yell at her for wasting time when she went to the pond for a swim.

Even more disturbing than his sudden outbursts of temper were the silent, scowling moments when he would sit pensively and study her as she went about her familiar household chores.

Finally, one day after a particularly stormy episode at breakfast, Charlee stalked into the kitchen and slammed the tray on the table. "What in hellfire's got into that man!" she exploded at Lupe, who was busy polishing silver at the big wooden counter by the window.

The shrewd old Mexicana had been working at Bluebonnet for ten years, and she had a hunch about what was setting both the *patrón* and his young charge at one another's throats. Chuckling, she said, "I have watched you watching him ever since you came here. Now he watches you back, and you do not like the taste of your own medicine, eh? Perhaps he begins to view you as a woman, not a child. Although I do not know how he can see through your disguise," she said, sniffing at the baggy boy's clothes Charlee wore.

When Charlee let out a gasp of indignation, Lupe only pressed her attack. "Why do you not wear the pretty things Lena gave you, or at the very least do something with your hair? You will never win him from Doña Tomasina if you continue to hide your charms."

"What makes you even imagine I want Jim Slade? Let Tomasina Carver have him 'n welcome. Two spite-meaner people I never seen."

"*Have* seen," corrected Lee from the kitchen door, a beatific grin spread across his dark, expressive face. He was as determined as his hero to instill the rudiments of proper grammar in Charlee's speech.

"You're eavesdropping, Leandro Velasquez," Charlee accused, the pink in her cheeks growing darker. "Why do you always have to take his part about schooling?" she questioned, changing the subject abruptly to distract him.

"Don Guillermo, Jim's father, came from an aristocratic family in Virginia. My own parents, like Jim's mother, were criollo, people who valued education. The difference between succeeding and failing, being happy or dissatisfied, the whole basis of a person's integrity is related to how much he understands. That's why I study. I don't want to be ignorant. I want to be worthy of the Velasquez name, and I'm very grateful to the Slade family for giving me a chance to learn about the Anglo culture as well as the Spanish. Some day I'll enter politics and help the *Tejanos* gain full representation in Texas."

"Well, I got all the education I want," Charlee sniffed. "My mama was a schoolmarm before she married Papa. She learned—taught me all I need to know," she added defensively.

"No one ever learns all he needs to know, *chica*," Lee said, tweaking her nose in brotherly affection and whistling his way toward the hall door. He paused with his hand on the knob. "You know, Lupe might be right about the clothes, but I'm right about the education."

Later that night, Charlee tossed and turned in her bed, too agitated to sleep. Finally, she rolled over on Hellfire, eliciting a sharp *whoosh* as the breath was squeezed out of him. She threw the sheet off and sat up, regarding the baleful green eyes that stared at her with wounded reproach. "Sorry, ole buddy. I reckon I'm just a poor sleeping companion tonight." The cat continued to glare as if to say, tonight and every night for the last two weeks!

Charlee reached for her coarse cotton robe, then crept downstairs toward the study. It had been a while since she had read a book, and the Slade family library was quite extensive.

The room was comfortably masculine, she decided as she padded silently across the polished plank floor laid with soft buffalo-hide rugs. The bookshelves on the north and east walls stretched floor to ceiling, and an oak library ladder sat in one corner. A long, low sofa covered with slick cordovan leather beckoned the reader, and a tallow lamp's brass fixture gleamed in the moonlight streaming through the large south window. Charlee lit the lamp and made a careful inventory of the library offerings on the walls. Lee was right. Everything was at her fingertips: Cervantes, deVega, Moliere and Goethe, Shakespeare, Emerson, and Thoreau. With a squeal of delight she even found her favorite, Robert Burns, and some scandalously wicked verse by Lord Byron. Mama had preferred that her daughter be edified by Edwards and Milton, but Charlee had always possessed a perverse streak of intellectual curiosity that had led her to pursue less moralistic modes of instruction. As she browsed she remembered Lillian McAllister's lessons to her and Richard Lee. Poor Richard Lee, always more like Papa than Mama, she thought. Charlee's brother had an amazingly inventive aversion to book learning. He played hookey whenever he could, often tempting Charlee to go fishing or swimming with him. As she remembered the sunny days of childhood, tears blurred her vision, but she quickly dashed them away. Silently she told herself, Your family's all gone, even Richard Lee, and you have to make a new life, Charlee.

Reading helped her cope with the loneliness. Over the next few weeks her late-night reading provided her a much-needed escape from the tensions of the day, as well as frequent topics of debate with Lee.

One afternoon Slade overheard a heated argument between the two of them concerning the relative merits of Locke and Rousseau on theories of government and human nature. Amazed, he stood in the shadow of the kitchen door listening to them talk. The damnable little minx had a brain after all! For some reason, her foul vocabulary and crude manners made him even angrier now that he knew she possessed the rudiments of a good education.

Jim spent the end of June and first part of July breaking mustangs and training the pick of the tough, wiry little broncs to be cow ponies for the Bluebonnet remuda. A sleek little paint filly had particularly caught his fancy, and he had spent an additional amount of time gentling her.

Lee had observed the extra attention and casually had inquired of his boss, "What are you going to do with this pretty girl? She's rather small for you to ride, *mano*."

Slade grunted. "As long as I have Polvo I don't need another horse, especially a runty filly like her, but she's fast and bright. Should make a helluva stock horse."

Lee's face was alight. "Speaking of fast, bright females, I imagine you've seen me teaching Charlee how to ride on Liso. For a kid who had only her father's mule for a mount, she's becoming quite a good rider. She could use a horse of her own and I was thinking . . ."

"One runty filly for another, huh?" Slade grinned sardonically.

"It would make a good peace offering, amigo. You've been a real *bastardo* around her lately." If Lee had any thoughts about the reasons for Jim's behavior, he did not volunteer them.

Slade only grunted and continued currying the little horse's gleaming coat.

The next afternoon Charlee backed out of the kitchen door with two steaming blackberry pies, hot and fragrant from the oven, one in each hand. Careful not to burn herself, she edged them onto the shady window ledge and then wiped her hands on her breeches.

"Those smell too good to be Weevils's handiwork," Slade ventured conversationally.

"Oh, I didn't see you," Charlee said, whirling around to confront her nemesis. "No, I baked them. Picked the berries, too," she added, as if daring him to jump on her for slacking off work again. These days there was always something eating him.

"Good. I've been real hungry for some blackberry pie. And one good turn deserves another. Come with me for a minute, Charlee. I have something to show you." His face was grave.

Puzzled, but relieved that he was not going to yell at her, she followed him down to the corral. There in front of the large fenced enclosure stood a beautiful filly with paint markings of black, white, and mahogany, all saddled and waiting—for who? she wondered. She had never seen the horse before, but she knew the men were in the process of training new remuda stock.

"Do you like her?" Slade's manner was casual as he reached out and patted the filly's nose affectionately.

"She's beautiful as an Ozark sunrise, 'n that's the truth," Charlee breathed, her green cat's eyes alight with pleasure.

"She's yours," he said, gently taking the reins and placing them in Charlee's hands.

"What? You can't . . . I can't . . . she isn't . . ." Charlee sputtered in amazement and consternation. "I could never afford a fine horse like this."

"We caught her with that last herd of wild mustangs. Only cost was the time it took to break and train her. She belongs to you free and clear, Charlee."

The last thing her prickly Missouri pride could stand was charity, especially from the likes of Jim Slade. "I know any wild horse that's broken and trained to saddle like this is worth a lot of money if you sell her. I can't accept such a gift," she said primly, "but I do thank you."

"Look"—Slade's voice was taking on an ominously grating tone now—"I own hundreds of horses, and if I want to give one insignificant filly away, I can damn well do it. You're riding Lee's gelding Liso now. You need a mount of your own."

"That's different. We're friends and I just borrow Liso now 'n then. I can't accept charity from you," she said with finality, although her hand had strayed to stroke the filly's velvety muzzle.

"It's not charity. I provide every other hand on Bluebonnet with horseflesh and you'll be no exception," he thundered.

"I'm not a hand, just a cook's helper and cleaning girl. And sometimes I put game on the table," she added puckishly. "Tell ya what, though," she continued, cocking her head and looking up into his forbiddingly handsome face. "I'll work out payment for her—a year's supply of squirrel, rabbit, deer, and whatever else I bring in for supper in return for her. That seem fair?"

Grimly Slade admitted defeat. "Yes, Charlee, that seems

more than fair, although you do try a man's patience. Didn't you ever have graciousness explained to you?''

"Didn't you ever have independence explained to you?" she countered, and was rewarded with a rare albeit grudging smile from Jim.

"All right, Cat Eyes, be a Missouri mule. I can see why that tom took such a shine to you—not just that you both have green eyes. You're both too independent for your own good, too."

When she smiled back at him, her face was luminous. Again he felt an urge to seize great handfuls of her hair and bury his face in its length, but as usual Charlee had it scraped into a bun. "Er...what will you name her?" he ventured, feeling for all the world like a schoolboy.

Charlee considered for a moment as she inspected the bright patches on the horse's shiny coat. "Patchwork," she said simply. "As pretty and bright as one of Grandma McAllister's hand-sewn quilts."

Early in the morning, Slade encountered Charlee and Lee out for a ride, laughing and talking gaily. They waved to him and continued on their way. The boy had been an excellent teacher. Charlee handled her horse superbly, but not all the credit could go to Lee, nor to his own training of the filly. Charlee had exhibited an uncanny way with animals, large and small, from the first day she had arrived.

He fleetingly wished he was the one riding alongside her but quickly suppressed the idea and went on with his morning rounds. Charlee was a continual surprise and irritation who it seemed had come to Bluebonnet just to turn his world upside-down. She was so damn proud, so self-reliant and seemingly innocent, yet he knew there could be no way in hell she got from Missouri to Texas without selling that sweet, slim body for passage. He was doubly certain of that since he had seen her frolicking naked in the water and singing bawdy songs. But now she was skittish and feisty, preferring the company of two old men and a boy to his. As he urged Polvo into a canter, he swore under his breath, "As if I need the aggravation of getting tangled up with that little she-cat."

Like Charlee, Jim had not been sleeping well for some time. Even his long, grueling day in the saddle didn't bring sufficient exhaustion for him to drift off easily that night. Then he heard the faint squeak of Rosie's door opening. No, it wasn't Rosie's room anymore but Charlee's, he corrected himself grimly. Damn, that was the trouble. He needed a night in a first-class brothel. He missed Rosalie just as she had said he would. He heard soft footsteps padding downstairs and rolled over. What was that urchin up to now? A quarter hour ticked by and she had not returned. Too long to have gone to the privy. Swearing, he rolled out of bed and reached for his pants.

Charlee was engrossed in her book when a cool, gravelly voice startled her. "What do you think you're doing?" His eyes scanned the room, ascertaining that she was alone. She was wrapped in a cotton robe and curled up on the big sofa, which seemed to envelop her. Her hair was down, secured in a long, thick pigtail. Her green cat's eyes seemed enormous, faintly frightened, an emotion he'd never associated with Charlee. "Well?" Impatience laced his tone.

She raised a book off her lap and held it clutched to her bosom, still speechless.

"What are you doing with that?" He strode across the room and took the copy of Robert Burns's *Poems, Chiefly in the Scottish Dialect*. Looking at the title he smirked. "You read this crap?"

Defensively she straightened. "I got readin'! I know what I'm doin'!"

He let out a snort of derision. "If you'd choose that dialect poet out of everything in this library, you haven't convinced me."

"I'm Scottish, a McAllister, and proud of it." She bristled like a small, pugnacious dog.

"I rest my case," he said archly.

"I suppose you'd rather read Shakespeare or Dryden," she replied suddenly. "I'll have you know my mama had me read all the Bard's plays and all Emerson's essays, and even Pope's," she added in a bored voice.

"And I'll bet you find Marvell and Pepys much more titillating," he said with a wicked grin.

Charlee let out a gasp, recalling in mortification how she had sneaked a copy of Samuel Pepys's unexpurgated diaries from her Grandfather McAllister's attic when she was barely old enough to understand barnyard facts of life. If she hadn't before she read it, she certainly did afterward!

Slade laughed now and sauntered over to the bookshelves. She watched his pantherish grace and noticed for the first time that he was barefoot, clad only in tight cotton breeches and an unbuttoned shirt. Suddenly he turned and tossed a book at her.

She caught it deftly and flipped the title page open. It was the poems of William Blake.

"I prefer the *Songs of Experience* to the *Songs of Innocence*," she said archly, closing the book.

"You would," he replied scathingly. "I suppose you've also read Swift and, of course, Byron?"

"Of course," she replied haughtily. " 'A Modest Proposal' is one of my favorite essays. I do love satire as well as bawdy."

He continued his search, reaching the high shelves from his position on the floor, she observed resentfully; she had been forced to resort to the ladder. Then he pulled a slim volume down with a muffled chuckle. "If you like bawdy lyrics, let's see how you do with something genuinely sophisticated and sensuous, Charlee . . ."

He walked measuredly across the room and handed her the slim volume. It was John Keats's *The Eve of St. Agnes*. She felt a small tremor when his warm fingers touched hers.

"I take it you've never read Keats?" At her nod of admission, he smiled. "Well, you might find it a considerable cut above 'Come to the Bower.' " The minute the words escaped his lips he could have bitten his tongue! What had ever possessed him to admit to her that he'd been an interloper that afternoon?

It took a moment for his words to register. Then Charlee's face took on a storm-darkened aspect and her deep green eyes fairly stabbed at him with fury. "You! You polecat, you damnable lowlife sneaky snake—you spied on me, you . . . you *saw* me!" She spluttered in rage, unable to think of anything sufficient to describe her mortification.

Slade watched her erupt, feeling alternately guilty, then disgusted with her hypocrisy. He had scarcely seen anything plenty of other men hadn't seen before. "Cool off, Charlee. If you go skinny dipping and screech out bawdy songs at the top of your lungs, you should expect company."

"Some company! A lecherous whoremonger," she spat furiously. "If you think just because I'm sleeping in Rosalie Parker's room I'll be your mistress too . . . well—"

"Don't flatter yourself," he cut in scathingly and spun on his heel to leave as silently and swiftly as he had entered.

Charlee spent another perfectly miserable night, unable to sleep. She finally resorted in desperation to reading the Keats poem that she had brought up from the library with her. She refused to consider why she had not discarded the volume after Slade stalked out. Instead she had clutched it unconsciously to her bosom and carried it with her to her room. By three A.M. she had finished *The Eve of St. Agnes*. Hating to admit she shared anything in common with Jim Slade, least of all this erotically enchanting poem, she nevertheless loved it. On a hot Texas night she drifted restlessly off to sleep with visions of two tragic lovers stealing away through a snowy English landscape.

The next morning Charlee was tired and miserable. How could she face Slade, knowing he had watched her cavorting naked in the water? No one had ever seen Chastity Charlene McAllister unclothed since she was a baby! She cringed to herself but doggedly pulled on her pants and knotted a baggy shirt over her midsection. Taking the long plait of hair, she wadded it behind her head and pinned it securely.

"I'll take Patchwork for a ride. That'll give me a chance to think," she told herself. Resolutely she headed downstairs, praying Slade was true to habit and long departed for the range. At least she wouldn't have to face him until supper.

When she entered the kitchen he was gone, but Lee was still sitting at the table with a cup of Weevils's bitter black coffee in his hands. Looking up, he greeted her with a sunny smile that lifted her spirits. "Good morning, *chica*. You've slept late today. So did Jim. He just left a minute ago."

"Lucky for me, then," she snapped, her mood instantly plummeting at the mention of his name.

"Your humor is as foul as his. Maybe a change of scenery would help, *quien sabe*? I'm going to San Antonio for supplies. You've been wanting to buy some new cooking pots. Come with me?"

Once more Charlee's irrepressible good humor surfaced. "Sounds wonderful, Lee. I hardly got to see the town when the wagon train arrived. I'm sure it's full of interesting sights and people."

The people and sights of San Antonio were indeed fascinating. Lee took Charlee on a tour of the area, swinging slightly southwest first, to approach the city by following the meandering course of the river for which it was named. Strung along its grassy rolling banks at intervals of a few miles sat four vast crumbling structures, recognizable as churches only by the bell towers still standing intact. Charlee could imagine the original beauty of the architecture.

"Such a waste," she sighed as they reached the largest and most impressive of them, San Jose de Aguayo. "Why has this happened?"

Lee smiled. "After Mexico won independence from Spain the government secularized the missions—took them away from the Franciscan order and tried to set up a system using secular clergy. It didn't work."

"Why not?" Charlee asked.

"Times change, politics in Spain, then Mexico City. Not enough priests willing to come this far north into the wilderness. The Indians who were supposed to be converted and educated never wanted to be made over into Hispanics any more than they want to be Anglos now. They trickled off; then the Mexican government used some of the buildings to house troops, as military bases."

"That's what happened to the Alamo, wasn't it?" She remembered reading that in a newspaper account years ago.

He smiled. "Yes. Both Mexicans and Texians used it that way."

"It sure is a shame, all these beautiful buildings becoming deserted rubble heaps. Anyway, I don't hold with churches being used by soldiers of any army."

"I agree," Lee said gravely. "You are not a Catholic, are you, Charlee?"

"No, I'm Presbyterian, but the Slades are, aren't they?" Why did she always seem to want to know more about that obnoxious man?

"Yes, *chica*, Jim's mama was, of course, and when an Americano came to Texas in the old days, he had to join the Church if he wanted to marry or own land here."

Charlee sniffed. "I've seen first-hand how religious his son is." When Lee looked curiously at her, she colored and changed the subject. "When I first arrived in San Antonio, I noticed how many Americans are settling there now."

"More every year, but the population's still mostly *Tejano*. Eventually, if Sam Houston's right and Texas becomes a state in the American Union, I guess it'll change," Lee replied.

"How do you feel about that—what if Texas loses her independence, becomes part of the United States?" Charlee found it hard to imagine becoming a foreigner in one's own land.

Lee shrugged. "I'm proud of my family heritage, but the government of Santa Anna was a bad one. Many people of Mexican ancestry in Texas, men of wealth and influence like Juan Seguin, Antonio Navarro, and Lorenzo Zavala, considered him a dictator. Seven of the men who died in the Alamo were *Tejanos*. So were many members of the assembly that declared independence and those who fought with General Houston."

"Men like Jim Slade? But he seems a lot more Texian than *Tejano* to me. It's only natural he'd want Texas to be American. Do you want the Republic to become a state?"

Lee considered as they rode along for a minute or two. "Jim and I have talked about it often. He has misgivings about the Republic's surrendering its independence to the United States. But Jim trusts Houston."

"And you trust Jim, right?"

"Yes, I suppose that's true, but it's a lot more complicated than that. You see while Lamar was president, he plunged Texas into debt. We're a weak, struggling new nation with a bankrupt government dependent on foreign manufacturing, unable to support a standing army. We don't even have a navy, or any railroads. Then look at our neighbors.''

"You mean the Mexicans who just raided San Antonio this spring?'' Charlee had read every news account about Texas she could lay her hands on since Richard Lee had come here in 1836.

"The Mexicans are only one threat. On our western frontier thousands of Comanche and Apache lie in wait to raid and kill. Then there is this giant to our east, the United States, locked in a power struggle with Great Britain for the Gulf of Mexico, not to mention ownership of the Pacific coast.''

Charlee considered. "I can see why Britain wants the Oregon Territory and even why they want to trade with Texas, but surely they don't plan to invade and conquer it?''

"No, no need. But if they want to keep their favorable commercial concessions with us, they have to keep Texas free of the United States. If Mexico reconquered us, its government is too weak to enforce any trade regulations. Some sort of token takeover by the Mexicans, who are in British debt, would be ideal from London's point of view. That way, the Gulf of Mexico is the Royal Navy's lake. And the United States is thwarted. We're just a chip on the bargaining table of the great powers.''

"But President Houston, I hear, is a pretty fair poker player.'' Charlee grinned.

"Yes, that much is true. I guess, to answer your original question, I'd rather see Texas as an independent Republic, beholden to no one, but if that can't be, like Houston, I'll do the best I can under the circumstances . . .''

"And that means statehood rather than being a British satellite or Mexican province.'' Charlee completed his thought.

"Yes, *chica*, that's about it. Look.'' He pointed ahead as they neared the main part of town. The spire of San Fernando Church towered over low clusters of adobe buildings, surrounded by tall stands of cypress and cottonwood trees.

"That church bell still rings to assemble the local Indian-fighting companies. Jim started riding with a company of rangers when he was fifteen. In those days, it was pretty bloody. Even two years ago, an actual shootout between Comanche chiefs and local residents took place in the Council House." He pointed to a building off the square.

Charlee shivered, finding the tales she had heard of Comanche depredations difficult to believe yet obviously true.

"That's another thing that causes us to mistrust the British," Lee said grimly. "There's pretty good evidence their agents have been supplying money to the Comanchero scum who trade whiskey and guns to the Indians, encouraging their raids."

"How horrible," Charlee said. "Still, I think the Comanche are sort of in the same boat as the Texians—caught between more powerful enemies on every side. They just choose a more basic way of fighting back."

Lee's face became shuttered, but he made a response of reluctant agreement to her logic. "I know no Indians have ever been treated honestly by Hispanic or Anglo settlers, but I also know what happens to women and children in a Comanche raid. I don't—speak of the devil . . ."

"What?" Charlee asked in confusion, following Lee's darkening scowl to where a dapper-looking man of indeterminate age stood beneath a tall copse of cottonwood trees. He was handsome in a dandyish way with curly white blond hair, straight aquiline features, and a startlingly fair complexion. His clothes were expertly tailored to fit a rather well proportioned frame of medium height. "Fancy dresser. Looks foreign," Charlee observed.

"He is. English. Ashley Markham's his name. He gambles and travels between here and New Orleans a lot." Lee watched the casual camaraderie between Markham and the three men he was talking to, all of them *Tejanos* active in local politics.

"A remittance man?" Charlee asked.

Lee scoffed. "Well, someone's paying him, but no one's sure if it's his family or a more official source."

"You mean he's one of them—those British agents you were telling me about?" Her voice hushed to a whisper and she stared harder.

"He's dangerous, whatever he is," Lee said. "Just remember that and stay away from him," the youth instructed her tersely. Slade would have his hide if he let Charlee get involved in this thing! "*Vamanos!* We have a lot to buy before we go home. I'll show you what splendid shops and stores there are in San Antonio, as well as some of the . . . er . . . more exotic amusements. Ours is a city of contrasts."

And indeed San Antonio was exotic and exciting. Charlee was not shocked by the first fight she witnessed outside of a cantina, for in crossing the Southwest on the wagon train, she had seen as bad. Armed, short-tempered men had always been a fact of life on the frontier. However, the casual nudity of the women and children by the riverside was harder for her to accept. Now that her own supposedly private ablutions had been violated, she was sensitive to anyone's bathing where they could be seen. The *Tejanas* had long reserved a quiet stretch of the river just outside town where they brought their washing and their young children. If all could get clean at once, so much the better. By evening, Charlee's senses were full with new faces, spicy foods, magnificent churches, and quaint marketplaces. While Lee drove the freight wagon home she drowsed, relaxed and happy for a change.

That same evening, Ashley Markham had an appointment. As dusk fell like a velvet kiss on the warm landscape, he stealthily made his way through the back entrance of the Carver town house.

"I trust no one saw you, including the servants," Tomasina Carver said, as she gave the suave Englishman a light kiss on the lips and ushered him into her upstairs sitting room. She was dressed in a thin silk robe of pale lilac, revealing a great deal of her voluptuous flesh.

"You did say you'd given the house man and maids the night off. That drunken livery boy was certainly in no condition to hear, much less see me," Markham said peevishly, pulling her once more into his embrace.

She let him kiss her and put his hands inside the thin silk wrapper for several moments, then pulled away with a seductive chuckle. "We must discuss business first, *querido*.

Do you have the money? Your contacts in New Orleans have been rather unreliable lately.''

He swore as he reached to his waist, showing her the money belt he wore. ''There it is, my love, all in gold, just as your Mexican friends specified. Oh, incidentally, I have a new contact right here in Texas now. He will be most reliable and most efficient. See to it that your friends get to their savage allies within the week.''

''It takes time to buy weapons and other things, Ashley, but I am sure they will manage. Who is this new agent, an Englishman? Anyone I know?'' Her black eyes glittered with curiosity and a sense of excitement at the dangerous game she played.

''No one you need concern yourself with,'' he said coldly. ''He's here on instructions from Lord Aberdeen himself and wants to maintain strict anonymity. Travels a great deal. An observant young chap, if a trifle idealistic for my tastes.''

She laughed. ''I used to be a Mexican patriot. Six years of living with Jake Carver cured me of all illusions.''

''Now you only enjoy the money—and the danger, I think.'' He wagged his finger at her in mock reproof. ''How far you've come from the innocent little schoolgirl I met in the English countryside eight years ago, Tomasina. In those days I thought you'd do anything for me. You were infatuated,'' he murmured as he stroked her arm, looking hungrily at her cleavage. ''What happened to change you?''

''My husband, that filthy pig of a Yankee, a crude, tasteless American!'' She ground the words out with loathing.

''You were the one who wouldn't let me touch you back in England, the one who had to be a virgin for her Texian senator. You chose him, Tomasina, a man twice your age, just because he was politically powerful and a good source of information for your friends in the Mexican government. I could have made the loss of your maidenhead infinitely more pleasant,'' he added silkily, caressing her back and buttocks now.

''Don't be a fool,'' she fairly hissed, swishing away from him. ''Every criolla is expected to be untouched on her wedding night. I could not let you complete your seduction,

Ashley. Jake would never have trusted me again if he even suspected I was not a virgin.''

"And Jake was such a good source of information for all those years, information to give to the Mexican government. Pity he had to find out our little game, dearest,'' Ashley said in a bored voice.

"He was of no further use anyway. It was time to kill him,'' she answered levelly.

"You mean you had spent all his money and wanted a richer husband. I'm the one who took a chance rigging that convenient accident and nearly got caught by that meddling young cowhand for all my troubles, too. You owe me, Tomasina dearest. Now, tell me what you've learned from your provincials here in San Antonio that might be worth passing on to my contact. Then, I'll reward you . . . and you can repay me . . .'' He punctuated his speech with several languorous kisses.

Tomasina writhed sensuously against him and let out a triumphant purr. "Where shall I begin . . . ?'' She told him bits of gossip about ranger movements and plans for actions against the Comanche. Then she renewed their embrace, already planning what she would wear to dinner with Jim Slade the following night.

Later that evening as he left the town house, Markham thought back over his relationship with the tempestuous woman whose bed he had just left. When did I cease to be the leader and become the led? he mused. He had met Tomasina Constanzia Aguilar when she was a dewy-eyed virgin in an English boarding school. Even then, Ashley Markham had been in the profession of espionage, and his government had wanted a contact in Texas. It had been easy for him to follow his instructions. The charming man of the world had swept the girl off her feet.

But he had not counted on her willful insistence in following her supposed religious tenets. In retrospect, Markham was certain Tomasina never had a spiritual impulse in her life. No, she simply had wanted a Continental admirer, a platonic girlhood fantasy with him as the principal player, but at the same time she calculatingly had reserved her maidenhead for a wealthy, older husband. Of course, he had guided her in the choice of gullible Jake, who had met his needs as a source of information about Texas politics.

He could still recall Tomasina's coming to him in tears after the disaster of her wedding night. Carver had been crude and rough, leaving her repelled and unsatisfied. All Markham's years of practice at seduction had paid off for him as he finally had succeeded in bedding his beautiful quarry.

She had become a practiced and inventive lover under his tutelage, but gradually he had begun to notice a restiveness in her. She took him for granted, held him at bay until she wanted to give in, demanded he get more money from his superiors. He had become fascinated with her, while she had become bored with him. Much as it galled him to consider it, Markham was sure her attitude had something to do with her resurgent romance with Jim Slade.

Even before Jake's funeral, she had announced to him that she would marry her former swain. Slade was politically influential, privy to Houston's inner circle, she argued. She had tried to convince Markham it would only be another marriage of convenience, but he was certain she was lying. He had observed her with Slade from a distance, watching the intrigue flicker in her eyes. She's fascinated by that young barbarian, a crude Texian, he thought in cold fury.

Well, if Tomasina loved to play with fire, Ashley Markham held a brace of matches. He massaged the handle of his .36-caliber Colt Patterson. The five-shot revolver was his newest toy, purchased on his last trip to London. Mr. Slade just might not survive the honeymoon.

chapter
6

"I certainly hope James has some decent help in the kitchen by now. That fat old buffoon who cooks for him is a

disaster. The food last time was virtually inedible.'' Don
Antonio Montaldo sniffed. Tomasina, who rode across from
him and his wife Beatriz in the carriage, replied, "I understand he has hired a new cook's helper, a young girl from
Missouri, who is quite skillful. Also, Lena Valdez is working tonight, and she is competent.'' Tomasina knew Don
Antonio's veiled question was his way of advising her the
Tejano community was aware of the relationship between
herself and Bluebonnet's owner. Well, damn them, let it be
a scandal if they wished! She was abiding by the propriety
of mourning, a mourning for Jake Carver she could scarcely
feel.

The Montaldos were Tomasina's cousins, slightly older
and very straitlaced, pillars of San Antonio's *Tejano* community. Also invited to dinner this evening at Bluebonnet,
and sharing the carriage, were the Sandovals, Don José and
Doña Esperanza, Jim's aunt and uncle, a vivacious, charming couple who actually seemed younger than Don Antonio
and Doña Beatriz.

Doña Esperanza dimpled and looked over at Tomasina.
"Well, it's about time someone took charge of James's
kitchen, and I am glad to see you are aware of who it is,
Tomasina. That poor man Jim's father hired may be a loyal
employee but he is a dreadful cook.''

At least she had one ally, Tomasina thought archly,
speculating about what the community would think if she
were to marry Jim Slade this fall as she had hinted to him.
Would it create too great a scandal? After all, Jake had been
an old man and an outsider to her *Tejano* circle. Slade, by
virtue of being a Sandoval descendant, was accepted.

As they rode toward the ranch in the swaying carriage,
the five passengers carried on a desultory conversation
about politics, the weather, the Indian menace, and other
matters of life in the Republic. Tomasina's thoughts were
miles ahead with the owner of Bluebonnet. Perhaps she
would marry him in October. A strange little quiver of fear
and excitement coursed down her spine as she contemplated
what it might be like to have him make love to her. He
would be no crude, clumsy oaf like Jake, nor a scheming
weakling such as Ashley. Both of them were so malleable,

so predictable. Of course, Ashley was by far the better lover, but he had become so tiresome of late. The element of excitement and newness in their clandestine affair had worn off long ago.

Slade was challenging and attractive, but he was also an unknown in many ways. Tomasina had already learned in the brief course of their resumed courtship that he was no longer a biddable boy, worshipful and adoring. There was a hardness, a calculated, measuring way he treated everyone now. He was truly dangerous, like a wild jungle cat, and he drew her in fascination. Do I dare to marry him and be at his mercy? she wondered. In part she longed to give in, to see what he would do; in part she cautioned herself to hold back. But she knew she would have him. If he proved too troublesome, well, there was always Markham to rid her of the encumbrance of another unwanted husband . . .

The dinner party would be arriving shortly, Charlee thought nervously. A hard knot of fear seized her just before she stepped in front of the mirror in her room. "Oh," she gasped in surprise, unsure whether the woman staring back at her from the glass was truly Chastity Charlene McAllister. Experimentally, she put her hands up to her face, then ran them down her throat and over her breasts, waist, and hips. So much was revealed by these clothes! The neckline of the blouse was rounded and dipped low to show a delicate expanse of collarbone. The blouse clearly revealed proudly upthrust young breasts. Her waist was incredibly tiny, and the gentle flare of her hips was sensuously revealed by every movement of the skirts as she walked and turned, posing and then gliding her hands over her body in wonder.

Maybe it would not be so hard to be a woman after all. Charlee had spent her whole life envying her father and brother all their male prerogatives and freedoms—to wear pants, to be able to spit and swear, to stay out late, and to go hunting whenever they wanted. But during the past several months she had begun to feel all sorts of new sensations, none of which she would ever admit coincided with meeting Jim Slade. She loved the caress of a soft sheer

night rail against her skin, the crackle of her hair as she
brushed it to the gleaming luster of polished bronze, even
the luxuriousness of soaking in a bathtub. And now here
she stood, taking inventory of her appearance, actually so
frivolous as to hope she was pretty. . . She was, wasn't she?

Charlee critically inspected her small golden face with
bright green cat eyes. Freckles, ugh! She wrinkled a small
pert nose in disgust. But they were only a fine dusting,
almost hidden now by her tan. Her brows were arched
nicely and her forehead high and straight. She had good
high cheekbones, she decided, turning this way and that.
Her chin was a trifle pointed and pugnacious. She smiled.
Good straight teeth, thank heaven, but her mouth was a bit
too large. No, perhaps not if she remembered to smile more
often. She practiced.

Jim quickly finished dressing and hurried downstairs
when he heard the crunch of carriage wheels on the drive.
Tomasina and the other guests were arriving. Her cousin
Antonio was one of the men Lee had seen in town convers-
ing with Ashley Markham. Slade was quite anxious to see
what he could learn about the Englishman from the pompous old goat. Don Antonio might be implicated in the
Mexican government's intrigue, but somehow Slade doubted
it. Montaldo had neither the wit nor the nerve to spy. More
likely he was simply a pawn of the clever Markham.

The guests were greeted in the *sala* by their host, who
treated the widow Carver with a studied familiarity that was
duly noted by the others. They were served cool wine by
Lena and chatted amicably on a variety of inconsequential
subjects. Slade gradually steered the conversation to politics, which set Don Antonio off on one of his tirades against
President Houston and the weakness of the government.

"Why, we have no dependable means of defending ourselves against Comanche depredations. Those savages raid
at will while that drunken barbarian and his cronies sit and
swap jokes in Houston City. It's a scandal, I tell you."
Montaldo's florid complexion was mottled with outrage.

"Considering how that profligate Lamar bankrupted the
government in a war against peaceful Cherokees, it's hardly

surprising now that President Houston hasn't the funds to keep standing troops against the real threat of Comanche,'' Don José retorted, keenly aware of the friendship between his nephew and the president. He himself, like many other *Tejanos*, had supported the general in his campaign for independence from Mexico.

Montaldo snorted, recalling the Sandoval affinity for marrying Anglos.

"We do still have the ranging companies, Antonio. They operate as effectively as we can expect on a volunteer basis,'' Jim put in, knowing full well Montaldo was aware of his participation in the dangerous work of the intrepid militiamen.

"Yes, but there is another thing to consider, James. The militia cannot possibly do the work of trained regulars, no matter how brave and dedicated they may be. Why just the other day I was talking to an acquaintance of mine, an English fellow, Markham . . .''

Tomasina, busy making small talk with her cousin and Jim's aunt, heard Ashley's name. Her senses prickled in warning, and she listened as that babbling old fool Montaldo ranted on about the flaws in deployment of the militia and how helpful Mr. Markham had been in suggesting ways to improve the city council's plans. Damn, she had warned Ashley to be careful about how he pumped information from talkative morons like Montaldo! Anyone shrewd enough to read between the lines of the narrative might well conclude that Markham was a spy! Her black eyes traveled surreptitiously to watch Slade's face. His expression seemed relaxed, even bored, but those cool golden eyes missed nothing, she was sure, sensing the coiled tension in his body. He was a militiaman of long standing and a friend of Houston's. Could it be possible . . . ?

Tomasina's train of thought was interrupted when that odious girl with the masculine name announced that dinner was ready. The waif no longer looked boyish at all—quite the opposite, in fact. Tomasina Carver's eyes narrowed as she took in the transformation of Charlee McAllister. One brief inspection convinced her that she must get rid of the girl before she replaced that disgraceful Parker tramp, who had created such a scandal. She would not be humiliated by having Jim flaunt a live-in whore again. Let him make discreet trips to those awful places in town if he must, but he would not keep a pretty young female living openly in his house while they were engaged! Then her eyes traveled from Charlee to Jim. Tomorrow was not too soon to have the girl sent away!

Slade's eyes widened, then narrowed in reaction to the fetching picture Charlee made in her simple campesina's costume. Now he could see that she was a girl, no doubt about it! The nymph at the pool flashed into his mind, and he felt an unexpected and most embarrassingly unwelcome surge of desire. God, how tantalizing she looked as she turned to go back toward the kitchen, with that mass of changeable-colored hair falling to her waist and those slender hips swaying.

"I say, James, is that the cook's new helper?" Don José questioned speculatively. "She certainly doesn't look like the creature Tomasina described to me at all!"

"Er...no...she doesn't, does she? The maid must have given her some of her clothes," Jim replied in agitation. That scheming little minx! Dressing up for the first time in front of Sina and a whole roomful of guests. He felt a sudden urge to wring that slim golden neck. He could see the amused smirks in José and Antonio's eyes. They were drawing the wrong conclusions, and he did not need any further complications with Sina. Slade swore under his breath as he strolled casually across the *sala* to escort his fiancée to the table.

All through dinner Charlee felt nervous and self-conscious as she moved in and out of the kitchen, serving the elaborate meal. She could sense the eyes of all three men on her, but she was concerned only with the narrowed golden gaze of Jim Slade. He seemed angry with her. In her naivete, she was bewildered as to why, considering all the times he had berated her for wearing her disgraceful boys' pants and urged her to dress like a female. Now that she had done so, he appeared angrier than ever.

And as if Slade wasn't distraction enough, Charlee could feel the hate radiating from Tomasina Carver. The conversation was in Spanish, which was natural considering that all Slade's guests were *Tejano*, but it made Charlee feel even more inferior, intruding on their old world elegance. Just after she had set a demitasse of coffee before Tomasina, she felt a rip as she straightened up. The bitch had caught Charlee's skirt beneath the heel of her fancy slipper and held it fast until it tore! Charlee struggled with an urge to pour the rest of the scalding pot over her tormentor. No, Charlee knew that would be playing into Tomasina's hands and would certainly earn Jim's immediate censure. With gritted teeth she pulled her skirt free and moved on to serve Doña Esperanza.

When the men adjourned to the study to smoke cigars and sip brandy, the women headed upstairs to freshen their toilettes. Tomasina lagged behind her companions and waited until Charlee was alone in the dining room stacking china. Swishing her dark blue satin skirt to get Charlee's attention, she stood imperiously in the arched doorway, inspecting her younger rival.

"Well, you do at least look like a girl, not a boy, now. I'll say that much," she said disdainfully in Spanish. How well she remembered the way Diego's eyes had fastened on the low neck of her blouse when Charlee bent over to place the steaming platters on the table!

"I . . . beg your pardon? Were you speaking to me?" Charlee turned from her task and nearly toppled a stack of china in surprise.

"Who else is here?" Tomasina switched to English. "I want to caution you, my dear, not to indulge in girlish hopes regarding Diego. He is my fiancé and we will be married this fall. All he will ever be able to offer you is a cheap and temporary liaison as his mistress." Tomasina watched the girl's face for any betrayal of emotion.

"You mean like Rosalie Parker? I don't reckon I hanker for that job, thank you." She stared back at the hostile obsidian eyes.

"Surely you aren't naive enough to believe a man like Diego would *marry* a girl from the Missouri hills, a cowhand's sister?" Her voice was laced with scorn.

"You don't need to fret, ma'am," Charlee said, with a

defiant toss of her mane of bronze hair. "I have no designs on Jim Slade, marrying or otherwise. You can have the surly sucker and welcome!"

With that she stomped from the room, recalling in fury the disparaging comments she had overheard the black-haired bitch exchange with her cousin Beatriz earlier. They had spoken under their breaths in Spanish, but Charlee understood well enough. She had a good ear for languages and after months around Lee, Lena, and Lupe, she was learning Spanish rather quickly. She still played dumb when any outsider was around. She had picked up a lot that way, including some rather inventive cusswords from Slade, which Lee had blushed to translate literally.

"Smartass foreigners, think they're too good for a Missouri hill girl, do they!" She slammed dishes into the sink in a fury of confused anger. What was it to her if Jim Slade married a prissy snob like that? She certainly didn't want him!

Then her hands trembled, almost causing her to drop a cup, as she recalled his scorching gold eyes raking her breasts when she bent over the dining room table. "Oh, admit it, Charlee, you wanted him to notice you tonight. You dressed up for him, to please him, and all he did was act as if your looking like a woman was a crime or something," she whispered brokenly to herself, suppressing the sudden urge to weep.

If Charlee was in doubt about her turbulent feelings, Jim was not in the least uncertain about his. He was mad clear through after sending a tearful, angry Tomasina home with the Sandovals and Montaldos. As he returned to the study to pour himself another drink, he mulled over their earlier conversation. She had asked to speak privately with him before the gathering broke up, so he had taken her for a walk through the flower gardens. The roses and daisies were blooming thicker than ever now that Charlee had weeded and pruned everything. Damn, why did *she* keep intruding on his train of thought?

Sina had looked hurt and walked in that haughty, tense

way she had when she was angry. Slade recalled her jarring words to him.

"That young woman you've taken in, Diego, she all but threatened me earlier when we were alone in the dining room. She . . . she actually had the nerve to accuse me of tearing her skirt and said she would pour scalding coffee on me the next time I came near her! She has a terrible temper and uses the most offensive language. I realize she is attractive in an earthy sort of way . . . but she's so common, Diego, and so presumptuous!"

A slow grin had lit his face then, replacing the earlier puzzlement. "You're surely not jealous of a scrap of a girl, are you, Sina?" he had queried teasingly. "After all, you can take care of that problem easily. Marry me now. If you're sleeping in my bed, you'll know for sure no one else is." He had taken her in his arms then and had kissed her hungrily, stilling her angry protests with his mouth and hands. It had been a long time since Rosalie left, and he had been tormented beyond endurance this night.

But Tomasina was not to be put off so easily. She had stormed, cajoled, and wept, pleading humiliation at the presence of a female servant with such impudent manners. No, she could not marry him until fall at the earliest and please would he consider dismissing the little tramp? Tomasina always knew how to play her cards, he would give her that, when to push, when to ease off, how to use her sexuality just enough to tantalize without going past ladylike bounds, how to play on a man's protective nature toward the weaker sex. Jim knew she was conniving as hell, but then he was sure all Hispanic women were.

Sina was every inch a lady, never uttering a vulgar word or doing anything ungraceful or crude, commanding servants imperiously, flirting with gentlemen discreetly, busying herself with dressmakers' fittings and dinner-party guest lists.

Slade suddenly tried to imagine Charlee fending off the amorous advances of a gentleman the adroit, inoffensive way Sina did. Charlee would flatten any man she didn't fancy; he'd bet Bluebonnet on that!

The more he considered the two women complicating his

life, the more confused he became about his feelings. When was the last time he and Sina had discussed literature or history? All she had ever read was the religious pap the nuns had fed her in convent schools. Even the years in England had been wasted on finishing-school skills such as painting watercolors, playing the pianoforte, and doing fancy needlework. He unwillingly recalled the heated political argument he had the other day with Charlee over the British abolitionist movement. She could take different sides of an issue and make a point on either side, yet do it in such an open, pugnacious fashion that she always rubbed him the wrong way. He hated for a bright woman to be not only right, but insufferably smug about it. Then, too, there was the matter of her gutter language and her penchant for doing hard, dirty, men's jobs such as hunting. She seemed to take delight in getting filthy and looking as masculine as possible . . . until tonight.

Slade shifted uncomfortably in his chair and took another stiff belt of whiskey. If that scheming little cat hadn't dressed so provocatively tonight, Sina would never have started in on him, and he wouldn't be sitting here now in a misery of sexual frustration. Damn, he knew Tomasina Carver was a lady and he must treat her as such, but he wanted her, wanted her voluptuous ivory flesh in his bed, that lustrous midnight hair spread out on his pillow. He closed his eyes in torture but found to his surprise that it was a slim, golden body with a wealth of silky bronze hair that flashed before his mind's eye.

He shook his head and got up to pour another drink. As he stood by the liquor cabinet, the door opened and Charlee stepped quickly inside. Slade spun on his heel abruptly and glared at her. "What the hell do you want in here?"

"I was just going to pick up the glasses you men left here after dinner. Do you mind? Or are you going to refill and drink from all of them?" she snapped, taking contemptuous note of his drunken condition.

"For an orphan who pleaded for a job, you've certainly lost your respect for your employer, *Miss* McAllister," he said sardonically, quirking one golden brow while his mouth hardened in a slash of displeasure.

"I show respect when it's due. You're drunk. Anyway, you won't remember what I said in the morning," she sassed.

"I'm not that drunk."

"You will be."

"You're a teasing little tart who has the mouth of a guttersnipe and the morals of that tomcat you adopted." He glared at her, taking in her heaving breasts, thrusting boldly through the thin fabric of her blouse. His eyes seemed to undress her as they raked her body down to her slim sandaled feet.

"You should talk, you randy stud! I know why you're such a bastard to me, mad as a bear drug out in January— your fancy ladylove won't let you touch her, and your whore's up and left you!"

"Keep your trashy mouth off Tomasina, Charlee. She's a lady, no mistake there, just the opposite of you. She speaks properly, acts with decorum, dresses beautifully—*and* has manners, an area sadly neglected in your haphazard education." His eyes raked her body scornfully.

"You've been on me ever since I came here, wanting me to get out of boys' clothes. Well, I dress like a woman and this is the thanks I get!" She stood with hands on her hips, daring him to say more.

He scoffed, "You've dressed the way you act now, I'll give you that much. A skirt doesn't make a woman a lady, but sashaying around in that low-cut costume sure leaves no one in doubt of your gender!" His golden eyes blazed like a prodded cougar's.

Charlee suddenly felt frightened, uncertain what was happening or what he intended. Deciding it was just the liquor talking, she gave up the argument and turned to leave, calling over her shoulder, "Just sit here and stew in your own juices—whiskey basted!" With a jarring slam of the heavy oak door she flounced out, leaving Slade leaning against the liquor cabinet, contemplating two courses of action. He could lunge after the chit and wring her neck, or he could do as she prophesied and get drunk. Reaching for a bottle, he decided on the latter course.

Quivering in rage, Charlee stormed back to the kitchen,

where Weevils was scrubbing the last of the pots. One look at her murderous scowl and he let out a raspy chuckle.

"Yew gone 'n tangled with th' boss man agin. Best leave him be after he 'n Miz Sina had them a go-round. He'll be madder 'n a biled owl fer a few days."

"How can you tell the difference? He's always got the disposition of a poked rattlesnake! I'll get the glasses from the study in the morning, Weevils. I'm going to bed. Where's Hellfire?" She scanned the room, but no orange furball was in sight.

"Must've gone out fer his nightly serenade." Weevils winked at her and his huge belly shook with mirth.

"Honestly, is that all males ever think about, human or feline?" She huffed out of the kitchen, more disconsolate than ever over the desertion of the boon companion who always slept at the foot of her bed.

By the time Charlee had undressed and brushed her hair with a fierce, crackling hundred strokes, she felt her anger abate, replaced by a terrible melancholy. What a disaster the evening had turned out to be! She had tried her best to look like a woman, to be feminine and attractive.

"Yes, I might as well face up to it and quit denying the truth." Charlee looked into the mirror and stared levelly at her image. "I didn't stay on here to find Richard Lee's killer. He probably *did* drown. First couple of weeks here I met everyone on Bluebonnet. No one's a murderer or had any reason to want one sweet, lazy cowpoke dead. I've been staying here because of Jim Slade. I want to be a woman for him."

She took a deep breath, relieved to have owned up at last to what had been tormenting her subconscious for months, maybe even from that disastrous day when she saw him for the first time, him and the elegant, beautiful Widow Carver.

"Why can't I be like her?" she asked her reflection miserably. "A lady! Harrumph! Mean and spiteful, but hiding it from the ones she wants to charm. If being a two-faced bitch is being a lady, he can have her and welcome. I'll never be like that and I don't want to be!" *But I want him.* With that, she slipped off her undergarments and pulled the soft, sheer folds of her night rail over her head. Then she curled up in a fetal ball on the bed, too awash in her own unhappiness to bother braiding her hair into its usual pigtail. "Maybe Hellfire'll come up to keep me company later on." The toll of great emotional turmoil soon claimed her and she drifted into a restless slumber.

A sharp, piercing screech coupled with a dull thud and a string of Spanish oaths awakened Charlee an hour or so later. Sitting bolt upright, she shook her head to clear it and listened for more noise. The wail of outrage had unmistakably emanated from Hellfire and the inventive cussing from Slade, but what of the thud? Tossing off the light sheet covering her, she hopped from the bed and raced barefooted from the room. She was sure no one else was in the house but Slade. Weevils and Lee slept in the bunkhouse, Asa had his own cabin, and Lena had been collected by her husband after the party.

What if Jim was hurt, or the cat? She ran through the long hall and plunged down the steps, where she narrowly missed trampling Slade's long-legged form, which was lying spread-eagle across the landing. The culprit in the mishap sat in the shadows, calmly grooming his back. He paused a moment and stared at her with basilisk green eyes, as if saying in disgust, "Really, what a cat has to put up with around this madhouse," then continued with his toilette.

Charlee knelt by Slade, who was groaning and rubbing his head gingerly with one hand as he tried to sit up. Gold eyes locked on the villain, and a few startling oaths led the tom to a swift and silent retreat upstairs to Charlee's bed.

"Are you all right?" Her voice was hesitant and breathless from her race downstairs after being awakened from a sound sleep.

"Why in hellfire didn't you let him in?" Slade demanded as he struggled to extricate himself from a badly crumpled pile of carpet.

Dazed and half asleep, she asked, "Who?"

"That son-of-a-bitchin' cat!" Slade rubbed his head again and stood up unsteadily. He looked at her puzzled face and continued, as if talking to an idiot, "He wanted in your room and you had the door shut, I guess. I heard him scratching. I was just coming up to bed when I suppose he got tired of waiting for you. He did his usual crash-the-barricade act and tripped me. If I'd been a few steps higher when I stepped on him I might've broken my neck." Now his voice was less angry and more aggrieved.

"Or the cat's neck," she put in, reaching out to steady him.

"Just like you to think of him first," he said morosely as he once more rubbed the knot on his scalp. Boy, that would help his hangover in the morning, yessir!

Charlee was fully awake by now and took note of his unsteadiness. She reached over to guide him into the kitchen. "I better get a look at that lump to see if you need a doctor or if it's just the whiskey causing your list." Before he could protest she had him in tow.

She quickly sat him down on a chair in the kitchen and lit a tallow lamp. "Now, let me see," she murmured, half to herself, as she parted the thick, straight gold hair and rubbed the goose egg.

"Ouch! You have any practice doctoring before?" He flinched and swore.

"Only my pa's mules. I can take care of the likes of you," she said calmly.

He raised his head and reached up to grab her wrist. Her soft palm brushed his stubbly cheek as he took his first real look at her. Good God, he could see right through that white thing she wore! Sitting with her standing between his knees put her breasts at his eye level.

Jim felt her grow very still, suddenly aware of where his gaze had trespassed. With one hand he continued to rub her open palm along his jawline while his other hand reached up to pull gently on a shimmering strand of hair that had fallen over her shoulder. Slowly, as his eyes now locked with hers, he pulled her closer by winding the bronze coil around his fist.

She did not resist, nor did she take any initiative, but moved woodenly, her green eyes huge and luminous. Her lips parted slightly as he pulled them to his own to brush them lightly, experimentally.

Her breath was sweet and the kiss soft and inviting. She let out a muffled little gasp of surprise and started to move back, but he pulled her closer between his legs, wrapping one arm around her tiny waist while keeping his grip on her hair.

"Don't," was all he said before his lips raised to hers once more, pressing more insistently this time as he held her trembling in his arms. She smelled of dried lavender, clean and natural.

Jim could feel her tremble but assumed it was an answering quiver of desire. It never occurred to him that it was virginal fear. It had been such a long time, and his need was so great that he considered no further. He stood and scooped her into his arms.

Charlee found herself being carried down the hall and up the stairs before she could muster her badly shaken wits. Jim placed soft, warm kisses along her temples and eyelids, then on her lips once more. She felt a languorous drowsiness overpowering her speech, turning her limbs to water. "Nn—" She couldn't even speak one word of protest before his lips silenced hers once more.

If Jim was slightly unsteady in his gait when he crossed the threshold of his room, Charlee did not notice it as she held onto him in a rush of dizziness. But when he deposited her abruptly on his large bed, her eyes flew open in shock. She looked around the strange masculine room, with its rough, dark oak furniture and animal skin rugs, realizing for the first time the enormity of what she was doing.

Slade stood towering over her by the side of the bed, methodically stripping off his fancy white shirt, whose studs had hours ago been discarded. As he continued to bare a broader expanse of densely furred chest and lean muscled arms, his eyes never left hers, willing her to lie complacently still in the center of the enormous soft mattress.

She forced herself to sit up, saying, "You're drunk, Jim," but she could not break the hold his eyes had on hers.

"Not that drunk, Charlee, not nearly that drunk." With that he quickly balled up the shirt and tossed it behind him, then knelt on the edge of the bed to take her small face between his hands and silence her protests with a deepening kiss.

He tasted faintly of whiskey and tobacco, compellingly

male, just as she had always known he would. His tongue outlined her lips, then pried them open and entered her mouth. She obliged him by opening wider in a small, whimpered gasp. He twined their tongues together while he explored the sensitive insides of her cheeks. His lips brushed and pressed, caressed and heated hers, until she was mindless and breathless, melting into him, returning the kiss with abandon.

He pressed her back onto the bed without breaking the joining of the kiss. Charlee placed her arms around his shoulders and felt the soft tickling of his chest hair as it teased her sensitive breasts. His hands seemed to be everywhere now, running down her sides, caressing her belly, squeezing and massaging her silky little buttocks until she writhed in wanton ecstasy. His warm lips left hers to trail soft, wet kisses down her throat and onto her breasts. Impatiently he loosened the tie of her night rail and eased it down past her shoulders to bare the delicate perfection of her breasts.

The moment his mouth fastened on one nipple, she arched up, clutching her fingers in his hair with a convulsive cry. His tongue teased and circled one hard little bud, then moved to the other, alternately licking and suckling them as she whimpered in pleasure.

When she was completely at his mercy, uncaring in the throes of her first passion, he regarded her flushed face and the mane of bronze hair spilled across the pillows as she thrashed, tossing her head to and fro. His own breathing was labored and erratic, his eyes glazed with lust. He quickly pulled off his boots and stockings, then stood up and unfasten his breeches.

Through heavy-lidded eyes Charlee watched him undress, realizing what was about to happen but too drugged by passion to stir herself or cry out in protest. *This was what you always wanted, from the first day you ever saw him, wasn't it*? Her eyes drank in his lean, sinewy body, following the thick dark golden whorls of hair covering his chest downward. He freed his hard straining sex and she saw the aroused male anatomy for the first time. Then he was back beside her, his hands and lips luring her into oblivious surrender once again.

Her arms were pinioned to her sides by the half-lowered night rail. Deftly he freed one slim arm, then the other, and slid the gown down past her hips and legs, tossing it to the bottom of the bed. She felt the hot hardness of his body. They rolled back and forth across the wide bed, locked in an embrace, rubbing and caressing, lips seeking, tongues entwining.

Charlee could have gone on like this forever, so new and wonderful was this exploration. How different his body was from hers, longer and stronger, hard and hairy. She buried her face in his chest hair and ran her hands down his narrow hips. But then he reached for one of her hands and pulled it between them, guiding it around the engorged shaft that had been prodding between her legs with such insistence.

She gasped at the hot velvety hardness of it. How could it grow to be so large and rock-hard, yet be so smooth and slick? She caressed him experimentally. Now it was his turn to let out a choked moan of pleasure. Then he rolled her onto her back and reached between her legs to caress the cluster of curls, feeling her wet readiness even before she began to writhe and whimper in wanting. He thrust into her in a frenzy of aching need, only to be shocked by the rending pressure of a breached barrier and Charlee's sharp cry of unexpected pain.

Charlee tensed at his swift, painful entry, but her own flesh was wet and eager, and quickly the hurt began to evaporate, replaced by a keen, aching need. He began kissing her feverishly as he moved inside her. She clasped him eagerly once more, her desire stoked into surging waves of pleasure. She joined him in what quickly became a natural rhythm. Once again she wanted time for all the wonderful new sensations to register, to weave their way through her and build toward some unknown completion. But Slade knew what he wanted, and he wanted it quickly. He increased the pace, and in a few long, shuddering convulsions, spent himself in her.

When he collapsed and withdrew from her, rolling onto his back, he cursed inwardly. Jim had never taken a virgin before, but he knew that he had done so now. The stricken look on her face and the hurt in her green eyes convinced him further. However, as he was satiated and still more than a little drunk, rational thought was fleeting indeed. He pulled her to him, rolling her to fit along his side.

Charlee snuggled down, still tense and aching for something which had not come, yet wanting the feeling of belonging that such cuddling gave her. Jim's soft, even breathing told her he had fallen asleep almost instantly. She reached for the covers crumpled at the foot of the bed. Pulling a sheet over them, she settled down to await the morning.

It arrived all too soon, for she had taken a long time to fall asleep, unused to lying beside a man and still excited from her incomplete introduction to making love.

Slade stirred first, rolling over against the slight body nestled next to him. Great masses of her hair were tangled around him, across his face and chest. He brushed the silky tendrils away and sat up. One look at Charlee, naked and asleep in his bed, was enough to bring last night back to him in a rush of remorse.

Damnation! He muttered several oaths under his breath and swung his long legs over the bedside, then swore again. Clothes were strewn all over the floor, and his pants were on the far side of the room. When he ran his fingers through his hair, he encountered the lump on his head. Wincing, he cursed once more as all the details of the preceding evening came into agonizingly clear focus. Grimly, Slade stood up and walked around the bed, realizing he had a pounding headache. "One part whiskey, one part tomcat, and two parts Charlee," he groaned as he bent over to retrieve his trousers. Once he had pulled them on, he looked again at the sleeping girl. She looked so young in the daylight, young and innocent.

He cringed and slipped silently out the door, heading for the kitchen. They had slept late, not surprisingly. Weevils gave him a peculiar look but made no comment. The cook served up coffee, muttering under his breath, then left the forbidding presence of his boss. If he saw any correlation between Slade's coming to the kitchen half-dressed in the late morning and Charlee's obvious absence, he did not mention it. Slade sat and contemplated what to do. No solution came readily to mind. Finally, he refilled his cup and poured one for Charlee. He would have to face her sooner or later, no use putting it off.

Deprived of Slade's body heat, Charlee had awakened almost immediately to hear his groans and curses as he dressed. Nervous and uncertain, she feigned sleep until he was gone, then sat up in bed, staring around the large masculine room she only dimly recalled from the night before.

"Now collect yourself," she scolded, shifting uncomfortably in the center of the bed. It felt strange to be naked beneath the thin sheet. She was sore between her legs. When she noticed the smears of dried blood on the sheets, she gasped. Still, it hadn't been that bad—in fact, a good deal of it had been downright wonderful, so much so she found herself wanting to try it again!

"I must be a terrible, wicked sinner," she sighed, but felt no genuine remorse. "Well, once we're married, it'll be all right for us to spend all day in bed," she said to herself, then blushed for her boldness.

Charlee sat hugging her knees with the sheet wrapped haphazardly around her. Closing her eyes, she relived every nuance of Jim's skillful seduction, including her own increasingly enthusiastic responses. He seemed awfully practiced at making love, despite the fact he had been drinking. That jarred her girlish reverie a bit, shaking her confidence in the fairytale ending she foresaw after their night of passion. What if he had seduced her only because he was drunk? Did men get more amorous when they were drinking? Remembering her father's tavern companions, she somehow doubted it, but her experience was rather limited. Then she recalled his muttering anger upon arising this morning. Clearly he had been in one of his foul humors when he stalked from the bedroom. Was that because of finding her in his bed?

No. She resolutely forced such disquieting thoughts from her mind. He simply had a hangover and a nasty lump on his head. Maybe he was one of those people who was always crabby when he awakened. Oh, how she wished he would return! Should she dress and go downstairs?

Just then her question was answered when soft footfalls sounded on the stairs. For a panicky second, Charlee struggled to remember if Lupe and Lena were supposed to be here to clean today. No, thank God, not until tomorrow. How mortifying it would be to be caught naked in Jim's bed by her friends. Then she reconsidered, maybe not exactly mortifying. "Oh, I guess I'll never make a proper lady." She sighed and hugged her knees again.

That was how Jim found her when he opened the door. Charlee looked up from her reverie, like some small, delicate doll with enormous eyes and flushed cheeks. Huddled beneath the sheet on the big bed, she looked like a lost, lovely waif. Wordlessly he strode over and handed her a steaming mug of coffee.

Charlee's eyes were riveted on the tall, half-dressed man. He was barefooted and bare chested, clad only in a pair of dark blue pants that hugged his lean frame scandalously. No part of him was unknown to her now. She blushed, thinking how powerful those narrow hips and wide shoulders were when he held her. His eyes were shuttered and his face grave as the silence between them thickened. She felt a prickle of unease as she took a scalding sip of Weevils's awful coffee and looked expectantly at him.

He, too, sipped his coffee and cleared his throat while he paced back and forth like a caged cougar. Suddenly, he stopped and looked squarely in her eyes. "You . . . you were never with a man before last night, were you?" He took one look at her stricken face and realized how obvious the answer was. "Shit! I'm sorry . . . that is, I didn't intend to . . ." He floundered into silence and resumed pacing.

"Just what did you intend?" She put the cup on the table beside the bed and clutched the sheet more tightly to her breasts.

"Not to seduce a virgin, that's for damn sure!" He rubbed one hand through his thick gold hair and winced again from the lump.

"And you thought I was some kind of whore, is that it?"

Her anger was beginning to tip the scales over her shock and hurt.

"What the hell was I supposed to think, you coming all the way from Missouri, an eighteen-year-old girl, all alone?" he said defensively.

"So that gave you leave to presume you could sleep with me?" She was almost yelling now, but her voice cracked.

"You were there, half-dressed in that see-through thing. I haven't had a woman in months! Hell, I was drunk!" Damn, what was he trying to excuse—his reasons for seducing her, or his poor performance when he had succeeded?

Charlee's mercurial mood swung once again to pain. Choking back tears, she swallowed hard and said, "So you were drunk and now you're sorry. Half the ranch must know by now we spent the night together. I can tell by the sun out there it's mid-morning. Any idea what we can tell Weevils or Lee or Asa?" She waited a few moments. "I didn't think so. Certainly not that you'd marry me, huh?" She held her breath.

He sighed angrily. "Look, I happen to be engaged to be married this October. You knew that before you sashayed around with that low-cut blouse hanging open, or picked a fight with Sina, or came downstairs with a see-through night rail on."

"You bastard! I suppose you think that I was out to trap you—that it was all a plot!" She was shrieking like a fishwife now.

"Come off it, Charlee. You're hardly the first virgin to try and trade her maidenhead for some marriage lines." Now he was getting angry. "Besides, you didn't exactly discourage me."

Stung by the truth of his statement, she lashed back. "Well, you oughta know about scheming women, since you're so hell-bent on marrying one, but I'm not like that. Even if I was, I'd for sure pick someone with a better disposition than you! You've got all the charm of a lantern-jawed jackass!"

This wasn't going at all well. Slade sat down on the big oak chair across from the bed and took a few deep, calming breaths. "Look, Charlee, I'm sorry about what's happened,

but you're just a kid. You don't know anything about life or
men, what you really want, or what's good for you.''

She ripped the sheet from the bed as she scrambled off,
wrapping it protectively around her as she stalked with as
much dignity as possible to the door. Haughtily she replied,
''I do know one thing about what I want and what's good
for me—it's not you!'' With that she practically tore the
door from its hinges and departed, slamming it deafeningly
in her wake.

chapter
7

''If I owned both hell and Texas, I'd rent out Texas and
live in hell!'' Charlee recalled the quotation from a newspaper back in Missouri, but she couldn't remember who said
it. ''Well, he was damblasted right!'' The evil gray weather
outside her window was in perfect accord with her mood. It
had rained almost constantly since she left Bluebonnet and
came to San Antonio, to Deborah Kensington's boardinghouse. As the rain beat a steady tattoo on the windowpane,
Charlee pressed her cheek against the cool, hard glass and
closed her eyes, replaying in her mind the events that had
brought her here.

After her disastrous fight with Jim the morning following
their lovemaking, she had marched off to her room and flung
herself across the bed to sob silently, humiliated by tears
that would not stop, tears for a man who did not love her,
did not even want her in his bed after his drunken lust was
slaked. She had heard him stalk downstairs and ride off
toward town shortly afterward. She had lain abed in misery
for over an hour and then forced herself to dress, since she
could not bear the further humiliation of having any of the
men come up to her room and find her in a red-eyed,

half-dressed state. After splashing cold water on her face to reduce the blotchy evidence of her crying, Charlee braided her hair, took a deep breath, and stuck out her chin pugnaciously. Just let anyone even look at her with scorn for her fallen state, or—worse yet—with pity! No one did. Weevils went out of his way to appear unconcerned about her tardy appearance in the kitchen. Asa and Lee ate lunch, making a bit more small talk than usual to fill the void in the conversation left by Charlee. Slade's absence was not commented upon by anyone.

As she peeled potatoes for supper, Charlee wondered if he would be gone for the night, seeking moral support from his fancy ladylove in San Antonio. "He's a chicken-hearted coward, that's what," she swore beneath her breath, yet her throat tightened when she even considered how she would face him when he did deign to reappear. "I for sure can't stay here, but what will I do?"

The forlorn, lonely question hammered at her relentlessly. She hated to admit that she didn't want to leave. Lee, Weevils, and Asa as well as many of the hands at Bluebonnet had become her family. She had found a true home in the spacious, lovely old ranch house, even if she had failed to warm the owner's cold heart. But it was obviously impossible for her to remain beneath the same roof with a man who had used and then discarded her so cruelly.

She had the money from selling the farm, which she could use to start a business in San Antonio maybe, or St. Louis, or New Orleans. But she didn't want to do that. It would mean never again seeing any of the friends she had grown to love. Besides, she had no citified skills. What kind of business could she operate?—a general store, a dress shop, or a milliner's? Hardly! All she knew how to do was hunt, work with livestock, garden, and cook. Scarcely the skills a young woman alone could call upon to invest in a business.

As it turned out, Charlee need not have concerned herself with any planning. Slade had done it for her. He arrived home that day having completed all the arrangements with a young widow who ran a large, prosperous boardinghouse. Mrs. Kensington had been looking for a cook and all around helper since her partner, a somewhat older widow, had remarried and moved away.

Dinner that night had been a nightmare, with everyone around the small table acutely aware of the simmering tension between the boss and the young woman who served the meal in sullen silence. Afterward, when everyone else had left the house, Jim approached her and perfunctorily informed her of his arrangements.

Charlee could still picture him standing there behind her in the kitchen. She had not acknowledged his presence until he had spoken in his low, rough voice. "You and I both know you can't stay here the way things are between us. I visited an old friend of mine in town who needs a helper, a sort of assistant manager at her boardinghouse. It's a really nice, respectable place and she'd pay you well. I . . . er . . . vouched for your cooking and housekeeping skills." His hands had been in his pockets and his level golden gaze fixed on the back of her neck when she had whirled furiously to confront him.

"Of course you didn't mention my other skills to the owner of such a respectable place! I'm just surprised you didn't arrange to send me to one of the local bordellos where you think I belong, you sanctimonious bastard!" Her green eyes were almost black with fury. She had restrained the urge to claw the calm, self-possessed look off his handsome face.

"I said Mrs. Kensington was a lady, from back east. She won't put up with your tantrums or your gutter language, Charlee. If you want a good job, you'll learn from her how to behave—or be out in the streets for real!" His stance had been defensive then, as if he was struggling to cover up a sudden rush of guilt with a black temper of his own.

Before her tears could betray her, Charlee had run from the kitchen, shouting over her shoulder that she would be packed and ready to go in two minutes.

Although she had been prepared to dislike Deborah Kensington sight unseen, Charlee found herself unable to do so, despite the woman's startling beauty and flawless manners. When they had arrived at the front of the big whitewashed building on a tree-lined side street, Charlee had grabbed her bundle of clothing in one hand and Hellfire in the other. "I can tell her who I am without your help, *Don Diego*," she spat sarcastically.

Slade had clamped a strong brown hand on her arm and propelled her toward the steps. With gritted teeth he said, "I will introduce you properly. I can scarcely drop you on her doorstep like a half-drowned kitten."

Rain had begun to fall during their late-evening ride to town, drenching them by the time they arrived. Just as they reached the steps, the front door had opened and a beautiful woman emerged to greet them in the dim twilight. Her gracious, warm welcome had been balm to Charlee's wounded spirit, and the fact that she loved cats put her several notches higher in the girl's estimation. The old cat even liked her, for heaven's sake!

A prickly lick on Charlee's arm brought her out of her reverie. The chewed-up furball gave his mistress a sharp nudge, dislodging her nose from the cold glass pane.

"Ouch! Oh, Hellfire, boy, I'm so glad I still have you." She straightened up from her crumpled pose by the window and scooped the large orange lump into her arms for a fulsome snuggle.

That's how Deborah found them when she knocked and opened the door to Charlee's room. "Good morning! I hope you slept well, Charlee. The first night in a strange place can seem very long. Is the room to your liking?" Her smile warmed up a striking face with lavender eyes and features that were finely molded but strong. A mass of silver-gilt hair was piled softly on top of her head, adding to her already imposing height, and her day dress of simple dark blue muslin looked as elegant as a ball gown.

Charlee smiled faintly as she looked around the cheery room, with its bright green gingham curtains and soft tan bedspread and rugs. "Thank you, I did sleep just fine. The bed is really comfortable and the room is beautiful. I'm beholden to you, Mrs. Kensington." Hellfire jumped from her lap and swished haughtily over to the proprietress to favor her with his presence.

"Please, call me Deborah. I hope we will be friends,

Charlee.'' With that she knelt gracefully and stroked the
preening tom beneath his chin, eliciting several loud purrs.
''I see I already have a friend in you. I hope you adopt
Adam so handily, too.''

''Adam?'' Charlee's voice was puzzled. ''I thought you
were a widow?''

Deborah's face clouded for a fleeting second, and her
eyes filled with a deep, nameless pain. She quickly suppressed
it and said brightly, ''I am. Adam is my five-year-old son.
He's named after his grandfather.''

''I'm sure Hellfire will love him. He always takes a shine
to folks I like, and I love kids.'' She smiled. ''I hope you
don't mind the name, but he's gotten sort of used to it and I
don't think he'd answer to much else now.''

Deborah was amazed at the transformation in the child
when she smiled. Why, she mused, she's really rather pretty
despite the awful snarled hair and the boy's clothing. ''I
assure you, the cat's name is fine. My son hears far worse
from the teamsters and cowboys on a daily basis, even if
they do try to be civil in front of a lady.'' She paused,
uncertain how to proceed. Jim Slade had told her very little
about the girl yesterday, only that she was an orphan and a
capable worker who had come to Bluebonnet looking for
her deceased brother. She needed a job and he wanted to
help her. Deborah read between the lines that Tomasina
Carver might object to a young single girl beneath his roof
and, hence, deduced his need to be rid of Charlee. But
Deborah expected a beautiful, voluptuous creature, not this
pathetic waif in boys' breeches.

''Charlee, I don't know what Mr. Slade told you about
your job here, but we do need to talk about some things
before we set to work.'' Her eyes strayed to the loose shirt
and patched pants the girl wore.

Charlee blushed furiously, recalling all the disasters resulting
from her ventures into dressing like a female. If the lechers
on the boat or in the hotel in Natchitoches were awful, the
humiliation with Jim Slade was the worst of all. She would
die before she'd wear that low-cut sheer blouse and free-
flying skirt again! ''I got me . . . er, I have no other clothes,
Deborah, at least none that fit me.'' Mustering all her

courage, she looked the immaculately attired older woman in the eye.

Deborah caught the girl's speech correction, and appreciated her natural grace and good bone structure. Charlee must have come from a good if highly unconventional family. Her own background had been considered unacceptable by some, Deborah thought bitterly. A kinship arose between the two women, who at eighteen and twenty-six had lived more than many a person twice their ages.

"I think I can advance you enough on your salary to purchase a few simple work dresses and other essentials, Charlee. You'll have to dress like a lady if you want to be assistant manager of this place. From what Jim Slade tells me, you're a wonder in the kitchen and know a great deal about running a big household. With twenty boarders most of the time, believe me, I need help along those lines."

Her warm smile softened the blow about having to wear dresses, and Charlee was interested in what her job might be. "I can cook, and I even hunt and butcher out my own kills." Just as she said that, her face clouded in remembrance. "Oh, I just realized I still owe Slade most of a year's supply of game," she blurted out before she could stop herself.

"That's a lot of hunting," Deborah replied in amazement. "However did you learn to shoot?"

"My pa and brother took me with them back in St. Genevieve County, in Missouri. I can knock a squirrel from a tree at two hundred yards," she added proudly.

Deborah pondered this, then asked, "But why do you owe Jim?"

"For Patchwork . . . my horse. I couldn't let him just give her to me, so we worked out a deal, sort of." She suddenly shifted her eyes to consider the cat, who had now deserted Deborah to sit serenely in the center of the bed.

"How long did you stay at Bluebonnet, Charlee?" Deborah was beginning to draw some conclusions about Charlee's feelings for the handsome young rancher, but she kept them to herself for the present.

"Oh, a couple of months, more or less. I don't rightly

recall," she said, with careless bravado that rang false even to her own ears.

On an impulse, Deborah walked over to the uncomfortable girl and took her small hand. "Charlee, how would you like to become a lady, as grandly dressed and smoothly polished as Tomasina Carver?"

Charlee's cat-green eyes widened and she let out a small gasp of surprise. "Oh, no, I mean, I could never . . . I don't want to be like her . . . I . . ." Her words trailed off.

"I know you could never *be* like her, Charlee. I wouldn't want you to, but you could learn how to dress and act the part of a young belle in polite society. Maybe you'll have a gaggle of young men come calling. You have the potential to be a beauty." As she spoke, Deborah examined Charlee's hair, noting the way the brightening daylight coming through the window turned its rich tan strands amber, red, and bronze. She took the ugly knot of braids down and unplaited it, then stood back to examine the girl's profile and figure. "Yes, yes, you can do a very great deal, if you want to."

"You rotten, no-good bastard! You took her to town and dropped her off on a boardinghouse doorstep like a stray puppy you had no more use for!" Lee was as close to tears as he could get without humiliating himself, yet his fury drove him to even greater emotion. All else failing, he took a roundhouse swing at Jim Slade, who ducked deftly and backed away.

"Cool down, Lee. You're acting loco." Slade blocked another blow.

"How could you do that to her? You seduced her, didn't you? Deny it—I dare you! You dishonored Charlee, slept with her so the whole ranch knew, and then forced her to leave." Lee stood still now, his slim shoulders shaking, while he clenched and unclenched his fists.

Slade put up a conciliatory hand, trying to reason with the infuriated youth, who had accosted him first thing that morning after he found that Jim had taken Charlee to San Antonio the previous night. "Look, *mano*, I don't deny I acted like a fool—all right, a dishonorable fool—but it's over and done with now. I can't change what happened."

"You could marry her—you *should* marry her," Lee accused.

Slade shifted impatiently. "I'm already engaged to Tomasina, Lee. We've set a wedding date for this October."

"Dammit, you're a fool, blinded by a pair of big teats while you let the real woman for you slip away!"

"Real woman, shit! She's a skinny little tease with a foul mouth and even fouler temper. Don't compare Sina with Charlee McAllister, Lee!" Slade was fast losing his temper, too.

Ever since he was a boy of eight, Lee Velasquez had worshiped Jim Slade. Now to see the man he had looked up to like a brother do such a terrible thing to the girl he loved like a sister was more than he could bear. Snarling an oath in Spanish he launched into the older and larger man with the vengeance of hell, landing several blows before Jim was able to wrestle him to the ground, where they thrashed furiously.

"Dammit, boy, you're getting too big to play like this." Slade was surprised at the wiry strength of the young man. In a few years he'd be a fighter to be reckoned with. Jim's jaw ached abominably and his right eye throbbed wickedly. The kid was getting too good! By the time Slade had subdued Lee, both of them were covered with mud and panting heavily in the dank, musky air.

"Now," Slade said, facing the murderous glare from the obsidian eyes glowering up at him as he knelt on the boy's chest, "let's get a few things straight. I'm not marrying Charlee, but I didn't just run her off Bluebonnet. We should never have stayed together in the same house. It's not the right place for her."

"And I suppose that boardinghouse is, huh?" Lee interrupted sarcastically.

"As a matter of fact, yes. It's run by a truly kind woman, a real lady who just might teach that hoyden some manners. Deborah Kensington's given her a good job. She'll treat her well." Slade rose and knocked what he could of the muck off his body.

"You seduced her and took her innocence! You have to

marry her!" Lee knelt on the ground, still glaring at Slade, poised, waiting for a reply.

Jim sighed in defeat, heartily sick of the whole fiasco. "Look, even if I was crazy enough to ask her, *she'd* refuse. In case you hadn't noticed, we really don't like one another very much. She left here telling me to marry Sina and be damned. She never wants to see me again. She hates me, Lee, and I can't say I blame her, but guilt isn't a very good reason to ask someone to marry you. Just cool off and think the whole thing over. Go talk to Charlee and ask her how she feels, if you don't believe me. But remember, it's between her and me to settle." Slade reached a hand out to the kneeling youth, who took it grudgingly and was pulled to his feet.

Lee whistled. "You're gonna have one hell of a shiner, Jim," he said with the faintest trace of a smirk. "All right, I'll go talk to her. Someone's got to keep communications open between you two fools until you come to your senses."

The noonday heat was far too intense for anyone to be abroad. It added to Tomasina's already sizzling temper, but she had to talk to that fool Ashley. After the disaster at Slade's dinner party the other evening, she could envision that moron Montaldo unwittingly giving away Markham's whole role in their operation here. Montaldo was a pompous ass, but Ashley was supposedly a skilled agent. *Men*, she thought disgustedly. All of them are fools! Well, perhaps not all. Jim Slade just might be a great deal more threatening and clever than she had previously intuited. Before, her anxiety had been sexual, a very private and personal fear. But now she realized it might have far more significance. She must discuss that with Ashley as well.

She had sent a servant with a note early that morning. They were to meet in the usual place, Don Felipe Rojas's city house just off the Main Plaza. His wife, Doña Serafina, was a vapid romantic whom Tomasina cultivated as a friend. Don Felipe was an idealistic firebrand who lived for the day the Mexican flag would once more fly over Texas. In the past several years, Tomasina had concluded they were both great fools, but their house was large and well situated for her clandestine meetings with Ashley. He could slip in a side entrance and join her in the garden, well hidden from the street by high courtyard walls. What was more natural and innocent than for the widow Carver to visit her old friend Doña Serafina for luncheon? The real drawback was that she must, on occasion, actually sit and converse with the vapid old bat, just to keep her happy. Today Tomasina decided to have a severe headache and beg off lunch after seeing Ashley.

"What do you mean 'my clumsiness'? Aren't you being just a bit presumptuous, my love?" Ashley Markham's brows arched with his sardonic query. Damn the nasty chit, to berate his espionage skills! When she was a mere virgin schoolgirl, he had been a master of the game!

Tomasina swished her gray silk skirts impatiently and whirled in anger when a jutting thorn caught the thin fabric and ripped it. Swearing, she pulled the garment free and proceeded down the path through the Rojas's flower garden. Ashley followed her angry, stiff strides and listened while she spoke. "You were milking Montaldo like a cow, far too blatantly. You should know how a fool like him will blather about his good English friend's sterling advice on the defenses of San Antonio. Anyone with half a brain could listen to him and realize what he had told you."

"Who would pay any attention to that stupid old windbag cousin of yours?" Markham looked disdainfully at Tomasina when they paused, facing one another, beneath the shade of the live oak in the center of the garden.

"Diego Slade," was her flat reply.

Markham's eyes suddenly narrowed to cold blue slits. "Precisely what do you mean, my dear?"

Contemptuously, she sat down on the wrought iron bench that encircled the trunk of the tree and smoothed her skirts before replying. She was hot and tired and thoroughly disgusted with Ashley's intransigence. "I mean that the other night when my dear cousin was holding forth on your sagacity, it was at a dinner party at Bluebonnet. The Sandovals humored him and I'm certain forgot the incident, but Diego listened far too intently and asked unobtrusive, leading questions all the while. When the British finance a full-scale Mexican invasion of south Texas, do you realize how dangerous it will be to alert Houston to our intelligence work in San Antonio?''

''Do you mean that because your war-hero fiancé is a friend of the president's, he might also be Houston's spy?'' Markham was drawing his own conclusions now and did not like them one bit.

Tomasina rose and paced in agitation. ''I'm not certain. It is possible. He goes to Houston City frequently and drops out of sight at odd times. He's evasive about just what he does.''

Markham smiled archly. ''You mean you can't get your lovestruck Lothario to confide in you. Tsk, tsk, Tomasina,'' he scolded mockingly.

Her black eyes flashed dangerously. ''Oh, never fear. After we're married, I'll get him to tell me everything, Ashley, everything . . .'' She let her voice trail off suggestively, taunting him.

''If he lives to talk, pet,'' Markham shot back in clipped anger. Play with him, would she, flaunting her crude Texian stockman!

''Don't be petty, Ashley. We need him and the direct connection he has with President Houston. He is still active in the militia and knows the numbers and positions of all the troops as well as Houston's plans in case of an attack by land or sea. My contacts in Mexico City tell me General Woll is ready to spearhead an invasion across the Rio Grande to San Antonio, then use it as a base from which to take Victoria and Goliad. After that, with naval support from their new armored ships, the forces can destroy Houston City and drive the Texian pigs north, past that wretched city of Austin, into the arms of the waiting Comanche.'' Her eyes glittered with malice and excitement.

Did she really believe such a fantastic scheme would work? Markham wondered. Aloud, he said, ''All of this is contingent on *Tejano* cooperation in San Antonio and British gold, is it not?''

''Yes, British gold to buy guns and whiskey for the savages and to equip Santa Anna's army. You get the gold for me and my countrymen. We will spend it wisely,

Ashley, believe me. And while you gather intelligence, do be more discreet, will you not?''

Markham slipped noiselessly from the garden and let himself out through the wrought-iron grill door at the side of the Rojas mansion. He had much to mull over, the plans from Mexico City as well as his relationship with the highly volatile Tomasina. There was also the matter of dealing with Jim Slade, who he was certain would prove a formidable adversary. Deep in thought, he did not notice the slight figure of a girl across the deserted street, who stopped in midstride and gaped at his secretive departure from the Rojas garden.

Charlee was taking a shortcut on her way home from the general store on the Main Plaza. Suddenly she saw a dapper-looking figure emerge from behind the gate, unescorted. Odd, she thought, that a gentleman would leave from a servants' entrance. His dress obviously bespoke upper class. Then he turned and she caught sight of his face. It was that Englishman, Markham, the one Lee had said was dangerous, who might be a spy!

That alone would have piqued her interest, since he was leaving the home of a *Tejano*, but what made it even more significant was that on her way to the store earlier, Charlee had seen Tomasina Carver enter the Rojas home by the front door. A queer coincidence, indeed. Could two such unpleasant people know one another? ''I'm just fanciful because I've been warned about him, and I don't need to be warned about her,'' she muttered to herself, deciding to tell Lee the next time he visited her.

Laughingly, she recalled his visit of yesterday. He had sported a nice set of swollen knuckles on his right hand and had assured her, under duress, that Slade had a matching imprint on his left eye. He was mortifyingly protective of her, she thought fondly. In many ways he had taken Richard Lee's place. If truth were told, he was a good deal more conscientious about her welfare than Richard Lee had ever been. She quickly pushed that thought aside as disloyal. Nevertheless, her young *Tejano* companion had cheered her greatly with his assurances that she still had a place in everyone's heart at Bluebonnet—everyone except Jim, of

course. Lee even tried to convince her that Slade was
genuinely attracted to her and would marry her if only she
would accept his suit! Ridiculous!

Charlee let out a proud, bitter laugh at that bit of fantasy.
Lee was surely a Latin romantic if he believed such stuff.
Lord only knew what fabrication Slade had made up to
excuse his own guilt, she thought disdainfully, and then she
dismissed the whole thing from her mind. She had more
than sufficient concerns to occupy her time and attention
now that she was living at Kensington's boardinghouse.

Deborah's establishment was run like clockwork, neat
and orderly, yet wonderfully spontaneous. The boarders
were an odd assortment of men and women of all ages and
walks of life, ranging from a prim schoolteacher who had
been left widowed in the War of 1812, to a gristly old
Indian fighter and scout named Racine Schwartz. She had
gone to the general store that afternoon to buy him pipe
tobacco. Mrs. Kensington did not allow chewing, thank
you. It saved a lot of washing the walls.

If the people were diverse in background and education,
all were basically respectable and surprisingly mannerly for
such a wild place as Texas. Even old Racine, despite all his
scars and hair-raising tales, never cussed in front of women-
folk, and minded his table manners surprisingly well for a
frontiersman used to the rigors of living in the wilderness.

Charlee was placed in charge of the kitchen after the first
evening, when she amply demonstrated her skills by roasting a succulent haunch of venison with wine and fine herbs,
as well as baking half a dozen luscious peach pies. The
boardinghouse larder was well stocked with a surprising
variety of fresh and salt-cured meats, and the backyard
boasted a large vegetable garden, several varieties of fruit
trees, and sundry berry bushes. In addition to overseeing the
kitchen, Charlee also was to take charge of the planting and
harvesting of all home-grown produce. She had a great deal
more to learn about bartering for meats, staples, and delica-
cies as well as keeping the linen closets stocked, the laundry
done, and the accounts up to date.

Charlee felt immensely fortunate in having the opportunity to learn all the intricate details of running a business and

at the same time using the domestic skills she had cultivated since childhood. She did not want to admit she owed her good luck to Jim Slade, but it could not be denied. "I'll just show him what I can do all by myself. I'll be a woman of property someday and never be beholden to him or any other man."

She would always be beholden to Deborah, however. In the first few weeks she lived there, Charlee learned to reword her ungrammatical speech, not to mention curbing her crude remarks and cussing. It was Deborah who first convinced her to embark on the precarious and unlikely task of refining dross to gold. She would become a lady.

"You're walking as if you have tacks in your shoes, Charlee." Deborah sighed.

"Well, it's these da—cursed high heels! It's not bad enough, having to slog around with a hundred pounds of petticoats and trip on long hems and cinch your waist in like a whey-belly horse, but now... high-heeled slippers!" She sighed and sat down on the large horsehair sofa in the front parlor.

Deborah came over and placed one elegant hand on Charlee's slim shoulder. "Take heart. Once you get in practice, it won't seem awkward at all. You're tiny and short, Charlee. You need the height and grace the heels give you. A great many tall, gawky girls would give anything to be petite and delicate like you and be able to wear such pretty shoes."

"What do you mean, 'be able to'? Any woman who's fool enough to want them can buy a pair," she replied in disgust.

Deborah's laughter echoed across the large room. "You never considered how great male vanity is and how fragile their self-image. A woman can't be taller than her dance partner or she'll soon be a wallflower."

Charlee harrumphed over that. "Seems to me men are a he—whole lot of trouble, more than they're worth. Anyway, if so many short men are worried about finding short girls to dance with I shouldn't have any trouble with partners."

"But Jim Slade is tall. He might like a woman he can

look in the eye." Deborah waited a moment. "Like Tomasina Carver."

That brought forth a display of temper. "Why in hellfire should I care! Let him marry that padded hussy and dance with her all night long!" The minute the implications of what she'd said dawned on her, Charlee crimsoned and cast a furtive glance at Deborah to see how she reacted to the unintentional double entendre.

Torn between mirth and compassion, Deborah chuckled for a minute and then sobered. She smiled warmly and sat down by Charlee's side. "You're in love with him, aren't you, Charlee?"

An angry denial formed on her lips and then died. What was the use? She had fought it and had denied it before that night. Then, after his cruel rebuff, she had denied it again—all to no avail. She sat still, awash in her own misery, saying nothing, revealing everything.

"If you want to, you can get him away from that conniving bitch," Deborah said softly.

Charlee jerked upright. Never since she'd met Deborah had she heard her utter one improper syllable.

"That's right, I don't like her either, and I know she's not right for him. You are." Deborah smiled winsomely.

"That's what Lee told me, too, only I didn't believe him. Oh, Deborah, you don't understand. He's so obsessed with polish and manners. He wants a real lady who's well read and traveled and has all the social graces, one from a fine old family, like his mother or father's. For certain, not a Missouri hill girl," she concluded sadly.

"In case you haven't taken stock, you've traveled quite a bit more than most women hereabouts, you're certainly well read, and your mother was a schoolteacher. I think your bloodlines will stand up under inspection. You have a lovely face and quite a perfect, fine-boned figure. You've just never learned to display your looks to advantage."

"I wore a skirt once for him and he . . . well, let's just say I didn't like his reaction," she finished in frustration.

"Your friend Lena's peasant costume? No, that was a tactical error. There's more to being a lady than being enticing looking and wearing a skirt, Charlee. You have to know how to dress appropriately and how to walk, talk, dance, serve tea. All the things you refused to let your mother teach you.''

''How'd you know that?'' she challenged guiltily.

''Let's just say I guessed, given your rather unorthodox mixture of skills. What I'm trying to tell you is, you can be as fine as any lady in Texas or anywhere else, but you have to work at it, no matter how silly or boring you think it is. Deal?''

''Deal,'' Charlee answered grudgingly.

It was baking day, and the last thing Charlee needed in the busy kitchen early that morning was Adam. But when Deborah left on an emergency call to assist Dr. Weidermann as a nurse, Charlee had to take on the responsibility of watching the active five-year-old. She loved the bright, handsome boy dearly and often played with him, discovering the delight of having a child to love, but five-year-old children and fifty-pound sacks of flour do not mix—at least not with very satisfactory results.

''Sadie, you start proofing the yeast while I measure the sugar,'' Charlee said to the elderly black woman who assisted her in the kitchen. Sugar, such a rare and expensive commodity, was used sparingly and kept in a special drawer in Deborah's pantry. Charlee set her huge crockery mixing bowl on the table and went to get it. While she was gone, Sadie carefully added warm water to the sticky dollop of yeast she had separated from the starter. Her back was turned to the boy, who played on the kitchen floor next to the heavy flour sack.

Just then, old Racine Schwartz called from the front hall, ''Miz Deborah!'' With a sigh Sadie set her wooden spoon in the middle of the bowl and walked ponderously toward the door to explain the missus's absence to the crotchety old man.

Charlee knelt in the pantry and measured a cup of sugar, careful not to spill a granule. When she rose, she suddenly realized how effortlessly easy wearing full skirts and petticoats had become to her, almost like second nature. She had on a simple rust-colored cotton dress, which brought out the bronze highlights in her hair and accented the tawny hue of her complexion. It was a cool gown with a slightly scooped neckline and elbow-length sleeves, serviceable for work, but still ladylike and pretty.

She was learning her lessons a day at a time, and so far it had not been impossibly painful. In fact, it was becoming rather fun to feel feminine and admired. A goodly number of young men, some of them boarders, some workers in town, had come to sit on the big wide veranda of Kensington's in the evening and sip lemonade with her. Charlee had never even thought about being courted before, and she was pleased to feel a real surge of female vanity when Billy Wilcox tried to kiss her the other night. She knew that with a little encouragement either Sam Knox or Paul Bainbridge would invite her to the dance next week, although she hadn't decided which one she would choose.

Realizing she was wool gathering, she smoothed her skirt and left the pantry to return to the main kitchen. The sight that greeted her almost caused her to drop the precious sugar. There sat Adam, with his beautiful black curly head bent in intense concentration . . . over a huge mountain of flour on the floor. In the center of the pile, he had painstakingly hollowed out a deep crater and filled it with water and the yeast paste from Sadie's bowl. He was stirring vigorously with a grubby wooden spoon and an even grubbier hand.

"I'm making bread, Aunt Charlee, just like you 'n Sadie do," he announced proudly, his big chocolate eyes aglow with pride. "I'm helping you . . . only I couldn't reach the table . . ." He stopped hesitantly when he saw the look of horror spreading across Aunt Charlee's face.

Taking a deep breath, Charlee calmed herself. "That's all right, Adam, but you—"

"What dat chile done now!" Sadie stood in the hall door, hands on her hips, with a look of mounting wrath in her eyes. "Lordy, Miz Charlee." She shook her head, scuttling to the other side of the room for a broom.

"No, wait, a broom will only make a bigger mess. The paste will stick to everything. It'll harden like plaster. Let's mix the water through the flour and then shovel it into the wheelbarrow Chester keeps out back. You fetch it while I get our pastry chef here out of harm's way."

With that, Charlee knelt at the edge of the boy-made volcano and extracted Adam's hands, which he promptly threw around her shoulders, coating her liberally with the sticky batter.

"Oh, I'm sorry, Aunt Charlee. I should've waited for you, only I never get to help," he hiccuped.

As she soothed the crying child, Charlee felt the tug of one of his little hands on her long plait of hair, which had fallen forward over her shoulder. The gleaming bronze braid was now covered with a grayish white ooze.

Sighing resignedly, she said, "It's all right, sweetheart. You help me finish making a big dough ball and then we can all shovel it up together. Here, help me." The dress and her hair were now covered with paste, as was Adam. Thinking of how much bath water they'd need that night, she began to gently work the squishy ooze of yeast water into the mountain of flour, careful not to break the dam and create a flash flood across the kitchen floor.

It had been three weeks since Charlee left Bluebonnet. Every day, Slade had worked furiously until he dropped, driving his men almost as hard as he drove himself. Finally, he had decided he must go to town to ask after the lumber he'd ordered. It wasn't likely to arrive for another week, but it salved his conscience to have an excuse for venturing into San Antonio.

Then, just by chance, he ran into Deborah Kensington walking across the Main Plaza as he left the freight office. "Good morning, Deborah. What are you doing abroad so early?" His inquiry was polite and casual.

"Oh, good morning, Jim. I've been up since five helping Dr. Weidermann deliver a fine baby girl to Mrs. Spurgeon. What are you doing in town?" As if she didn't know!

"Oh, I just inquired at the freight office about some lumber. I'm building a new corral. How is Charlee working out?" He fell in step with her easily, since her tall stride was nearly as lengthy as his own.

Oh, so casual, aren't you? she thought in secret amusement, but she said, "Come see for yourself. I left her and Adam baking bread this morning."

By the time they arrived at the side porch, they could hear squeals of delight from Adam and soft chuckles from Charlee. They quietly climbed the steps, and Slade looked through the open door over Deborah's shoulder.

Hearing footfalls, Charlee looked up from the blob that was rapidly engulfing her, the boy, and the kitchen floor. The laughter died on her lips when she saw a dark blond head behind Deborah. "Oh, Deborah! I didn't expect . . . I mean, Adam and I were . . ." She held the boy protectively in her arms, at a loss to explain the debacle, when an irate Sadie came through the back door for the next wheelbarrow load.

Looking at her employer, Sadie pointed an accusing finger at the boy and said sternly, "Dat chile gone 'n done it dis time, Miz Deborah, I declare—"

"No, really, Deborah, it wasn't a malicious trick. He was only trying to help us," Charlee put in.

She could never imagine what an endearing sight she made, kneeling on the messy floor with the pretty rust dress all smeared with flour, her long braid curling softly over one shoulder and a dab of flour on the tip of her freckled nose as she comforted the disconsolate child. Slade took in the startling transformation. She looked, for all her disheveled state, like a lovely little madonna, all soft and feminine. He felt a strange tightening in his chest and swallowed hard.

Before he could gather his wits to say anything, Deborah broke the tension with a hearty laugh. "Well, it looks as if my son has struck again. I'll relieve you of him and head for the washroom, Charlee. Good luck to you and Sadie with the cleanup. I'll send Chester to the store for another sack of flour."

As Deborah departed with Adam, Charlee stood up awkwardly, humiliated to have Jim see her in such a hideous mess. Forcing a smile, she said ruefully, "I think this is where you came in last time."

Slade laughed and gestured over to the sill where Hellfire watched with an air of tolerant boredom. "Well, he's here, but I don't see a dog on the premises."

She joined him in the laugh. "At least it's not mud this time."

The awkward silence extended after that until Sadie began to shovel another load into the wheelbarrow, muttering under her breath all the while.

"I . . . I have to help with this and then start another batch of bread. We're out, and we need at least eight loaves a day around here. Friday's always baking day." Charlee knew she was babbling.

Watching her flush pinkly and push a stray lock of hair off her smudged cheek, Slade smiled, stifling the impulse to reach over and caress her small, lovely face. How had he ever thought her boyish or homely? "I have to go now. I just wanted to see how you were doing in your new job. Deborah can't sing your praises enough. See, I told you you could make it, Charlee."

Misinterpreting his praise as another excuse for his desertion of her, Charlee bristled and said stiffly, "Yes, I can and I am. I do appreciate your help finding me this position in town. I'm learning a great deal from Deborah, and I have a real social life for the first time."

"Social life?" he queried darkly, his thick, dark gold brows furrowing over fierce amber cougar's eyes.

"Yes." She preened as she plopped a big scoop of paste into the wheelbarrow. "Billy Wilcox and Ray Larkin took me for buggy rides last week, and next Saturday either Sam Knox or Paul Bainbridge is escorting me to a dance at the Pearsons'. I haven't decided which one yet. It's really a lot of fun living here in town."

"I'm ever so glad you've found so many ways to amuse yourself," he said evenly just as Sadie bumped him with the wheelbarrow. Glancing from the old woman to Charlee, he nodded to her and stepped out of the way. "I have to be at Sandovals' for luncheon with my aunt and uncle, and Sina, of course."

"Of course," she echoed acidly, distaste for his fiancée written all over her face. For a fleeting instant she considered telling him about seeing Markham and Tomasina at the Rojas place but immediately changed her mind. He'd only think she was fabricating a wild tale out of jealousy.

''Perhaps I'll see you and Mrs. Carver around town from time to time,'' she said as she helped Sadie put the last of the goo in the barrow and deposited the shovel on top of it. ''If you'll excuse me, I have to change these clothes before they harden on me.''

Before Slade could reply, she swished past him and vanished through the hall door,

chapter
8

Charlee twirled around the floor of her small upstairs room and then looked over at Deborah for approval. Her transformation over the past month had been incredible indeed. Slowly, wonderingly, she ran her hands over her face and down the curves and contours of her body. Was this beautiful lady really Charlee McAllister?

Thoroughly enjoying her handiwork, Deborah sat on the bed after assisting Charlee with her toilette. Gleaming coils of her incredible multicolored hair were piled high on Charlee's delicate head, while the rest bounced over one shoulder in long, soft curls. Deborah had shown Charlee how to apply the lightest hint of kohl to her eyelids and darken the tips of her thick, brushy lashes so that her green eyes looked larger and brighter than ever. Her sprinkle of pale gold freckles was toned down with a light dusting of powder, which was enhanced by the tawny color of a sun-kissed complexion, flawless and glowing.

The revelation of all those soft, slim curves in her tiny figure was even more amazing. Deborah's ability to see beyond the raggedy ill-fitting clothes had not prepared her for Charlee's truly elegant if petite proportions when properly dressed. She had helped Charlee select the fabric, color, and style for her gown. It was made of a soft silk chiffon, light and airy for the warm Texas night. The color was anything but cooling, a deep, fiery crimson that brought out the golden bronze highlights in her hair and contrasted with her deep green eyes. They had sewn the dress themselves, Charlee becoming almost as adept with needle and thread as she was with a squirrel rifle. The neckline of the dress was low in front, coming to a deep cleft to reveal the curves of her high young breasts. It was caught with a satin ribbon just beneath the bustline. The skirt was very full, flaring out from a waist circled with the same satin ribbon. The sleeves were long and elegantly fitted at the cuffs, emphasizing her delicate wrist bones. The red satin ribbon was repeated at the hemline of the frothy skirt and on the cuffs. The simplicity of the dress enhanced the dazzling color and the delicate form of its wearer.

"Do you think I need anything else?" Charlee asked nervously, smoothing the silk skirts for the hundredth time as she peeked down at the dainty red satin slippers on her feet.

As Deborah pinned a tiny cluster of white rosebuds in Charlee's hair, she smiled and replied, "No. Only the cameo." She referred to the white cameo necklace on a slim gold chain, suspended in Charlee's cleavage. "It adds a touch of innocence and delicacy to the fiery, sophisticated dress. You, Miss McAllister, will be the most beautiful woman at the ball."

"Only because you refuse to accept any of your suitors' offers and aren't going. Why not, Deborah? It would be so much fun. I feel guilty going without you." Charlee's deep green eyes took on a pleading look. Why did Deborah persist in her grief? Surely five years was long enough to mourn any man!

That familiar, oddly hurt look flashed across Deborah's face once more, only to be carefully erased as it always was. "No, I can't, Charlee. I've had my fill of dances, parties, and beaus. I have a child to raise and a business to run. You go and have a wonderful time with Paul. And who knows, perhaps someone else might show up?"

Charlee snorted crossly. "If you mean someone tall and blond, forget it. He only goes to the *Tejano* fandangos. His fancy ladylove wouldn't dirty her skirts associating with a room full of Texians.''

"If she married Jim Slade, she'd have to, wouldn't she? But then maybe she won't marry him, if you play your cards right.'' Deborah gave Charlee a shrewd, assessing look.

"You sound just like Lee. Honestly, Deborah, I'm not interested in getting married at all just now, least of all to that conceited, boorish snob.'' With that she kissed her friend on the cheek and twirled out of the room, holding her full skirts as gracefully as any lady to the manor born.

Jeb Pearson and his wife Mavis owned one of the largest freight lines in Texas. With thousands of settlers pouring into the Republic every year, the demand for supplies of all kinds, from dry goods to hardware and lumber, was phenomenal. The Pearsons had become wealthy in the space of five years, not an uncommon occurrence in the wide-open new nation.

Desirous of displaying their wealth, Jeb and Mavis had built a huge two-story house on the outskirts of the city, complete with a ballroom, which was now festooned for the gala dance that evening. The rugs were rolled up, and the polished plank floor gleamed, reflecting the light from hundreds of imported candles, winking from handsome brass chandeliers. The big double doors to the grounds were open on three sides of the house, admitting a pleasant breeze through the crowded room. An eight-piece "orchestra" was tuning up for some hearty reels and hoedowns. The Pearsons even boasted a piano, where a man was plunking out lively tunes in time with the fiddles and guitars.

Charlee made inconsequential small talk with Paul Bainbridge as they entered the ballroom after greeting their host and hostess. Still nervous over Paul's effusive compliments on her appearance, Charlee scanned the room in search of a familiar face, taking in the long white linen-covered tables groaning under the weight of roasted pork loins, crispy fried chicken, golden corn dodgers, garden peas smothered in freshly churned butter, flaky apple pies, and even freshly turned ice cream. Immense bouquets of wildflowers were everywhere, filling the air with their fragrance. Women decked in their gala finery swirled in time to the music. Paul gallantly assured Charlee she was the most beautiful woman there.

Could it be true? she wondered. If so, only one man would convince her of the fact, and he was not present. Pushing that thought aside, Charlee decided to have a good time. And, quite magically, she did, garnering envious looks from many a Texas belle whose partner deserted her to vie for a dance with the lovely lady in red. Whirling across the floor in the arms of one admirer after another, Charlee was grateful for all Deborah's patient instruction, including lessons on how to avoid the stomping feet of one's partner without losing one's sense of rhythm or sense of humor. Despite clumsy dance partners, sweltering heat, and a slightly off-key piano, the evening was pure enchantment to Charlee. She found herself laughing and trading quips with cowboys, store clerks, blacksmiths, and teamsters.

Slade stood in the hall doorway after making his obligatory salutations to Mavis and Jeb. He knew Charlee must be here. Then he caught sight of her gleaming bronze curls far across the room. God, she was the most vibrant, breathtaking sight he'd ever seen, in her flame-colored silk. Just then she threw back her head and laughed at her partner's sally. He could see her smile and it dazzled him, as did her superbly proportioned petite body, flying gracefully around the floor in a waltz.

He found himself drawn hypnotically across the crowded dance floor to cut in on Billy Wilcox, who rather ungraciously turned Charlee over to him. "Well, Deborah certainly is to be complimented on working miracles," he breathed as he scooped her into his embrace and whirled her away into the waltz.

He felt her stiffen in his arms for a second. Then she relaxed and snapped back brightly, "And I suppose I deserve none of the credit myself?"

"If you're fishing for more compliments than you've already received, milady, yes, you do look beautiful in that dress. But your waltz step is half a beat off." His amber eyes were alight with a mixture of impatience and some other unnamed emotion.

Her smile was withering now as one tiny foot came down on his instep with its sharp little heel digging in. "Oh, dear me, how clumsy, Mr. Slade, but then I'm still new at this waltz thing, as you just pointed out yourself."

"*Touché*." His smile spread slowly, warmly.

She could not help but feel the magnetic pull of him. Damn, why must he affect her this way? At her slight softening, he tightened his grip around her waist and she felt her breasts tingle as they brushed against his chest. Charlee stared raptly at his brown satin cravat, faultlessly tied inside a white silk shirt and tan linen jacket. "I'm not the only one decked out in my finery tonight, James August. Since your fiancée isn't here, whom are you trying to impress?" She waited a moment and smiled to herself.

Slade's reply came like a bucket of ice water dashed over her head. "I always dress to fit the occasion, Charlee. I'm only glad Deborah has taught you to distinguish the difference between trail clothes and evening wear. After hiding in boys' rags all these years, it's past time you learned. But that's beside the point," he rushed on when he saw her gasp and begin to frame a retort. He lowered his voice and eased them over toward a deserted alcove in the east corner of the room. "What I have to know concerns your . . . ah . . . health. I've counted a full four weeks since the night you left Bluebonnet, or, should I say, the night *before* you left." He waited to see if what he said had sunk in.

Lee and Weevils had both made it clear to him what they thought of his cavalier treatment of the innocent girl he might have left carrying his baby. He was not at all certain what he would do if she was pregnant, but he would at least be obligated to support the child. He must ask. Looking straight into her luminous green eyes, Jim saw obvious embarrassment and confusion there.

Why was he reminding her of their night together? It obviously meant nothing to him, so why dredge up humiliating memories just to taunt her? She tried to break free of his imprisoning grasp. "If you want to celebrate the anniversary of my loss of innocence, you can do it alone!" she whispered furiously.

"I want to know if you're pregnant, you dense little

fool," he hissed hastily, holding onto her wriggling, silk-clad body. "You were raised on a farm. Surely you can't be that naive." One look at her stricken face convinced him that she could be.

Oh, Lordy, she'd never thought of *that* unlikely possibility! She stood very still now, frozen in horror, her mind gone blank.

Not daring to breathe, Jim asked in a quiet and deadly voice, "Have your courses come in the past month?"

She felt certain her face was as red as her dress when the realization dawned on her. How utterly stupid! He must think her a complete moron now as well as the hoyden he'd always believed her to be. "Yes. Mr. Slade. You can wipe that stricken look of terror from your face," she spat icily. "Not that I'd marry you even if I *were* with child."

Just as she broke free, he whispered tauntingly, "As I said once before, don't flatter yourself. I only intended to take care of my responsibilities toward the child. That didn't include an offer of marriage." He stood there watching her stalk toward the side door of the ballroom, head held high with no backward glance. *Why did you say that, dammit! You know you'd have married her if she were carrying your child.* An inner voice confronted him with the truth he was loath to face.

What was it that always made the two of them incite one another to do and say such rash, cruel things? Slade swore to himself and walked over to the table where servants were handing out generous glasses of whiskey to the gentlemen. He needed one.

Charlee could hear Paul Bainbridge's voice calling to her as she fairly ran out the side door, narrowly avoiding a collision with several dancers in the process. Once the blessedly cool night breeze hit her flaming cheeks, she took some calming deep breaths and forced down the tears. *Please don't let me humiliate myself by crying,* she pleaded silently to no one in particular. The sour taste of bile was still lingering in her mouth when Paul finally found her sitting on a garden bench, but at least her face bore no telltale evidence of tearstains.

"I brought you some lemonade, Charlee."

Paul was built solidly as a tree trunk, with crisply curling brown hair and wide brown eyes. Many of the girls in town fancied him, since he was attractive and his father owned the largest general store in San Antonio. Charlee had accepted his invitation to the dance more out of curiosity than anything else. He was one of the few bachelors in town who had not courted her yet. Now, after one brief evening, she decided the other girls could fight over him. He was boring and tended to put his hands in places where she didn't want them.

Smiling thinly, she accepted the glass and said, "Thank you, Paul. The fresh air out here is wonderful tonight."

"I think the climate's so healthy in Texas a body plumb has to go somewhere else to die." His eyes were fixed on her cleavage as he spoke.

She considered the joke about renting out Texas and living in hell, then decided against sharing it. "Well, a few folks have died, I think, Paul, even here in Texas," she said gently.

"I don't want to talk about dyin', pretty lady. No siree. You and I have a whole lot of livin' to do," he rasped, while one hand took the empty glass from her hand and deposited it carelessly on the ground. Then he reached for her shoulder and her waist, pulling her to him before she could protest.

For a minute, Charlee let him kiss her, just to see what it felt like. Billy Wilcox's kisses were boyish and sloppy, as were Sam Knox's. She was becoming a connoisseur of technique, she decided, grudgingly admitting that none of the callow youths in town measured up to Jim Slade. Bainbridge certainly didn't—ugh! She tried to break free, but her struggling only seemed to inflame him more, unlike the other boys who had quickly and apologetically desisted.

"Why so prim 'n cold, Charlee? I seen you dancin' with Jim Slade like he was a prince or somethin'. What's he got that I ain't? My family's rich as the Slades, 'n we ain't got no greaser blood in our veins neither. You oughta be glad to be shut of him, honey."

With that he renewed his assault. Charlee gasped and then went limp against Bainbridge's chest. When he loosened his hold on her in surprise, she reared back in his arms and gave him a sound smack across his square, stolid face. Before he could retaliate or she could continue her counterattack, a cool, gravelly voice interrupted.

"I think the lady wants shut of *you*, Paul. And this is one greaser who'll damn well see to it you honor her wish. *Comprende?*" Slade emerged from the shadows. He presented a tall, lean, decidedly menacing figure silhouetted in the moonlight. He had left by the front door, thinking to avoid the unsettling chit, then had heard the sounds of their struggle carried on the still night air. He'd consumed just enough whiskey to be spoiling for a fight, and Bainbridge's slurs were a perfect opening.

Charlee sprang free of Paul now that he was distracted by Jim. Brushing her skirts and rubbing her hand across her mouth, she whirled on her rescuer in humiliated fury, killing mad at men in general. "I could have handled this without your help. All you want, both of you"—she shot her fiery glance back at Bainbridge, who was standing with fists clenched now—"is to have a fight. Neither of you gives a tinker's damn about me!"

"Stay out of my way, Charlee. I brung you, 'n I'll take you home, but first I'm gonna fix one meddlin' half-breed."

Bainbridge easily outweighed Slade even though he was several inches shorter. His chest and torso were massive, and he had a reputation in town as a brawler. But Slade was lightning fast, a veteran of dozens of Indian fights, a survivor of deadly combat in war. His reach was longer than Paul's, his aim surer, and his wits cooler. After half a dozen roundhouse swings that stirred the breeze but failed even to ruffle Slade's cravat, Bainbridge charged in like an enraged longhorn.

Slade's face split in a slash of white teeth as he grinned like a shark. It was all over so quickly Charlee could scarcely see what happened. One minute Paul was ramming his body toward Jim, the next he was sprawled on the patio, rather like the sack of spilled flour in her kitchen last week. Slade had punched him once in the solar plexus and chopped the back of his neck wickedly as he went down. Bainbridge lay groaning.

"Well, are you satisfied? He's scarcely more than a boy. You could've broken his neck," she seethed.

"A skull that thick has to be carried on a neck that can withstand a lot more punishment than I gave it. He outweighs me by a good thirty pounds, for Christ's sake! Anyway, in case you've forgotten, he was getting rather familiar with you. Or was I mistaken? Did you really enjoy his classy seduction? Just playing coy, Charlee?" Each accusation was laced with sarcasm as his golden cougar's eyes raked her disheveled form.

"You rotten, arrogant bastard! Ooh!—I promised Deborah I'd quit swearing, and I haven't slipped once in the past month—not until I encountered you! Now just why do you think that is, *Don* Diego?" She pulled herself up to her full height, now glad of the extra inches the high-heeled slippers added. Glaring murderously at him, she stormed, "Don't use me as an excuse for any more of your drunken brawls, you abominable—"

Her words were cut short as Slade grabbed her and pulled her to his long, hard body without warning. Gold eyes dueled with green eyes as his lips descended slowly, inevitably down to fuse with hers.

The intensity of the kiss stole the breath from both of them, then sent them plunging into a hot, panting frenzy as they pillaged each other's mouths. He growled deeply and lifted her off the ground, molding her tightly to him. As she melted into him she ran one slim little hand up to tangle in his thick, gold mane of hair, pulling him down to kiss her all the more savagely. Their hips pressed intimately, instinctively together.

Charlee could feel his arousal even through her layers of skirts. Blindly, heedless of their surroundings, she teased him and rubbed her lower body against his, answering from some deep, unsatiated wellspring of need. Oh, she wanted this, wanted him, wanted something so desperately, something only he could give her. She could feel Slade tremble as he reached down to pick her up, scooping her tiny body into his arms effortlessly without breaking the fiery seal of the kiss.

What in hell was he doing? What had she done to bewitch

him? Jim could feel her abandoned response, as well as his own need to show her what she craved, to give her what he had not that first time. He took a few long, uneven strides, and then Bainbridge, reviving, gave a long, plaintive bleat of pain and began to struggle into a sitting position. Slade cursed as he nearly fell over the youth.

Quickly he set Charlee down and tried to collect himself, all the while eyeing Bainbridge, half with anger, half with gratitude for preventing a rash act, the consequences of which he preferred not to even imagine.

Charlee stood on wobbly legs, fighting waves of dizziness and breathlessness, yet too proud and humiliated to reach out to Jim for support. She could see that he, too, was shaken and laboring for breath. At least there was that consolation. Whatever had possessed her to react so instantaneously and obviously to his rough advance? She called herself every name she could think of, foolish and foul. How would she ever live this down? If it hadn't been for poor, stupid Paul, she'd have let Slade drag her into the bushes and ravish her. Who was she kidding? She'd have ravished him!

Suddenly she felt Jim's strong fingers on her elbow, propelling her toward the front of the yard. "Polvo is tied out front. I'll take you home."

"No, I won't go anywhere with you," she hissed, wrenching free with a mulish set to her jaw.

He stood still then, dropping his hand and looking her up and down in contempt. "And exactly what do you plan to do? Let your gallant escort back there waltz you home? Or perhaps go back into the Pearsons' house with your hair half unpinned and your lips swollen from kisses. You give yourself away, lady." He reached out and lightly touched the pink flush across her collarbone and the tops of her breasts. His fingertips affected her like a burning brand, and she gasped, suddenly aware that he was right. She was disheveled and disoriented. He had marked her, and her reputation would be ruined if she appeared inside in this condition.

Hating him for his knowing smirk, and aware that he was as glad as she that Bainbridge had forestalled their folly, she grudgingly said, "I'll go back to Deborah's with you."

Slade swung effortlessly onto the big buckskin and then
bent down to pull her up in front of him. He kept an arm
around her to hold her steady on the bouncing horse. Her
stiff, unyielding posture told him that she was willing him
not to touch her. He could see her profile in the moonlight,
her little chin stuck out mutinously as she forced down the
tears welling under her thick lashes.

She had pride, he would grant that, as well as startlingly
unexpected grace and beauty, he added grudgingly. That
must be what led him to that fit of furious temper, seizing
her and beginning the savage kiss that had nearly undone
them both. What had come over him?

They rode in silence down the wide, tree-lined streets,
deserted at this late hour in the sedate residential neighborhood. They finally came to Kensington's boardinghouse
and Slade reined in Polvo. He could feel Charlee begin to
wriggle down, eager to escape his presence. A flash of
perverse anger coursed through him. A few minutes ago she
would have let him take her right there on the ground in
Pearsons' garden. Now she acted as if he were a leper. As
quickly as it came, the anger fled. He had acted abominably,
just as she had said, certainly aiding and abetting Bainbridge
in spoiling her gala evening. He sighed, gently but firmly
holding onto her until he could dismount. Then he helped
her down so as not to tear the beautiful dress she wore.

Charlee froze in terror when she felt his hands on her,
keeping her from fleeing as she so devoutly wished to do.
She had controlled her tears and her temper so far, but she
could not stand to have him touch her much longer without
breaking down completely. When he reached up and lifted
her from Polvo, she shivered as her breasts brushed across
his shoulder. She could feel the warmth of his breath on her
face. *Coward*, she cursed herself, yet she was afraid to look
into his face. She turned toward the front of the house the
instant he released her, but then his voice stopped her
retreat.

"We have to talk, Charlee." It was that same low gravel
voice she had heard in her dreams so many nights, and it
still had a hypnotic effect on her. Her step slowed, but she
did not turn. Then his hand reached out and caught her wrist

with surprising gentleness. "Please wait." Perhaps it was the firm warmth of his big hand over her tiny wrist, perhaps the plea in his voice; she turned and faced him.

"What do you want of me?" She hated the plaintive wail in her voice and forced herself to meet his eyes.

"First of all, I apologize for my conduct tonight. I had no right to say what I did inside, or to grab you just like Bainbridge did in the garden." He released her wrist now and stood very still. His eyes left her face and fixed on a point high over her right shoulder.

She stood frozen in surprise. The last thing she expected from Jim Slade was an apology! Before her dry throat would allow her to speak, he began to pace and to talk in low, intense tones, running his hands in agitation through his hair.

"Look, whatever it is that happens between us . . . it's pretty damn explosive. But I guess you know that as well as me." He shrugged in rueful bewilderment. "I don't think it's love, but it's nothing as uncomplicated as lust either. Hell, I don't know what it is!" He threw up his hands in frustration, then looked at her, his golden eyes reflecting confusion and pain to match her own.

"I don't understand what came over me in the garden either," she said breathlessly, feeling the heat of a flush steal up her throat and face.

"I guess what I'm trying to say is that we both should take some time to think out our feelings." Slade paused and looked expectantly at her.

"You already made yours crystal clear to me last month, as I recall." Her voice was ice cold now, each word a whiplash of condemnation. What did he want—to make her his mistress? "You're going to marry Tomasina Carver."

"Dammit, I don't know what I'm going to do," he exploded.

"Shh, you'll wake half the boardinghouse with your yelling!" she whispered fiercely, her heart beginning to drum furiously in her breast. What did he mean? Would he break his engagement? "As I asked before, Jim, what do you want from me?" She would never again make the

mistake of presuming anything with this complex stranger
whom she loved.

"Just accept my apology for now and stay out of harm's
way. For God's sake, keep away from Bainbridge and the
rest of those clumsy schoolboys who'll maul you every
chance they get." Damnation, that sounded too much like
jealousy to his own ears! The slow smile spreading across
her piquant little face made him wince. She had interpreted
it just that way, obviously.

"I'll try my level best to retain what small measure of
virtue I still possess," she said primly. With that she
vanished into the shadows on the veranda, leaving him
standing alone in the moonlight, feeling a complete fool.

Charlee spent a restless night, tossing in her lonely bed,
furiously angry at the ruin of her debut as a lady, but
breathlessly excited at Slade's parting words and actions.
Upon rising, she once more reviewed their tempestuous
interchanges that preceding evening. Though he was unsure
he loved her, he was undeniably attracted to her and certainly jealous. At least that much had been established. She
debated confessing to Deborah what had happened. Her
older friend might be able to coach her in how to act around
Jim the next time she saw him. Of course, it would be a
considerable embarrassment to tell Deborah *everything*.

Charlee's debate was quite unnecessary, as it turned out.
By the time she had dressed and gone downstairs, she was
late for church. The Methodist circuit minister was in San
Antonio for a rare visit, and all Protestants of various
denominations flocked to hear him preach that Sabbath.
Being raised Presbyterian, she had planned to attend the
service with Deborah, a lapsed Episcopalian. It was to be
held on the lawn of the Chalmers place, just off Dolores
Street.

Deborah was waiting with Adam, who looked for all the
world like a small, dark cherub. Charlee glanced from
Deborah to her son and wondered for the hundredth time
how such a blond woman could give birth to the chocolate-
eyed, black-haired little boy. Once she had asked Deborah
about Adam's father and had received such a poignant,

crestfallen refusal to discuss him that she had never pried again.

"I'd almost given you up, Charlee. Come on. Reverend McGiver won't wait to begin, even if I am giving him free room and board for the week he's here." Deborah noted the circles beneath Charlee's eyes. Well, she must have had a full evening of fun and dancing all right. Why was she so quiet then?

Smoothing her pale lavender skirts and straightening her straw bonnet, Deborah quickly inspected Charlee's outfit as they left the house. The deep yellow cotton gown she wore set off her hair and made her look as fresh and bright as a spring buttercup. Charlee had naturally good taste in styles and an eye for color as well. Her social graces were coming along, too. She could dance, pour tea, and converse without using profane or vulgar expressions—well, at least most of the time, Deborah amended to herself with a small chuckle.

"How was your debut as belle of the ball, Charlee? Did Paul step on your toes much?" she queried brightly as they were helped into the carriage by the handyman Chester.

"Well," Charlee said carefully, "let's just say it was eventful and the least I had to worry about from Paul Bainbridge was his stepping on my toes!"

Deborah gave her a quizzical glance, but said no more, as Adam began to chatter excitedly while they rode through the streets of the awakening city.

When they arrived near the Chalmers's big rolling front lawn, a kaleidoscope of thronging men, women, children, mules, horses, and dogs greeted them. Color and noise were chaotic. Calico skirts swirled and ruffled parasols twirled as the women and girls giggled and gossiped. Farmers, stiff and uncomfortable in starched shirts and suit coats, sweated in the hot mid-morning sun. A small spotted dog darted in and out between skirts and boots, chasing a boy whose irate mother caught both by an ear, eliciting similar yelps from child and canine alike. One teamster, obviously suffering under the duress of the Sabbath, was forced to move a pair of recalcitrant mules without benefit of swearing. A group of would-be choir singers, woefully out of practice, were braying an off-key version of "Shall We Gather by the

River?'' It was joyous pandemonium, a typical Texas excuse for socializing, significantly more respectable than a horse race, but only slightly more subdued.

"Thank heaven we aren't late. Before he left the house, Reverend McGiver lectured me on the importance of punctuality and decorum in all things,'' Deborah said mischievously. "His congregation may be on time, but I can't imagine anything anyone can do to a Texas crowd to make it 'decorous.' ''

Charlee joined her in laughter, then sobered when she caught the murderous glare in Suzannah Wilcox's eyes. The pretty brunette had been the belle of San Antonio's Yankee community until Charlee had come upon the scene. Suzannah's brother Billy was one of many swains who flocked to pay court to the new girl in town. Last night Suzannah had watched Charlee dance with a succession of men, unconcealed hate in her pale blue eyes.

"Let us down here, Chester, and then good luck finding a place to tie up the team. Oh, there's Hannah Wilcox and her daughter, Charlee. You know Suzannah, don't you?'' Deborah asked.

Charlee saw no help for it but to endure the pouting little schemer as she stepped down from the carriage with a graceful flourish. Sally Butler and Nesta Tilden were clustering around Suzannah.

Faint threads of their conversation caught Charlee's attention as she approached. "She danced indecently close with him and then they had a fight in a secluded alcove. The next thing, she was outside with Paul,'' Sally hissed conspiratorially.

"You should have seen the way he was beaten up. That Jim Slade is nothing but a half-breed Mexican bandit,'' Suzannah added spitefully. "It's understandable that he seeks out his own kind—those *Tejanas*—but to be engaged to Tomasina Carver and then dally with that McAllister tramp, well!''

If Charlee was cringing inwardly, her outward show of coolness would have done a Boston librarian proud. "Good morning, Mrs. Wilcox, Suzannah, Sally, Nesta. Lovely morning for a prayer meeting.''

The frosty silence was complete in the small circle of

women. Deborah cast a sympathetic look at Charlee. "It is a lovely day, isn't it? Charlee, I think Adam is off pestering Mr. Soames. We'd better go rescue the poor man before our amateur teamster talks his ear off about those horses." With a brief nod, she departed with Charlee in tow.

"Well, I told you it was an eventful evening, didn't I," Charlee said with a rueful sigh. She should have realized leaving the dance with her former employer after said individual had flattened her escort would create a slight stir in polite society.

"Perhaps you'd better fill me in after the service," Deborah replied dryly.

"I will if the multitude doesn't stone me first," Charlee agreed bleakly. First she was humiliated in front of all the men at the ranch, now all the women in San Antonio. *Damn Jim Slade!*

chapter
<u>9</u>

"Just remember, look everyone you meet squarely in the eye and disdain any rudeness from anyone." On Monday morning Deborah attempted to buoy up Charlee's faltering courage. "You'll find most people are fair-minded. If Paul Bainbridge got drunk and made improper advances, it was perfectly all right for Jim Slade to escort you home after rescuing you."

"You know there's a whole lot more to it than that boiled-down version," Charlee said crossly. She had confessed everything to her friend, including her disgraceful response to Slade's fierce kiss. As to their relationship at Bluebonnet, well, she guessed a woman as shrewd as Deborah Kensington could figure out the rest.

"I've carefully told that boiled-down, or at least rinsed-

out, story to several people who accepted it readily enough.
Just remember,'' Deborah admonished, "not everyone has
the spiteful mind of Hannah Wilcox. Anyway, Suzannah set
her cap for Jim three years ago and failed to interest him.
She's been hatefully jealous ever since. Disregard her and
her friends.''

"What would I do without you?'' Charlee's green eyes
darkened as she said gravely, "I . . . I never had a real friend
before . . . not a woman friend, that is, a real honest-to-
goodness lady. I treasure our friendship, Deborah.''

Deeply touched by this lonely young woman's declaration, Deborah put her arms around Charlee and replied,
"Believe it or not, my in-laws would give you quite an
argument about my being a lady. I've done some pretty
wild, unconventional things myself. Maybe someday I can
tell you all about them. Now, young lady, you take your
kitchen supply order to that general store and act as cool and
proper as if you never laid eyes on either Jim Slade or Paul
Bainbridge.''

"Even though his father owns the store?'' Charlee questioned
weakly.

"*Especially* because his father owns the store,'' Deborah
said stoutly.

Charlee walked straight into Bainbridge General Mercantile and up to Simon Bainbridge, who was behind the cash
counter where the ledgers were kept. Thank heavens his son
Paul was not in the store today! Dealing with old Simon
would be difficult enough without facing a scorned suitor as
well.

Although she was certain he saw her, old man Bainbridge
did not look up from his books until she stood directly in
front of him and cleared her throat. "Good morning, Mr.
Bainbridge. I have a large order to be filled for the boardinghouse kitchen.'' When he nodded a curt acknowledge-
ment, she smiled primly and plunked the list down in front
of his bespectacled eyes. "The wagon is outside, and
Chester is there to load things. I need a few patterns and
some trim, so I'll just take a stroll upstairs to the yard goods
in the alcove. Call if you need me.'' Again the silent, surly

nod as he grasped the list and headed down one overcrowded aisle to begin filling her order.

Charlee wandered into the back corner of the store's second floor, entering a small, rather dingy addition where the bolts of fabric, dress patterns, and sewing accessories were kept. The place was virtually deserted so early on Monday morning. She picked up a big pattern book and carried it over to a dusty window ledge. Setting it down, she grimaced at the grime on the wide sash, found a bit of rag to wipe the worst of it off, and sat down for a good long browse.

Charlee lost track of time, vaguely hearing Mr. Bainbridge bark orders to Chester and his clerk now and then. The bright sunlight filtering in was warm, so she reached up and pried open the swollen casement window and was rewarded with a cool breeze. "I must remember to close it when I leave or all these bolts of cloth will be soaked first rain," she said absently, then became immersed once more in the world of hoop skirts and lace fans.

Suddenly, her attention was brought back from the fashion book when she heard the crunch of boots on the loose stones in the alleyway behind the store. Someone was walking into the deserted narrow space between the big mercantile and a windowless office building across from it. Jutting out into the alley, the addition to the mercantile offered the only view of that area from its second-story window. Who would be back there at this hour and why?

As if in answer to her questions, a meticulously dressed man in a tan worsted suit and frilly silk shirt rounded the corner and stepped into the shadows below her. When he doffed his wide-brimmed hat, Charlee recognized the unmistakable white-blond hair of Ashley Markham. She sat very still, curious yet prickling with some premonition of danger. Another set of footsteps crunched on the rocks. Charlee leaned out expectantly, pressing her face near the dirty window sash to see who it was.

She recognized the glossy black hair of Tomasina Carver even before she heard the low-hissed voice with its heavy Spanish accent. Charlee strained to hear what they said.

"Here is the information you need, all I could glean from

that fool councilman. His son is a ranger, but I could not question him too openly about troop strengths and locations without making him suspicious."

"If your people south of the border weren't so clumsy moving their army into position, the rumors making everyone suspicious would never have begun," he said nastily.

"Do you have the money?"

"Don't I always, pet?" He smiled sarcastically and offered her a small leather sack that she quickly slipped into her reticule.

"I do not like meeting here out in the open," she said petulantly, looking back down the alleyway. "What if I were seen back here?"

"There's no one about this time of day, and I need to get this information to my contact within the hour. He just arrived in town at daybreak. We could scarcely use the Rojas place at this hour without arousing even more suspicion, now could we?" His very reasonableness was irritating to her.

"Very well, just do not come to my town house anymore. The time is too near for us to risk being discovered now."

Tomasina turned to leave, but before she could get more than a step away, Markham grabbed her by one arm and swung her roughly into his embrace, kissing her passionately until she began to wriggle free, pushing at him with her hands and tossing her head back to avoid his mouth.

Tomasina's eyes opened wide and a loud hiss of shock escaped her lips as she arched back and looked up at the open second-story window of the mercantile, where Charlee sat frozen in horror. For a second, black and green eyes locked. Then Markham followed Tomasina's gaze upward to see Charlee. "You fool!" Tomasina spat at Markham and turned, pulling him down the alleyway.

Charlee had been sitting in the window listening to the quick snatches of conversation between Tomasina and Markham. When her rival looked up and saw her, she did not move, but stared in shock as their words and actions hit her with wrenching impact. Jim's fiancée was a spy for the Mexicans, in league with a British agent! She stood up numbly as they hurriedly left the alley. What should she do now? Lee would know. He could convince Slade of the truth. Quickly she went downstairs and instructed Chester to load the wagon as soon as Bainbridge had all the supplies assembled and go directly to the boardinghouse. Then she began to walk briskly toward the livery to get Patchwork. She would ride to Bluebonnet as fast as she could.

Once they were out of sight and earshot of the horrified girl, Tomasina said breathlessly to Markham, "Kill her, at once, or we're both as good as hanged for treason!"

"Don't be a fool! I can scarcely go rushing in there and shoot her in front of half a dozen people," Markham retorted, his eyes squinted in concentration. "We can't just have bodies turning up all about town and country, now can we? Quite a few people would ask questions. Nor do I fancy pushing her from the second-story window in hopes she'll break her neck in another of your unfortunate accidents! Who is the child, anyway? Pretty little thing."

Tomasina seethed. "She is a nobody, Dick McAllister's sister, a waif who turned up on Diego's doorstep a few months ago."

Markham laughed in spite of himself. "You mean that new girl at Kensington's boardinghouse, the one who created such a furor at Pearsons' Saturday night when your beloved beat her escort senseless? Are you quite certain you're not using this as a new grotesquerie for eliminating rivals, Tomasina?"

She gave him a withering look, then said calmly, "You said you had to meet your Comanchero friend this morning. What is his name——Brady? Before she can babble this to anyone, let Señor Brady take her to his allies. She'll hardly be the first white slave to die in a Comanche camp." Tomasina's eyes glowed like black fire.

Though he was a hardened espionage agent, Ashley Markham quailed at her lust for violence, especially directed against an innocent young girl. Carver and the meddling brother, now those were other matters, but this . . . well. He considered with his usual detachment, ignoring her agitated expression. It must be done, unpleasant or not. The McAllister girl must vanish, and Rufus Brady was perfectly equipped to handle it. A job was a job, after all.

* * *

The Comanchero was a big man, over six feet five, with greasy, sand-colored hair and pale gray eyes, wide set in a square, pockmarked face. He walked with an oddly lumbering grace, and his smile showed large, straight teeth. The grin would have been boyishly engaging were it not for the dark, tobacco-stained enamel and the twisting leer created by a deep scar at one side of his mouth.

He grimaced at Markham, then leaned back in his chair. They were seated in a sleazy cantina, where Brady sipped a glass of cheap whiskey. Before noon the place was deserted, but nonetheless they met in the back and spoke in whispers. "Took ya long 'nough, English. Ya got th' money 'n places fer us ta hit?" When Brady stood up he dwarfed Markham's slim, dapper five-foot-ten form.

"Yes, I have your information and the whiskey money for your red friends. But first there is a small matter in town you must take care of for me . . ."

As she hurried up the street, Charlee was so immersed in the jumble of thoughts ricocheting through her mind that she didn't notice him until he collided with her. He was the biggest man she had ever seen. She looked up to face the stranger and apologize for her absentminded clumsiness. The words died on her lips when she met his cold gray eyes and saw the evil-looking scar that rent his face into a grotesque mask. Before she could move or say anything, he grabbed her around her waist in a lightning-swift gesture, literally squeezing the breath from her. She struggled to clear her swimming head and cry out, all the while flailing impotently against his grasp. Her head rolled around and she searched frantically for someone, anyone to help. The alleyway where she had been intercepted was deserted; not a soul was in sight.

"Fer a little bitty thing, ya shore kin wriggle somethin' fierce." Brady's huge hand clamped over her mouth just as she let out a loud cry. His meaty palm covered her whole face and virtually suffocated her as he lifted her effortlessly and swung her tiny body around the corner into a narrow side street. At the end stood a small, rickety shed with its door ajar.

"Markham sez ya gotta go ta th' Comanch. Pure shame. Dunno if'n they'll keep ya long." He regarded her small, fine-boned frame, running his hand over her breasts and hips as he lowered her to the filthy floor of the shed. "But then, yore stronger'n ya look, 'n ya got all th' right parts. Yep, Iron Hand'll like yew."

Charlee felt nauseated as his words struck her with terrifying force. He was a Comanchero, one of those hated and feared outcasts, desperate cold-blooded cutthroats who traded whiskey and weapons to the Comanche. And he was going to sell her to the savages!

Brady reached in his hip pocket with one hand while the other still covered her face, muffling her desperate cries. Quickly and efficiently he stuffed a foul, smelly rag into her mouth and then threw her face-forward onto the dusty floor of the storage shed, once more knocking the breath from her. She was bruised and suffocating, but her terror overshadowed all else as she struggled to spit out the wad of stinking cotton. Rufus Brady laughed cruelly as he tied her hands tightly behind her back, then looped the rough rawhide around her ankles, hogtieing her. When he had tied another rag around her face, securing the gag in her mouth, he stood up and looked down at her, helpless at his feet.

"I got me some bizness over at th' Tres Hermanos Saloon. A feller owes me money—'n lady, I always collect my debts. Yew remember thet," he said with a chilling grin.

Once he had her away from town, what might he be capable of doing to her? Thinking of that, she felt her blood freeze.

As if reading the terror in her huge green eyes, he let out a low, evil laugh and opened the door. "I'll be back fer ya afore long. Once't we're clear o' Santone, wall . . ." He left her then, with his threat hanging in the air like an ax ready to fall.

Soon she would be missed and Deborah would institute a search. But who'd look for her here, on a deserted back street in one of the poorest sections of town? By the looks of the shack, it had once been a small warehouse or stable, long ago abandoned.

Think, Charlee. Be calm and think. She forced herself to stop struggling, since that was only using up her limited supply of strength in a totally futile endeavor. The killer was an expert with ropes. She began to inventory every inch of the shed from top to bottom. There must be a way. She had to figure a way out of this.

Asa Ketchum, too, had a problem that Monday morning. As he sat in the big ranch house kitchen listening to Weevils clank pots and pans in the dishwater, he threw a rock-hard biscuit on top of his leathery gray eggs and forced down another swallow of the spunkwater coffee. Since Charlee had left, the food had suffered a marked decline. In addition, there was an ominous air of tension at mealtimes. Lee would discuss his frequent trips to town to visit Charlee, while everyone covertly watched Jim's reaction.

Slade was alternately hostile and taciturn. Always quick to anger, the boss now exploded at the most insignificant things. He and Lee had a terrible brawl the day after Charlee left. Asa had seen Slade's black eye and the boy's bruised knuckles and quickly put two and two together. "Whole damblasted place's goin' ta hell faster'n a cornstalk lawyer can get a man's mark on a quit-claim deed," he swore, absently rubbing his aching jaw.

"I kin fix thet toothache fer ya, Asa," Weevils offered as he watched the foreman wince in misery.

"Pshaw, I'll wait till I can get to Doc Weidermann next week," the Virginian drawled softly.

"All's he'll do is pull it. I kin stop th' pain without yew openin' yer mouth."

"You 'n your home remedies," Asa scoffed, taking another sip of the foul coffee.

"Best cure fer toothache in th' world is ta take a rag 'n rub some cat shit on it. Wrap it round yer jaw fer a day er so. Works ever' time," Weevils averred.

Asa spit a stream of the vile coffee across the table. "That what you're puttin' in this here coffee?"

"Naw. Don't talk foolish. Onliest thing ya use animal dirt fer is poultices on th' *outside* o' a body."

"Well, smellin' it'd for sure take my mind off my tooth," Asa said sarcastically.

"Whut'd I tell ya. Works ever' time. 'Course, what with Miz Charlee gone 'n thet critter o' hers with her, I'm right pressed for th' makin's, so ta speak."

Asa stood up. "That's just what I've been thinkin' on, Weevils—Charlee, that is."

"Yew miss her, too." It was a simple statement of fact.

"Yep, I do, 'n so does that hardheaded youngun' of Will's. Damn if Will didn't make the mistake of his life askin' that boy to marry the Aguilar girl. I liked her pa right enough, but she's not the one for Jim. It's Charlee McAllister he should marry."

"Yew 'n me know thet, 'n so does Lee, but who's gonna convince th' boss?" Weevils shrugged, causing his mountainous frame to ripple.

"Someone's got to. I . . ."

Just then Slade came striding rapidly up the back steps and into the kitchen. "Asa, two men are down with a sprained back and a stomachache—or at least that's what the malingerers tell me. You're supposed to handle the men. It's a good hour past sunrise. What's the holdup?"

Asa took one look at the agitated young man before him and motioned for Weevils to leave them alone. The fat old cook was happy to oblige, quickly scooping up his dishpan and heading out the door.

"Two good-for-nothin' hands more or less won't make no mind, Jim. It's Wyler and Kellerman, right?" At Slade's surprised nod, Asa motioned for him to sit down at the round oak table.

"You've had a burr under your blanket for quite a while now, son," he began carefully. "It's time I talked ta you the way Will would've if he was here."

"I know what my pa wanted me to do, Asa," Slade said wearily, with a touch of defensiveness in his voice.

"I wonder. Oh, I know what he told you when he died, but that was over six years ago, before the Aguilar girl married Jake."

"She's a widow now and I'm going to marry her," Jim said doggedly.

"Lots of things change, son. You, her. You ever think if Will was still here he'd change his mind, too? Maybe see you with someone else, someone you really care about, who cares about you?"

"You mean Charlee." Slade stood up stiffly, in an abrupt angry motion, nearly overturning his chair. "Let me alone, Asa. It's between her and me."

"Appears ta me, after what went on here that night, it's gone a little too far for you ta just pack her off ta town 'n go about your business. Charlee McAllister is a good girl, young and inexperienced. What you did shamed her 'n you know it." He put up a hand to stay Slade's angry retort and continued, "Now, it'd be different if she didn't care for you or you for her, but anyone with eyes 'round here knows that purely ain't so. Charlee belongs at Bluebonnet. Mrs. Carver don't, 'n Will'd be the first ta tell you the truth of it, if he was here." He stood up as he spoke, fixing Jim with his level blue gaze. For all the rebuke in his words, his voice and manner were gentle.

Slade could accept accusatory anger like Lee's, but losing the respect of this proud, honorable old friend was a bitter draught indeed. He felt helpless, angry, guilty, and very confused. "Look, Asa, I appreciate you speaking your piece and I understand what you mean. I . . . I just don't know what I'm going to do. My whole life's turned upside down since she came into it." They both understood which "she" he meant. "Just let me sort things out for a while."

Asa nodded, reaching for his hat and heading for the door. "All right. You do what you got to, son."

Jim spent the entire morning catching up with paperwork in his office. He needed to keep busy, that was the answer. If he put enough time and distance between himself and Charlee McAllister, he might be able to see things clearly.

Asa's condemnation sat heavily on him. First Weevils's accusatory looks, then Lee's furious attack, now Ketchum's reluctant sermon. Was everyone on Bluebonnet her champion? Of course, that didn't account for the debacle in town Saturday night and resultant furor the next day.

After he had left her at the boardinghouse, Slade had ridden to the Sandovals' to spend the night, too emotionally wrung out to feel like making the long ride back to the ranch. When his aunt had accosted him in the *sala* the next morning, he had cursed himself for a fool over and over. She had been to mass at San Fernando Church and had heard the latest gossip about his fight with Paul Bainbridge.

Tia Esperanza had been furious. What was he doing, disgracing the family name and shaming his fiancée by consorting with a kitchen trull, and worse yet, engaging in a street brawl with a shopkeeper's son? His mother and father would both be appalled at his crass behavior. What would Tomasina say?

Slade did not wait to find out. Placating one furious woman in twenty-four hours was enough trouble. He would handle Sina later, after she had a chance to cool down. The devil of it was, he didn't know what he would tell his fiancée about his feelings for Charlee, or for that matter about his feelings for *her*.

Was Asa right? Would Will have approved of Charlee and have freed him from his promise to wed Tomasina Aguilar? That morning, as he sat slumped at his desk with his head in his hands, there was only one thing Jim Slade wanted to do, and that was be shut of both females.

Dammit, I don't want to get married at all! He wanted neither a manipulative beauty like Sina nor a raging termagant like Charlee. What a choice, he thought bitterly to himself.

Just then a knock sounded on the open door and Lee stepped inside. The youth had not appeared at all chastened after their terrible fight, but rather seemed to be biding his time, the same as Weevils and Asa. Well, they could wait till the Gulf froze over. He'd do what he wanted when he wanted, not before.

Glaring up at Lee, Slade motioned silently for the youth to enter. "What is it, Lee?"

The slim young man shifted uneasily and then sat down on the edge of a large leather chair across from the desk. As

he began to speak, he looked distinctly nervous. "I . . . er
. . . heard about Saturday night in town, Jim. I'm glad you
didn't pull your punches with Bainbridge the way you did
with me."

"That all you came in here to tell me?" Slade replied,
with a faint grin tugging at the corner of his mouth.

"No, but it does concern Charlee, or at least, she's the
one who saw it. I should've told you sooner, but I wasn't
sure you'd believe her, but now that you went to town to see
her, and all that's happened . . ."

"Can you get to the point, *mano*? I have a lot of work to
do today." He gestured impatiently at the cluttered desk.

"Well, last week, when I went to town to see Charlee,
she told me about a strange coincidence. She had gone to
the store and was cutting back across the plaza, past the
Rojas house . . ." Lee relayed the whole tale to Jim, half
afraid of an eruption of unreasoning anger as his boss
defended his fiancée from such an accusation, half afraid of
a killing fury if Slade believed Tomasina Carver guilty of
such perfidy.

Slade stood up and began to pace, his mind racing back
to the evening of the dinner party with the Montaldos; the
way Sina disliked Serafina Rojas yet still had luncheon with
her every week; the many other small, odd events over the
past months . . . "Why didn't you tell me this sooner?"

Lee darkened and muttered something unintelligible, but
Jim interrupted him. "All right, you thought I was so mad at
Charlee I'd think she was lying. Well, I don't believe Sina
is a British agent, but maybe, just maybe, she's a misguided
Mexican patriot. Hell, I don't know. Maybe the whole
thing's a damned coincidence and Sina's never even met
Ashley Markham."

"Then you do believe Charlee saw them both at the Rojas
place at the same time?" Lee looked immensely relieved.

"Yes, for all that proves. The important thing is that our
friend Markham has been a busy boy here lately. I've heard
rumors that there have been sizable Mexican troop movements south of the Rio Grande and the Comanche are
raiding more frequently to the north of here in the past
weeks. Someone is financing a lot of dirty work." Slade

stared absently at the dispatches he'd received yesterday from Houston City.

As if reading Jim's mind, Lee smiled and said, "Your source for all this information, would it be our president himself?"

"You've got a shrewd and observant head on those young shoulders, *mano*. Take care that it stays in place. Keep away from political intrigue. It's bad for your health."

"What are you going to do, Jim?"

"Just what you hoped I would," Slade snapped, "go to San Antonio and talk to Sina and Charlee. Maybe even look up a sidewinder named Markham. It's time I had some answers."

"Now, what you want, ole evil-eye debil, you?" Sadie glared down at an agitated Hellfire with rancor in her piercing black eyes.

"Sadie, I haven't seen Charlee all morning. It's after one now and she's still not home. Chester said she was going to Bluebonnet for some emergency or other, but I just looked in the stable and Patchwork is still there. I'm worried." Deborah's face reflected her concern as she absently eyed the pacing old tom.

"Dat critter been drivin' me loco fer hours, Miz Debrah. Doan Miz Charlee go nowheres without him." Sadie, too, was worried.

"This isn't like Charlee," Deborah said as she knelt and stroked the restless cat.

"What isn't like Charlee?" Jim Slade questioned as he opened the kitchen door and stepped inside, pushing his wide-brimmed hat back on his head.

"Oh, Jim, I'm so glad you're here!" Deborah rose and quickly relayed what she, Sadie, and Chester knew of the morning's events.

"You say she was off to the ranch to see Lee?" His face was drawn in alarm by the time she had finished her tale.

"Yes, that's what she told Chester at Bainbridge's store, but Patchwork is still in the stable. She never came home, and that was at least two hours ago."

Slade cursed and turned to leave. "I'm going to the store

to see what I can find out. Maybe someone's seen her along the way.''

Before he could get out the door, a blur of orange brushed by him and was down the back steps, waiting uneasily near Polvo, well out of reach of the horse's large hooves. As if to express his disgust with human slowness, the cat looked up at Slade.

"You wouldn't . . . no." Slade dismissed the feline almost instantly as he mounted up and headed toward Bainbridge's Store, taking the most direct route. All the while, Charlee's sighting of Markham and her suspicions about Sina replayed fearfully in his mind. God, what might the fool girl have blundered into?

Slade paused to look down the twisting narrow labyrinth of alleyways near the store, a two-story landmark of sorts surrounded by various one-story frame and stone structures, many of them shoddy and deserted. "Not exactly a classy neighborhood, eh, Polvo?" he muttered, trying to decide which course she might have taken. Did she strike out on foot to reach her house first or go directly to the livery? Then a flash of color caught his eye, and he turned to see Hellfire dart down one narrow alley toward a dilapidated shack at its end.

"Damn fool cat still hanging around. Still, Charlee always did have a queer way with him. Maybe it's worth a look," he said, half in disbelief, and nudged the big buckskin down the narrow back street.

When he dismounted, the cat was clawing furiously at the splintering wood of a door on a very deserted-looking frame building. Looking cautiously around him, Slade sensed no one nearby, but nonetheless he drew the rifle from his saddle scabbard. When he tried the door, its wooden bar latch slipped up with a creak and it opened easily. He peered into the dim interior.

There in the far corner, with her back against a filthy, cobweb-infested harness rack lay Charlee, hogtied and gagged. Slade's reflex action was to check all corners of the room for any hiding kidnappers. But the cat scurried quickly over to his mistress and began to butt up against her face, yowling angrily.

Satisfied that the shed was empty except for Charlee, Jim quickly knelt beside her crumpled figure and propped his rifle against the wall. He slipped a wicked-looking knife from its sheath and cut her bonds, then the rag that held the hateful gag in her mouth.

It hurt too much to try to talk, for her throat and tongue were parched, but when the circulation began to return to her hands and feet she let out a low moan. Even with Slade's help, she found it agony to straighten her legs and attempt to sit up.

"Don't try to move for a few minutes until the blood starts pumping again. Let me get a canteen off the saddle and give you a drink." As he rose, he said over his shoulder, "Your feline friend here found you. Better give him a whole churnful of butter tonight." He was back in a second with the water, warm and brackish from the hot metal container, but heavenly to her injured mouth. "Take is slow, that's it . . . easy." Jim found his hands were trembling. If he hadn't found her . . .

"Son of a bitch!" The expletive ripped from Rufus Brady's throat as he aimed his gun and fired.

Slade had been absorbed in caring for Charlee, but his reflexes were still sharp from years of survival on the frontier. He rolled to his left with lightning speed and scooped up his rifle. Brady, standing in the bright sunlight, peered into the dim interior of the shack but could not see clearly. His first shot went wild, showering jagged splinters over Charlee, who rolled to the right, holding Hellfire tightly in her arms. Ignoring the girl and cat, Brady pulled a second pistol from his sash and aimed it at the man with the rifle. His shot found its mark at the same instant Slade's found the Comanchero, but Brady's .54-caliber martial pistol did not carry the impact of Jim's .54-caliber Pennsylvania Long Rifle. Slade's shot knocked Brady back from the door frame into the hot yellow dust of the alley, where he lay very still.

Slade lay crumpled with his back against the harness rack. Using a heavy iron hook for support, he pulled himself up unsteadily. As quickly as she could get her stiffened legs to move, Charlee was by his side. "You're shot! Where? Oh, Jim, is it bad?"

"I've been shot lots of times. It's never good, believe me." He grimaced as he shook his head, trying to clear the sudden spate of dizziness overtaking him. "Just a crease in my side, I think. Let's hope our friend out there is in worse shape." Using the rifle as a crutch, Slade cautiously walked out the door and prodded the Comanchero's inert figure. "Yep, he's worse," he said tonelessly. Then he swore several particularly vile Spanish oaths. "Rufus Brady," he breathed.

"Who . . . who is . . . was he?" Charlee could not make herself look at the corpse for more than a second, although the cat was sniffing it as he circled warily.

"Christ, you're lucky to be alive! Brady's a Comanchero."

"I know that," she said with a shudder. "He told me what he planned to do with me—send me to a chief called Iron Hand."

Slade swore again, then reached his hand to her shoulder to steady himself.

"You *are* hurt bad. Lordy, I can see the blood seeping through your shirt. Let's get you over to Polvo. Can you mount up?"

He shook his head. "First I have to check his body and his horse for any information. If he was on his way to Iron Hand, he'll have something for sure." Using her for support, he knelt and began to go through the cutthroat's pockets.

"Dammit, you'll bleed to death!" Seeing he would not be dissuaded, Charlee stopped her protest and began to tear strips methodically off her petticoat. "Here, at least let me wrap it before you pass out from losing blood." She knelt beside him and began to pack the long reddening slash across his left side. She tied the makeshift bandage around his chest as he continued doggedly with his task.

"Go through the saddlebags on his horse." He nodded to the big roan tied down at the end of the alley.

"What am I supposed to be looking for? Why can't the law do it?"

"Anything like dispatches, maps, any notes about ranger

or militia movements. Or money—gold for buying whiskey or guns—you get the idea. Jack Hays is the only law I trust and he's out of town now. Forget the local law. I want this information for Houston.''

When he mentioned the president's name, she hesitated, then turned and quickly ran toward the roan. ''Whoa, there. You're as ugly as your owner. Oh, got a disposition to match, huh,'' she said as the big beast laid back his ears. She grabbed the reins with no nonsense and held them steady, all the while talking to the horse until he calmed. Then she methodically went through the saddlebags. All the usual possibles were there, hard biscuits, a bottle of cheap whiskey, cooking utensils. Then her small hand dug out a heavy leather sack. She opened it. Gold—a whole pile of American ten-dollar gold pieces!

''Jim, I've found a sack of money, just like you said!'' Coming to the end of her search, she hefted the pouch and ran back to where Slade was kneeling.

He was quickly scanning a scribbled list of dates and place names. ''Someone in San Antonio had one hell of a source of information. I have to talk to our friend Ashley Markham,'' he said grimly as she helped him up.

When she gasped at Markham's name, he looked at her sharply. ''Markham's the one who sent him—Brady—to kidnap me. I saw him and Tomasina together. They were . . . Jim!''

Slade's face had been growing increasingly ashen as blood pumped through the soaked rags binding his torso. Suddenly he could see Charlee's face grow fuzzy and dark before his eyes. Her words did not register as he began to black out.

Charlee grabbed him, staggering under the vast weight differential between a one-hundred-sixty-five-pound man and a hundred-pound woman. ''Get on Polvo. No more arguments or you'll bleed to death!''

Somehow she managed to get him on his horse, all the while marveling that a full five minutes must have elapsed since three shots were fired and no one had even peeked down the deserted alley to inquire about it. ''I see why he didn't want to bother with the law,'' she muttered to herself as she led the big buckskin and its crippled rider from the alley.

The next hour was pure pandemonium. By the time she had reached the Plaza, a crowd had gathered and a boy was sent to bring Dr. Weidermann to Deborah's place. With the assistance of several townsmen, Charlee had gotten Jim back to the boardinghouse and upstairs into her bedroom.

While Dr. Weidermann cleansed and sutured the ugly gash in Slade's side, Charlee held him and threatened to box his ears if he didn't lie still and let the doctor finish. Brady and Markham could wait.

No sooner had the doctor left, giving her instructions for the care of her recalcitrant patient, than he was attempting to get out of bed. She sat on him. Once assured he would not move and further injure himself, she promised to give the note and the gold to Lee and tell him all that had occurred. She agreed to talk to no one else about Brady or what had happened to her. Swearing she would not venture from the premises unescorted and chance another kidnapping, she finally got him to take a light dose of laudanum and rest.

Deborah had been beside herself with worry when a very bedraggled Charlee had trudged up the front steps with two strangers behind her carrying a bleeding Jim Slade. Following Slade's instructions, Charlee had told Deborah only that she had been grabbed by Brady and rescued by Jim.

After Slade drifted off to sleep, Charlee dispatched Chester to bring Lee to town and then was persuaded by Deborah to take a soak in the tub. She felt unclean from Brady's touch and was more than willing to bathe after checking on her sleeping patient once more.

That night Charlee brought a light supper to Jim who had awakened from his drug-induced nap in a signally foul humor. Looking around at the dainty pale green curtains and seeing Hellfire stretched out comfortably in the window sill, he quickly surmised whose room he had been settled in at the boardinghouse.

"I can't stay here, and it's not safe for you, either," he said before she could even set the tray down.

"You can, and I'll be fine. Lee's right down the hall.

He'll sleep in Mr. McCurdy's room tonight. I told him everything and I gave him the note and the gold. That ranger friend of yours, Mr. Hays, returned to town. He's ridden to the president for you. Now, are you satisfied?'' She stood with her small hands on her narrow hips, bronze hair spilling on her shoulders like a curtain of metallic satin. A green silk robe was belted tightly around that incredibly tiny waist, outlining her petite curves in a very disconcerting way.

Slade looked her up and down. Flushed and smelling of wildflowers, she was obviously fresh from a bath. He shifted uncomfortably in bed, struggling to sit up and let the pain take his mind off how desirable she looked, standing there like a miniature Valkyrie.

''Watch out, you'll reopen those stitches.'' She quickly slipped over to his side and helped him sit back, plumping up pillows behind him. ''Try and eat something. You'll feel better.'' Seeking desperately to hide her nervousness, she reached over for a bowl of chicken soup and a spoon. Why was it, every time she wasn't mad enough to clobber him, she was skittish enough to run from those burning golden cougar eyes?

''I can feed myself,'' Slade growled, wincing as he shifted to avoid the spoon she was hefting with determination toward his mouth.

''Open.'' Her voice was calm and authoritative, but she feared her hand would start trembling if he didn't cooperate immediately.

Ungraciously he swallowed the hot liquid and then placed a strong brown hand around her wrist, neatly removing the spoon with his other hand. ''Just hold the bowl.''

She acquiesced, letting him finish the soup by himself. When he complained he needed more solid nourishment, she said primly, ''Dr. Weidermann said only a liquid diet until tomorrow.''

He grimaced, then laughed. ''I'm surprised he didn't offer you a sample of his Indian stew. Bet he's still got some bubbling in that ghoulish office of his. Crazy Russian.''

Charlee looked puzzled. ''What do you mean, 'Indian stew'?''

"I forget you're a recent arrival in San Antonio. About two years ago, a big fight between the town fathers and a group of Comanche chiefs ended in a massacre of the Indians."

"Lee told me about it," she said.

"Old Doc was in on that shootout and wanted to gather a few specimens, it seems." He smiled in remembrance.

"Specimens?"

"Skeletons. For his anatomy laboratory. He selected two of the likeliest-looking of the dead braves and took to rendering them down to be reassembled for the edification of his patients."

Charlee gulped in revulsion. "You mean he *cooked* them? That nice, harmless-looking man with the courtly European manners?"

He laughed at her horrified expression. "Well, they *were* dead and cluttering up the council house."

"But to cook them!" Her green eyes were enormous.

"How else could he get the meat off the bones?" he asked reasonably. "The real trouble came a few days later when he emptied his 'stewpot' into the town sewage system. The women out to do their laundry were a trifle upset."

"I guess that's for sure," she retorted vehemently. "I assume he was suitably punished."

"Oh, yes, by Texas standards he was. The court fined him ten dollars. I imagine he's kept his cooking to himself ever since." His golden eyes were dancing as he chuckled at her discomfiture.

"And to think Deborah works with him as a nurse!" Charlee grimaced, irritated at the cavalier attitude Slade was exhibiting. Texas violence and crudity were still hard for her to accept at times.

"He's a good doctor, trained at the best European universities. He's just not very... ah... orthodox for a Russian," he added, unable to resist the awful pun.

In spite of herself, Charlee grinned as she set the bowl on the bedside table. Although reluctant to break the charm of their momentary camaraderie, she knew she must tell him about Tomasina and Markham.

"Jim, I already told Lee this afternoon, but he said I

should talk to you about it . . ." Her words trailed off, and she avoided meeting his eyes.

Something niggled at the back of his consciousness, but Slade could not remember what, only that it was decidedly unpleasant. "Go on, what is it?"

Nervously she stood up and began to pace as she recreated the whole series of events leading up to her abduction, carefully repeating verbatim everything she could recall of Tomasina and Markham's conversation. When she had finished, she looked over at him warily, uncertain of how he would take it.

Jim sat very still, listening intently and sensing her agitation as she spoke and paced. Something inside him tightened painfully when she described Markham's grabbing Sina, the action that had led to her catching sight of Charlee in the upstairs window.

"Lee told me you saw Sina and Markham at the Rojas place over a week ago," he said tonelessly, his best poker face in place.

Charlee stood very still now, crossing her hands over her chest, skewering him with cloudy green eyes. "And do you think I'm telling the truth?" She had to know if he loved Tomasina Carver enough to cover for her.

"Yes" was his level reply. His cool golden eyes met her challenging green ones. "Sina's involved with a British agent—that much is clear. Just leave it to me now. Stay out of the whole dangerous mess."

"With pleasure," she said sharply and scooped up the tray, departing the room with an abrupt slam of the door. So, he'd protect the bitch even if she was spying for two hostile foreign powers. The big war hero, willing to betray his conscience for a cheating, conniving woman who had tried to have her killed!

chapter
<u>10</u>

Charlee tossed and turned in the makeshift bed she had set up in Deborah's room. It was past midnight and she still could not sleep. Finally she threw off the covers and glanced over at Deborah, sleeping peacefully. Silently she swung her legs over the side of the cot and sat up. It was either get up and go raid the pantry, or lie in the stillness of the night, tortured by her thoughts, until she gave way to tears. She had already shed too many tears over Jim Slade.

She resolutely pulled on her sheer silk wrapper and belted it securely. Barefooted, she padded silently from the room and down the hall, hearing old Mr. McCurdy's loud snores and Adam's soft voice as he babbled in his sleep. When she came to her own room, Charlee stopped and placed her hand on the knob. She must have stood frozen in indecision for several moments, debating with herself. Should she check on him? He seemed stronger tonight, and Sadie said he had refused the laudanum before going to sleep. Still, he had been shot, even if he was too perverse to admit he was in need of help.

Charlee told herself she was a fool, grieving for another woman's man. She was just about to turn away when a muffled moan issued from behind the door. With a soft click the latch lifted and she swung the door wide. Her room was bathed in moonlight. Flickering shadows made by the gently swaying cottonwoods outside her window stretched across the gleaming plank floor. The room was cool and the rustle of the shiny leaves was soothing.

As she closed the door carefully, her eyes quickly swept to the bed, where Slade's long body lay. All the covers had been kicked off. He was naked, save for the wide swaddling of bandage around his waist. He's probably the type who always sleeps in the altogether, she sniffed to herself, unable to stop her eyes from traveling the length of his lean frame. One long foot dangled over the bottom of the bed, while the other leg was pulled up and bent at the knee. One hand was flung, palm open, across his forehead, and the other hung off the side of the bed, its fingertips touching the rug lightly. He was too long to fit comfortably on her small mattress.

Like a sleepwalker, she approached the bed, listening to the sound of his steady, even breathing, hearing no more moaning. The bright moonlight made the thick hair on his chest and legs gleam like gold. That startlingly handsome, forbidding countenance was half hidden by his hand, the unsettling cougar eyes closed in sleep.

Almost against her will, she reached down and felt his cheek. Cool. No fever. Satisfied that her mission of mercy was unnecessary, she began to straighten up, only to have her wrist enveloped by Slade's lean, powerful fingers. His compelling eyes pierced her as he held her fast, roughly pulling her to a sitting position on the edge of the bed. With his other hand he reached beneath the pillow and pulled out a wicked-looking Bowie knife, then slid it back to its resting place.

"A good way to get killed is to sneak into a man's room, Cat Eyes."

Charlee gasped at the sight of the knife and tried to pull free of his bruising grasp. "Let me go," she croaked.

"What the hell are you doing here?" His voice was whispered and harsh.

"I didn't come in to slit your throat in the night, if that's what's bothering you," she answered tartly. "I heard you moan in your sleep."

"From all the way down the hall?" he shot back dubiously.

"I couldn't sleep. I was just going to get something to eat." Realizing what it looked like, walking up to a naked man's bed in her thin silk wrapper, she blushed furiously, then cursed herself for getting into such a predicament. "Cover up before you catch your death," she added crossly, reaching down for the sheet lying on the floor.

He still did not relinquish his hold on her wrist. "It's warm enough, Charlee," he said softly. "I don't need the cover. Just how long did you plan to stand there gawking before you left?"

She let a seething hiss of breath escape as she tried in vain to jerk free of his grasp. "You vain, presumptuous peacock! Let me go or I'll poleax you, you bastard!" As she thrashed to get free, her voice was rising dangerously loud.

He laughed. "Now that's the Charlee we all know and love. Genteel to the end."

Just then she spit out another oath and tried to push away from him, only to have her elbow inadvertently connect with his injured side. He let out a strangled gasp of pain and swore in a colorful mixture of Spanish and English, releasing her and doubling up while lying on his side.

"Oh, Jim, I'm sorry! Are you hurt?" She knelt by the bedside and reached out to touch his arm gently.

"I was shot this morning, if you recall—damn yes, I'm hurt!" He swore another string of invectives and rolled onto his back.

"Let me check the bandaging and see if you've started bleeding again." She sat up on the bed once more and leaned over him, intent on looking at his wound.

As she gently loosened the thick wrapping, she leaned forward. Slade felt her hair, gloriously unbound, trail onto his chest like tickling strands of silk. Her wrapper had come undone in their struggle, but she seemed unaware of it. He saw the soft swell of breasts, straining against the sheer white silk of her night rail. In vain he sought to concentrate on his pain, on the rustling night sounds from the cotton-woods, the wail of a stray dog, anything but Charlee's soft hands on his body, the faint wildflower fragrance of her.

As she touched him, Charlee knew her fingers must be clumsy with her trembling. She took a steadying breath and said, "Well, you're not bleeding, thank God."

As she replaced the bandage and refastened it, she dared not meet his burning eyes, which she knew were riveted on her. He reached up with one hand and ran it lightly across her collarbone, then down the slope of her breast. With a gasp she realized that her robe was open. As she jerked back, she felt the swollen proof of his maleness, hot yet velvety.

His trespassing hand continued its path around her breasts, first one, then the other, and she felt a familiar tightening of her nipples. His other hand tangled in her hair and pulled her head down to where his lips were beckoning. She did not resist but hypnotically pressed her mouth over his. He teased with his tongue and parted her lips. His tongue darted in and traced circles on the roof of her mouth, then insinuated itself around her own, drawing it back into his mouth.

Jim could feel her trembling, feel her small hands run up his chest, caressing the thick hair, curving over the muscles of his shoulders, clinging. He began to peel the robe off her shoulder.

When he broke the joining of the kiss and trailed soft wet licks and gentle bites down her throat, she gasped out, "Don't, please, Jim, ooh . . . you'll hurt yourself . . . start bleeding."

"You just said I'm not bleeding, but I do ache, for you, woman, for you," he growled roughly. "Let me love you, Charlee," he added more gently. He never slowed his assault on her senses, all the while kissing her breasts and tracing delicate patterns across them with his tongue. His hot, wet mouth burned through the sheer silk of the night rail, while his hand continued to pull the robe down, freeing one of her arms, then the other. Like a sleepwalker she cooperated, letting him slip the long sleeves off and discard the robe until she was sitting on its crumpled length, clad only in her gossamer gown.

"You are so tiny and perfect," he groaned against her throat, pulling her closer to him and feeling her respond. He ran his hand down her back, across the tops of her small silky buttocks, then down one thigh and back up between her legs. She gasped and let out a whimper of surrender. "Stand up and take off that gown for me," he breathed into her neck. She hesitated and he kissed her throat once more, murmuring, "It's only fair, you know. You can see all of me. Let me see all of you, my beautiful little darling. Please."

His hands reached around her waist and urged her gently
off the bed, where she was half sitting, half lying over him.
She stood up on shaky legs, weak as a newborn foal,
quickly sliding the sheer piece of silk over her head, tossing
it carelessly to the floor in one graceful motion. He reached
up for her and clasped her hands in his, holding her poised
at the edge of the bed for a moment, his eyes devouring her
sleek, slim curves. She met his gaze boldly, unashamedly
reveling in being female and being desired.

A strong new sense of confidence and purpose suffused
her as she feasted her eyes on the man before her. He
wanted her now; she would make him want her always. Her
eyes were smoky with passion, darkened and glowing as she
came into his embrace, wordlessly surrendering to him,
making a vow to herself.

Jim ran his hands over her delicate body, marveling anew
at such perfection in miniature. What was it about this
child-woman, contentious, wild and headstrong, the opposite of every ideal and value he held about the lady he
would wed, what was it that drew him so irresistibly to her,
over and over? He knew he had never, even in his most
infatuated youth, desired Sina this way.

Feverishly he caressed her, feeling every silky inch of her
flesh, forcing himself to go slow this time, to take her all the
way with him. Her own busy little hands and mouth were
driving him wild with her spontaneous, untutored responses.
"Shh . . . love, we have all night," he crooned, slowing her
hungry movements. Careful to favor his injured side, he
rolled himself up and half over her, reversing their earlier
positions.

He used his fingers to spread the masses of her long
gleaming hair over the pillow like a silk fan, all the while
kissing her temples and eyelids, then trailing soft, wet
kisses down her throat and over each aching, pointed little
breast. When she writhed and moaned, thrusting them
eagerly into his mouth, he suckled them, using his teeth and
tongue to tease and pleasure. His hand traveled lower, over
her belly and hip. Soon his questing mouth followed in a
scorching path.

He held up one little leg by its fragile ankle and nibbled

on her instep. When she let out a soft gasp of unexpected pleasure, he continued downward, tracing the curve of her calf with his lips, licking the tender skin behind her knee, then moving to her inner thigh, only to repeat the process with her other leg, until he had her writhing in a need as desperate as his own.

Still he held back, gripping her slim little hips firmly with his hands, leaning down slowly, first breathing into the curling triangle of tan silk, tantalizing her until she cried out. He reached one lean brown hand up and placed his fingertips softly over her lips to silence her, then lowered his mouth once more into the wet, honeyed and eager core of her. He could feel her convulsive trembling as he licked and stroked softly, skillfully, waiting patiently to feel her crest of passion. It did not take long.

Charlee lay with legs spread, back arched, head tossing from side to side, mindlessly awash in a strange blending of pleasure and need. She wanted it never to end, she hungered for something more, alternately torn in ecstasy, in want. Then with a startled gasp she stiffened, feeling the shock waves ripple through her in sharp spasms.

Jim held her, reaching up to embrace her and kiss her lips, whispering into her ear soft love words in English and Spanish. "I owed you that one, little Cat Eyes." He pressed her against him full length and felt her resurging awareness of her surroundings, of him.

Charlee clung mindlessly to him, raining feverish, grateful kisses over his face, neck and shoulders, running her hands up and down his arms. As breath and sanity returned, she realized he was as yet unfulfilled, holding her close, his hips gently, rhythmically thrusting against her own with the hard shaft of his desire straining between her legs.

Experimentally, she ran her hand down over his hard thigh, then back to the core of him, grasping the phallus securely. She was rewarded with a deep groan and a deepening kiss. His hot shaft felt wonderfully alive in her hand, and she realized the desperate mindless craving she had felt earlier was reciprocal. Now he needed her in that same primeval way. Before she could carry this new thought any further, he let out a sharp breath of pain-pleasure and grasped her busy little fingers, prying them away from their newly discovered delight.

"Lord, woman, what you do to me," he gasped as he levered himself up and over her, spreading her legs and thrusting inside her. He felt her stiffen for an instant, knowing she recalled her first clumsy initiation. But that remembered pain was quickly forgotten as she received him full length in a warm rush of pleasure. She arched up to meet his second thrust. Once more, he gentled her with his hands, slowing them to steady, even strokes, keeping a narrow edge of control over his own passion while he incited her once more to a blinding pitch of need to match his own.

Finally, sensing that she was nearing the brink, he increased his rhythm to the frenzied, ecstatic thrusts of their first mating. But this time as he trembled and convulsed, she joined him, clinging and shivering, crying out his name, just as he murmured hers. Realizing that his weight was an uncomfortable burden, Slade rolled off Charlee as soon as he could regain his breath and composure. As he lay back across the bed he pulled her slight form with him, nestling her against his uninjured side. She nuzzled his neck and beard-roughened cheek.

She lay in the crook of his arm with his fingertips lightly grazing her shoulder, gently, peacefully caressing her. He was content in knowing that this time he had brought her pleasure equal to his own. Satiated, exhausted, and weak from his injury, he was badly in need of some sleep.

Charlee lay quiescent, her body still singing from the magic he had wrought on her, yet desperately wanting something more—the spoken words, the commitment from him that she had vowed to have. Silently she willed him to speak but he did not.

All at once she realized what it must have cost him, with a newly stitched gash in his side, to go through all the wild exertion of making love. "Are you bleeding? Here, let me see the bandage." Deftly she began to examine his side as he let out a weary chuckle.

"Isn't this where you came in?"

"Don't be crude."

"Ouch! Damn, that aches now," he hissed, tightening his abdominal muscles as she rebandaged him.

"I can't imagine why," she whispered dryly. "I'll get you some laudanum from the kitchen."

"No, all I need is to get some sleep." He pulled her down beside him and proceeded to do just that.

Sighing, she stretched one arm over the bedside for the wayward sheet and covered them, content for now just to lie with him.

Feeling the heat of the early morning sun pouring through her bedroom window, Charlee awakened at daybreak. She felt another source of heat as well, the very warm, solid flesh of the man who slept peacefully beside her, with one arm beneath her neck and the other draped possessively across her breasts. One long hairy leg was flung carelessly over her. She studied his naked body and unshaven face in the golden light. Even with those magnetic eyes closed, he looked like a lean jungle cat, a predator, tawny and sleek.

Taking care not to awaken him, she gently disengaged herself and slid from the bed. She must be dressed and out of here, with all evidence of her presence erased before Deborah or anyone in the boardinghouse found out. After sliding into her robe and gathering up her night rail, she quickly scanned the room for any other evidence. None was present save for the faint essence of her perfume and the mellow, musky scent of male and female sweat commingled in lovemaking. With a sigh she turned to leave, then on sudden impulse bent down and gave Slade a light, brushing kiss before she fled the room.

It took only twenty minutes to bathe, dress, and get to the kitchen, where she and Sadie prepared a hearty breakfast for the boarders. If the old cook noticed a new sparkle in Charlee's green eyes or a flush to her cheeks, she said nothing.

Once the food was on the dining room table, nearly two dozen hungry people enjoyed buckwheat pancakes and molasses, crisp bacon, and hot black coffee.

Charlee went to the kitchen and fixed a tray for herself and Slade, nervously anticipating their next meeting. All her confidence, engendered and emboldened by passion, evaporated in the harsh light of morning. He had seduced her once again, but still had made no vows of love. Yet, as she recalled his tenderness, the slow, careful way he had held his own passion in check while bringing her such unimaginable pleasure, Charlee could not help but feel that he did care for her a great deal. She carried the tray upstairs, humming determinedly.

Slade awakened slowly, dimly aware of a sense of loss after the small, soft warmth had left his side—a woman, Charlee. He could still smell the faint hint of wildflowers in the room. It wasn't a dream. She had been here last night, hadn't she? He sat up, shaking his head and running one hand over his side, which by now only ached dully. He'd taken no laudanum last night, he was sure. "That was no drugged fantasy," he said to himself, chuckling ruefully.

As he became more alert, all the details of their erotic night together came back to him. God, what a wild, passionate little creature she was! She was like a cactus flower, her delicate beauty surrounded by protective thorns. He'd been pricked by those thorns on more than one occasion. Yes, she was his Cactus Flower. "His"—Slade suddenly realized how possessive he had become overnight. He was sure they had exchanged no words of love; he'd made her no promises. But he had seduced her again and he couldn't even plead that he'd been drunk this time. Why did every event, every quirk of fate seem bent on drawing him to Charlee McAllister?

His ruminations were disturbed by a call of nature, which he quickly answered. Then he scrounged through her closet until he located his breeches. The shirt must have been bloodstained beyond redemption, he surmised. Running a hand over his beard stubble, he decided a wash and a shave were in order. He padded down the hall to the men's washroom and cleaned up amid good wishes for a quick recovery. Feeling too weak to hazard the stairs after his exertion, Slade walked unsteadily back to Charlee's room and sat in a chair by the window. He was peering out at the street below when the sudden pounce of Hellfire caught him unawares. The orange blur landed neatly on the windowsill after leaping cleanly past his outstretched legs. The cat didn't touch him, but he was so startled that he jerked back, painfully twisting his injured side.

"Hellfire and damnation," he swore at the cat, glaring into slitted green eyes that stared back with much the same color and fire as Charlee's own. Smiling to himself, Slade relaxed and reached a tentative hand to the feline, allowing him to sniff and accept or reject this peace overture.

Crooking his fringed ear, Hellfire squinted and approached the proffered hand warily. After several experimental sniffs, the cat suddenly snaked out an abrasive tongue and planted several licks across Slade's knuckles.

Scratching the cat's chewed ears in amazement, Jim chuckled. "So, I'm all right now that I have her scent on me, am I? Well, just remember, my scent is on her, too."

The bedroom door opened and Charlee backed in carrying a tray laden with a stack of steaming buckwheat cakes and a pot of fragrant coffee. She was wearing a pale green muslin dress, plainly cut but softly curving to her petite body. Her bronze hair cascaded down her back, held loosely in place by a matching green ribbon. Softly flushed from climbing the stairs with her heavy tray, she looked the picture of feminine grace and delicacy. As he quickly moved across the room to help her with her burden, he wondered how he had ever thought her boyish or plain.

"What are you doing up?" Charlee felt a jolt as his warm hands covered hers, taking the tray from her and depositing it on the bedside table. She felt the blush heat her cheeks as she looked at his cleanly shaven face. "You've shaved," she added idiotically, unable to think of anything else to say.

He smiled dazzlingly. "I went down the hall and Mr. Rubins was kind enough to lend me his razor. I could hardly be abed all day, unless, of course, the chef could be persuaded to forsake her post for the duration . . ."

At that insinuation, she turned to fuss with the food on the tray, saying, "You may not be interested, but I've worked up quite an appetite." The minute the words were out of her mouth, she went crimson with mortification.

Shaking with silent laughter, Slade stood behind her and put his hands on her slim shoulders. Planting a kiss on her neck, he whispered, "I've worked up an appetite, too, but let's eat first."

She whirled, intent on chastising his levity or fleeing, she was not sure which, but then he caught her chin in his hand and forced her to look in his eyes. The glinting devilment of his humor was contagious, and immediately a bubble of laughter escaped her.

He bent and kissed her nose, then moved over to the bed and reclined against the headboard, hands behind his neck, feet crossed at the ankles. "Now, wench, what about those buckwheat cakes?"

They ate in companionable silence for a few moments, he on the bed, she sitting next to him on the room's only chair. Then Hellfire jumped down from his perch on the sill with a thud and meandered toward the smell of food, especially the butter slathered across the mounds of brown cakes. Bypassing Charlee, he jumped neatly onto the bed and boldly walked up to Slade's plate.

"Hungry, eh? Well, seems to me I did mention something about a churn of butter," he said, scooping a generous dollop onto his spoon and feeding it to the voracious cat.

"Why, you fickle old devil, you! Why did you—" Charlee's accusing eyes went from the blissfully busy cat to Slade. Suddenly she knew why the cat had finally accepted Jim. Once more she felt the color stealing up her throat and face.

With the hint of a smile tugging at the corners of his mouth, he looked smugly at her. She suddenly found herself returning the smile, idiotically, mindlessly happy despite her shyness.

They sat wordlessly, tawny gold and cat-green eyes locked in communion, when a sudden click of the door broke the spell. It was flung open and Tomasina Carver swept into the room.

chapter
11

Tomasina came to a halt just inside the door, her eyes narrowing as she took in the intimate tableau. Slade sat bare-chested, reclining against the headboard of the bed with that hateful cat perched next to him. Charlee was much too close, sitting in a chair beside the bed.

"Diego, I just returned from the ranch this morning and heard you had been shot! I came immediately." Ignoring Charlee, she swished her chocolate taffeta skirts dramatically and swept over to the opposite side of the bed. Placing her hands on his shoulders, she kissed him on the lips in assertion of her position. Let the little tart be warned. After all, Charlee was only a scullery maid!

Slade had never seen Tomasina act so forward, and he was certain of what had prompted her boldness. Smiling rather cynically, he carefully freed himself and prepared for a difficult confrontation.

As Charlee rose and gathered up the tray, her eyes met his once more. "I'll take these things to the kitchen, Jim. Just yell if you need help."

Watching the unspoken interplay between them, Tomasina suddenly knew they were lovers. There was a certain intangible tension between a man and woman who had lain together. A murderous fury seized her as she watched the mere slip of a girl vanish out the door.

Slade observed the quick flashes of jealousy and calculation play across her beautiful face, realizing for the first time how little he knew her. What a blind spot for a man who prided himself on being such a shrewd judge of people!

Quickly regaining control of her emotions, she turned to

confront her fiancé, remembering that she had to walk a tightrope carefully between Jim and Ashley Markham.

She sat on the bed and placed one hand, now minus its glove, over his own, which rested limply on the covers. "Diego, are you badly hurt? I feel so guilty that I was not here, but those tiresome men at Jake's ranch got into a fight. I will be so relieved to have you assume the burden of running the place for me, *querido*."

Ignoring her question about his injury, he said, "A Comanchero named Rufus Brady, an errand boy for Ashley Markham, tried to kidnap Charlee." His cougar's eyes skewered her, looking for a reaction to either name.

"Why would anyone want to bother with a kitchen maid? Really, Diego, I do not understand." With her black eyes limpid and her forehead creased in a frown of puzzlement, she looked as guileless as a newborn foal.

"I wonder, Sina. You see, Brady didn't get away. I killed him and searched his body. He was carrying a bundle of gold and some very interesting information on ranger and militia movements." He paused for effect, then continued, "Charlee told me everything, Sina. She overheard you and Markham in the alley yesterday morning."

She put one small beringed hand to her throat in outrage. "That's absurd! She's either lying or she saw another woman and mistook her for me!"

"Give it up, Sina. You and that damned English spy were seen at the Rojas place last week, too. I always did wonder why you martyred yourself, spending so much time with that old harpy, Serafina. How long have you and Markham been conspirators—or, should I ask, lovers as well?" Odd that he didn't even feel a flicker of jealousy as he made the accusation.

As he spoke, Tomasina watched his face. There was no chance of bluffing her way out. Damn Ashley and his careless rendezvous! She decided to take a desperate gamble. Both her hands were in her lap now, shredding an expensive brown silk glove as big, shiny tears welled up in her eyes. She let them fall down her flawless porcelain cheeks as she sobbed and threw herself on Slade's chest.

"Oh, James, forgive me. I never meant for you to be

hurt, my beloved!" She switched to Spanish, feeling more comfortable fabricating her tale in her native language. "Ashley was wild when that girl saw us. He arranged to have her disappear. I swear, I did not know about any Comanchero. I would never have let such a man try to kill you. You must believe that!" She looked imploringly into his eyes.

"Then you'll tell me everything about you and Markham?" His voice was toneless, cold.

She took a deep, sobbing breath and began. "I met him in England. I was only a schoolgirl, darling. He was gallant and charming, and I had a foolish infatuation for him. Then I returned home and did not see him again until about a year ago. He is not my lover, James! I do not find his pawing advances at all appealing."

"Then why do you do his dirty work for him?" Slade's eyes were like amber glass as he waited for her to answer.

She flung her head back, and with eyes flashing she announced, "I am a patriot, a Mexican citizen. Markham and his government only aid our cause—to free Texas from Houston and return it to the *Tejanos*."

He sighed, expecting this to be her reasoning. "Sina, I'm one of Houston's men. I've always supported his government. I fought to drive Santa Anna and his army out of Texas. So did Seguin, Navarro, Zavala—lots of us *Tejanos*. Texas will never be reconquered by Mexico. The British are only playing a game of balance of power, pitting Mexico against the United States, for their own interests."

She shook her head, then rubbed her temples with her fingertips. "I . . . I do not know, James. I used to believe Ashley Markham's lies, believe he and his money could supply an army to raise the Mexican flag over Texas once more."

"By giving the Comanche whiskey and guns, knowing they'll slaughter innocent settlers? That's what he and his friends are doing, Sina." He took her shoulders in his hands and gently shook her. "Think, Sina. I'm not lying to you. Markham was going to sell Charlee to Iron Hand as a white slave!"

She broke down completely then, crying piteously against

his chest while he stroked her hair softly and held her, uncertain how much of her hysteria was real, how much feigned. Doubtless she was frightened. She had excellent reason to be!

Finally she quieted and looked up at him with trembling lips and swollen eyes. "James, I've been a fool, but I am sorry. When I think they might have killed you! I love you more than anything, more even than Mexico. You will still marry me, give me the protection of your name? I promise I will be a good wife. I—"

"Sina, I can't promise you everything will be just like it used to be, but I will protect you." He quirked a crooked grin. "President Houston is rather chivalrous when it comes to the ladies, after all. But you have to tell me everything about Markham's schedule, where he goes, who he meets, *everything*. He's dangerous, and I mean to stop him."

Briefly, she gave him an edited outline of Markham's activities, the Indians he and his friends dealt with, their irregular rendezvous; she even told him about some shadowy intermediary with connections high in the British Foreign Office, although she denied knowing his name or whereabouts.

Jim slid off the bed and paced about, running long brown fingers through his golden hair. Tomasina watched him, still fascinated despite her fear and anger. If she could just get him to marry her, she'd be beyond the law. But would she feel the same glow of satisfaction so obviously radiating from Charlee McAllister this morning? In part she wanted to find out, in part she did not. No man had ever had that hold on her. Still, if Jim became unmanageable, there was always Ashley. She listened attentively as Slade gave her instructions.

"Go home and wait for Markham to contact you. Tell him no one believed Charlee and that you're both safe. Then wait until he sets up another meeting with his Comanche friends. As soon as you know when and where, you tell me so I can stop him and his killers for good. And, Sina, when your friends from Mexico contact you about their plans, anything like that little romp of General Vasquez's in March, you'd better tell me that, too. Agreed?" He looked at her levelly.

She took a deep breath and looked him in the eye. "I promise, James. I'll do anything you ask."

He escorted her to the door and then down the deserted hall. When they reached the stairs, he stopped, feeling a brief surge of lightheadedness. Damned wound! He held onto the banister and reached for Tomasina's hand to give her a chaste kiss goodbye. He must placate her to gain her cooperation in this wretched intrigue. Although he hated the idea of using a woman, especially one whose family had been so close to his own, he knew what he must do. His other feelings toward her would have to be sorted out later. Right now he was confused and simply wanted to settle with Markham.

As he raised her fingers to his lips, Tomasina again surprised him and came quickly into his arms, backing him up against the banister for a thorough kiss on the lips. Without appearing ungallant, there was little to do but return her kiss. Strange, ever since Jake died, he had tried with infrequent success to get her into his embrace. Now that he had finally succeeded, he couldn't help but compare his lack of response to Sina with the galvanizing feelings Charlee's touch gave him.

What Slade did not see was Charlee standing at the foot of the stairs watching the embracing pair. Hellfire at his most baleful could not have conjured up a more lethal look than his mistress did. After using her so tenderly last night, he once more cast her away, to fall beneath that murdering bitch's spell!

"Careful, I'm not sure the banister can take all that strain," she called with acid sweetness.

Slade, who was indeed leaning back against the rail with Tomasina pressed intimately against his bare chest, jerked forward as if burned, dislodging her. The quick movement strained his already aching side and he swore beneath his breath, wincing in pain as he attempted to straighten up.

Archly Tomasina smiled down on the girl below, then gave Slade another light salute on the lips and began to descend the stairs. "Really, Diego, you must speak to Mrs. Kensington about the forwardness of her kitchen help. It ill becomes those of such low station." That last sally was

delivered directly in front of Charlee, whom she passed with
one smug curl of her lips. *"Hasta luego, querido,"* she
called over her shoulder.

Charlee stood there smoldering, fighting the urge to lunge
after the hateful aristocrat and significantly rearrange her
glossy hair, not to mention her face. Inside, Charlee McAllister,
Missouri hill girl, just wanted to slip quietly from Slade's
sight and sob her misery into Hellfire's warm, reassuring
pelt. But she was stubborn and proud as well. Hadn't
Deborah taught her to act like a lady? With spine stiff and
head erect, she turned her back on Slade and walked toward
the kitchen.

Furious with Sina's snobbish arrogance and her deliberate
staging of that embrace, Jim swore beneath his breath. He
considered going after Charlee and attempting to explain to
her, but decided against it. He was dizzy, and his wound
ached abominably. Moreover, he didn't want to endanger
Charlee by telling her too much about his role as Houston's
agent. He would lie down and rest while he considered how
to handle her when she brought his lunch.

When Lee rather sheepishly entered the room with his
luncheon tray, Slade knew Charlee was seriously angry.

"Charlee told me you'd be needing your strength, so
you'd better eat," Lee said, with the faintest hint of a smirk
playing around his lips.

Slade resisted the impulse to groan aloud. "I suppose
she's let that rotten little temper loose on every hapless
piece of crockery in the kitchen," he said sourly.

"Temper? Charlee?" Lee's face was alight with unholy
innocence. "You're a poor one to talk of temper, *mano*, and
I think you know it." In spite of Slade's darkening counte-
nance, the youth went on, "And she didn't break one dish.
As a matter of fact, she prepared this especially for you.
She said something about your wanting solid food despite
Dr. Weidermann's orders," he added innocently, depositing
the tray in front of Slade and whipping off the napkin.

Slade looked down on a steaming bowl of Charlee's
slow-simmered chili con carne. A stack of crisp, toasted
tortillas and a small granite pot of coffee completed the
feast. The thick reddish-brown dusting on the tortillas might

have given him a warning, but perhaps a man sees only what he wants to see.

His face split into a grin as he grabbed the large spoon beside the plate. "Well, I guess she can't be in such a snit if she made my favorite, chili."

He hadn't realized how the morning's exertions had fired his appetite until he smelled the spicy fragrance of the chili. It was divine! Dipping deeply into the thick, reddish stew, he grabbed a crisp tortilla with the other hand and stuffed it all in his mouth. Intent on assuaging his hunger, he shoved a second heaping spoonful in before the first had hit bottom.

The burning began in the pit of his stomach and moved like a sirocco-fanned brush fire up his throat, racing across his tongue, then exploding out of his mouth to sear his lips in a billowing surge of agony. He was being incinerated alive! Frantically, he searched the tray for water. There was none. Ignoring the cup, he grabbed the granite coffee pot, yanked off the lid, and downed several gulps of the scalding, inky brew. It was thick as river silt and boiling hot. Now his hands were almost as burned as his innards. Rather than dousing the fire, the java fanned it. Tears and sweat trailed down his face as he slammed the pot and its evil contents back on the tray with a string of exceedingly filthy, guttural curses.

His voice was so hoarse, Lee could scarcely understand the words, but they related to a slip of a girl and her parents' aberrant sex practices. Careful to conceal the laughter that threatened to erupt, the vaquero turned and reached behind him for the water pitcher and glass on the table.

Lee had watched Charlee dish up the food and had noticed a sizable pile of seeds and cores from green chilies on the kitchen table. How was he to know she hadn't put the hot chilies into the large cookpot simmering on the stove, but rather into this one small bowl? Of course, he had seen her liberally sprinkle the tortillas with cayenne, but then Jim had at least that much coming. Watching his friend gulp the water while clutching the glass with both burned hands, Lee was certain that he never wanted to be on the wrong side of Charlee McAllister.

"For a *Tejano* raised on chili, *mano*, you sure act as if

you never had anything hotter than a strip of salt pork," he said ingenuously when he could see Jim was finally catching his scorched breath. The tears had abated, but he was still sweating profusely.

With another foul oath, Slade flung the napkin over the lethal mess. "Take this back to the kitchen and tell her to poison wolves with it—or better yet, have her cat bury it. It'll melt the claws off that son of a bitch!"

Slade spent the afternoon resting and building up his strength to confront Charlee at dinner. At least she couldn't very well poison all twenty boarders at the table just to spite him! Asa brought him some clean clothes that afternoon, and Jim bathed and shaved again with his own razor. Seething as he dressed, he donned a crisp homespun shirt that he left open at the throat and a snugly fitted pair of butter-soft buckskin breeches. Last, he pulled on a gleaming pair of Cordovan boots. He was dressing for battle.

Slade conveniently encountered Deborah in the hall and told her he would be eating downstairs tonight. She bustled off with a smile to set another place at the table.

During dinner, Charlee looked daggers at Slade, setting each bowl and platter on the table with jarring force. At one point she narrowly missed depositing a large pitcher of scalding brown gravy in his lap. When she "accidentally" dropped a sharp carving knife, point down, between his legs, he retrieved it and set it carefully on the table. Then he reached behind her surreptitiously and grabbed a buttock, pinching it painfully. Smiling as blandly as if he were discussing the weather, he whispered a succinct and rather vulgar threat in Spanish, which he knew she understood quite well thanks to Lee's unorthodox tutoring.

When he released her, she hurried to the kitchen like a stampeded jackrabbit and did not come anywhere near him for the rest of the meal.

Jim went to the kitchen after dinner, looking for Charlee. Sadie was cleaning plates. She laconically informed him that Charlee was out back somewhere.

He stepped out and looked around. No Charlee. Just then the cat sprinted between Slade's legs, nearly knocking him off the porch steps. Hellfire had already shown that he had a better nose than anyone when it came to finding his mistress. Slade followed the cat, who led him to the ice cellar behind the shed.

He lifted the heavy door and climbed down the stairs into the cold, dim interior, cut deeply into the earth. When he got near the bottom, a low moan broke the silence. When his eyes adjusted to the dim light of a single candle, he was greeted by an arresting sight.

Charlee stood with her back to him, bent over one of the large blocks of straw-covered ice, her petite derriere delightfully exposed beneath her hiked-up skirts and lowered pantalets. She was applying a generous chunk of ice to a reddish mark on her buttock.

"I imagine if I place my hand over that print, it'll be a perfect fit." He leaned against the thick earthen wall with nonchalant ease and waggled a finger at the gasping girl. "It's not nice to dump gravy on a man's only clean buckskins, even worse to drop a sharp knife on the precise anatomical position you were aiming for, my sweet."

Throwing down the ice, she whirled around and furiously straightened her clothes. "I'm only sorry I missed," she hissed.

He looked at the bristling girl, dwarfed by the giant ice blocks surrounding her. "Careful, with all that steam, you might melt the ice and drown yourself."

"If I could take you with me, it'd be worth it. You miserable son of a bitch, I'll scarce be able to sit for a week!"

"That's too bad, because you're riding to Bluebonnet first thing in the morning," he said levelly, daring her to defy him. All thoughts of reasonable explanation had fled his mind during his near brushes with scalding and castration at dinner. She would do as she was told with no more nonsense!

A dangerously coy look flashed across her face and she smiled, fluttering her lashes as if she were a halfwit. "Lookee heah, 'Don Diego,' us Missoorah hill gals, we knows ourah place—it's right heah in Miz Debra's kitchen, jest like yore ladylove done tole me this mornin'."

"If this noon's cooking was any sample, I seriously doubt

it,'' he snapped. "Will you forget about Sina and be sensible, dammit!" His voice vibrated in the cavernous depths of the cellar.

"Forget that murdering bitch!" She was shrieking now, her tone matching his in stridence. "You'll just have to forgive me for being a wee bit upset! It's not every day I get kidnapped by a Comanchero and almost sold into white slavery!"

Remembering what she had been through, he struggled with his temper. "Charlee, I know you won't believe me, but there's a chance Sina wasn't involved in your abduction. I don't know yet, but I do know for certain Ashley Markham was. He's the one I mean to stop, any way I can."

"But you'll still protect your precious *Sina* 'any way you can,' too—even if she's a spy and a traitor," she accused.

He stood with one foot poised on the stairs, too angry to trust himself any nearer to her. "I am through arguing. Whether or not you enjoy my company, you are going to Bluebonnet with me first thing in the morning." He turned and began to ascend the steep steps, trying in vain to ignore his aching side and the shrieking girl behind him.

"Compared to you, *Mister* Slade, Iron Hand is beginning to sound pretty damn good!"

The next morning Charlee woke alone in her own bed. Insisting he felt much better, Slade had moved in with Lee and Mr. McCurdy, leaving her to sleep in peace. Some peace, she bitterly admitted to herself. All night she had tossed and turned, tortured by dreams of Jim and Tomasina in torrid embraces, then of herself and Slade and their breathtaking passion of the previous night. Sweating and trembling, she had awakened over and over.

Then toward daybreak she woke one final time after reliving their lovemaking, recalling Slade's question to her the night of the dance at Pearsons'. *My God, I could be pregnant! I've gone and done it again, and that lowlife philanderer is still planning to marry his fancy ladylove. What will I do?* Her mind whirled in turmoil. He had insisted she return to Bluebonnet—to keep her as a mistress? Of course, he would meet his responsibilities to any bastards she might drop as a consequence. She lay with her fists clenched in the sheets, tears overflowing and running down her temples, into her hair. Aloud she whispered to the empty room, "I won't do it! I won't live that way and be shamed like that."

"If"—she paused and gulped at the enormity of the idea—"if I am pregnant, I'll take my nest egg and go to New Orleans. I could always pretend to be a widow, start my own restaurant or boardinghouse . . . Hell, I'll do it anyway." Feeling utterly bereft, Charlee threw off the covers and leaped out of bed, startling the cat awake. The sheet fluttered over him when she tossed it carelessly to the foot of the bed. Like a mole emerging from a hole, Hellfire tunneled out from beneath it, his fringed ear and balefully glowing green eyes visible. He sat in his white shroud, watching Charlee bustle about in the dim morning light.

"Hellfire, old boy, how'd you like to see New Orleans?" With that she gave the protruding ear a scratch and began to dress. So intent was she on packing that she did not notice when the cat slithered from beneath the bedcoverings and slipped silently out the open window.

She had washed her face, plaited her hair into a thick, serviceable pigtail and donned a cotton blouse and sturdy skirt, split down the center to allow for riding astride. Charlee felt ready for her undertaking.

"I'll just have to leave some of my cash money to pay the rest of what I owe for Patchwork," she sighed. "I'll tell Deborah to give it to him in my note to her." Leaving all her friends here in Texas would be difficult, but if she stayed, her situation would be impossible. Sitting down at the small table across from her bed, Charlee thought of Richard Lee for the first time in a long while. If only he were alive the two of them could start over again. She wouldn't be so alone. Resolutely she forced the bittersweet fancy from her mind and pulled some paper and a pen from the drawer. The letter must of necessity be brief, for she had to make good her escape before anyone else was awake and stirring.

After several hasty and inadequate tries, she penned a succinct note to Deborah, thanking her for all her kindnesses and assuring her that she must leave rather than return to Bluebonnet with Slade. She felt certain her friend would surmise the reasons for that decision.

Placing the note and the payment for her horse in an envelope, Charlee grabbed her possible sack and looked for Hellfire. "Damblasted critter. He's probably in the kitchen. I'll leave the note for Deborah there and collect him."

When she made her stealthy exit from her room, the halls were deserted. The only one at all likely to be up was Sadie, and Charlee felt confident she could swear the old woman to secrecy. However, when she tiptoed into the kitchen, neither Sadie nor Hellfire was around. She swore to herself about feline perversity and moved toward the back door, the forgotten note still clutched in her hand. Knowing she dare not call aloud this close to the house, Charlee decided to walk toward the livery and hoped the cat would be near enough to respond to her call from that distance. She began to descend the creaking stairs. Balanced in mid-stride on the first step, she was brought up short by a sarcastic gravel voice.

"Well, up so early, all packed and ready to go. Thoughtful of you, my little Cactus Flower, but we really should eat breakfast and say goodbye to Deborah first." Slade had come around the veranda from the side porch and was leaning indolently against a banister column. Hellfire was twining around his legs, with matching indolence.

"Why you, you pusillanimous hunk of moldy flea-bitten fur, you . . . you traitor, you . . . you . . . *tomcat!*"

"Is that any way to speak to the cat who saved your life?" He pointed his finger at her accusingly and in a couple of long-legged strides was beside her, relieving her of the possible sack. He eyed the note clutched in her hand but made no move to take it. "Don't think you'll need that," was all he said.

They went back into the kitchen and Slade helped her begin breakfast for the large household. Shortly they were joined by Sadie, who, if she thought it odd for the pair to be in the kitchen starting the cook fire, said nothing.

By the time Deborah, Lee, and the boarders made their

appearance, Charlee had several pots of fragrant black coffee brewed, a mountain of fluffy eggs scrambled, six dozen crusty biscuits browning, and two heaping platters of spicy pork sausage fried.

Watching her economic and graceful movements in the kitchen, Slade said, "Asa'll sure be glad to see you back, Charlee. Weevils can't boil coffee and talk at the same time, much less get a digestible meal on the table."

"Asa won't be the only one glad for this kind of food," Lee sang out, snatching a piece of sausage from the platter as she carried it into the dining room.

Charlee did not deign to reply to either man.

By the time the horses were saddled and Lee and Jim were ready to leave, Deborah came out to say goodbye. Standing on the porch, Charlee glared at the assembly. When she saw Hellfire sprawled limply across Slade's saddle, she clenched her jaw. The cat eyed her with characteristic feline indifference, as if to say in a bored tone, "Well, aren't you coming?"

Her eyes narrowed to green slits as she saw her luggage tied onto a pack horse. "Who—?"

"Jim asked me to pack the rest of your things while you were making breakfast, Charlee," Deborah replied. She walked over and put an arm about the young woman's shoulders. "It's not that far to Bluebonnet. We'll be able to visit often." Then she gave her young friend a hug and whispered so that only she could hear. "Don't give up so easily. Tomasina hasn't won yet!"

With a sigh of resignation, Charlee bid Deborah farewell, and strode down the steps. When she mounted Patchwork, Slade nudged Polvo next to her horse and transferred the cat to Charlee's saddle. Hellfire gave her hand a few rough licks and settled down, purring loudly.

"Just like a male," she snapped. "Get your own way and you're happy as a drunk in a moonshine still."

chapter
12

"And I say, my love, that it's time to cut our losses and escape with our whole skins. My government will assign me elsewhere, someplace my escapades aren't so . . . er . . . well publicized." Markham's polished black boots and faultlessly tailored cream suit were out of place in the frontier parlor of Jake Carver's old ranch house with its hideously clashing rose and maroon upholstered furniture. Tomasina had always hated Jake's house, so she had never attempted to redecorate it, only to escape it.

Looking down on the immaculately attired man with his perfectly barbered hair, Tomasina wondered how he had managed to ride all the way from town without getting a lock out of place. He was neither dusty nor wrinkled. Did he ever sweat? If so, the memory failed her. He was draped rather effetely over the atrocious sofa. Tomasina turned her back on him and looked out the window at the desolation of the Texas landscape, whipped by the hot morning wind.

"Where would we go, Ashley?" she asked wearily. God knew she was sick of the frontier; she longed for civilization, but *her* civilization, where Spanish was spoken, an unlikely probability with Ashley Markham. "It's not likely your government will reassign you now with General Woll so close to invasion. If he takes San Antonio and moves east to the Gulf while the Comanche rise in the northwest, Houston's government will crumble."

Ashley threw back his head and laughed, a brittle, unnerving sound that lashed her frayed nerves. "General Woll, indeed. What the hell do you think he is—another 'Napoleon of the West'?" He scoffed at the title Santa Anna had claimed for himself. "Well, at least Woll *is* a Frenchman, but don't forget, dear heart, we defeated the original article. I suspect Sam Houston can handle *El Presidente* and his French mercenary."

"How can you sit there and say such a thing? This is a full-scale invasion. Your own government has sunk millions into it." Tomasina's black eyes blazed as she stood glaring down at him.

Once more he laughed. "I'd never realized the depth of your patriotism, my darling, or the extent of your political naivete! Christ, no wonder we've been exposed by a stupid chit of a kitchen maid! Bloody incompetence."

"*Your* incompetence, not mine! I did not want to meet you there. Anyway, I told you, no one believes the girl. She is just a servant in love with Diego. He thinks she made up the whole story in a fit of jealousy over me."

"Including her abduction by Brady?" Markham looked cynical and bemused. "I only wonder what fox-lynx game Slade's playing." He stroked his chin contemplatively.

Tomasina's eyes narrowed. "Forget the girl and Slade. What do you mean by 'my political naivete'? I've been in touch with the highest sources in Mexico City. You and other British agents have circulated a fortune across Texas, sowing counterrevolution."

Markham sighed and looked at her, half in fondness, half in frustration, as if she were a favorite child who had just failed to perform adequately in front of visiting relations. "Tomasina, really, be realistic. General Woll will make an incursion, a raid just like Vasquez's in March. It's a simple act of defiance, a fishing expedition by wishful, doomed dream spinners back in Mexico City. They hope to spark a popular uprising of the *Tejanos*. Rubbish! That clever French mercenary won't hold San Antonio a week, much less march to the Gulf! And as to the 'millions' Lord Aberdeen has supposedly spent arming Mexico, remember the source of those reports: inflammatory American newspapers, scarcely the most reliable sources," he said with heavy irony.

"You've given me thousands to pass along to the Mexican partisans, even more for your Indian allies," she insisted, with rising anger.

"Little enough for Her Majesty's government to spend containing Yankee avarice in North America," he sniffed blandly.

With an icy chill, Tomasina realized his words had a familiar ring. What had Slade said to her only a few days ago about the balance of power, Mexico versus the United States?

"You don't expect us ever to reconquer Texas, do you?" Her tone lent a cutting edge to the question. "You never intended that we would. You wanted only to placate my government and maintain favorable relations with us."

"Well, darling, your compatriots do owe British banking interests rather a large sum of money. They'd hate to see the Mexican government topple. Nasty business, that." He regarded his nails idly. "As long as your Mexicans are playing soldier games in Texas, they aren't cutting one another to pieces at home, and with our good offices mediating between Texas and Mexico, the Americans are held at bay as well. Not exactly neat and orderly, but a plan of sorts, nonetheless. One does what one can."

Markham stood up and walked over to Tomasina, who had turned once more, this time to stare at the portrait of Jake still hanging over the mantel. They used to joke about him. Now it seemed the joke had turned on them.

"Tomasina, my beautiful, fiery little patriot, let go. It's over. We can return to Europe. I'm sure my brother in London can arrange me a decent post somewhere on the Continent." He placed his hands on her tense shoulders and began to massage deftly, interspersing his strokes with soft, light kisses across the nape of her neck.

Tomasina took long, deep breaths, trying desperately to remain calm, not to turn on the man behind her and rend his handsome, cynical face to shreds, as he had just done to her dreams. Used. She had been used, her body, her mind, her hopes of returning to Mexico City to live in triumph— Ashley had begun his game with her seven years ago. Was it really her idea to marry Jacob Carver, or his? Her idea to contact old family friends in Mexico City, or his? Every step of the way, since she was an infatuated schoolgirl sneaking away from her *dueña*, Ashley had coached her, seduced her, used her.

With a brittle smile, she turned to his embrace. She would let him use her once more, use her body at least, but only once more. "If you really think we must leave, *querido*, I suppose we must, but first you will have to meet your Comanchero friends one last time. After all, you cannot leave your superiors in the lurch. They will expect that diversion just before General Woll's attack."

"Hmm, I suppose so. Such devotion to duty, my lovely firebrand . . ." His mouth claimed hers in a fierce kiss.

"I'm beginnin' to think Weevils put some of them dangblasted home remedies of his into the cookin' 'n that's why it tasted like it did, Charlee." Asa sat in the large cool kitchen at Bluebonnet and watched the late afternoon sun's faint rays cast rich bronze-and-red highlights on Charlee's hair as she stood by the window kneading bread.

She rubbed her nose with her wrist and wrinkled up its flour-dabbed tip in a bubble of laughter. "He is a dickens for folk medicine. 'Good slab o' raw bacon'll cure near ever'thin'," she averred, mimicking Weevils's accent perfectly.

"Wal, it's purely true, fer yore infermation," a high, wheezing voice cut in as the obese old man came in the back door, struggling under the load of a full flour sack. "I do like wheaten bread a damn sight better'n cornbread, but hellfire 'n damnation, this stuff's expensive, not ta say heavy 'nough ta give a body a hernia." He sat down as Asa relieved him of his burden.

"You got any cures fer the hernia, Weevils?" Asa asked gravely.

The cook snorted in disbelief. "Course I have. Any fool knows ya let a big summer onion set out in th' sun fer a couple o' days, till it's nice and soft. Soak it with cow piss 'n tie it ta th' lower belly fer 'bout three days."

Asa grimaced and Charlee giggled. Just then Lee walked in, still brushing trail dust from his clothes. His smile lighted on Charlee and its radiance filled the room. "Aah, smell that! What sweet aromas come from this kitchen since you've returned to us, *chiquita*. Only last week the fragrance of sulphur, blackstrap molasses, and castor oil greeted me at the end of a long, hard day on the range.''

Weevils shrugged. ''Them's th' fixins fer th' best damnblasted tonic in six counties!''

After they all shared a laugh over the vile brew the old cook was always foisting on ailing cowhands, Lee sobered. ''Seriously, I wish there was something to help Jim's side heal better. He's in a lot of pain, even though he tries to hide it.'' He looked at Charlee as he spoke.

She gave a disgusted shrug and said, ''And he calls *me* a Missouri mule. Dr. Weidermann told him not to ride so much until those stitches come out, but that stubborn, willful, *gunshot* man just won't listen!'' With a sigh of exasperation she returned to her kneading.

''Best thing in the world fer any wound, gunshot, knife, whutever...''—Weevils paused and looked speculatively over at the window where Hellfire reclined, eyeing him warily—''is fer a person ta take th' first two joints o' a cat's tail, rub 'em over th' sore place, then bury 'em. Two days 'n th' wound's healed. 'Course, a body's gotta find a cat thet's willin'...'' His voice trailed off as the feline in question flicked the appendage in question in a most agitated manner, glaring hostilely as if he understood every word.

The fat man shivered. ''Sometimes I git me th' most eeriest feelin' 'bout thet critter.''

Everyone laughed.

''What's the joke?'' Slade stood slouched in the kitchen door, his casual pose belying the ache in his side that only the tight set of his mouth revealed.

Asa guffawed, ''Weevils here's got a cure for your injury, but friend cat won't see clear ta cooperate.''

Again everyone burst out laughing except Jim who saw no humor at all in the abominable throbbing of his slowly healing wound. Asa explained the proposed cure while Charlee put the finishing touches to shaping six large, neat loaves. Lee watched her efficient but tense movements as she worked furiously, noticing that she was careful not to look at Jim.

In the three days since her return, she and Slade had barely spoken, avoiding one another like the pox. Although

Charlee refused to tell Lee what had happened in town, he could venture a fair guess that Tomasina Carver had much to do with the rift. Shaking his head sadly, the youth wondered how things would ever sort themselves out. At least they were both back at Bluebonnet together. Just then Slade's words jarred him from that train of thought.

"I have some business in Houston. I'll be leaving in the morning, Lee."

"But Dr. Weidermann specifically said those stitches should come out this week. You've got to—"

Interrupting Lee's angry plea, Slade turned to Charlee. "I haven't got time to ride the opposite direction. We've got a lady here who can sew a fine stitch. No reason she can't unsew a few just as easily." He looked at Charlee with a challenge lighting his eyes to amber fire.

She blanched. "I never did anything like that! Deborah's trained as a nurse, not me."

"Either you do it or my clumsy *compadre* here gets a stab at it, and he can't even buckle a cinch without getting his fingers caught in the straps." Slade gestured carelessly to Lee, who immediately took several steps backward, consternation written like a brand across his face.

Charlee's eyes slitted and glowed with an unholy light. "You asked for it, but I won't guarantee you'll be riding anywhere tomorrow."

Charlee carefully washed and scalded her mending scissors and a small crochet hook that Jim had dug out of one of his mother's old trunks. She had heard Deborah discuss such sanitary precautions with Dr. Weidermann and understood that they occasionally prevented infections.

Slade was standing in his bedroom, calmly stripping off his shirt, when she came in with the instruments, fresh salve, and bandages. She stood in the doorway, silently watching the ripple of lean, corded muscles across his back as he flexed his shoulders and carelessly tossed the shirt onto the bed. Remembering how those strong arms had felt embracing her, Charlee experienced a surge of that old, hateful weakness deep inside her belly. Damn and damn again! He turned and looked at her as if he had read her innermost thoughts. Smiling, he stretched out on his bed and awaited her ministrations.

She was nervous, not only because such a delicate operation was beyond the realm of her experience, but because it meant sitting close to Jim on the very bed where he had first seduced her. She took a shaky breath and set the tray on the bedside table. Acidly she said, "This is going to hurt like hell."

"No doubt," he agreed, seeming completely unconcerned.

Once she had unbandaged the puckering slash and looked at the crusting dried threads protruding from the reddened flesh, she felt her concentration return. At least there seemed to be no great degree of swelling or discoloration to indicate suppuration. The thread was easily visible, and with a steady hand she should be able to snip and pull each stitch free. Mechanically she set to work, surprising even herself with how quickly and efficiently she was able to complete the unpleasant task. When it was finished, she allowed herself to look at Slade's face for the first time. He had made no sound or movement all the while she had worked. Now he looked faintly pale beneath his tan, with sweat beading his forehead, but otherwise he was unshaken.

"Did it hurt much?" she had to ask.

"Not nearly as much as you'd have liked," he replied with a grin, touching the slash gingerly with his fingertips. "Actually, it's a relief to have those itchy drying threads out. They were what was aching me the most."

"Now just don't pull the whole da-...accursed thing open again," she shot back angrily, reaching for the bandages and salve.

He grabbed her wrist and then took the little hand in his. "Still determined to be a lady and not cuss—at least unless you're really good and mad."

She tried to pull her hand free, but he held it fast. "Let me go," she snapped, unsteadily.

Slade's eyes moved over her face, the long plait of hair tossed carelessly over her right shoulder, then settled on her hand, which he pulled over to his mouth. He kissed the palm softly with his warm, persuasive lips. She felt herself melting beneath this curiously gentle assault.

As if sensing her temporary paralysis, he said, "Charlee, I have to talk to you before I go. I want you to wait here until I get back, not try another escape. Markham could kill you yet if he decided to."

"I can take care of myself," she retorted hotly, once more trying to pull free.

"The way you did with Brady?" he questioned gently.

"Why should you care? If I'm gone, your ladylove is safe. That's what you really want, isn't it, Jim?" Her eyes made a silent plea to him for a denial.

He made none, but still he did not relinquish her hand. "I won't deny I want to protect Sina if I can." He felt her stiffen and grabbed her other hand, holding her prisoner on the bed as he willed her to listen. "She's a fool, but maybe no more than that. Markham's used her for his own ends, and right now the first thing I have to do is take care of him. Then maybe I can sort out some other things. But for now I want you safe, out of his clutches."

"And I'm supposed to accept that," she said almost wistfully. " 'Just sit tight, Charlee, wait until I can make up my mind whether to keep you on as my mistress or discard you once the danger's over.' I may not be a fancy lady like your Sina, but I am a woman with finer feelings, too. I have my pride."

Slade's face darkened as he fought the inescapable logic of her forthright statement. "If I told you that I needed to convince Sina that we were still going to be married, would you accept that?" He struggled with the unaccustomed need to confide in a woman, something he had not done since boyhood.

"You aren't going to marry her?" Her eyes were clouded, but a glimmer of brightness began to surface. She waited.

As he swung his feet off the bed and sat up beside her, he uttered several exceedingly vile Anglo-Saxon vulgarities. "I never had much respect for a man who'd use a woman the way Markham has. Now I'm in the same position with Sina. Dammit, I don't know what I'll do . . . what I'll *have* to do! I owe her family. Her father and mine settled here together, were lifelong friends. Now everything's changed. She's changed."

"Do you still love her?" The question seemed to ask itself. Charlee had to know, since he was using *her* without qualms.

He didn't blink on that one. "No, not the way I did when I first met her, or even the way I did last spring when Jake died and I came courting again. But it's more complicated than that. Hell, I'm not sure I'll *ever* know what love is, at least the kind you read about in books. What I'm trying to say is that I have obligations I can't get clear of yet, but I want you here, safe, waiting for me so we can settle this thing between us.

"I don't know if I love you, either, but I can honestly say no other woman has ever affected me the way you do. Say you'll stay, Charlee, please?" He raised both her hands to his lips now and kissed the backs of them while his eyes locked with hers. It was as near a plea as she would ever hear from Jim Slade, and Charlee knew it. Wordlessly she nodded her agreement.

The next morning Slade was gone at first light, off on another of his mysterious errands. If Lee knew where he went in Houston or why, he would not speak of it. Charlee fretted about his half-healed injury and wondered how several grueling days in the saddle would affect it, but she knew no one could keep Jim from doing what he deemed necessary.

Slade rode for nearly two days, making a dry camp the first night, pushing Polvo hard and himself harder. He must meet Houston face to face quickly. However, he was not going all the way to Houston City as he had told everyone, but only to the junction of the San Marcos and Guadalupe rivers, for a meeting they'd arranged earlier.

As he camped the second evening, Slade watched for signs of the president and for signs of Indians and other marauders. Anything was possible in the wilds of Texas. A man traveling alone was easy prey if he was inexperienced, something Jim Slade decidedly was not. A matched set of .36-caliber Wilkinson over-and-under pistols nestled securely in the sash around his slim waist, and two Pennsylvania Long Rifles were primed and ready on Polvo's saddle scabbards.

When Houston and his entourage arrived around dusk, Slade had coffee made and waiting for them with a small thirst-quenching libation to cut the bitter taste of the strong black brew. Without looking up, he poured a tin cupful and spoke. "Your scouts are slipping. I've heard you clumping around in the brush for the past quarter hour."

"Don't you know I'm supposed to be in Galveston inspecting a customs house? No wonder I lost my way, stumbling around through the bushes!" Houston's laugh boomed out as he reached for the proffered mug. Waving aside the flask, he said, "I no longer imbibe, Jim-boy. Mrs. Houston has reformed a thoroughgoing scoundrel, I'm sad to say at times like this." With obvious discomfort he squatted on the ground, favoring his bad leg slightly. The shattered ankle had never healed properly.

Slade greeted two of the rangers who accompanied the president, men he'd known and worked with since he was a new recruit in a Bexar ranging company. They were rough and unshaven, hard-eyed men who never relaxed their guard while out in the open, seldom even when in civilization. He offered them coffee and then set to fixing a simple meal of beans and hardtack as he and Houston talked. He knew there were at least four more men standing guard at strategic points around the campsite.

"I figure we have all night to talk, then I have to ride like hell to Washington-on-the-Brazos in the morning. I received your little pecuniary offering, courtesy of the Comancheros, along with the written communication." Houston's eyes were fixed on Slade, waiting for him to speak his piece, noting the way he favored his injured side. Little escaped those penetrating, shrewd eyes.

"*Little* offering," Slade retorted. "Then your treasury isn't as bankrupt as you report, Sam. The money's only a small part of it, though, you're right there. I was glad you asked for this meeting. Since we sent that package to you, I've found out a good deal about our friend Ashley Markham." Slade watched the older man's face, but as usual, the poker expression gave nothing away. Quickly Slade reviewed Charlee's kidnapping, Brady's death, and

Sina's confession. Houston listened to the whole recitation in silence, sipping his coffee and staring into the fire.

"You trust her to tell you the truth after all that's happened?" It was a straight question with no overtones of cynicism.

"I don't know. God help me, I don't know. Now that I look back over the past years, I see all kinds of things that I never put together before, patterns in her behavior that would've made me suspicious of anyone else."

Houston's face took on a faraway expression for a brief moment as he said, "I know the feeling. One woman in the world you never expect to—" He stopped abruptly, and the poker player's mask slipped into place once more. "I assume you have someone watching both her and Markham?"

Slade nodded. "I'm pretty sure he has to make connections with his Comanche friends soon, as soon as he gets more money from his New Orleans source. Now he doesn't have Brady to do his dirty work for him."

"But he still has Mrs. Carver," Houston said almost gently.

Slade looked up abruptly, then tossed the dregs of his coffee into the fire. "She only has contact with some renegade *Tejanos* who relay information between San Antonio and Mexico City."

"Antonio Perez?"

Slade sighed. "I'm almost certain his band supplies the couriers, but I don't have a complete list of all the local *Tejanos* who are involved, only Felipe Rojas, and Sina, of course," he finished bitterly.

"Well, Jim, about the same time I received word of your scrape, some other intelligence came my way. It seems the captives from the Sante Fe expedition are on their way out of that stinking Mexican prison, thanks to the good offices of our American friends, although the British are taking a few bows, too."

Slade snorted and Houston continued. "But that's not the half of it. Everything's still in turmoil with those idiots in the legislature passing declarations of war and appropriations for an army to invade Mexico." He threw up his hands in disgust. "Where they expect to get the money to feed and arm this grand 'levee en masse' I'd love to know! I suppose they expect Texian soldiers to eat cactus and then club Santa Anna into submission with the chewed-up pulps.''

''What we need are more men like Jack Hays and his rangers, who can live off the land and keep Santa Anna at bay on the border,'' Slade said with a crooked grin. He and the president had long agreed on the futility of a full-scale war Texas could never win and could not even finance.

''Men like Hays and you, Jim-boy.'' He paused and looked levelly at Slade. ''I have special need of your intelligence in San Antonio now, although I'm not any more certain of the widow Carver's reliability than you are.''

As Houston carefully chose his words, the thought crossed Slade's mind that his chief may have had another source report to him about Sina's connection to Markham. But he held his peace. The president would tell him only what he wanted him to know. ''What's happening on the border, Sam? Troop movements? We've only heard rumors as far north as San Antonio.''

''Maybe a big invasion this time, bigger than Vasquez. If it is, it'll take them a while to organize it, but one way or another, something's in the wind. I have a Yankee friend in Mexico City who says a certain French mercenary named Woll has a new command, orders unknown to outsiders as yet.''

''And his orders involve Texas,'' Slade surmised. There was little doubt.

Houston nodded. ''If your . . . fiancée''—Slade noted his tentative use of the word—''is in touch with Perez, she'll know. He's under Woll's command.''

Slade considered this. It all fit. A strike sometime before winter. ''Hear anything more about those warships coming from the British?''

''One's arrived. The other's still tied up across the pond, but I'm certain Santa Anna will get both his new toys if Pakenham has anything to say about it. However, Aberdeen himself may have changed tack, to use a nautical term.'' Houston's eyes lit up. He loved the complexities of international politics and its intrigues.

"The British Foreign Secretary's done something to please you?" Slade was incredulous.

"Let's just say the American Secretary of State, Daniel Webster, has. It seems he and another diplomat on the British side named Ashburton have concluded the long wrangled-over Canadian-American border dispute in Maine. Webster won the chess game. Pushy, those New Englanders."

Slade nodded, beginning to see where Houston was leading him. "And so, having gotten their tails scalded in the north by President Tyler's administration, the British have decided the Yankees just might cast their greedy eyes south—to Texas."

"Exactly," said the president, with gleeful malice unconcealed in his voice. "Lately my correspondence with the Foreign Office has been exceedingly cordial. Mexico is in their hip pocket—if they can only keep her from unraveling at the seams. But Aberdeen will do anything to avoid having the Americans, flushed with their diplomatic triumph in the north, cast their eyes toward Texas in the south. He proffers us undying devotion."

Slade broke into a broad grin now. "You plan to cozy up to Her Majesty's government and rattle a few chains back in Washington." He was beginning to think like his chief. Houston would use the British to goad the United States Congress into voting for Texas annexation.

"Sooner or later, we've got to jump, Jim-boy. It's either statehood in the American Union or disintegration into a satellite of some European power. Most likely the British lion would gobble us up."

"Here's to a royal case of indigestion," said Slade, hefting his refilled coffee cup.

With a roaring laugh, Houston returned the salute. Then he sobered. "Look, I am sorry about Tomasina Carver. I understand what you're going through better than you might imagine. Don't trust her, but do listen to her. And watch her. If any of Perez's people try to contact her or Rojas, you may hold the key to nipping a full-scale war in the bud. Or, the Mexicans may just wait on the Comanche to do their dirty work for them and strike when we're marshaling ourselves to repel the savages."

"All the more reason to break the chain that links guns and whiskey to belligerent Indians," Slade answered softly.

"Markham," said Houston.

"Markham," echoed Slade.

chapter
<u>13</u>

Tomasina Carver was on a mission of desperation. It was the second-to-last of her considerable repertoire of fallback plans. It shouldn't be too difficult. After all, if she'd just managed to convince Ashley Markham of her continued ardor after what he had done to her, surely she could handle one Texian frontiersman. She would seduce Jim Slade and trick him into marrying her.

She had it all figured out. It was near sundown, a warm late summer evening. Jim would be finishing dinner, not expecting a visit from her. She would give him all the information about Ashley's rendezvous with Iron Hand. Then she would break down and weep copiously over her betrayal of Mexico and her own fall from grace with that cad Markham. Slade would take her into his study to comfort her and calm her down, she would unbutton her basque saying she was faint, ask for some brandy, get him to share it with her. No, it should not be too difficult at all, she concluded with a small shiver of anticipation. Always a lover of danger, Tomasina reveled in the challenge.

Once he had taken her honor, he would be duty bound to marry her, no matter what his ridiculous attachment to that harlot of a scullery maid. She would deal with Charlee McAllister later. For now, Tomasina realized she needed the name and protection of Jim Slade, and Tomasina Aguilar had always gotten precisely what she needed.

* * *

As he retraced his grueling ride from Bluebonnet at a far more sedate pace, Slade reviewed his parting words with Houston. The white-haired giant had been the first one up, waking Ben Jonson to relieve the man standing night guard duty. Then he had made coffee, terrible coffee, but coffee nonetheless, and Slade had drunk it gratefully.

Noticing the haggard appearance of his young protege, the shrewd old Texian cleared his throat and searched for a way to console Jim over Tomasina's betrayal. "Jim, you're young, you have a lot of life ahead of you. Even if you've been dealt a losing hand twice now with that widow lady . . ."

Jim smiled at his chief's unease. A man who could filibuster the United States Congress into submission and let loose a volley of bombastic oratory strong enough to cow the French ambassador was actually fumbling for the right thing to say. "For a man who could write love sonnets while lying wounded on a battlefield, you seem at a loss, Sam."

Houston's leonine brow creased. "Believe it or not, my press reports often exceed my elocutionary abilities."

"Somehow I doubt it, but I appreciate your concern."

"Hell, son, you look like a man with a leak in his canteen who's just watched his horse piss in the water hole and then dropped his last bottle of whiskey on a sharp rock."

"No. It's only my side stiffening up after sleeping on hard ground. I'll live, just like you said. Don't worry about me and Tomasina. I guess it was never meant to be between us anyway. My father's deathbed request, cemented by a boyish infatuation, nurtured through six years of jealousy over old Jake Carver." He shrugged philosophically.

Houston arched a shaggy white brow. "Don't sell us old fellows altogether short, you young pup." He paused, then said slowly, "I was disillusioned in my first love too. But when I met Margaret, I could never have envisioned how blissful my second chance at matrimony would be."

"Maybe I've already found my second chance, too. I'm not certain yet, but don't grieve over Tomasina and I won't either."

"That young fool McAllister's pretty little sister?" Houston's eyes sparkled.

"You crafty son of a bitch! How did you find out about Charlee?" The man's sources of information and ability to put things together never ceased to amaze Slade.

Houston's shaggy white head tipped back in laughter. "Hardly a state secret. Your young friend Lee is quite certain it's a match made in heaven. Is it, Jim-boy?"

"I honestly wish I knew."

As he neared Bluebonnet, Slade pondered that question and his answer to it over and over. Could he really marry that wild little hellion, who made him burn with lust one moment and drove him to homicidal frenzy the next? He shuddered to think about spending the rest of his life with her. Yet when he considered the alternative of losing her, as he almost had twice that week, it made him feel desolate.

Slade pulled up at the corral, looking over toward the ranch house. It was good to be home. Charlee was probably in the kitchen with Weevils, cleaning up the remnants of supper and feeding that crafty old cat. Suddenly he was eager to see her, to put his arms around her slight body and lift her up in the air, spin her around and kiss her soundly. He would see her green cat eyes light, be warmed by the radiance of her smile, feel her response to his kiss. As he swung down from Polvo and vaulted up the kitchen steps, he realized that he had the answer to Houston's question.

"Where's Charlee, Weevils?"

At the familiar gravel voice, the old cook turned and his beefy face split in a toothsome grin. "Didn't expect ya back so soon, boss. Charlee's down at th' pond. So blame hot this afternoon, she decided ta take a cool-off." He no more than got out the words when his young employer spun on his heel, calling over his shoulder, "Sounds good to me, too!"

"Yeehaw!" Weevils let loose with a string of whoops as he watched Jim kick Polvo into a brisk canter, heading toward the pond. The boss hadn't looked that animated or happy in a month of Sundays!

Hellfire basked in the early evening sunset while Charlee splashed, dived, and floated. The water was soothing to her restless spirit. She didn't know how long Jim would be

gone, probably at least a week's travel all the way to
Houston City. What would happen when he returned? If
only he would realize what Tomasina Carver really was, that
she didn't love him, and in fact was using him, not the other
way around. But an inner voice nagged her, *Little fool, he is
using you and that doesn't bother him.*

She rolled over and began to swim with fast strokes back
toward the edge of the pool, her agitation evident in the
vigorous way she knifed through the water. Like a naked
sylph, she quickly slapped the mass of her hair back so that
it clung to the curve of her spine as she climbed the diving
rock with sure, easy steps. Her gleaming, sleek flesh caught
the golden hue of the setting sun as she stood on the top of
the small promontory, poised to dive, her silhouette outlined
against the azure and orange of the evening sky.

Slade stood rooted to the ground, watching her in much
the same way he had months ago, still amazed at the grace
of her tiny body. But now he felt no surprise or guilt, only a
fierce, protective urge to enfold her in his arms. As he
watched her dive, he began to strip off his dusty trail
gear—gunbelt, shirt, boots, pants. He considered the bandage around his side, then shrugged and stripped it off. Four
days after the stitches had been removed the wound was
healing nicely. Silently he walked around the edge of the
water, keeping the thick cover of underbrush between him
and Charlee's line of vision as she floated in the center of
the pool.

"Little Cat Eyes, sunning yourself, just like your feline
friend here," he whispered, crouching down to scratch a
fringed ear. Without a sound he climbed the diving rock
from the back while his feline conspirator kept watch over
the drifting girl.

He cut cleanly into the water and came up a scant three
feet from where she had heaved herself upright and was
furiously treading water. That great mass of dark hair went
flying wildly about her shoulders as she craned her neck
searching for the invader.

"You!" she fairly shrieked as he snaked out a long arm
and brought her into his embrace. Her writhing, flailing
body quickly quieted under the skilled ministrations of his

hands and lips. He could touch bottom near a shallow area of the pool and quickly gained solid footing in the water, holding her small, silky frame melded to his own. In the water she weighed less than ever, butterfly light. Her skin felt soft and slick as he caressed the curves and hollows of her backbone, waist, hips and buttocks, never freeing her mouth from the ravaging assault of his lips and tongue. When he felt her respond with all the fierce, sweet abandon bundled up in her small body, he growled his triumph aloud and carried her from the water to the mossy bank.

Charlee's fright and confusion when she was startled by the sharp splash of a diver had quickly turned to anger at his unexpected reappearance in such a cavalier manner. Once he touched her, her mood shifted again to passion. God, but she could deny him nothing. The sensual part of her craved his touch; yet another small voice cried a warning.

Jim laid her gently on the cool, damp moss, reclining beside her. The setting sun made the droplets of water on their flesh amber and shimmering as they ran eager hands across one another's skin, sending the water flying. He bent over her and buried his mouth along the curve of her jawline, kissing her earlobe and throat, then trailing down to her collarbone and breasts.

When his hot mouth fused over a hardened nipple, she arched and gasped, her hands clutching frantically at his shoulders. He teased and suckled her upthrust breasts as she ran one palm up and down his back, her other hand tangling in his wet gold hair. They devoured one another frantically.

When he slid one hand down between her legs and caressed the glistening tan curls, she made a small whimpering cry and opened for him. In one smooth motion he raised himself over her and slid inside as she welcomed him. If his movements were fast and frantic, hers matched them in desperation. After the initial surge of hot, sweet pleasure assaulted his senses, he slowed them both to an easier, gentler rhythm, prolonging the ecstasy. He raised his upper body as he thrust in long, slow, delicious strokes, and looked into the depths of her eyes, glazed now with passion and some deeper, painful emotion he could not fathom.

"Charlee," he whispered as his mouth descended to rain

kisses on her eyelids, temples, nose, all over her face, until
he could hold back no longer. His lips once more claimed
hers, and he twined their tongues together in a consuming
kiss, while the steady rhythm of his thrusts once more
accelerated.

When he felt her stiffening in the tight, clamping
contractions of orgasm, he could hold off no longer.
Shuddering in exquisite release, he gently rolled them to
their sides, still holding her tightly to him.

It was just like the last time—the moon, the stars, and all
the planets exploding inside her, she thought in awe. As she
held tightly to him, Charlee was unwilling to break the
glorious joining of their bodies and face the harsh light of
reality.

He gave her nose another soft, swift kiss and then pulled
away from her, rolling onto his back to ease the wrenching
ache in his side. Rubbing the wound, he marveled at the
human body's ability to sublimate pain. Then he sensed
rather than heard her distress. Turning his head to look at
her, he could see the crystalline tears mingling with water
droplets on her soft golden cheeks.

"Charlee, love, what's wrong? This is hardly an appropriate response after what we just experienced together." He
reached one hand out to trace the tears' path down her
cheeks, caressing the silky skin softly. He leaned over her
with a puzzled expression on his face. "Why?" he questioned
again softly.

She turned her face away, but his strong, persuasive
fingers forced it back, forced her to look into his hypnotic
cougar's eyes. "All you have to do is put your hands on me
and I...I just melt...I do whatever you want," she
finished helplessly.

"Only what *I* want?" He teased gently. "It seemed to me
you rather enjoyed it, too, my prickly little Cactus Flower."

She wrenched her face away from his fingers, spitting out
the words, "Yes, I enjoyed it...I loved it." *I love you.*
Taking a deep breath she let the words go in a frightened
rush, "And I might get pregnant, I might already *be* pregnant!"

He stroked her jaw with his fingertips, coaxing her face

around once more, smiling wistfully at her. "And would that be so terrible?"

"That's easy for you to say. You're a man. No one would blame you, only me. I'd be the one alone, with an illegitimate child. I—"

"No!" He interrupted her, feeling a fierce surge of protectiveness. "So that was it, the reason you were trying to run from me at the boardinghouse?" She nodded imperceptibly with her thick bronze lashes still shielding her eyes. Slade sighed raggedly. "I suppose I deserve that, after what I said to you the night of the dance. Oh, Charlee, I said it because I was jealous and angry. God, I didn't mean it! Why is it we always seem to bring out the worst in one another? Except when we make love, that is." He planted a soft butterfly kiss on her lips.

"But there's a danger in that," she said, trying to free herself from his grasp.

"Damn right there is. It's habit-forming. All I could think of on my ride home was you. I could get scalped being so preoccupied, woman. Only one answer to the whole situation, seems to me."

Her heart froze in her chest as she found herself staring up into his mocking golden gaze. "What's that?" Her voice was surprisingly steady.

"We'll just have to get married, and work on that baby business, too. Not necessarily in that order..." Without waiting for her reply his mouth came down on hers with hot, sweet persuasion.

Tomasina pulled her gelding up in front of the big house at Bluebonnet, waiting impatiently for one of the young vaqueros to help her dismount. When a boy assisted her, she briskly handed him the reins and smoothed her skirts, turning to ascend the front steps. She gave a brief, perfunctory knock, then entered the front hallway, glancing into the parlor and dining room.

"Good evening. Diego? Is anyone here?" She stood in the center of the long polished hall, tapping her foot impatiently. Then she heard the floorboards groan, and the shanbling bulk of Weevils filled the kitchen doorway.

Wiping his meaty red hands on a towel, he greeted her. "Evenin' Miz Carver."

"I've come to visit Don Diego. Please tell him I am here."

"Wal, ma'am, ya see . . ." Weevils did some quick calculating. Jim had gone after Charlee around three quarters of an hour ago. If he found her in the water, the old cook would have bet his best batch of spring tonic on the two of them being there together for quite a while yet. "Mr. Slade went up ta th' pond, on sorter whut ya might call an inspection visit. Now I reckon I could send someone . . ."

"No, that is quite all right. I can find him myself," she said with a predatory gleam in her eyes. The sharp tap of her high-heeled riding boots quickly faded out the front door.

Weevils's smile went from ear to ear, revealing a fulsome amount of gums and tobacco-blackened teeth. "Yep, ya'll find him all right, 'n a whole lot more'n yew bargained fer, I betcha, Miz Prissybritches!" Whistling, he shuffled back to the kitchen, towel slung rakishly over one shoulder.

Before she rode clear of the thick, brushy cover surrounding the pool, Tomasina heard the clear, strong peal of masculine laughter. Perfect. If she found him in the water, undressed and alone, she would find her bargaining all that much easier.

Then another bubble of laughter erupted, a high, clear soprano! It could be none other than the McAllister tramp. The sounds of mingled voices, laughter, and splashing water drew her nearer. Her rigid Hispanic pride demanded she turn her horse and ride away. But an insidious, unwilling female jealousy and curiosity drew her closer. She dismounted and began to walk silently through the shrubbery, mesmerized by the sounds beyond.

Peering through the dense cover of willow branches, she watched Jim and Charlee cavorting, splashing one another, diving and chasing, playing like two young otters. Their laughter rang across the water. When he finally caught her, she turned in his arms and they stood up in the shallows. They were both quite naked as they murmured soft endearments, unashamedly embracing, molding lips and bodies together. Then Slade cupped Charlee's small face in his hands. Their playfulness stopped, and they stood still and silent for a moment as he stared intently into her eyes. Then he lowered his head and she strained upward for a soft, sealing kiss.

At that precise instant, Tomasina realized Slade would never marry her. He was smitten with that scrawny, hoydenish kitchen maid. A sudden surge of fury seized her, washing over her in red waves, but she was rooted to the ground in voyeuristic horror, unable to tear her eyes from the couple in the water as they moved to the shore.

They sank slowly onto the bank and embraced once again, caressing and murmuring indistinct love words as they joined their bodies. Jim lay back, pulling Charlee's slight weight on top of him, urging her to grasp his shaft and guide it into her welcoming warmth. Slowly, savoringly she impaled herself; then with his hands guiding her rhythm, she began to move.

When Slade made one final hard thrust upward and Charlee let out a cry of fulfillment and collapsed on top of him, Tomasina wrenched herself away from the tableau, feeling the simultaneous urges to retch and to run out and claw the small tan-haired vixen from his embrace. She succumbed to neither. Instead, she turned and silently retraced her steps toward her mount.

On the way back to the ranch, she had time to compose herself and plan a new course of action. There was always one last desperate gambit, her last fallback plan, one which allowed for the encumbrance of no men in her life. Markham had betrayed her. Now so had Slade. Well, she could eliminate them both and let both be damned!

Returning to the big house, she smiled sweetly at Asa Ketchum, who greeted her in perplexity at the door. Weevils had gone off to his cabin for the night, Charlee was swimming, and, as far as he knew, Slade was traveling from Houston.

"Good evening, Señor Ketchum. Your cook informed me that Diego was somewhere near the pond. I searched, but was unable to locate him. It is getting dark and I must return to my ranch. Please, may I write a message to leave for him when he returns? It is a matter of some urgency.''

Later that evening, Slade paced in his study. He'd received a cryptic communication from Asa saying Tomasina had stopped by and left him a note. He sent an exhausted Charlee upstairs to bed, and went in to his desk to open the missive. Apparently Markham had contacted her. He debated heading over to Jake's ranch immediately, but decided against it. He'd had enough trouble soothing Charlee's ruffled feathers once today. Tomasina's information could not be acted upon until daylight anyway.

So reasoning, he climbed the stairs and opened the door to his room. Finding no Charlee, he stripped off his clothes, then padded barefoot into her room down the hall, whisked her sleeping body from the covers, and carried her back to his large bed. He sank down beside her and she snuggled into his arms. As he drifted off to sleep, Jim was almost certain he heard the faint noise of a cat purring somewhere in the darkness of the room.

Tomasina turned from the window when she heard Chana usher Slade into her parlor. She had dressed carefully for the occasion, in a demure brown linen skirt and jacket with a starched white blouse. Businesslike and simple. No distractions or blandishments to make him wary.

''Good morning, Sina.'' He stood in the door, looking her squarely in the eye, not a hint of guilt or remorse, not even a hint of unease marring his handsome face. The bastard!

She smiled coolly and glided over to offer her usual perfunctory kiss. Keep the routine, do nothing to make him aware that she knew of his filthy liaison with such low-class trash as Charlee McAllister.

''Your note said you'd heard from Markham.'' He looked down at her and waited, his face unreadable.

Nervously, she turned and began to fidget with a stray curl at her shoulder. ''Yes. He came out here yesterday and told me he meets with Iron Hand and his band around the twelfth, at a place along the upper San Marcos River.''

"I take it he'll be traveling with an escort?" His voice was laced with harsh irony.

"Yes, more of his Comanchero friends. They'll have the guns and whiskey."

"He's bringing information on how to avoid ranger patrols," Slade guessed.

She nodded tightly.

"Anything else in the works, Sina? From south of the border? Hear from Antonio Perez or Enrique Flores lately?" He poised on the balls of his feet.

She faced him with clear black eyes wide open. "No, nothing yet. They will move before winter, I am certain, but Tonio or one of his vaqueros will tell me first."

"So you can gather all the current information on defenses and militia positions?" His brow creased in a harsh frown.

"Please, Diego. I have promised you I would wait and watch, tell you whatever you want. Do not be cruel..." She sobbed and let the tears fall as she turned into his arms. He held her, awkwardly trying to soothe her, and for the first time she felt some of his guilt seep through the poker facade he had erected over his emotions.

By the time she had dried her eyes and seated herself, white-faced and trembling, by the parlor table, he was assuring her everything would be all right. He would deal with Markham and protect her from the authorities. Slade promised she would be free of the Englishman and need have no more involvement in espionage and treason. He believed her. It was the performance of her life.

When Tomasina was ushered into Don Felipe's vault-roofed library, she was once more struck with how singularly appropriate the dark, cavelike, decaying palace of a house suited the Rojas family. Unctuously smiling, Don Felipe appeared a moment later, rubbing his hands in nervous anticipation of their midnight meeting.

"So delighted to be of service to our glorious cause, Doña Tomasina. I cannot express to you—"

She interrupted his flowery oration in an impatient, agitated voice. "Save your speeches for the parade ground when

General Woll arrives, Felipe. Is Cordova here yet? I've been awaiting word of his arrival for weeks.''

''But of course. I am always a most punctual man, as punctual as the condition of Texas roads and the aim of Texian guns allow.'' The sibilant voice was low and insinuating. Vincente Cordova had always disturbed her, with his lithe, pantherish elegance and penetrating black eyes; the eyes of a visionary or a fanatic, she was never sure which.

''Since you are here, Captain Cordova, I assume General Woll's army is now a day's march at most from the Main Plaza.''

''Quite so. A day, two at the most. Don Adrian sends his regards,'' he replied.

''Good. I salute him and anxiously await his deliverance of San Antonio, but it is of another matter that I must speak to you. One of the greatest delicacy and secrecy.'' She eyed Don Felipe, who had been hovering silently in the background like a tame crow. With a stammered blush and stiffly affronted gait, he quit the room.

Cordova smiled thinly. ''I assume you wish to speak of our mutual acquaintance, Mr. Markham, or is it perhaps of other mutual friends . . . ?'' He let his words trail off, gauging her reactions. What game did this childish woman play?

''As to Ashley Markham, he no longer signifies.'' That got his attention, rather more penetratingly than she would have wished. His black eyes were narrowed to slits as he waited for her to continue. ''He has let his cover slip rather badly, I'm afraid. My fiancé discovered his connection with Iron Hand weeks ago. Right now Markham is walking into a trap. No one can save him. He is of no further use to our cause anyway.''

''If he is known as a British agent dealing with the Comanche, you are, of course, correct. But British gold—now that is always of use to our cause.'' Once more he waited like a chess player.

''I can supply the British gold. You can contact the Comanche.'' She turned from the mantel, where her fingers had been tracing nervous patterns in a thick accumulation of dust, to watch his reaction.

Unexpectedly, he threw back his black, curly head and

laughed. "You, a respectable lady, go-between for foreign spies and marauding savages? How dazzlingly unexpected, especially when you will be married to a pillar of the Yankee community, a friend of Sam Houston!"

"I am not prone to carelessness, as was Ashley. I will assuredly fulfill my end of the bargain." Her cold black eyes challenged him openly.

"I believe you just may do so at that, Doña Tomasina." He walked over to Don Felipe's large oak desk and unstopped a crystal decanter. Pouring two small cordial glasses of deep ruby liquid, he handed one to her. "To Ashley Markham's successor."

Measuring each other over the tilted rims of the prismed glasses, they drank in silence.

When she was safely back in her own town house, at the other end of the shady, tree-lined boulevard, Tomasina felt the sense of triumph, so tightly held on her ride home, suddenly evaporating. With trembling hands she once more opened a grimy fold of paper and reread the message on it, a message she had copied over a week ago from a note in Markham's pocket. Sated and drowsy from his long bout of lovemaking, he had slept soundly that day at Jake's ranch, slept the sleep of the damned as Tomasina stole away from the bed and methodically and noiselessly searched his clothes. The besotted fool never suspected a thing.

Men were all such fools. Diego believed he could use her while keeping that Americana trash; Ashley thought she was going away with him after his last mission to the Comanche. It would be his last mission anywhere, once Slade and his rangers caught up with the unfortunate Englishman. Perhaps the two men would kill one another. Tomasina smiled at the thought. With the information she'd given Slade, Ashley was dead for certain. If Slade returned to San Antonio, he would walk into the welcoming embrace of the Mexican army. They knew how to deal with turncoats, *Tejanos* like Diego who worked for the Texian usurpers.

Even Vincente Cordova was a fool. He patronized her, thought she could not gain access to the higher circles of British espionage. But she had, without Markham ever discovering it; she had found the name of his mysterious

contact, the direct link to the British Foreign Office and all
that grand Imperial gold. He was William Kennedy, author,
traveler, diplomat with a startling affinity for changing
sides, first supporting the Republic, then working clandes-
tinely for Aberdeen to suborn the Mexicans and Comanche
who worked against Texas. And Kennedy was arriving in
San Antonio on September twelfth with a special pass
through the occupation army lines. Tomasina smiled. She
was counting the gold already.

September eleventh dawned with a warm, still mist hugging the city, enveloping everything from the tallest church
spires on the plaza to the deepest ruts in the roads leading to
them. Word of a surprise invasion had circulated the preceding day, brought by a drunken Mexican spy who lingered
too long in a local bordello. A delegation of frightened
Tejano shop keepers who had gone in search of the Mexican
army to plead for peace did not return. Another hardier
corps of Texian and *Tejano* volunteers fortified themselves
to do battle, rendezvousing before dawn in the court building and other houses facing the Main Plaza.

Out of the swirling mists, the sounds of martial music
echoed across the open expanse of the plaza. General Woll's
army arrived in full military splendor, right down to the
accompaniment of bugles and drums. One young drummer
fell, the only Mexican death in the opening fray that resulted
in the fall of San Antonio.

At first the defenders were certain of victory, having been
misinformed as to the size of the invading force, so well
concealed by heavy fog. While the Mexicans scaled the
heights of several church towers under Woll's precise direction, the Texians kept up a lively fire into the fog bank,
yelling and cheering. Then, as suddenly as the lifting of a
curtain, the brilliant Texas sun cut through the mist, revealing
to the eyes of the horrified defenders over a thousand
Mexican soldiers surrounding their meager fortifications.
The invading force was ten times what they had been led to
expect. Cannons faced them from across the plaza, rifles
were trained on them from the heights of San Fernando
Church. They were surrounded. They surrendered uncondi-

tionally, and General Woll, French mercenary, career soldier and man of essential decency, spared their lives and guaranteed them the rights of prisoners of war, a nicety his own commander-in-chief in Mexico City had not always observed.

All together, discounting boys and the badly wounded, fifty-two prisoners were captured, while many more escaped as the fog once more spread like a blanket over the city. As the alarm went out across the Texas countryside, the city remained the essence of placid order. Martial law was, of course, in effect. A proclamation was issued on the morning of the twelfth assuring the citizenry that all peaceful people, *Tejano* and Texian, were to be unmolested and their property rights respected. They were reminded, however, of their renewed allegiance to the Supreme Magistrate of the Mexican Republic, the illustrious General Santa Anna.

Widely varied feelings prevailed across the city—anxiety, anger, deliverance, vengefulness. For Tomasina, none of these emotions mattered. Her mood was one of anticipation. Tonight she was to meet William Kennedy. If her bargain with him could be as well struck as the one with Vincente Cordova, she would become an arbiter of Mexican-British diplomatic relations, covertly manipulating generals and cabinet ministers. Eventually she'd live in a palace in Mexico City, shaking the dust of Texas from her skirts forever.

William Kennedy was not at all what Tomasina expected. For one thing, he was a boyishly young-looking man whose smooth features and carefully tailored clothing belied the measuring look in his piercing gray eyes. As he bent to coolly salute Tomasina's fingertips, one thick, straight lock of light brown hair bounced carelessly on his forehead.

"May I offer you what hospitality these modest furnishings afford—a glass of sherry? Or some rather nice claret?" While he poured, Tomasina felt his eyes on her, assessing her as if she were a piece of livestock.

"I am not being auctioned, Señor Kennedy," she said coldly, accepting the claret but not tasting it. No finesse, she thought pettishly; at least Markham had a facade of gentility about him.

"Please forgive me," he said briskly, his tone indicating quite perfunctorily that he cared not a whit if she forgave him or not. "I was expecting to meet Ashley Markham tonight. If I had known a lady would be taking his place, I would have suggested a less compromising location to meet than this hotel room."

Tomasina's laugh was brittle. "Being involved in espionage is compromising enough, I warrant. I shall not fear for my reputation, and you need not fear discovery. Unlike your lackadaisical countryman, Mr. Markham, I am most discreet."

"Nicely spoken, Madam. From your remarks, I assume Markham has been compromised. Is he dead then?" His icy gaze riveted on her.

She decided to give up all pretense at coyness and play her role with the same startling coolness as he did. "Ashley is a coward who planned to run when he was discovered. Even as we speak, my Texian fiancé is tracking him down. If he is not dead now, he soon will be. I've been his right hand for years, his main source of intelligence in the *Tejano* community here and his sole source from the government in Mexico."

"And now you offer me those same services you rendered to Mr. Markham?" Was his tone mocking, tinged with innuendo?

"I am in communication with a high-ranking officer in General Woll's army who has been an irregular with Colonel Perez in the past. He has contacts with the Comanche."

The slashing tan brows arched in distaste. "Those irregulars are little better than cutthroats and savages themselves."

"Then what does that make the foreigners who finance them, Señor Kennedy? At least we fight on our own land, for our rightful government."

"So do the Indians, Doña Tomasina, in their own benighted way." His rebuke was quietly stated, considering her sparklingly furious accusation.

Deciding she must take a more diplomatic tack, Tomasina forced herself to calm down. "The fact remains, Markham is gone and you need me as liaison to the Mexican government, as well as my contacts, who can equip the Comanche to fight the Texians."

"All bought with English money—Mexicans and Comanche alike. Damn the things we do in the name of political expediency." He ran a hand through his hair and affixed her with another of those measuring stares. "All right, Mrs. Carver. I have a rather substantial amount of gold, to be turned over to Mr. Markham . . . doubtlessly a good portion of it intended for you and your irregular friends in the Mexican army. I see no objection to dealing directly with you. Felipe Rojas speaks highly of you, and lord knows, your position once you marry Jim Slade will be invaluable. We know he's a close confidant of President Houston, and he's done special assignments for him from time to time."

At the confirmation of her suspicions about Slade, Tomasina's eyes widened in surprise. She said scornfully, "What use is it to know about that Yankee pig Houston? He will die a traitor's death, like all the American usurpers, once the Mexican army reclaims Texas."

"Perhaps," was his noncommittal reply.

"Need I remind you, Mr. Kennedy, that you are in San Antonio under a safe conduct signed by General Woll, who is now in command of the city?"

"Point taken." He shrugged, rather too carelessly.

"Then you may have the gold delivered to my town house tomorrow night at precisely midnight. My servants will be dismissed for the night and the back courtyard gate will be open. It is most secluded."

"I shall expect a full report about your irregular soldier's activities. Also a complete inventory of all expenditures. Fussy, those bureaucrats. You do understand me, Doña Tomasina?"

"Perfectly, Señor Kennedy."

chapter
14

Charlee sat by the pond, feet dangling in the cool water, lazing in the late afternoon sun. She looked peaceful, but she was deeply troubled. Jim had been gone for nearly a week, and she had no idea when he would return. It could be weeks, or it could be never if Markham and his lethal friends were lucky and Slade was not. With a shudder she forced that thought from her mind. As if sensing her malaise, Hellfire butted her chin with a wet, cold nose, letting out a soothing series of murphs. He rubbed sinuously back and forth against her arm, and then began to knead furiously on her lap.

"Ouch! That hurts, you rascal. This skirt's too thin for your long claws." She stroked the scarred head, and he settled down in her lap. Charlee frequently came to this quiet place to dream or to work out her troubles. Whether she was alone or with Slade, Hellfire always followed.

She closed her eyes and remembered their last time here, two days before Jim had left on this desperate mission. He had loved her so deliciously, passionately, tenderly. No, she corrected herself with a wrench in her heart: he *made* love to her. There was a difference. Did he love her? He had asked her to marry him after she had blurted out her fear of being pregnant. But had he only done so out of some misguided sense of honor, or guilt for having stolen her virginity? He had never said that he loved her, only that he wanted her. But he had told her that he once thought he was in love with Tomasina. Could he still be in thrall to that cold, calculating beauty?

Disturbing the purring cat, she lay down on the warm grass, curling into a ball and stroking Hellfire while she relived their conversation the morning he had returned from visiting Tomasina.

Slade had been very brusque and short-tempered, busy loading weapons when she had interrupted him.

"Weevils says you and Lee are going on some sort of vigilante raid," she said in concern.

He had looked up in agitated surprise, seemingly viewing her as an unwelcome intruder. Continuing to pour powder down the barrel of a Pennsylvania Long Rifle, he had answered as he worked. "Hardly vigilante, Charlee. Lee and I are duly sworn-in members of the Bexar County Militia, and we're legally empowered to go after any gun and whiskey runners trading with the Comanche. I only wish Jack Hays and his men weren't scouting to the south. We could use their help.''

''You mean you're going after Ashley Markham and Iron Hand?'' she had questioned, with dread in her voice.

He nodded absently, putting down one rifle and picking up another to begin the meticulous process of preparing the single-shot percussion rifle for firing.

''This all has something to do with that note you got from Tomasina Carver, doesn't it?'' Lord, she sounded like a shrewish wife already, even to her own ears!

He put down the gun and walked over to her. Taking her hands in his, he ushered her to the big chair behind the desk. He slung one long leg across the corner of it and sat facing her.

''Yes, Sina sent for me. It seems she received word from Markham that he's meeting with his Comanchero friends, even going with them to deliver the goods now that Brady's dead. It's our big chance to nail him once and for all.''

''But it's so dangerous . . . what if . . . what if it's a trap? Can you trust her?'' She really wanted to cry, *How can you trust her!*

Jim smiled rather ironically. ''I think she's telling the truth about Markham. She wants him out of her life now that their illegal activities have been uncovered. She believes we're still engaged, and she definitely needs my protection from the authorities,'' he finished darkly.

Charlee felt a stab of alarm, but she struggled not to show it. She had to ask, ''Are you still engaged to her?'' *Are you still in love with her?*

Jim had sighed, as if realizing it would not be easy to explain. ''I have to rendezvous with the other men in only a few hours. There isn't time to go into it all. It's very complicated, a long tale of family obligations and youthful romanticism. Only remember now that—''

Charlee would have given anything to have had him complete that sentence, but just then the door had swung open and Lee burst in, fairly bristling with guns and knives. She had never before seen such a cold, hard expression on his face.

"We're late, Jim. Where's the extra shot for the Wilkinsons?" Lee seemed not to notice Charlee, so great was his preoccupation.

Tossing him several heavy pouches of shot, Slade had stood up and bent to plant a swift, carelessly aimed kiss on Charlee's nose. "Take care, Cat Eyes. We'll be back when we finish this. It may take a while to track him to his filthy friends, so don't worry if we're gone for a few weeks. Remember, I've been doing this since I was fifteen, and I know how to take care of myself."

"Yeah, and you have all the scars to prove it," she had shouted at his retreating back, unreassured and frantically worried.

That had been last week. Now she lay by the cool, unbroken waters of the pool, afraid for him and uncertain of what would happen when he returned. He must return; she could not bear to consider otherwise.

Giving Hellfire a solid pat, she sat up and began to put her shoes on. "No use sitting here daydreaming. Humph, might as well pull petals off a daisy. 'He loves me, he loves me not,'" she said in a singsong voice.

When Charlee returned to the ranch kitchen, it was past time to begin dinner. Smiling at Weevils, who was peeling a large pot of potatoes, she donned an apron and grabbed a fat, freshly killed chicken. Carefully she reached into its body cavity and extracted the entrails, cleaning and cutting where they adhered to the flesh.

Looking up, Weevils said, "Be shore yew save me th' gizzard."

"Oh, Weevils, that's Hellfire's favorite piece. Oh well, I guess he can make do with the heart. I love the liver. What do you want the gizzard for anyway? You never eat anything but the white meat."

"Ain't fer eatin'," the old cook said patiently. "Jist need th' linin' from th' gizzard."

"Let me guess," she interjected. "It's a folk remedy for rheumatism."

"Nope," he said with evident disgust at her willful ignorance. "Biled chicken gizzard linin' 'n pepper 'n vinegar are th' best cure there be fer th' stomachache."

"Who's sick?" Charlee was so preoccupied the past week worrying over Jim and Lee that she hardly took note of the rest of the men at the ranch.

"Thet young feller Josey Kellerman's been complainin' somethin' fierce 'bout his gut," Weevils replied.

"Maybe he should go see Doc Weidermann," Charlee said uncertainly.

Weevils let out a loud oath in his high-pitched whine. "Why, thet loco ole Rooshin'd kill th' tad. All's he needs is a good dose o' my medicine 'n he'll be fit—"

"Ta puke, but then, I reckon that might cure th' lazy tramp from malingerin'," Asa interrupted as he entered the room, tossing a dusty hat on the wall rack and sinking into a chair.

"You're sure he's not really sick, Asa?" Charlee began to smile despite her earlier depression. "If not, I'd love to see him take his medicine!"

Asa guffawed. "No more'n Lee would, I bet. Last time he was down with the grippe, Weevils here sat on him and poured near a gallon of that stinkin' broth down his throat." He added in puzzled afterthought, "Never saw a feller get well so quick."

"Oh, Asa, why did Lee have to go with Jim and the rangers? He's only a boy, not an Indian fighter."

"Just remember, Charlee, I watched Jim's pa send him out when he was lot younger'n Lee. Boys have to become men hereabouts, real quick. 'Sides, he has his own personal reasons for goin'," Asa finished darkly.

"What do you mean?" Even her friend and companion Lee had secrets, it seemed.

Asa cleared his throat, uncertain how to tell the girl such a ghoulish thing. "Jim's pa took Lee in when he was only a tad, an orphan."

"I know. He told me that," she said impatiently.

"Well, what he didn't tell you was how he got orphaned."

With a sickening dread, Charlee intuited what Asa was about to tell her. "The Indians killed his parents," she said in a choked voice.

"Not only his ma and pa, but his older brother and sister, too. Burned the house to the ground. Will found him crouched over the bodies of his ma 'n pa. Figgered he'd been there for at least a day, mebbe more. Only reason he escaped was because his ma'd hid him in the root cellar afore she went after the other children. He was only six years old, but he'll never forget, I reckon. The Comanche were all drunked up on Comancheros' whiskey,'' Asa finished sadly.

"No wonder he looked so harsh and cold the morning they left. How awful. He never told me anything about it,'' Charlee said, with a break in her voice, remembering how she had defended Indians' rights to him and he had let it pass without comment. But recalling the look on his face the day he left with Slade, she knew that his hatred for the Comancheros was a fierce and terrible thing. If only it didn't blind him to danger when he went into battle against a cunning and deadly foe like Markham.

"Rider comin', Asa,'' Weevils piped, interrupting the tragic tale of Lee's family.

"Is it Jim?'' Charlee asked hopefully, then at once realized her foolishness.

Slade would not be alone and would not come to the front door. She leaped up and raced past the wheezing old cook. At the end of the long hall, a tall, thickset figure huddled against the door frame, looking over his shoulder at the deserted front road.

Whalen Simpson owned one of the largest liveries in San Antonio. A big, muscular bear of a man with a brushy handlebar moustache, thick tan hair, and bright blue eyes, he was considered by many of the town's spinsters and widows to be a prize catch. He had courted with Deborah and was obviously smitten with her, but she was as persistent in ignoring his overtures as he was in making them.

"Evenin', Miss Charlee,'' he said nervously, doffing his hat and entering as she opened the door for him.

"What are you doing out here this late, Mr. Simpson?'' His fearful manner was odd. Was someone following him?

"You folks ain't got the word? Figured not. That's why I stopped here on my way to meet up with our volunteers. I spent near a week ridin', spreadin' the alarm. Lucky to escape with my life, I was.''

"What in tarnation you tryin' ta tell us, Whalen?" Asa interrupted impatiently as he stalked up behind Charlee.

"San Antonio's been captured by the Mex army! Thousands of them. We tried to fight, but they cut us to pieces. Sneaked up on us in a fog, they did, cannons and all. Some of us got away when the fog came rollin' back in. We're gettin' volunteers to march on the city under Matt Caldwell and Jack Hays. Where's Jim?"

Charlee let out a horrified gasp and Asa swore. Weevils just shook his head in silent consternation.

"Reckon I'll be ridin' with ya, Whalen. Let me go down ta the bunk house an' take a tally of who's game for action 'n fit ta ride. Oh, Jim's not here. Jim 'n Lee are out on militia business, after Comancheros."

Charlee fumed. At the same time a full-scale attack on San Antonio occurs—how convenient! She only wished to have Tomasina Carver in front of her at that moment. She knew she'd kill the lying, betraying bitch with her bare hands. Then another thought flashed across her mind: "Deborah! My God, Deborah and Adam—are they all right?"

Simpson flushed a bit sheepishly and mumbled, "We had to get away and spread the alarm so fast, I never got me a chance to see to her. But I'm sure no harm'd come to her, ma'am. It was a regular army under command of a general."

"So was the one at the Alamo, as I recall," Charlee retorted, turning to dart upstairs.

Asa had already departed for the bunkhouse, but Weevils turned to call after the girl. "Now, Charlee—whut yew fixin' ta do?" Already he didn't like it.

"Charlee! How did you get into San Antonio?" Deborah's voice was laced with alarm as she rushed to the kitchen door and embraced her friend.

Charlee hugged the taller woman exuberantly, then broke free with a giggle and pirouetted around. She was dressed in an old black shirt of Jim's and her ever-faithful boys' breeches. "Sometimes it pays to dress like a boy, especially if you're an old squirrel hunter on a secret mission in the dead of night!"

Deborah was not mollified. "But there are sentries posted everywhere, and they have orders to shoot anyone out after curfew!"

"They have to see you to shoot. Hell, Deborah, I could take any of those sappers into the best squirrel woods in St. Genevieve and they'd never bag a thing! Anyway, I'm real good at squeezing through small places."

"Still, it's dangerous. Now that you're here, you'll have to stay. Unless Jim is—"

"Jim isn't with me," Charlee cut in. "He'd skin me if he knew I sneaked in here. He and Lee are off chasing Comancheros. We only got word today that the city was occupied. I came right away. Is Adam all right?"

"Yes, he's fine. Overjoyed, in fact," Deborah rejoined in an oddly agitated voice.

Puzzled by her friend's demeanor and words, Charlee looked at her face. Deborah's lavender eyes were almost purple, dilated in fright or fury. Charlee had never seen the cool, composed Mrs. Kensington look so tense and nervous before. "Those Mexican soldiers really have you strung up tight, haven't they?"

"Oh, Charlee, it isn't that, it's—oh, you have to get out of here! It isn't safe. You'll be missed at Bluebonnet."

"I second the motion," a deep masculine voice interjected in a low, silken growl.

Looking over Deborah's shoulder, Charlee saw a man framed by the kitchen doorway. With pantherish grace he came into the room and put one arm possessively around Deborah's waist.

Charlee stood mute, staring at the most beautiful male she had ever seen. He had longish curling black hair and aquiline, sculpted features taken straight from a Renaissance painting of a Spanish grandee. In spite of his rough buckskin clothes and the brace of pistols at his waist, he carried himself with the assurance of a born aristocrat. A wide-brimmed, flat-crowned hat set with silver conchos was pushed to the back of his head. He took it off and tossed it absently on the table, never letting go of Deborah's waist.

Finding her voice, Charlee squeaked, "Who are you?" embarrassed at her gawky reaction.

He looked down at Deborah and some subtle interchange took place between them. He seemed to be waiting for her to speak, willing her to do so. When she did, Charlee was stunned.

"Charlee, this is Rafael Beaurivage Flamenco, my husband." The words seemed dragged out of her.

"Also known as Rafe Fleming," he added dryly. A dazzling smile lit his face, which was oddly enhanced by several intriguing small scars.

"You're Adam's father," Charlee fairly shrieked. The nagging familiarity of his swarthy beauty suddenly came into sharp focus. No wonder the boy didn't favor Deborah! "But how... why...?"

"It's late and we'll have a long ride tomorrow, Miss... you never did introduce her to me, wife," he said, turning from Charlee to Deborah. His low voice held a softly taunting note that was not lost on Charlee.

"Charlee McAllister. I used to work for Deborah," she replied quickly. "She and Adam are my friends," Charlee said protectively. Something very odd was going on here, and she meant to get to the bottom of it.

Just then Adam came bounding down the hall and burst through the door to catapult into the stranger's arms. "Papa! You been gone," the boy shouted, hugging his father. Seeing the two of them together, there was no doubt of the child's paternity, nor any doubt that Kensington was not Deborah's married name. What had she called him—Flamenco, Fleming? Charlee's head was abuzz in confusion as she hugged Adam. The boy returned her greeting, but he still would not relinquish his place in his father's arms.

"I'll explain it to you later, Charlee," Deborah said, taking her friend's arm. "Can you get her safely out of here, Rafael?" She looked worriedly at her husband.

"It'll be no problem. I have a safe conduct from the general. I should be able to escort an old family friend back to *his* parents," he said, quirking one black brow wickedly.

"How did you get a pass... Oh!" Charlee felt her cheeks go pink in embarrassment.

"You're mistaken in your assumption, Miss McAllister," he said coldly. "I'm not part of General Woll's army, regular or irregular. Merely a Texian rancher from up north.''

"What Rafael means is that he's from an old Creole family in New Orleans. As one of French-Spanish ancestry, he has no love for the Yankee usurpers in Texas,'' Deborah said bitterly.

"At least that's what the general thinks, and I'd be a fool to disabuse him, wouldn't I, love? Now, why don't you see to getting your friend some food and a place to rest while I tuck this sleepy young rascal in?'' He tousled the black head resting quietly on his shoulder. "I'll be waiting for you in our bedroom.'' Without another word he strode imperiously from the room with the tired child.

"Have you eaten?'' Deborah queried of Charlee, all the while watching the retreating figures.

"Yes, before I got to the outskirts of town. Deborah . . . if there's anything I can do . . .'' Charlee felt awkward and uncertain of what to say.

"No, there's nothing, but thank you, Charlee. I . . . I guess you must be wondering why I changed my name and lied to everyone here, saying I was a widow.'' Deborah's eyes were cloudy, and she turned to pace across the kitchen floor, attempting to regain control of her emotions.

"You don't have to tell me anything you don't want to, Deborah,'' Charlee said softly, sympathetic to her friend's distress.

"I need to talk, Charlee, to face it all myself, I guess. You see, we were married in Boston nearly seven years ago. It was a whirlwind courtship and we never really knew one another. I went with him to New Orleans, to live with his family.''

"They didn't approve of a Yankee foreigner. You weren't Southern, weren't French, weren't even Catholic,'' Charlee supplied, recalling many cryptic comments Deborah had made over the past months. Now they all made sense.

"Yes. His family heartily detested me, but the real problem was between Rafael and me. I . . . I wanted different things from a marriage than the traditional Creole wife was entitled to expect.'' She sat down and put two slim, trembling hands over her face for a moment. "Anyway, we quarreled. I knew he wouldn't change, and I couldn't compromise my principles that way. So I fled. But I couldn't go to my father in Boston. It's the first place Rafael would have followed to retrieve me. Even under enlightened Yankee law, we women are chattel, you know," she said in an attempt at ironic humor, belied by the wistful sadness in her eyes.

"And Rafael wanted you back? Would he have followed you all the way to Boston?"

"Oh, yes!" Deborah's eyes flashed. "You see, I tried to leave once before, openly. I got no farther than the bottom of the stairs at our summerhouse."

"But if he was so adamant, maybe he really did love you," Charlee said uncertainly, finding it hard to imagine Jim Slade traipsing half way across the United States to retrieve her.

Deborah's beautiful face hardened into cold, patrician lines, set with determination. "No, he only wanted to keep what he considered was his . . . his property! He would have lost face in Creole society if his wife deserted him. Anyway, he knew about Adam, that I was pregnant. He wanted his child, his heir. And now he's won," she finished with a sigh that tore at Charlee's heart.

"Adam, I take it, is overjoyed to have his papa materialize out of nowhere." At Deborah's nod of resigned agreement, Charlee considered the picture of father and son. "Deborah, you said Rafael Flamenco was a planter, a New Orleans Creole from an old French-Spanish family?"

"Yes, Rafael's parents can trace their bloodlines back centuries to Valois and Hapsburg princes. By comparison, the Manchesters of Boston are mere nouveau riche upstarts."

"I understand the competition, believe me," Charlee said, recalling her feelings of woeful inadequacy as a St. Genevieve farmer's daughter in love with a Slade from Virginia. "But then why does he . . ."

Charlee fell into embarrassed silence when the soft footfalls of the tall Creole echoed down the hall. Almost immediately his long-legged stride carried him into the kitchen, where he stopped behind Deborah's chair. With one brow quirked at Charlee in a faintly insolent challenge, he put his hands on Deborah's shoulders. "Past time for bed, wife. Adam's sound asleep, and I'm sure after her adventure Charlee here is tired. Better show her to her room." It was a command, not a suggestion, and both women knew it.

Not wanting to be drawn further into the confusing emotions she felt swirling around husband and wife, Charlee rose and said, "I guess I am tired. I know the way to my old room, and I can help myself to sheets and make up my bed." When Deborah nodded, Charlee turned to go, feeling oddly embarrassed to watch the Creole trace soft, sensual patterns with his thumbs across Deborah's shoulders and up the nape of her neck. From those small caresses and Deborah's unconscious response to them, Charlee understood that there was desire, tenderness, perhaps even love. She knew herself how it felt to want a man's touch even when she knew she would pay bitterly for it.

She found the bed in her old room already made up. Depositing her armful of linens on the table she decided to wash off some of the trail grime before slipping between the clean sheets. Charlee stepped silently into the hall and walked down to the far end, where the ladies' washroom was located. After a swift sponge bath from a porcelain basin, she felt much refreshed. She unbraided her hair and brushed it, then dumped the dirty water in the bucket for Chester to empty in the morning. "I'd better refill the pitcher for Miss Clemson or I'm sure she'll complain to Sadie about there being no water for her morning ablutions," she mumbled.

Charlee slipped downstairs and out the kitchen door. Barefooted, she made scarcely a sound as she padded to the pump. Just as her hand touched the handle, she heard voices coming from the side veranda. Unable to move without betraying her presence in the shadows, she became an unwilling audience to the scene unfolding in front of her embarrassed eyes.

"Hiding out here won't solve anything, Deborah. If I have to, I'll carry you kicking and screaming to bed; boarders, neighbors, the whole Mexican army be damned."

Rafael's voice was a low growl that carried across the yard with knife-edged intensity.

"I am *not* hiding. I just wanted a breath of fresh air before retiring," the angry female voice answered primly, eliciting a snort of male disbelief.

"Come here, wife." The words were low, seductively spoken, like velvet. Charlee couldn't tear her trespassing eyes away as she watched the way Deborah moved into his embrace. He stood still, willing her to come to him, not touching her until she stood directly in front of him and placed her hands tentatively on his chest. Then he enfolded her in a fierce embrace, lowering his mouth to her neck, nuzzling and kissing her throat as he tangled his hands through the long hair falling down her back like a silvery waterfall.

Deborah melted against him and let out a weak cry as she surrendered to his kisses. After a long, torrid embrace, they broke apart, both breathless and trembling with unspent passion.

"You may have taught me desire, but you care nothing for my spirit, my soul," she said in a poignant whisper.

He laughed or gasped, Charlee could not tell which, as he said, "It is your spirit, your very soul that I wish to possess most of all, Deborah."

"Then you will leave me nothing!" Her soft cry was desolate as it carried on the still night air.

He murmured something indistinguishable as he scooped her up and carried her down the long side porch and into the house. As the lovers vanished from the moonlight, Charlee could see the outline of Deborah's slim white arms twined unresistingly around Rafe's dark neck and shoulders.

chapter
<u>15</u>

Charlee slept restlessly that night. In her dreams she saw Rafe and Deborah locked in torrid embraces; the visions quickly blurred to ones in which she and Jim were the lovers. She could feel the warmth of his breath and the soft, sweet persuasion of his kisses, when just as abruptly it was Tomasina's glossy black head he cradled, caressing her, loving her. With a sharp cry of "No!" on her lips, Charlee awoke at daybreak, her covers kicked off, her flesh sweaty and warm despite the cool dawn air.

Nervous about how she would react when she faced Deborah and Rafe that morning, Charlee prayed that she would not betray her unwilling role of intruder the previous evening.

Having brought no respectable clothes with her, she rummaged through the chest in her room and found the hideous old red gingham dress Deborah had not packed for her when Slade took her back to Bluebonnet. Grimacing at its ugliness, she donned it and made a makeshift belt from some extra hair ribbon to give herself a waistline. How vain she had become since learning that she wanted to be a woman!

Breakfast was not quite the usual pandemonium, because all but the oldest of the male boarders had been involved in fighting the Mexican invaders and had either fled or had been captured. Only three men were at table that morning: crusty old Racine Schwartz; Otis Bierbain, a German tanner; and Hiram Lucas, a young Quaker who did not hold with fighting. When Rafe came down, he would be joining them as well.

As Charlee and Sadie prepared the meal, Deborah did not appear, which was most uncharacteristic of her. Of course, Adam was not about either, but then he had been allowed to stay up well past his bed time last night. Just as she was beating up the last batch of biscuits, Charlee heard Adam's burbling laughter erupt down the hall, intermingled with a warm baritone chuckle.

Rafe entered the room carrying his son, as naturally at ease greeting the boarders as if he had lived there all his life. If they were at all surprised or shocked at the sudden resurrection of Deborah's husband, none appeared to show it. Rafe sat Adam in his special chair at the corner of the long table and assumed his place at the head.

When Deborah entered, she pointedly ignored her husband's usurpation of her place as proprietor of the establishment and helped Charlee and Sadie serve the food, then sat demurely beside Adam, across from Rafe.

Charlee spent most of the meal chatting with the boarders, explaining her absence from Kensington's and describing her duties at Bluebonnet in vague terms. She did not mention Jim Slade, and no one was so impolite as to bring up his name, although she was certain everyone had heard the gossip about the fight at Pearson's dance and about her kidnapping and rescue.

After breakfast, Charlee began to help clear the dishes, but Teresa, the new maid, arrived breathlessly and began to assist Sadie. Then Deborah said, "Charlee, let Teresa do that. You've helped enough already. Anyway, Rafael wants you to be ready to ride in less than an hour, so you'd better get back into your boy's disguise."

Deborah's face revealed much about the previous night to Charlee's discerning eye. Deborah's skin was faintly flushed, her eyes lustrous and heavy lidded. Passion-sated. *God, is that how I looked to everyone at Bluebonnet after I'd been with Slade?* she wondered.

After bidding a hasty good-bye to Deborah and Adam, Rafe and Charlee slipped out of the boardinghouse. When they passed the sentry at the end of Robles Street, Rafe turned to her and spoke for the first time. "Now where is this paragon of a horse you left obediently awaiting your call?''

Charlee bristled, then saw the honest good humor dancing in his black eyes. ''Patchwork is down in the arroyo past those willows. She'll wait, I know. I trained her myself and left her in a well-hidden spot wih plenty of grass and water. She knows how to be quiet.''

He grunted in approval as they headed toward the arroyo, then watched in admiration as Charlee leaped off the livery horse she had ridden from town and flew to the pretty little paint, who nosed her joyously and then stood still while the slip of a girl jumped effortlessly onto her back.

They left the rented horse tied securely in the copse for Rafe to reclaim on his way back to town, then rode for several minutes without talking.

As the silence lengthened with the miles, Charlee covertly studied the forbidding stranger who was Deborah's husband. His profile was classically handsome, but there was something dangerous, uncivilized in his mien, as if the Creole elegance was masking terrible violence, perhaps pain. Had Deborah's flight caused the hurt? Charlee dismissed the idea almost immediately. Women grieved over men, not men over women. Any fool knew that.

As if privy to her thoughts, the Creole finally spoke, startling her from her reverie. ''You don't much like me, do you, Miss McAllister?'' There was a mocking glint to his eyes that gave his face a hard look.

''I don't know you, Mr. Flamenco,'' she answered cautiously, struggling to remember how Deborah pronounced the Spanish name.

''It's Fleming now, but call me Rafe. Everyone in Texas does. That doesn't answer my question, but I'll answer it for you. I've, ah, sensed your . . . shall we call it reserve toward me ever since we met.''

''How'd you expect a body to treat someone raised from the dead?'' she snapped, suddenly peevish at all men and their unreasonable demands.

He nodded, a gesture of concession. ''I suppose it was a bit of a shock, especially to someone as close to Deborah as you are. I've heard about how she took you in, sort of remade you into the belle of San Antonio." His piercing dark eyes locked squarely with her level green ones.

Looking self-consciously down at her hoydenish boy's disguise, Charlee broke the spell of his gaze and said, "I scarcely look like the belle of anything now, but you're right, I do owe Deborah. And I don't want to see her hurt," she added, daring again to face the liquid depths of his eyes.

"Neither do I," he replied gravely. "That's why I want to get her out of the city as quickly as I can. She's been raising hell, bringing food and medicine to the prisoners, complaining about the way they're treated. She's made a few enemies."

"Surely aiding the men held prisoner in the Maverick house isn't seditious. I'd think General Woll would be glad of help feeding and caring for them."

He sighed patiently. "General Woll is honorable enough, more than enough for a foreign mercenary, but he's got some irregulars in his command who aren't exactly bound by the rules of conventional warfare," he finished bitterly.

Remembering that she had believed him to be just such a partisan raider, she colored in mortification. "She's been threatened?"

He continued, unaware or unconcerned about her embarrassment. "Yes. It's complicated because of me, I'm afraid. Flores might not have come after her if he hadn't found out she's my wife. Or maybe he would. He's always been a jackal."

What were Deborah and Adam caught up in? "You sound like you know this fellow from a ways back," she said, with fear beginning to gnaw at her vitals.

"Captain Enrique Flores, now of the Rio Grande Defenders, was late a spy and raider of General Canalizo's from Matamores. He and I tangled up near Nacogdoches a while back. Let's just say I bear him a grudge," he finished darkly.

"And he'll take it out on Deborah and Adam because they're your family?"

"I need to get them away, but I'm being watched. As soon as Flores is scheduled to go out on a scout, I'll see Woll and request permission to take my family out of San

Antonio. He's a reasonable man and has already reprimanded Flores for harassing Deborah once. I hope he'll let me leave with them. The problem is taking them somewhere they'll be safe from Flores and his band of cutthroats.''

"Bluebonnet,'' Charlee supplied.

"Bluebonnet,'' he agreed. "Once I know she's out of his reach, I'll deal with Enrique myself.''

The absolute coldness of his voice sent shivers down her spine. She almost felt sorry for the raider as she watched the deadly-looking man at her side eye the countryside around them with a frontiersman's instinctual wariness. She was afraid of him, but she was also intrigued by him. After all, he was married to her best friend. "You don't act like any planter or Creole gentleman I ever heard of,'' Charlee said tentatively, daring to pry into his life.

He shrugged. "It's been so long ago I scarcely remember that life. I was a spoiled young fool, rich, bored...'' He let his voice fade. After a few moments of silence, he said, "When I lost Deborah, I finally took a look at myself and the people around me. I didn't like what I saw. But I was still restless. Once my ties to my family in New Orleans were broken, I was rootless. My grandfather left me the deed to some land in Texas, a rancho. When Joe and I got there it was nothing but a rockpile overrun by Indians and wild mustangs.'' He smiled twistedly in bitter remembrance. "I went to work for the first time in my life. Ruined my hands for playing the piano.''

But not for shooting a gun, Charlee thought grimly to herself. Aloud she said, "So, you're a different man from the one Deborah married. Should that make things better between you, or even worse?''

When she looked at her, Charlee expected to see another thunderous flash of anger but was surprised to see the clear etching of pain instead.

"I don't know,'' he said quietly. "Just what did she say last night? She did tell you she ran off, pregnant and alone?''

"Yes,'' Charlee answered uncertainly. "Little else, only that you disagreed over what your marriage should be like. She hurts a lot, though. I could always sense that, even when I thought she was a widow. Whatever the trouble is, be good to her, Rafe. She deserves kindness, for all the good turns she's done other folks.''

As if he were struggling against some inner agony so intense he dare not reveal it, he nodded, his expression drawn and taut. Did all men mask their finer feelings so? Did Slade?

"Good afternoon, Mrs. Carver. Fancy your arriving just when I had need of speaking with you." Vincente Cordova's black eyes sparkled with irony. Obviously he was waiting for her in the shade of the giant cypress outside the milliner's shop.

"What do you want?" she queried, nervously scanning the indolent crew of men and dogs sleeping in the midday heat in the park. She might visit with General Woll and other pro-Mexican leaders in the community now, but raiders connected with the Comanche were still people with whom she did not deem it safe to associate openly.

He smiled as if reading her mind, then took her arm in a proprietary manner and steered her around the corner. "The drunks will tell no one of our meeting, have no fear."

Shaking free of his grip, Tomasina forced herself to show none of the disquieting emotion he evoked in her. "What do you want with me? You cannot possibly be reassigned to your former duties so soon."

He shrugged carelessly. "Word straight from the general himself. We march on the twentieth for the Rio Grande. Once I report to the garrison commander, I will be returning to Texas and my other duties. I need the gold now. With the army of occupation withdrawing, it will be awkward to return for it later."

Tomasina paled and grasped the wall behind her for support. It felt hot and scratchy through her gloves. "What do you mean, after the army withdraws?" She could hear the sick, sinking sensation in her voice.

"You did not expect General Woll to hold San Antonio indefinitely, surely? The Texians are amassing volunteers right now. If we stay here in this trap, they will do to us what our illustrious president did to them a scant six years ago,'' he said in grim humor.

Tomasina's shock gave way to furious, sparkling anger. Was there no end to the perfidy of men! Only a few evenings ago she had dined with the general, who had revealed nothing about leaving. ''Apparently this was the plan all along, these were the orders—to leave if any resistance was shown by Texas riffraff?''

''There are too many of them, not enough of us now,'' he said in an infuriatingly rational voice. ''A thousand men cannot fight five times that many. Someday, perhaps, when they are not so well led, when we can raise a full army to take all the major cities. Until then, I obey orders and seek out my Comanche friends. They'll keep the Texas militia busy, or at least, very distracted.'' His smile was blinding.

Her mind spun wildly as she groped for some way to stall him. ''Well, you surely cannot come home with me now and just carry it out. If I am to be left here to the mercies of those Texian pigs, I must maintain appearances as James Slade's betrothed. The night before you are to leave, at midnight, enter by the garden gate, which I will leave unlocked. I will meet you in the cellar.''

''Good. Until the nineteenth.'' He was gone, vanished into the deep shade at the end of the alley before she realized she stood alone.

And she did stand alone, never more alone in her life. Ashley was dead and Slade would not marry her. She realized now that Kennedy as well as Cordova had known of Woll's orders to retreat. The army, her glorious liberating army, was deserting her.

I will be damned to hell if I leave all that English gold for filthy savages, she swore to herself. Let Cordova fight his petty war, sniping at the Texian swine in skirmishes, holding nothing, proving nothing. I will take the gold, and curse them all, English, Texian and Mexican!

Quickly she went home. It would not take her long to pack her belongings; by tomorrow night she could slip out by bribing a sentry and be long gone before Cordova suspected anything. She hated leaving many valuable things, gifts Jake Carver had lavished on her, but she would have enough English gold for a new start. Her cousin Elmira in Mexico City was in for a surprise visit.

It had been a hellish ten days, Slade thought grimly as he wiped the sweat from his brow with his sleeve. Tossing the thick mane of gold hair off his forehead, he replaced his hat and nudged Polvo to catch up with Lee, who was riding several lengths ahead of him.

The younger man, too, was soaked with perspiration as he rode near the head of the string of rangers. They had made a dry camp the night before and were badly in need of water. Markham and his friends were certainly leading them on an exhausting chase through some of the wildest and most desolate land of west Texas, land that even Slade, a lifetime resident, had never seen.

Quincy Laber, a heavyset, tall Tennesseean, rode up next to Jim and Lee. "Yew two fixin' ta give th' rest o' them boys heatstroke afore they git a chance at th' Comanch?" His twangy Tennessee accent matched the devilish gleam in his eyes.

Laber never seemed to mind dust or heat, going thirsty, or being shot at. He was one of the original San Antonio minute men who had responded over the years to the tolling of the San Fernando church bell when it was the tocsin for Indian raiders. Carrying only saddle, bridle, and blanket, provisioned with sugar, salt, and coffee, they set out heavily armed to fight and live off the land as they moved in fast, deadly sweeps across south central Texas.

Slade had gone on his first ranging expedition with Laber and had always appreciated the older man's patience with a green boy. "If I didn't know better, I'd swear you like eating dust and cactus, you old sidewinder," he told Laber easily.

Laber let fly a thick burst of tobacco juice and laughed. "I niver seen me any livin' body in sech a rush ta ketch up with his Maker. Me, I'm jist here fer th' scenery. Right interestin' sights, too. Kinda open 'n bare."

"You mean no signs of Markham's friends," Slade supplied in a level voice. "You suppose he's onto us and leading us on a false trail?"

"Naw. Beecher and that Cherokee pal o' his'n woulda knowed right off th' minit thet tenderfoot tried any fancy stuff."

"I agree," Lee said to Quincy. "That Cherokee scout is the best tracker in west Texas."

"His name," Jim said gently to Lee, "is Solomon Tall Chief. I just want to find Markham and his friends. The sooner we get this settled the better."

Lee looked oddly at Slade, as if sensing his undercurrent of urgency. "I have my own reasons for wanting to find Comancheros. *Any* Comancheros," he added broodingly.

"Niver yew fear, neither o' ya. We'll git them bastards," Laber vowed softly, blinking back the film of sweat and dust from his eyes.

The string of weary riders filed silently along the trail toward the setting sun, twenty men on a mission of death.

Death also stalked the low-lying thickets along Salado Creek that day, September eighteenth. Jack Hays and his hand-picked scouts lured General Woll and his men from the city into an ambush. However, before the Texian commander, Matthew Caldwell, could bring up his reinforcements and spring the trap, the crafty tactician Woll recognized the precariousness of his position and withdrew. Almost simultaneously with the clash at Salado, another detachment of Woll's force under Colonel José Maria Carrasco had engaged Captain Nicholas Dawson's volunteers in a brutal hand-to-hand encounter a few miles away, killing all but fifteen of the fifty-three Texians who had been rushing to the Salado. Texian losses were tragic, but the Mexican Army also suffered significant casualties; among the dead was Captain Vincente Cordova.

When Woll's exhausted troops returned to San Antonio, it was after midnight. The city was breathlessly still, its citizens awaiting their return or hoping for deliverance.

Tomasina Carver knew the army's return signified nothing since they would so shortly be leaving for good. However, when her maid came in early the next morning with news of the battle, she had some reason for rejoicing.

"Doña Tomasina, it is such a pity, so many brave soldiers

wounded. I heard the groaning all the way across the plaza this morning. And so many killed. Why, that handsome Captain Cordova—''

Tomasina spun on her heel, barely catching what Dolores was saying until then. "What did you say about Captain Cordova? Is he . . . is he dead?"

At Dolores's doleful nod, a sudden exultant sense of freedom surged through Tomasina. She fought revealing it and made some simple commiserating remarks to her servant, then turned to leave. She had much more time to plan now. Yes. It would all work smoothly, beautifully.

That same day, late in the afternoon, Solomon Tall Chief rode back toward the column of dusty riders who inched their way in a widening arc from south to north around San Antonio. He headed for Jim Slade, the commander of their mixed band of volunteers and meagerly paid rangers.

"See anything ahead that might give us a clue, Solomon?" Slade signaled the men to stop while he and the scout talked.

The tall, raw-boned Cherokee's impassive face was covered with grime, but his dark eyes were brilliant with the excitement of his discovery. For such a large, lanky man, he unfolded himself from his mount with surprising grace and squatted on the hot prairie soil to mark a crude map in the dust. "Markham is here." He indicated a spot with a stalk of Spanish dagger he had just cut from the surrounding brush. "Four, maybe five miles south. He has moved in a circle, just as you guessed he would."

Slade nodded, pushing his wide-brimmed hat back on his head. "He's moving in an arranged pattern, arcing back and forth until they intercept him, when they think it's safe. So what's the story, Solomon? Have Iron Hand's scouts spotted us or not?" Slade asked, already suspecting the answer from his friend's demeanor.

"They wait here, Iron Hand and thirty, maybe forty braves." He used the stalk to indicate another place just to the north of the first. "Here is the San Marcos, here the English and his friends, here the Comanche. They meet tonight, I think." He looked expectantly up at Slade who was studying the crude map in the dust.

"They'll stay and whoop it up for at least a day or two. Give us time to scout the site and pick our best way to hit them. Any suggestions? You know the river in that area better than any of us." Slade waited.

The Cherokee grunted and made a few more marks, speaking as he drew. "Here is the river plain, wide open, maybe thirty, forty yards across on the west side. Good campgrounds, easy ford, plenty firewood, shallow water. Here on the east side, a high bluff, maybe forty feet up."

"They'd put sentries there for sure. How are the north and south ends of the valley?"

"Narrow here." Tall Chief marked the north end. "Here, open, low brush, no cover," he said of the south.

Slade scratched his head. "Seems like we've got to get up that bluff and knock the sentries off, real quiet, then bottle up the north end of the river valley. If we hit them from the north and east and they try to scatter south and west into the open with no cover, we can pick them off from the bluff before most of them get away. Especially if we can rout the horses."

The Cherokee nodded. "We better. There are two of them to our one, at best. Tonight, you come with me and we look at the exact place where they feast. It should work."

The noise of the drums and the bark of drunken laughter carried across the prairie. Lying on his belly with the cold, gritty sand of the riverbed chilling his bones, Slade listened and watched the activity upriver. It was a cloudy night, with the moon appearing in sporadic bursts to illuminate their progress, yet slowing them; for when it came out full, they had to lie behind the inhospitable cover of stray cactus, Spanish dagger, and scrub mesquite. When they got to the river, the willows were a merciful relief from tearing thorns.

Watching the campfires, Slade spotted Markham and two other white men, far more crudely dressed than the obviously uncomfortable Englishman.

"Looks like he has a fence post up his ass," the Cherokee whispered, echoing Jim's thoughts about the dandified spy, who was doubtless loathing every moment of this exchange with the savages.

Grunting in grim amusement, Slade said, "Inconsiderate of me to have killed his stand-in, now, wasn't it?" He looked up at the bluff rising steeply on the other side of the narrow river. "We hit them at daybreak. They ought to be good and drunked up, sleeping it off. I imagine most of the powder and shot for those Brown Bess flintlocks is still in the packing crates."

The sun rose quickly, sending its warm gold shafts to strike the cold flatness of the prairie, bringing the desert's night coolness to swift, searing heat. In charge of the men taking the bluffs, Laber gave several terse hand signals and the men spread out.

Lee felt his fingers tighten on the cold handle of his knife. He had volunteered to take out the Comanche sentry at the northeast end of the bluff. The climb was steep and tortuous in the dim predawn glow. It had taken him several hours to get into position, since he had to be careful not to make the slightest noise. He was the youngest member in a brigade of seasoned veterans and was anxious to prove himself to them, to himself, and to the memory of Josefina. Most of all for Josefina, his sister who had been so brutally murdered all those years ago. His parents and older brother had been killed quickly, but his sister had been raped and tortured first. He still heard her screams of anguish in his nightmares sometimes.

As he maneuvered into position, Lee watched the squat, powerful-looking Comanche survey the river basin below his vantage point. The savage stood in profile, one of Markham's .75-caliber Brown Bess muskets in his thick, dark hands. Lee felt the sweat roll down his temples and down between his arms and torso. He felt the sour, choking taste that was nature's blend of fear and hate, well leavened with the keen nervousness of anticipation. He was ready. Now!

The Comanche turned and looked out to the southwest. In one panther-quick lunge, Lee was across the space between them with his knife flashing in the pink dawn light. The

musket made a small thud as it hit the rocky soil, released
from the nerveless fingers of the savage who crumpled to
the earth beside it, one soft, bloody gurgle forming on his
lips as his windpipe was cleanly severed. The dying Comanche
had dragged Lee down with him. Kicking the body out of
his way, the youth crawled to the edge of the bluff and
signaled Laber. Several men quickly climbed up to join him
in preparation for the fireworks.

Ashley Markham's head throbbed wickedly from good
French cognac, not that hideous rotgut swill the others had
drunk, thank God. He had brought his own private stock
and kept it hidden from Yates and Slocum, not that the
filthy gunmen would discern the distinction between fine
brandy and cheap whiskey any more than would the Comanche.
He was penitent for his overindulgence last night, but one
had to do something to bear the stench of the savages and
endure the heat, dirt, and inedible food. He swore and
scratched several mosquito bites with one hand, taking an
oath never to camp by a low-lying riverbed again. The
others seemed impervious to the blood-sucking horde, but
their body odors probably were natural repellents, he surmised pettishly. Yes, this was definitely the last excursion in
Texas: Godforsaken pisshole of carnivorous insects, gale-
force winds, and dust clouds sufficient to choke a camel.
The Sahara, he concluded grimly, would be a preferable
assignment.

Just then he heard the high-pitched screech of a mountain
"yeehaw" and the thunder of horses coming down from the
narrow, brushy ravine to the north. They were under attack!
Cursing, he dove behind several bales of blankets and cheap
calico brought for the Comanche squaws, clawing for his
gun, only to realize it was back in his saddlebag across the
clearing. He had slept away from the savages and Comancheros, loath to hear their inebriated snores or be urinated
upon by staggering drunks. He crouched and took inventory
of the fight. As Iron Hand furiously directed his raiders to
scramble for their ponies, the band of Texians thundered
across the flat, sandy riverbed, splashing water as their
horses crossed the shallows. The Comanche ponies scattered

in neighing terror at the yelling and shooting. Few of the braves could catch a mount as the chaos erupted on all sides of Markham's makeshift shelter. The Comanche made a fight of it, zigzagging between rocks and brush, shooting and clubbing at the men on horseback. The Texians galloped among them, cutting them down in cool efficiency with bullets and rifle butts.

As soon as Yates showed his bright red head, he was picked off by a shot coming from the bluff across the river. His body lay half submerged in the shallow stream, coloring the water pink as his life ebbed away with the current. Slocum was in the thick of the melee clubbing at a ranger to get his horse. Markham could see the puffs of smoke and glinting rifle barrels on the bluff as he crawled toward his saddlebag and his Patterson Colt. Once the five-shot revolver was in his hand he felt much better. With cool calculation he looked for an avenue of escape without exposing himself to the deadly fire from above.

As he was eyeing one lone rider at the periphery of the battle and considering his chances of killing the man and taking his mount, Markham saw Jim Slade in the thick of the action, directing men to move left and right, cutting off retreating Comanche. No mistaking that tall half-breed on the big buckskin!

Gripped with rage, Markham felt Tomasina's betrayal wash over him. The bitch! There was no way Slade could have known about this parlay without her telling him. Markham had been scrupulously careful. His rendezvous with the Comancheros and the long, grueling course they had ridden for the better part of two weeks, all his precautions were in vain because of Tomasina's treachery. And she was safe in San Antonio—with Kennedy's gold! The gold . . . of course! He knew as certainly as he was under attack that Tomasina had contacted Kennedy and gotten the gold from him.

Using the boxes and bales for cover, Markham inched his way across the space between him and a riderless mount trapped between two boulders by the stream's edge. A dead ranger's foot was caught in a stirrup and his body lodged in the rocks, rendering the horse immobile. When a stray

Comanche saw the same opportunity present itself, Markham waited until he cut the corpse free and grabbed the horse's reins. Then he flung himself full force on the savage's back with a large rock in his hand. With all his strength he brought the sharp stone down on the back of the thick brown neck. A soft, crunching sound coupled with the inert collapse of his victim convinced Markham that his aim had been true. He was saving all five bullets in his Colt for Tomasina Carver!

He grabbed the Comanche's gun and knife and the ranger's hat, then swung into the saddle. His only hope of escape lay to the north, back through the narrows from the direction the rangers came. Now that the bulk of them were in the camp, finishing off the dazed remnants of Iron Hand's men, he might be able to slip by. No chance of escaping the withering fire from the bluff if he headed into the open country to the southwest.

The Indians realized they were being cut to pieces from the bluff, but were unable to return fire because of the rising sun's blinding rays behind the snipers. As best they could, they retreated west with heavy casualties. Two of the treacherous white men lay dead, and the third had vanished.

Slade searched the melee around him again as he shot and clubbed his way to the center of the campsite. The two whites in greasy buckskins lay dead, but where the hell was Markham? Swearing, he continued yelling orders and dodging bullets.

Finally, the resistance ended. A small group of bloody Comanche were being herded together by those rangers who were still mounted. Slade signaled for Laber to bring his men from the bluff for cleanup.

"Look's like yer English falcon's done flew th' coop," Laber said, spitting in disgust.

Slade's face was a granite mask of restrained fury. Looking over to the Cherokee scout, he said, "Any chance of picking up his sign in this muck?"

"Anyone seen th' fancy-dressed dude hightail it outta here?" The cry went up amidst the ranks as the men came in, some limping, others helping wounded comrades.

"He got through the narrows to the north." Lee's calm voice cut through the babel of noise. "I saw him from the bluff but he was out of range . . . looked to be on Chauncey Durham's horse.''

"Yeah, Chauncey's daid right 'nough," a sad voice chimed in. " 'N his horse's gone.''

"You know what to do," Slade barked to Laber, who nodded briskly and began to give orders.

"I'll stay to help with the cleanup." Lee's comment was casual, but his voice was tight.

Slade turned to his young friend, shaken by the blood lust he saw in Lee's eyes. "No, *mano*, I'll need both you and Solomon if we're going to catch that bastard Markham.''

Lee's eyes glittered like cold obsidian. Then suddenly he laughed, breaking the terrible tension between himself and Slade. "You're right, Jim. I promised Charlee I'd keep your hide in one piece. I can't go back on my word!''

chapter
16

"Almost two weeks and no word yet from Jim and Lee. I don't like it, Lena," Charlee said as she gave the rug a smart thump, then dodged a thick dust cloud that the wind whipped her way.

Lena smiled as she took a whack at the rug. It was cleaning day, and if beating rugs took Charlee's mind off the absent men, then Lena would beat rugs until sundown. "Do not worry about Don Diego. He can take care of himself. So can that young rascal who rides with him.''

"I still don't like it. Markham's a sneaky snake, and I've seen what those Comancheros are like firsthand." She shivered as she recalled Brady.

"I am only glad *los diablos* are gone and their dictator-loving friends with them, those plunderers," Lena said as she beat the rug more vigorously.

The army of General Woll had departed the preceding day in slow stages, escorting around a hundred *Tejano* families who had chosen to flee from San Antonio under the protection of the army rather than stay and risk reprisals. They felt that angry Texians would see them as sympathetic to the central government of Mexico, whether they were or not. Others like Lena, staunch allies of President Houston's government, were furious with their fellow *Tejanos* for running, rendering everyone of Mexican ancestry suspect.

"You should have seen the confusion," Lena went on. "Carts loaded with all sorts of things, mostly stolen," she sniffed. "And cattle. Where did all those cattle they drove with them come from, eh?"

Charlee shrugged. The oddities of Texas politics still confused her, with English-speaking and Spanish-speaking people aligned on both sides of the sovereignty question. "I'm glad Rafe didn't have to hide Deborah and Adam. I only hope that dreadful Flores person went home with the rest."

Despite the heartening news about Woll's retreat, Charlee was still worried about everyone's safety. Tomorrow she vowed she'd go to San Antonio and see if the Flemings were safe. As to Jim and Lee—she forced herself not to dwell on morbid thoughts.

One thing to rejoice over was the end of this wretched subterfuge between Jim and Tomasina Carver. If Markham was caught, then the ring of spies who had been supplying the Indians would be uncovered. Slade would have no more reason to pretend being affianced to Tomasina. That was, if it *was* just a ruse, Charlee considered uneasily.

He asked me to marry him, she reminded herself. But that had been during a tender interlude between bouts of lovemaking. Maybe he was just carried away with the moment. Knowing full well the wild swings from good humor to black anger that characterized Slade's moody behavior, Charlee was hesitant to count on his constancy, especially where the beautiful Mexicana was concerned.

Lena's voice interrupted her uneasy reverie. "I will finish this rug, Charlee. It is time for you to start dinner. Weevils will make the biscuits if you do not hurry." Grimacing as she remembered the dense slabs of dough the fat old cook called biscuits, Lena took Charlee's rug beater from her hands.

As Charlee headed toward the kitchen door, she moved with unconscious grace, her long plait of hair swinging in rhythm with her steps. The maid noted approvingly how pretty the young woman looked in the full cotton skirt and low-cut white blouse, sensuously molded to her lithe body. It was a warm day, and Charlee had chosen the cool and comfortable peasant's garb. Her day dresses were long sleeved and required several cumbersome petticoats, while this outfit needed only one underskirt. Remembering how she used to look in ragged, baggy boys' clothes, Lena was delighted with her friend's transformation. So, she had heard, was Don Diego. If only Charlee would be the new mistress of Bluebonnet, not that haughty Doña Tomasina!

When she had beaten a batch of biscuits, larded and seasoned a venison roast, and pared a nice selection of fresh garden potatoes, carrots, and onions, Charlee looked around the big kitchen and nodded to herself in satisfaction. Removing her apron, she headed upstairs, but before she had walked halfway down the long hall, Asa's voice stopped her.

"Charlee, Billy Crea found this under his bunk when he went to clean it. I thought you'd want to have it." His voice was kind but hesitant as he handed her a battered old leather volume.

Touching it, she let out a small gasp of recognition. "Oh, Asa, it's Richard Lee's diary, the one he began the year before he left for Texas. I assumed he'd stopped writing it when he moved here, since it wasn't with his other things." Lovingly her hands stroked the worn leather cover. Poor Richard Lee, dead so young, killed in a senseless accident. She had been so caught up in her own trouble, with her fascination for Jim Slade, she had seldom given her only brother a thought in months!

With tear-shiny eyes, she thanked Asa and returned to the privacy of the study to think. Should she read it? To read another person's diary was an unthinkable breach if he were alive, but Richard Lee was dead. She had laid spring bluebonnets and primroses on his grave, wept disconsolately as she sorted through his clothing. But so much had happened to turn her young life upside down since she had arrived in Texas that the resiliency of youth made his memory fade. Until now.

With trembling hands she opened the familiar-looking volume. Since childhood, her brother had always been an erratic chronicler, going for months without making an entry, then spending hours writing, depending on his moods. Quickly she scanned some of the earlier entries, written before he had left St. Genevieve.

> Feb. 4, 1835. Papa died last night. It seems strange to write the words and look at them. I still don't believe he is gone. Mama is white as chalk, I fear she will not survive him long. What will I do—just Charlee and she only a babe?

So, he did worry about her. But, she recalled sadly, even then she had been more practical about their survival than her brother.

> Aug. 10, 1835. More news in the papers about Texas today. Mr. Devlin has a whole pile of broadsides written by a fellow named Burnet. If ever the call of destiny reached out to me, it does today. What riches, what paradise, but only for the boldest takers . . .

More entries about Texas, all idyllic, boyish dreams spun by an incurable romantic who would rather skip chores and slip off to the swimming hole than do an honest day's work. After their father had died, Lillian McAllister had faded like a summer rose caught in October frost. At least he had been perceptive about that, Charlee thought sadly. But he had always been a schemer, caught up in fantasies about getting rich or becoming a hero. How ironic that he had arrived after San Jacinto. Then she was struck by the thought that Jim Slade had fought at San Jacinto and in countless other dangerous and decidedly unglamorous battles long before he was Richard Lee's age. Shaking her head, she turned to August 17, 1836, and read his account of how he had planned to leave Missouri behind that fateful next morning.

Richard Lee's entries during the journey to Texas were sporadic, but still imbued with the boundless optimism of youth. He had spent over a year drifting from job to job, going hungry, never able to get a stake together for the tools and livestock it took to homestead any of that marvelous "free land" he had boasted he would own. Finally, a much chastened Richard Lee McAllister had arrived in San Antonio just shy of his twenty-first birthday, in time to be hired by a prominent young rancher named Jim Slade, or as her brother described him in the diary: "Of oddly mixed parentage, half Mexican, half Virginian, he seems on good terms with the very Mexicans he fought at San Jacinto, a man in his late twenties, very hard-looking . . ."

Charlee realized fate had played tricks. Richard Lee, for all his immaturity, was twenty-one. Jim Slade at the date of this entry could have been no more than nineteen or twenty!

The further she read, the more Charlee was struck with a subtle change in her brother's personality, revealed between the lines, shifting from naive buoyancy to charming cynicism. He watched others around him prosper through unremitting toil, something he had ever been averse to trying. He had chosen to work as a ranch hand, living a day-to-day existence, dreaming of the time that he would be rich and able to shake the dust of Texas from his boots for good. The Republic had lost its romance when he had learned only those who sweated long and hard achieved what Will and Jim Slade had. He wrote amusing accounts of how he had fobbed off work on other men and played hooky in town, but Charlee could well imagine how Asa and Jim must have viewed his actions.

Suddenly, as she was wistfully smiling and flipping through the diary, a name leaped from a page: Tomasina!

Jan. 10, 1842. Saw Tomasina Carver again today in town, coming from the Rojas Mansion. She is really something to look at . . .

* * *

Charlee's cheeks flamed as she read her brother's rather explicit fantasy about the beauteous young matron. It would have been embarrassing enough to read such private thoughts about any woman her brother might have taken a fancy to, but Tomasina Carver! What was it about that calculating bitch that set men afire—even her poor, lovestruck brother?

She skipped the rest of his sexual ruminations and read about his days off, which he mostly spent in town. He frequented several saloons, even mentioned being introduced to Ashley Markham and several other gentlemen at the Red Heart. At Markham's name, Charlee felt a tingle of premonition. Apprehensively she read further.

> Feb. 3, 1842. Saw them together again in back of her modiste's shop. Markham waits for her at the rear entry. What I would not give to kiss her and pull the pins from that mass of raven hair. Just watching them made me quiver with passion. Her the fancy lady, too good for a common ranch hand, but not too good to commit adultery if the man in question is a fancy English dandy! Oh, Sina, my beautiful Sina . . .

Charlee's fingers were nerveless by now as she turned the pages. The whole sordid relationship between Tomasina Carver and Ashley Markham was chronicled in her brother's crabbed hard-to-read handwriting, seen through his jealous eyes. It seemed to her that Richard Lee became obsessed with the trysting couple, even going so far as to follow Markham. He was suspicious of the Englishman's motives for carrying on an affair with a prominent rancher's wife. Also, Markham lived well and dressed to the nines, lost at cards more than he won, yet always seemed to have money. Money—or the lack of it—had become her brother's fixation, leading him to his death when he followed Markham to the Carver ranch one morning.

In horrified fascination, Charlee read Richard Lee's detailed account of how Ashley Markham and Tomasina Carver murdered old Jake and then made it appear to be a riding accident. Recalling her own surprise about the close succession of Carver's and Richard Lee's deaths, she remembered that she had at first blamed Slade.

Now a cold, killing dread infused her soul as she continued reading, even though her intuition told her what would happen next. Richard Lee went to Tomasina Carver and blackmailed her, threatening to expose her as an adulteress and murderess if she did not pay him. After all, if she could support her English lover so well, she could certainly spare a modest sum for him to ensure his silence on such a delicate issue!

The last entry had been written the day Richard Lee died. He was to meet Ashley Markham at the pool on Bluebonnet land to receive his money from Tomasina. But instead he drowned, another convenient little accident. Just like Jake Carver, who must have found Markham and Tomasina out. Charlee let the book drop to the floor as waves of nausea swept over her, followed by a fierce trembling. They had killed him, that spy who could well be stalking her Jim right now, and that bitch, that murdering, conniving, cold-blooded bitch!

If Slade dealt with Markham, she could damn well take care of Tomasina Carver herself! Jumping up, she looked over to the big glass case against the far wall of the study, the gun case. Resolutely she went over and opened it. Jim and Lee had taken the best of the long arms and several handguns, but a .51-caliber single-shot Derringer remained. It was small enough to conceal, yet quite lethal at close range. She could easily smuggle it inside the Carver house and pull it neatly on the murderess. She'd make Tomasina Carver sorry for the day she had first laid eyes on Richard Lee McAllister. Tomasina would be even sorrier that his sister had come to Texas!

San Antonio was ominously still, mourning for the Texians who had been killed defending the city during the attempt to retake it. Many were fearful for the prisoners carried off with the retreating army of General Woll. It had taken nearly two years for the sad remnants of the earlier Santa Fe Expedition to be returned from Perote Prison north of Mexico City. They had told tales of horror—of starvation, filth, and disease. What would befall those now being led to confront Santa Anna's wrath?

Charlee was too preoccupied with her own loss, her own sense of righteous anger at Tomasina Carver to take note of the chilly tension pervading the usually fiesta-minded city. She rode past silent *Tejano* children whose liquid brown eyes reflected sorrow over events they could only dimly understand. The shops and homes of those who had fled with the army were standing open in mute testimony to the hysteria that still gripped San Antonio. Charlee thought fleetingly of Deborah and Adam, but assured herself that if Rafe Fleming was half as fearsome as he looked, he would be well able to see to his family's safety.

Before she knew it, she had arrived in front of Tomasina's town house. Deciding she might be denied entry, she turned Patchwork to the rear, where she hoped the garden gate would be open. The gate was locked, so she was forced to climb the wall, which proved a bit more arduous than it might have been had she taken time to change from her Mexican clothes. After several tries she succeeded in boosting herself onto the top of the wide, high adobe wall, using Patchwork's back as a ladder. Dropping to the ground with a resounding *thunk*, she looked about to see if she had been discovered. No one was in sight as she peered through the thick green leaves of a fig tree, looking toward the house. After checking her gun once more, she stealthily crept toward the large stucco structure.

When she reached the side door, she slipped the weapon into a deep side pocket, hidden in the voluminous folds of her skirt. She had to use both hands to turn the latch. The door creaked open. No one was in the hall as she made her way toward the front of the house and the sound of voices. One of the voices was Tomasina's, raised in strident complaint to a maid. She spoke in rapid Spanish which Charlee could understand only partially. It didn't matter. Tomasina seemed to be alone except for a few servants.

Positioning herself behind the heavy pine doors, she waited until the maid slipped out of the room. Tomasina stood by a wide window overlooking part of the garden. She wore a simple but elegant day gown of soft mauve that set off her black hair and pale complexion.

"Very striking gown, Mrs. Carver, but not in keeping with the last vestiges of mourning for the man you murdered."

At the sound of Charlee's voice, Tomasina whirled and gasped, her eyes narrowing in shock at the last words.

Before she could speak, Charlee continued in a tight little voice, "Or maybe I should say *two* men you murdered, but I guess you'd scarcely consider mourning for my brother."

Tomasina looked around quickly, reassured that no one was with the dangerous chit. No one had overheard her startling accusations. Edging toward her writing table, she smiled archly and replied, "I am afraid the only witness to the deaths you describe is Ashley Markham. And your *lover*"—she spat the word like an oath—"is disposing of him right now. You can prove nothing."

"I have Richard Lee's diary, describing how you and Markham killed Jake Carver and made it look like his horse threw him. My brother followed *your* lover to the ranch that morning and saw the whole thing. Anyway, it doesn't matter, because I also have this." She pulled the Derringer from her pocket and leveled it at Tomasina. "And, lady, I can knock a squirrel out of a tree at three hundred yards!"

Tomasina crumpled onto the chair next to the writing desk rather like a wilted rose, then began to speak in a voice so muted and low Charlee had to walk closer to hear.

"My aunt insisted I marry the old fool. He was a brute who hurt me on our wedding night. I imagine Diego is not like that, is he?" She really did not seem to be asking Charlee, just musing to herself over some long debated point. "No, he would be a forceful but skilled lover, the kind to bend a woman to him through passion.

"I could have had him, you know, many times in the past years, long before he ever met you. But I waited for marriage, and then you came along. I will never understand men. What a fool, to take a serving girl, a *fregonzuela*, to his bed when he could have had me in only a few months."

Charlee felt the sting of those insulting words, doubly so because she was unsure of Jim's true feelings. If Tomasina felt betrayed, there was no denial of the possibility that

Charlee had been deceived as well. "You have an awfully
high opinion of your own charms, Miss Richbritches. What
happened to your devoted admirer Ashley? Did you tire of
him and decide to feed him to Slade . . . or did he tire of
you?"

Tomasina threw back her head, her lips curled in a sneer
of contempt. "The poor besotted fool, he's off on one last
mission for queen and country. He never knew I was
sending him to his final reward out there with those hideous
savages. *Quien sabe*, maybe he and Diego will kill one
another."

As Tomasina made that last cutting sally, Charlee paled
for a second, although her gun did not waver. If only she
were not so afraid for Jim!

The tiniest flicker breaking her concentration was all
Tomasina waited for. Sensing the younger woman's agitation over Slade, she tried another tack, reversing Charlee's
thrust at her. "You stand so assured, asking me if Ashley
tired of me. What of when Diego tires of you, eh? Surely
you must know he will never stoop to marry a *puerca* such
as you! What will *you* do when he turns you out as he did
Rosalie Parker?" She flung the taunt and it had the desired
effect.

Charlee lunged for Tomasina, the gun still in her hand,
forgotten in her fury. How she itched to get her fingers in
that carefully coiffed black hair and rip it out in big
handfuls! Suddenly, Tomasina slapped at the gun, which
discharged its shot out the *sala* window harmlessly. Blindly,
Charlee grabbed a hunk of glossy hair with her left hand and
pulled it free of its pins with a brutal yank. At the same time
she dropped the now useless firearm and used her right arm
to block Tomasina's raking long nails.

Tomasina was slightly taller and considerably heavier, but
her size yielded her none of the advantage that she had
anticipated. Charlee was incredibly strong and slippery,
tenaciously holding onto her antagonist's hair. While her
free hand gouged and punched, her small booted feet kicked
wickedly. Unlike Tomasina she was not hampered by stiff
stays and heavy petticoats. She used a slim leg to sweep

Tomasina's encumbered feet from beneath her, plunging them both to the floor in a writhing welter of arms and legs.

Charlee landed on top, but Tomasina's hands fastened on her long braid and ripped it free from its ribbon. Soon two masses of waist-length hair were flying together as the women rolled and thrashed, hiking their skirts above their thighs. Each clawed for an advantage, shrieking and cursing in Spanish and English. The writing table collapsed first, sending a tallow lamp and a profusion of papers and books clattering to the floor.

Somewhere in the mess another gun was hidden. As she fended Charlee off, Tomasina's free hand clawed frantically through the litter on the floor searching for the cold smooth metal grip, but not finding it.

Dust-covered, with grimy beards and bleary eyes, two slim riders hunched against the hot blast of late afternoon wind as they entered San Antonio. They were unaware of the Mexican occupation and withdrawal that had taken place in their absence. They rode toward the Carver house as swiftly as their exhausted mounts allowed. Solomon Tall Chief had tracked Ashley Markham for them until the spy's destination was clear: San Antonio. Then Slade had sent the scout home to rejoin his family. Lee, however, would not be dissuaded from continuing the pursuit. Once in town, the most logical place to begin their search was with Tomasina, Markham's co-conspirator.

Jim dismounted from Polvo, his bloodshot eyes scanning the front of the big house. No sign of Markham, but he did not expect there would be. From the trail signs, they could be no more than an hour behind him at most. Just then a shot whistled through a side window, leaving the telltale tinkle of shattered glass in its wake.

Lee was on Jim's heels as they rushed toward the front door, drawing their pistols as they ran. "You watch for Tomasina. Markham's mine," Slade shouted to his companion as he tried the door. It was locked, but a few swift, hard blows from their combined bodies splintered the wood frame and it swung ajar.

As they rushed down the hall and veered into the *sala*,

Jim and Lee were stunned by the chaos that greeted them. The elegant room was a shambles. A round-eyed maid who had been watching the melee fled past them and vanished down the hall. China was smashed and furniture overturned, chairs were splintered and drapes torn from their heavy iron rods. Charlee and Tomasina rolled, kicked, and cursed. Charlee emerged on top once more, methodically choking the breath from Tomasina as she straddled the gasping woman. Her skirts were hiked to mid-thigh and a blanket of tan hair spread across her shoulders.

As soon as he recovered his wits and saw that Markham was nowhere in sight, Slade scrambled across the debris and pried the tiny form from atop her fallen adversary, whose face was approaching the same shade as her dress. Getting Charlee to relinquish her kill was no easier than it would have been to get her cat to relinquish his. Jim required Lee's assistance as he raised the flailing, swearing girl and transferred her with a swish of her cotton skirts to the youth's gently restraining arms.

Slade then knelt and assisted a coughing, choking Tomasina to her feet. She alternately pulled the tatters of her gown together and cried piteously as she clung to him, babbling in Spanish. "Oh, James, thank God you saved me! She is insane, coming here with a gun, saying she was going to shoot me! She fired, but I jumped aside. See, see the window?" She flourished one hand toward the shattered glass, her pride and joy, imported all the way from New Orleans.

Charlee wrenched free of Lee's hold and lunged again at the woman Jim perversely shielded. He threw himself between the two spitting females as Lee once more restrained Charlee saying, "Easy, *chica*. Calm down."

"What the hell is going on?" Slade thundered, leveling a black scowl at Charlee. He looked fierce with a two-week growth of bristling beard on his wind-beaten countenance. Seeing the Derringer that had discharged and broken the window, Slade scooped it up, recognizing it as the one left in his case at Bluebonnet. "Did you try to kill her?"

"No!" Charlee calmed somewhat and stood straight despite Lee's restraint. "I did bring the gun, but I wasn't going to shoot her in cold blood. She knocked it from my hand. I . . . I guess I lost my head. I came here to face her down after I found out she and Markham had killed Richard Lee . . . and Jake Carver.'' As she finished, she flashed a venomous look at Tomasina, daring her to deny the accusations.

Before Tomasina could reply or Slade intervene further, a sardonic voice interrupted them from the *sala* door with a chilling command.

''Drop your weapons, gentlemen, if you'd be so kind, else I'll be forced to shoot one of the, er, *ladies*.'' Ashley Markham no longer looked dapper, nor felt devil-may-care. He was exhausted, filthy, and furiously angry, not to mention frightened out of his wits by his near brush with death on the Texas plains. He watched through narrowed eyes as the young *Tejano* and his dangerous companion complied with his orders.

When Slade removed his pistols and tossed them to the floor, Tomasina crumpled in a heap over the overturned writing desk, still sobbing but watching the scene from the corner of her eye.

Lee and Charlee stood slightly apart from Slade and Tomasina, both very still now, waiting to see what the harried Englishman would do next.

''So touching, Tomasina, rescued by your own true love from the hands of his hoyden mistress. Too bad he shan't be able to rescue you from me, you treacherous bitch!'' The hatred gleaming in those icy blue eyes was enough to make Tomasina's already pale face blanch once again.

''Ashley, I do not understand. I—''

He cut her off with a dismissive oath. ''Save the dramatics. I found Kennedy's gold in your cellar, all packed up and ready to go, rather as I had suspected. You must realize I had a great deal of time to figure out your machinations on my journey back to San Antonio. A bit too much of a coincidence, your *amour*, here, turning up in Iron Hand's camp with a company of rangers, don't you think? . . . unless you told him where I'd be. Did you hope we'd kill each other?'' He spat the words at her venomously.

Charlee gasped as she recalled Tomasina's exact words to that effect only moments earlier. Then her eyes shifted from

the shivering, cowering woman on the floor to Slade, who
diverted Markham's attention with a question of his own.

"What now, Markham? There are four of us. Even with
that English-made Colt there's no way you can kill us all.
Give it up and get out of here. You've got a good running
start."

"Oh, no. Leave you alive to bulldog my trail from Texas
to London? I rather suspect you're that tenacious, aren't
you, *Don Diego*? No, indeed. I'll get rid of you, all of you,
except for my conniving companion Tomasina. For her, I'll
reserve something special along the way. . . when I tire of
her. . ." He let his words trail off in a softly menacing hiss.

When Markham aimed his Colt at Slade, Tomasina took
her only chance. The instant his eyes shifted from her to
Jim, she seized her small pistol, for which she had so
desperately and covertly searched. But as she raised it
toward Markham, he saw the barrel glint from the corner of
his eye. Instantly he turned from Slade to the woman and
his revolver barked at close range. The slug hit Tomasina in
the chest and threw her backwards. Markham stepped back
with Slade once more in his sights, but Jim had dropped to
one knee and was lunging toward his gun on the floor at the
same time Lee was diving for his. The split second it took
Markham to glance from one man to the other and decide
where to aim first was one split second too long. It cost him
his life. Slade's shot hit him in the chest and Lee's followed
it. The force of two bullets propelled Ashley Markham
through the *sala* door into the hall.

While Lee inspected Markham to be certain he was dead,
Jim knelt by Tomasina who was crumpled on the rug. Blood
ran everywhere as he pried her hand away from her chest.
"Charlee, give me your petticoat—quick! I need something
to stop the bleeding." Obediently she tore her one thin slip
into strips. Slade grabbed them without even looking at her.

"Easy, Sina. Lie still while I bind this tight to stop the
bleeding. Dr. Weidermann will be here soon." He looked at
Lee. "Shoot that son of a bitch again if you aren't sure he's
dead, then run for Weidermann!"

chapter
<u>17</u>

The stoop-shouldered Englishman puffed on his pipe, looking absently out the window at the dismal, muddy street scene of the capital city. Some capital, he harrumphed to himself, but then it fit this godforsaken Texas Republic. Washington-on-the-Brazos was named after Washington on the Potomac, which, he had been given to understand, was only marginally more civilized.

Just then young Mr. Miller entered the small anteroom and cleared his throat. "The president will see you now, Mr. Elliot." Sweeping up his white planter's hat from a table, Charles Elliot, British chargé d'affaires in Texas, entered Sam Houston's office.

"Good afternoon, Mr. Elliot. I trust you are settled in as comfortably as circumstances permit in our crude frontier town," Houston said, offering a vigorous handshake.

Elliot had the grace to blush, having made known his preference for remaining in Houston City. "Yes, Mr. President, I am tolerably well set up." As he sat down in the horsehair chair Houston offered him, he indicated his pipe, which had gone out, and asked, "Do you mind?"

"Not at all. Tobacco is a gift from our red brothers for which we shall be forever in their debt. I do not view it as a vice, but rather a providential deliverance from the grind of our daily tasks." As he spoke, he took a seat behind his large desk, which was covered with its usual eruption of papers and books.

"I've had some heartening news today." Houston continued, watching the Englishman's watery blue eyes for a response. Elliot's slouching demeanor made him devilishly tricky to read. "It seems a general invasion of our south ern borders is not forthcoming from Mexico. In fact, General Woll has retreated from San Antonio with several groups of militia in hot pursuit. They gave him a sound trouncing at Salado Creek. I do appreciate your good office as a mediator between the Republic and Santa Anna's government. However, it would seem Texas can handle the situation on her own in the immediate future."

"But surely you aren't considering reprisals? Her Majesty's government cannot condone a Texian invasion of Mexico any more than the ill-fated Mexican invasion of Texas." As he watched Houston, his fingers played on the pipe.

Bombast still gives me the edge, Houston thought in wry amusement, noting how small gestures could give a man away, while the flamboyant theatricals he staged were a superb smoke screen for his real motives. So Elliot was upset at the prospect of Texas invading Mexico? As if Texians could afford to finance any such thing! Houston said, "I have been forced by this heinous invasion and the resultant public outcry to order Brigadier General Somervell to organize the militia and volunteers who are massing in San Antonio. They will make a special patrol of the border, in numbers no less than those of Woll's forces. We can muster the manpower any time El Presidente chooses to try us, sir." He omitted mentioning that Somervell had been given strict instructions not to cross into Mexico.

"Well, yes, I suppose it is rather a face-saving necessity, what?" Elliot nodded, once again puffing and tapping. "Just so you understand Lord Aberdeen's position regarding Britain's good offices between the Republics of Texas and Mexico. We can be of inestimable value to your cause."

And your own cause, which is to keep us as a buffer between the Americans and the Mexicans, Houston added to himself. "I do appreciate that. You know how earnestly I desire to keep my sovereign republic free from foreign dominion. To that end I have always cultivated the friendship of the French, the British, and the Americans." As he delivered the last line, he noted Elliot missed a tap on his pipe bowl, but only one. Houston gave him credit. At forty-one, Charles Elliot was beginning to learn a few things about cloaking his missionary zeal.

Wishing to change the subject from the ticklish situation of Anglo-American rivalry over North American real estate, Elliot turned to his reason for calling that day. "I've come to beg a favor, Mr. President. One of a rather confidential nature, I'm afraid. If you can see your way clear to assist me, I give you my personal assurance that Her Majesty's government will be well disposed to look the other way when General Somervell's army . . . er . . . 'patrols' the Mexican border." His slouched form leaned slightly forward in the chair.

Houston gave him a wintry smile. You're really sticking your neck out on this one, Charley-boy. It must be a very large favor indeed. "I'm always disposed to be cooperative with Her Majesty's government, Mr. Elliot." He waited.

"Well, it seems we, that is I, having just arrived here a month ago, find myself in rather an awkward situation regarding a British subject. He has no official ties with Her Majesty's government but has been traveling in North America for several years."

"All of North America is rather beyond the scope of my authority, not to mention my interests," Houston put in drily.

"Er . . . quite. But this chap has been in Texas now for several months and has made a bit of a blunder, overstepping his authority."

"I thought you said he has 'no official ties'?" This was beginning to be fun.

The tapping resumed. "I shall be most candid, Mr. President, in admitting to you that Mr. Kennedy has contacts of no little influence in the Foreign Office, as well as being a well-known author at home and abroad and a friend of your Republic."

"Ah, young William Kennedy. His views expressed on an independent Texas completely coincide with my own. I've read his work, both volumes."

Charles Elliot let both eyebrows rise. The old barbarian

was startlingly literate at times. "I am so pleased you are disposed to help him, then. You see, he is being held by a local ranger commander outside of San Antonio."

When Elliot paused to collect his thoughts, Houston urged him on. "Pray, continue."

"It seems Mr. Kennedy has run afoul of some rather unsavory locals, men who deal with the hostile savages, and was in their company when they were captured. Naturally, the lawman assumed he was one of these contraband dealers."

"Naturally," Houston echoed innocently.

"Well, he is a friend of your Republic and, additionally, well thought of in Foreign Office circles. If you could clarify this to your subordinates, Her Majesty's government would consider it a signal favor, a sign of closer ties between our nations."

Houston sat back in his large oak chair behind the desk, head thrown back, staring at the ceiling, appearing to consider the matter on which he had made a decision earlier in the day. He had first received notification of Kennedy's arrest from the same courier who had brought word of Woll's retreat.

"I should imagine a man of Mr. Kennedy's scholarly inclination to be an ill-suited companion to Comancheros. I shall see to his release forthwith, Mr. Elliot."

The chargé d'affaires hesitated, obviously in grave discomfort now. "There is one more problem, Mr. President."

Houston waited, saying nothing but nodding for Elliot to continue.

"Mr. Kennedy was entrusted with a rather substantial amount of gold for a purely innocent trading venture under the sponsorship of some private investors. It has fallen into the hands of local authorities in San Antonio, where he had left it for safekeeping with one of your citizens, a Mrs. Jacob Carver."

This was getting better and better! So, the British government was willing to expose Tomasina Carver's involvement in British espionage, right down to her lace underdrawers! Houston hoped Slade would take it well. "And you need to recover the evidence"—he pretended to correct himself—"I mean, the *investment*, for Kennedy's friends." Just so Elliot thinks I'm doing him a really big favor, he gloated. "Of course I'll see to it, Mr. Elliot, never fear."

After Elliot left, pipe long cold but heart aglow with triumph for the success of his delicate mission, Houston called his faithful secretary into his office. "I need to send several communications, Miller, all of them exceedingly unofficial, epecially the one that goes to our Ambassador on the Potomac. First, let's give Jim Slade some doleful news."

Slade carried Tomasina gently from the *sala* to the kitchen, where the doctor instructed him to lay her on a sturdy table. While the skillful Russian extracted Markham's bullet, Jim held her down, stilling her agonized thrashing with the weight of his body. Charlee assisted, filling in for Deborah in the emergency.

As Tomasina drifted into a moaning, laudanum-induced slumber, the doctor sewed up the angry red wound. "Such a pity for one so beautiful to be scarred. I will try my best to make the stitches small and neat," he said to Slade.

"Yes, she is beautiful," Jim replied. Beautiful and treacherous, he added silently.

His preoccupied silence damned him in Charlee's eyes. She saw his gentleness with Tomasina and his fury at Markham for hurting her. Nothing else seemed to matter to him, least of all a disheveled and sorrowing Missouri hill girl, who hid her pain behind a wooden facade of resentfulness.

As soon as the surgery was done, Charlee helped the doctor clean his instruments. Weidermann instructed the wide-eyed maids to prepare their mistress's bed. When Slade curtly told them to prepare a bed for him in the next room, Charlee slipped away without his even taking notice.

She returned to the *sala* to find Lee anxiously pacing. Markham's body had been removed by one of Jack Hays's rangers, who served as the law in San Antonio since all the officials of the court were prisoners on forced march to Mexico. Lee looked up and asked uncertainly, "Is she going to live?"

Charlee sighed, partly in resignation, partly in anger. "Yes, I expect so, with Jim to tend her. The way she's holding on to him, she'll either live or drag him into the next world with her! I hope they both roast,'' she muttered darkly under her breath as she headed toward the back door.

Lee hurried after her. ''Where are you going? Wait up, I'm coming with you.'' He went around the front of the house and retrieved Liso, then met her in the rear as she slipped onto Patchwork. Wordlessly they headed for Bluebonnet, taking Polvo with them as there was no one to care for the horse at the Carver house.

On the slow ride to the ranch, Lee outlined the long, grueling pursuit of the Comancheros and the battle that ensued, ending with Markham's escape and flight to San Antonio. Charlee described the taking of the city by General Woll, the amazing events at Kensington's boardinghouse, and her discovery of Tomasina's perfidy in Richard Lee's diary.

''I want her hanged,'' she stated baldly to the young vaquero.

He nodded bleakly, empathizing with her over the loss of a brother. ''I understand how you feel. My brother and sister died with our parents. In revenge for them, I've killed many men, Comanche and those who deal with them. But you must realize, *chica* . . .'' He paused, uncertain of how to go on, to explain to her.

''You mean, Slade won't let anybody lay a hand on her, don't you? She's guilty as sin of two murders, her own husband's as well as my brother's!'' Her face was set in tight lines of outrage and hurt.

''No, it's not Jim, or at least it's more than Jim. Charlee, the law in San Antonio would never hang a woman, especially one from an old respected family, a woman of property and influence, a lady despite her treachery.''

Charlee whirled on him, furious over the logic of his argument even though she knew he was no admirer of Tomasina's. ''She deserves to die just as much as Markham did. I suppose Jim'll nurse her back to health and marry her just to cover up the whole ugly mess.''

''More likely he'll try to ship her off to relatives in Mexico when she's well,'' he responded, praying he was right and Charlee wrong. ''You misunderstand his feelings over her, I think, *chica*. He doesn't love her—if he ever did—but he feels guilty, obligated to her. Or, more properly, to her family and the old agreement between his father and her father. It's the past that holds him, Charlee, not any love for Tomasina now.'' He could tell by the look in her tear-blinded jade eyes that she did not believe him.

''Just let me pack my things and collect Hellfire. I'll be gone in the morning. Jim Slade can do whatever he wants. It doesn't signify to me anymore.''

That night, snuggled up with the old orange cat in her bedroom, Charlee cried herself into an exhausted sleep. She dreamed of the last night before Slade had left, when she had nestled in his arms, savoring what she foolishly thought was his love.

True to her word, she packed her clothing the next day and had an unwilling Lee load them on a spring wagon.

''I'll leave this in town. Maybe Slade will want to bring *her* back here in it. If not, you can always pick it up at the livery.''

As she vanished down the road, Asa, Weevils, and Lee watched dolefully. The cat's steady green eyes held theirs as he sat facing backwards on the seat, taking the jouncing ride in stride, as if he knew a secret no one else did.

When she arrived at Kensington's—no, Flemings'—boardinghouse, Charlee jumped off the wagon and reached for Hellfire, who disdained her assistance and sprang gracefully to the ground. Sniffing to reacquaint himself with his surroundings, he trotted toward the side door to the kitchen, no doubt to beg some milk or meat drippings from Sadie. Chester informed Charlee that Deborah was upstairs in her room. Just then Adam burst down the steps and ran into her welcoming arms.

''Oh, Charlee! I'm so glad you're here. You can take care of this house. Now that mama's back, we're going to live at papa's house, way far away.'' He wriggled as she knelt and hugged him.

''Now, what's all this about your leaving and your mama being gone?'' She held him at arm's length for mock inspection.

Breathless with information, he plunged on. ''When the army left, that bad man who came here with General Woll, he took mama and put her in one of those carts. Then when

papa came back, she was gone and he followed them and
there was a big fight. My papa is the bravest man in the
whole world! He saved her and now she's packing all our
things so we can go with him to his ranch! Isn't it great?''

"Yes, I'm sure it is," Charlee replied uncertainly.

"Come on, you can help!"

Bemused, she followed him up the steps and into Deborah's
room where everything was being packed into trunks.

Deborah was kneeling on the floor, surrounded by a pile
of shoes and several jewelry boxes. Hearing Adam's and
Charlee's chatter, she looked up, then rose and rushed into
her friend's embrace.

"Oh, Charlee, I'm so glad to see you! So much has
happened I scarcely know where to begin." Her face looked
pale and drawn, her beautiful features haunted and sad.
"Adam, darling, I need to talk to Charlee about grown-up
things. You go to the kitchen and let Sadie get you some
cookies and milk."

With a quick hug for each of the women, the joyous child
fairly flew down the steps. "Bet Hellfire's in the kitchen,"
he shouted over his shoulder.

"I take it a lot's happened since I left San Antonio on the
sixteenth," Charlee said dryly. Then, noticing the tension in
Deborah's expression, she pulled her friend to sit on the bed
beside her. "Now tell me what's going on."

Deborah explained the tumultuous events of the past days
in outline, obviously finding some things too painful or too
personal to relate in detail. Captain Flores had abducted her.
Rafe's old enemy had lied to the general, accusing Rafe of
spying, and had convinced Woll to put a price on his head.
His safe conduct into San Antonio was rescinded and he
was nearly shot. When he finally reached Adam and Sadie,
they hysterically told him about her disappearance. Rafe had
trailed her and rescued her during a fierce battle.

Charlee sat rooted to the bed while Deborah narrated the
incredible events.

Despite the fact that she was back home and safe,
something was definitely wrong. Deborah was not as happy
as her son.

"Where is Rafe now? Adam said you were leaving soon," Charlee volunteered uncertainly.

Deborah ran a hand through her hair and swallowed. "Oh, he's at Bainbridge's, ordering supplies for our trip. I guess we'll leave in a few days," she finished distractedly.

"You don't want to go with him, do you?" Charlee asked it gently, oddly surprised at her friend's reaction after all Rafe must have gone through to save her.

Deborah sat mutely, her silence an assent of sorts. "I . . . I honestly don't know. A part of me wants to be with him, to follow him anywhere, like some mindless creature, but I'm afraid. He's become a stranger—a violent, even savage man, so different from the Creole aristocrat I married. I guess I resent losing all the hard-won freedoms I've come to treasure the past years. A woman needs her own . . . sovereignty, her own sense of individuality." She stopped and looked uncertainly at Charlee. Deborah was flushed in embarrassment for having revealed so many of her private thoughts. "Oh, I suppose I'm rambling. It's too complicated and too painful to rehash, better left alone. I'm married, and under the law I have certain obligations from which I can no longer hide."

"And Adam, what about him . . . and his father?" Charlee added hesitantly.

"You've seen how it is. He adores Rafael. If there was nothing else, I'd have to go back to him for Adam's sake." She sat disconsolately. "At least he'll be happy, and living on a ranch will be good for him." She said it as if trying to convince herself.

Charlee did not know what to say, feeling some of Deborah's agonizing ambivalence herself, torn between love for Jim Slade and pain over his desertion. "If there was nothing else," Deborah had said. But after the episode she had witnessed in the yard, Charlee knew there was obviously something else, something more to the relationship between Deborah and Rafe than the son they shared. She vowed she would talk to Rafe Fleming to see what he planned for his family.

Charlee placed her arm around Deborah's shoulders as they huddled together on the bed. "Wherever you go, I just want you to understand that I'm your friend and I'll always be here to help you any way I can. We can write, maybe even visit from time to time."

Deborah hugged Charlee back. "Oh, you don't begin to know what your friendship has meant to me. I'll always be so grateful."

"I'm the one who should be grateful. You took a scraggly, foul-mouthed waif and taught her how to speak, dress, even walk, for heaven's sake," Charlee replied as she ruefully remembered her painful metamorphosis. "That's part of what I need to talk to you about. I learned a business skill from you, too. I can run the boardinghouse for you, or even make a down payment and buy you out if you want. I have a little nest egg from selling my parents' farm in St. Genevieve. I could pay the rest in installments, I'm sure . . ." Her voice faded nervously as she looked away from Deborah's worried eyes.

"I'd love for you to own the boardinghouse, Charlee, and I'm sure you would do an excellent job. But I can't believe that you and Jim . . . that is, I'd hoped you would make up your differences and get married. I know he loves you, not Tomasina Carver. Charlee, are you certain—"

"Yes, I'm certain," she interrupted impatiently, pain and anger clearly written on her small, vulnerable face. "He's staying at her house right now, sleeping in her bedroom." At Deborah's look of horrified incredulity, Charlee went on to explain about the shooting, and Tomasina and Markham's collusion in murdering Richard Lee and Jake Carver.

"So, you can see he's chosen his side," she finished coldly. "He's willing to protect a murderess from facing her just punishment."

"Taking care of someone near death is scarcely the same thing as shielding her from the law, Charlee," Deborah gently remonstrated.

Charlee's face clouded and she sniffed. Walking nervously to the window, she said, "You should have seen him, Deborah, when she was shot. He was so tender, so gentle with her. When Doc Weidermann sewed her up, Jim was devastated over the scar it would leave to mar her porcelain perfection," she spat hatefully.

Taking a deep breath, she turned and faced her friend. "Well, may I run the boardinghouse for you or not?"

"I can scarcely take care of it from the wilds of north Texas, can I?" Deborah replied with a wobbly smile.

Having settled her own future, even if not to her satisfaction, Charlee decided she could not rest until she was assured about Deborah and Rafe. Throughout the day she worked up her courage to confront the darkly mysterious Creole gunman. But where to do so? The boardinghouse was always crowded with people busily coming and going. She could hardly ask Deborah's husband to go for an after-dinner stroll with her! But she must talk to him.

As it turned out, Rafe took the initiative for a private conversation just after the midday meal. She was carrying a heavy tray stacked with dishes from the dining room table when he suddenly stood in front of her.

"May I take that for you? It looks to weigh more than you do, Charlee." His tread was cat-silent and his voice low and silky. Charlee gasped in surprise, almost dropping the rattling china before he eased the weight from her hands. Rafe negligently set the tray on the work table in the center of the kitchen.

"Don't you ever make a sound before you creep up on a body?" she asked churlishly.

He turned and flashed her a white grin, which seemed to erase the menace from his scarred, swarthy face. He was as beautiful as some dark satanic god. Heaven help Deborah, Charlee thought suddenly.

"Sorry if I frightened you, but there are a few matters we need to discuss. No one is in the office now. Would you join me?"

Nodding, Charlee swallowed, and preceded him down the hall into the small, comfortable room where Deborah kept her books and records for the boardinghouse. When he closed the door behind them, she took a deep breath and turned, feet planted squarely apart, hands on hips. "Well, Mr. Fleming?"

He quirked one black brow at her feisty stance and said, "I'm not going to devour you, Charlee. I've asked you to call me Rafe. I know you're Deborah's friend and feel protective of her, but I'm her husband and I think my rights take precedence over yours.''

Of all the smug, arrogant male vanity! ''You're a regular Creole version of a certain *Tejano* I know, damned if you aren't!''

He ignored her outburst and slung a long leg casually over the corner of the big oak desk, sitting back on its cluttered top. With a sweeping gesture at the books and papers on the desk, he said, ''Think you could handle all this, run this place if we sold it to you?''

Charlee arched one eybrow. She strolled over to the window and said, ''Oh, so that's it. I guess you didn't have time to ask Deborah what she planned to do yet, did you?'' She turned like a triumphant little cat, her green eyes glowing. ''I'm buying *her* boardinghouse. We arranged it all this morning. I have a small nest egg and we agreed upon a fair price.''

Rafe nodded with a self-deprecating grin. ''So, it's all settled. No need to ask if you feel capable of running the operation.''

''Deborah did it for the past six years. She was scarcely older than I when she came to San Antonio, and she raised her son beside making a success of her place.'' Her tone of voice dared him to dispute the facts.

''Yes, she did raise *our* son. Like this place and the ranch up north, everything we have, we share, from here on, for the rest of our lives.''

His voice was conciliatory, Charlee grudgingly admitted. Still, her anger at men in general and one fickle Texian in particular led her to say, ''I suppose us Texas women seem pretty independent to a Creole gentleman.''

''I've lived the last six years in Texas, not New Orleans. It's been a long time since anyone considered me a Creole . . . or a gentleman,'' he added with a wicked gleam in his black eyes. Then his expression turned grave. ''I guess I approached you before talking to Deborah because I wanted to smooth over the transition of her selling this place.'' He hesitated, then stood up and paced across the floor. ''No, that's not the real reason,'' he confessed reluctantly.

"I guess I was afraid of another confrontation with her before I convinced her to go home with me." The tension in his body was as evident as the strain in his voice.

"You sound afraid she might not go with you," Charlee said. "From the way she talks, I didn't exactly get the impression you were giving her any choice."

Rafe's face became shuttered. "No, I won't give her a choice . . . or a chance to refuse me. I've searched for her and Adam for six years. Now that I've found them, I'll never give them up again. But I don't want to hurt her any more either. I hoped to win you over as an ally."

"You already have a pretty staunch one in Adam. You won him over the minute he met you," Charlee said, recalling Deborah's pain over the child's adoration of his father.

Rafe smiled then, love and pride written across his face. "Yes, Adam is glad I found him. He's talking about going to our ranch and getting his own pony to ride . . . even having brothers and sisters. He wants to be like the other children he knows, to be part of a real family."

How could she argue with a child's joy? "I suppose he has the right to expect those things," Charlee replied thoughtfully. "He told me once that he wanted a baby brother."

Rafe's face was alight now. "His mother and I've been working on it, believe me."

Charlee reddened at that remark, visualizing the scene between them that she had witnessed in the backyard. Then recalling her own near brushes with pregnancy the times when Slade had seduced her, she turned away angrily. Men! "You think you can solve all your problems in bed?" she bristled, too furious to be embarrassed any longer.

Puzzled by her sudden anger and not knowing its cause, Rafe replied gravely, "No. I was disabused of that naive idea back in New Orleans when she left me. I don't expect it'll be easy and I know it'll take time, but I intend to rebuild my life with Deborah just as I rebuilt Renacimiento, my grandfather's old rancho. I love my wife, Charlee, but I can't chance losing her again by giving her too many choices here and now, not until she learns to trust me again.''

''And that means getting her away from San Antonio and all its ties, showing her the home you've made for her?'' Charlee asked with dawning understanding. The honesty of his confession and the earnest entreaty in his black eyes touched her. Despite Rafe's barbaric appearance and arrogant manner, Charlee had a gut instinct to trust what he said. ''I guess you have yourself another ally, Rafe Fleming, but I plan to write Deborah regularly and she'd better answer me every time... and I'd better like what I hear from her. Agreed?'' She cocked her head with a gamin grin.

Fleming was taken aback by her mercurial moods. Nodding, he replied, ''Agreed, Charlee.''

The weeks of Tomasina's recovery were miserable ones for Slade. It seemed that he was in a well of depression and preoccupation so deep that he would never scale his way out of it. The day of the shooting, he had been so keyed up over finally disposing of Markham, so exhausted physically and emotionally by all that had happened in the preceding two weeks, that he could scarcely think straight. Then Tomasina Carver lay bleeding, near death, and all the bittersweet memories, the old guilts and lost dreams of his youth, came rushing back to assault him. He had helped the doctor save her life and then had put her in her own bed, to rest in a drug-induced sleep.

Finally he had the presence of mind to realize Charlee was gone. Then the conversation preceding Markham's entrance flashed into his mind. What had Charlee said—something crazy about Ashley and Tomasina killing her brother and old Jake? He had sat by Sina's bedside that first night, sipping a glass of brandy, too bone tired to sort it all out. Near daybreak he fell asleep in his chair, too exhausted to consider whether or not the woman he had nearly married was really a murderess.

Two days later Tomasina regained consciousness. She saw Jim across the room, asleep in a chair, unshaven and fully dressed in his same blood-stained clothing. It was her blood, she realized with a sudden gasp of agony! Her chest throbbed in screaming pain as she tried to sit up. As the horrendous events of the past week refocused in her mind, she looked at Slade and calculated what he might do.

Obviously she could go nowhere for a while. Assuredly the English gold had been confiscated and Ashley was dead. But Jim had saved her. She forced her mind back through the haze of agony as Dr. Weidermann had performed surgery on her, recalling Slade's tenderness. He had left his trashy American mistress and stayed with her. Perhaps he would not believe the cheap tart's wild accusations about the murders. She must do everything in her power to convince Slade of her innocence and Ashley's duplicity. If he would protect her from the charge of spying, she must now be sure he would also save her from a hangman's noose!

Because she was gravely ill and in pain, her role-playing was easier in the ensuing days. Jim was the soul of compassion and protectiveness. If part of the reason he treated her with such concern stemmed from his own guilt for using her to trap Markham, she accepted that with well-concealed rancor. Just as long as she could hold him by her side, she was safe.

"You have been so kind to me, darling," Tomasina said softly in Spanish, looking soulfully into his gold cougar's eyes. Despite his solicitude, those eyes were frighteningly unreadable to her. "What were you thinking just now? You seemed so far away." She reached for his large dark hand and fondled it delicately between her own small pale ones.

"I'm just glad you're finally out of danger, that's all," he evaded. In truth, he had been thinking about how he was going to approach Charlee and explain his stay with Sina.

Lee, who had come several days ago with a change of clothes and other personal items for him, accusatorially informed him that Charlee was living at the boardinghouse once more, having moved lock, stock, and tomcat from Bluebonnet. He had affirmed Charlee's story that Tomasina was involved in a double murder. The testimony of Richard Lee McAllister's diary had convinced the young vaquero just as it had Charlee. Slade had a gnawing dread deep in his gut that told him they were right. Then he had read the diary.

He looked down at the drawn features of the beautiful woman in the bed. He had used her, to his dishonor, no doubt, but she had used him, too. His golden gaze locked with her fathomless black eyes and he said, "Sina, I need to know about Jake and that McAllister kid." He could feel her hands tighten involuntarily over his.

Then her eyes became liquid with big, shiny tears and she turned away. "You believe them, don't you? They are all against me. They hate me, James. Once I believed you loved me, but now. . ." She let her words trail off and held her breath.

He sighed. "I am not in love with you anymore, Sina. That much I told you a month ago. I also said I'd protect you from the charges of espionage with Markham. I hadn't counted on murder."

The coldness of his voice when he made the last statement caused her heartbeat to accelerate. Grasping his arm, she tried to pull herself into a sitting position, clinging to him and sobbing in a mixture of pain, frustration, and fear. "Markham did the killing, James, not I! Jake found out about my working for him. All our plans for liberating Texas hinged on secrecy. Ashley said he had to die."

"And McAllister?" He sat very still.

"He . . . he blackmailed Ashley, saying he'd seen Ashley with me, seen Ashley kill Jake. When he asked Ashley for money, Ashley went crazy. He set a trap—he did it!" She shivered and cried.

Carefully but coldly he laid her back against the pillows, then stood up and gazed at her with a sad, resigned look on his face. "Sina, give it up. Lee brought me the boy's diary and I read it. He was a graphically accurate reporter. You were there when Jake had his accident. God only knows how you and Markham contrived to get rid of Dick, but it was you, not Markham, he approached with blackmail."

With that Slade walked deliberately out of the room, shutting the door with finality. He went downstairs and asked the old man who did heavy chores to bring him some hot bath water.

He would shave, bathe, and change, then go to Flemings'. No, he amended ruefully, it was McAllister's now. He had been as amazed as anyone in town to hear the tale of Deborah's resurrected husband who had whisked her and their son off to his ranch up north. Of course, it did explain a great deal about the reclusiveness of such a beautiful young widow these past years.

Now Charlee was the new proprietor of Deborah's establishment. Independent, willful little creature! Yet he knew she'd make a go of it. He swore at his own gullibility, realizing that she had possessed sufficient money to actually buy a boardinghouse, all the while convincing him she was an impoverished waif who needed a job! That little cat would land on her feet no matter what.

Slade reviewed their less than satisfactory relationship as he soaked the aching exhaustion from his bones. Indeed, he had done little but sleep and brood about her brother's diary the past three days as he watched over Sina, making sure the flighty maids cared for her properly. Now that she was safely on the road to recovery, he turned his attention back to Charlee.

Charlee . . . damn, he didn't even know her real name until he read it in Dick's diary: Chastity Charlene. He could scarcely blame her for dropping Chastity, although he rather favored the feminine sound of Charlene. Still, she would ever be Charlee, an odd mixture of hellion, waif, and seductress. He snorted as he remembered his own words to her the night of the dance—something about feelings more complicated than lust but surely not love. Was it love?

After so badly misjudging Sina and his relationship with her, he reconsidered his proposal to Charlee McAllister that day by the pool. At the time it seemed the most natural thing in the world to say he'd marry her. He ached for her even now, desiring that lithe little body, so wondrously passionate and responsive, made just to fit his own. Chastity she was not! But that was merely lust . . . well, perhaps "merely" was not the right word . . .

Certainly he enjoyed their sparring conversations, her ready wit and earthy common sense, her unexpected flashes of erudition, perhaps most of all her continual perseverance

in becoming a lady, a paragon who was always faultlessly
attired, never swore or made an ungraceful move. He
enjoyed it so much because she never completely succeeded.
He realized with a surprising start that he never wanted her
to. He had been raised to admire the cool, polished exterior
of women like Tomasina Aguilar Carver, but the woman he
most enjoyed being with, laughing and loving with, was
neither cool nor in truth highly polished at all. He must
straighten things out with her right now.

It was nearly dinnertime when Slade came downstairs,
still mulling over how to discreetly handle Sina's perfidy
once she was recovered enough. At the same time he must
convince Charlee to marry him. It would be a neat juggling
act at best.

Lee waited for him at the foot of the stairs, hat in hand,
looking dusty and agitated; obviously he had just ridden to
town in great haste. "The president's messenger just arrived
from Washington-on-the Brazos with this." He handed Slade
a sealed envelope. "All kinds of high-power politics going
on, and he needs your help . . . that is, if you think the
widow can spare you," he added sullenly.

Jim sighed, ignoring the youth's continuing hostility,
which had resurfaced when he had stayed in town with Sina.
Running a hand through his still damp hair, he swore. "For
your information, Sina's past the crisis and I was on my
way over to the boardinghouse to see Charlee. Now I guess
that'll have to wait."

Slade went into the study with Lee on his heels. Motioning
the youth to sit down, Jim tore the missive open and began
to read.

> Jim-boy:
> Some news you will doubtless find unpalatable
> but which I trust will come as no surprise. I find
> Tomasina Carver is more ambitious than ever we
> thought. She has made contact with William
> Kennedy himself. It is his blood money your local
> people confiscated from her. I expect you will fill
> me in as to the particulars of that episode in due

course. (I also trust Markham is no longer a problem.)

Kennedy, however, remains one. He has rather conveniently, for our purposes, gotten himself arrested by Captain Kessler's rangers while he was in the company of some Comancheros. I have sent official word he is to be let go, although the rest of them will doubtless hang. It is because of his influence in British politics and his high visibility in American circles that I am doing this, despite the sour taste it leaves in every Texian mouth.

Be that as it may, I am anonymously apprising some American sources of this special dispensation given the British Foreign Office. Kennedy will arrive on your doorstep shortly to collect his evidence—Mrs. Carver's ill-gotten gold. Give it to him, however you must arrange it.

As ever,

Houston

Postscript: If you have no match at hand, please feed this indigestible missive to Polvo!

Slade scowled darkly, then shrugged. He knew how badly Houston hated letting a dangerous man like Kennedy go, but he understood the chess game well enough. A discreet favor to the British government, carefully leaked to the Americans, brought the president's master plan one step nearer completion. Sources high in the Tyler administration were growing increasingly alarmed at the Anglo-Texian friendship that Houston was fostering. The more old Sam courted the British Lion, the more quickly the American Eagle would stretch out its talons and annex Texas.

He sat down and started to compose the report about Markham's demise and the expedition against Iron Hand, which he had been postponing writing since his return to San Antonio. As for Kennedy and the gold, he began to form a plan in his mind that might solve several problems at once.

Slade looked up at the scowling youth who had been fidgeting silently while he had read Houston's letter. "Lee, how'd you feel about delivering a message to the president for me?"

"Want to get me out of your hair for a while?" The young man grinned in spite of himself.

"Well, you were going to Galveston to pick up that breeding stock anyhow. Washington-on-the-Brazos is a detour, I know, but not too long a one."

Shrugging, Lee replied, "I guess you and Charlee have to sort this out for yourselves."

chapter
<u>18</u>

After the long, hot ride to Washington-on-the-Brazos and a lengthy interview with Sam Houston, Lee was tired and annoyed, still stewing over Jim's estrangement from Charlee and the mysterious goings-on with Tomasina Carver. What would his boss do with the scheming woman? And how did Jim's letter to the president figure into it all? Houston had questioned Lee about Markham's death, the raid on the Comanchero camp, and the state of Tomasina's health after her near brush with death.

When the president had quickly perused Slade's letter, he had burst into gales of hearty laughter but had not offered to explain the source of his mirth to Lee, only telling the youth that several thorny problems were about to be neatly solved. Lee had left the office feeling very frustrated indeed. It was as if they thought him still a child, too young to be trusted with state secrets. But not too young too fight Indians and Comancheros, he thought grimly.

However, he had another mission of some importance entrusted to him, Lee consoled himself: the new breeding stock—two prize mares Jim had purchased from a plantation in Alabama. The boat would dock in Galveston Harbor any day now, and he was in charge of bringing them back to Bluebonnet. Since Slade was so busy tending to his wounded fiancée, Lee was handling ranch business in his boss's stead.

It took him two days to ride from the present capital to Houston City. "Sure wish they'd settle on a place," he groused to himself. Since the Republic's founding, the government had shuttled between Washington-on-the-Brazos, Houston, and Austin, not to mention Columbia, Harrisburg, and several other obscure places. Lee arrived in the booming city named after the president late the second afternoon.

Early the next morning, after a horrible breakfast in a modest Houston hotel, he set out to purchase a ticket on one of the steamboats that shuttled back and forth the fifty-mile distance between Houston City and Galveston Island. Nostalgically recalling Charlee's fluffy biscuits and comparing them with the dreadful dough balls he'd just ingested, Lee hoped for better fare in the port city, or failing that, a brief stay. The trip between Mobile and Galveston was usually accomplished in a few days, weather permitting. Since it was a brisk late fall day without severe storms, Lee was optimistic. The horses should be ready and waiting for him.

"Maybe I'll even try one of those oyster houses Asa and Jim are always telling me about," he said to himself as he strolled down the landing on the San Jacinto River. Grinning, he also recalled that oysters were supposed to be an aphrodisiac. If time permitted, he decided he would investigate the houses of pleasure on the Galveston waterfront as well.

Having had his initiation into sex over a year ago, Lee felt very much the man of the world, alone on a business trip in an exotic coastal city, hundreds of miles away from the rolling hills of the Texas interior. The flat gulf plain was certainly different from the San Antonio area. He had thought Houston City flat, but as the boat headed into the

open waters of Galveston Bay, he was astounded at the
dead-level, grassy marshlands.

When the boat passed Point Bolivar and pulled up to a
long wooden wharf, Lee stared in amazement at the bobbing
latticework of hundreds of oceangoing vessels, sloops and
schooners, all floating at anchor. The sky was the usual
blinding Texas blue, and the wind was brisk, but laden with
the unfamiliar tang of salt. He saw gulls circling overhead
and heard the screams of cranes in the distance.

"Never seen th' ocean before, young feller?" a wizened
old seaman said, spitting a wad of tobacco juice into the
clear turquoise depths of the bay.

"It smells different, all right. I've never seen land so flat
and treeless before," Lee confessed, suddenly feeling younger
and less sophisticated.

The old-timer laughed. "Figger we got us three trees
worth countin' on th' whole dangblasted island. Got us a
new church, six hotels 'n all sorts o' warehouses and
businesses. Place is growin' fast. Be th' biggest port on th'
gulf someday... if one o' them hurricanes don't wipe it
out!"

"I need to find a shipping line, name of Morgan-Kollar.
Know where it might be?" He might as well check on the
horses first, then decide how much time he could allot to
seeing the sights.

The old seaman gave him directions and Lee set out,
feeling oddly secure to have his feet planted on dry land
once more after hours on the vibrating deck of the boat.
Taking in the international flavor of the seaport, he quickly
wended his way down the long pier. Ships of all nations
were tied up across the harbor, and he could hear German
and French mixed in with the lazy drawls of Alabamans and
clipped tones of British merchants. Other more exotic eastern European accents sounded guttural and harsh to his ears.

Just then the strident tones of a clear soprano carried
across the waterfront. The voice was that of a child, or a
very young lady, judging by her educated vocabulary, speaking English with the faintest trace of a French accent.

"And I tell you, that is the price we agreed upon!" The
speaker was indeed a child, although her slightly curved

figure hinted at the woman she would become. She was tiny, with raven locks that bounced in girlish curls as she stamped her foot in pique.

She was arguing with a large beefy American dressed in seaman's clothes, apparently an officer of the schooner from which they'd both just debarked. His florid face was mottled in rage as he towered over the feisty girl. "You see here, you told me your pa was meeting you and he'd pay. I'm not letting you go until he pays me the difference!"

"My father's family is one of the finest in New Orleans. I assure you my father will make good for such a paltry amount. I need the cash I have now for lodging until he arrives . . . any day. You'll get your money, Monsieur Phillips."

Her voice carried the cultured tones of wealth with its accompanying arrogance, no doubt there, Lee thought wryly. As he observed her expensive gray silk traveling suit and matching bonnet, he wondered why a girl of such tender years was traveling alone.

The ship's officer had apparently become impatient with the debate. He reached out and grabbed the girl. "I'm beginning to be suspicious about your family, missy. No pa here to meet you 'n no one traveling with you from New Orleans. If you want to pay for a hotel room, I got me an idea about how you can do it . . . after you give me the rest of that cash."

The girl was small and quick as she twisted from his grasp with a furious hiss. "You Yankee pig! My father owns one of the biggest ranches in Texas, Renacimiento! Rafael Flamenco will kill you for even saying such a thing!"

Lee debated whether to interfere on behalf of the girl. Lord knew, her battle with the burly sailor was most uneven. But when he heard the names Renacimiento and Rafael Flamenco, he was rooted to the wharf in shock. Rafael Flamenco was Deborah's husband, the lethal-looking Texian Rafe Fleming, who had appeared at the boardinghouse during the Mexican occupation of San Antonio. Charlee had told him all she knew about the bizarre situation just before Fleming had taken his wife and son back to his ranch. Now it seemed the mysterious gunman had a runaway daughter as well as a runaway wife!

"Let the girl go," Lee said quietly to the seaman as he walked up behind the struggling pair.

Phillips whirled, loosening his hold on the shrieking, flailing girl. "Who the hell are you—another kid of this here Flamenco fellow's?" With a mixture of amusement and contempt, he looked Lee's youthfully slim form up and down.

"Just a friend of the family, so to speak," Lee replied levelly. "What seems to be the problem? Maybe I can pay you what she owes in her father's place."

The sailor noted Lee's worn boots, cotton shirt, and cord pants, the clothes of a cowhand. In addition, he had the Hispanic features of a despised Mexican. "Huh, you're one of them greasers without a peso or I miss my guess. Get lost, sonny, or I'll loosen your teeth." Phillips turned back to the girl, whose small, heart-shaped faced looked pale in breathless fright as she clutched her reticule tightly.

"In Texas, men respect women and girls. Keep your hands off her." Lee's voice was soft but cutting now as his anger ignited. "And, any man who calls me a greaser had better be prepared to back up his insult."

Something in Lee's tone of voice set off a warning bell for the American. He turned again to face the slim younger man. "All right. I can back it up, greaser." He raised a big fist for a roundhouse swing.

As Lee ducked, he jabbed, thankful Jim Slade had given him lessons over the years. Still, he was sure that his wiry quickness would not match the big brute's strength for long. Another quick jab to the enraged seaman's midsection and then he danced back toward the edge of the pier.

At the very instant the burly American lunged past him, Lee felt an agonizing sting in his right arm. The girl was beside him with a pair of tiny scissors in her hand. She had stabbed at her antagonist and caught her rescuer instead!

Before Lee could do more than let out an oath of pain, the sailor was swinging again. Lee caught sight of the girl from the corner of his eye, scissors once more raised. This time she found the right target, but not before the distraction of her sudden movement caused Lee's reflexes to slow. The brute caught him squarely in the midsection, knocking the wind from his lungs in a hissing *whoosh*. Luckily, she distracted Phillips just long enough for Lee to suck some air into his aching chest. The seaman gave her a brutal swat, sending her flying back onto the rough boards of the wharf, then lumbered after Lee once more.

"Now, greaser, say your prayers," he growled, nursing the reddening furrow across his left arm.

Phillips lunged at Lee, intent on grappling him into a killing bearhug. At the last second, when the bigger man almost had him in his clutches, Lee twisted to the left, colliding with the girl. Having lost her scissors, she swung with her reticule, landing a surprisingly solid blow for one so slight—against Lee's temple, narrowly missing Phillips. "Get the hell away before you kill us both!" he yelled, toppling her roughly backward as he simultaneously dodged his opponent.

Lee moved away, shaking his head to clear it. He'd better end this fast before the damblasted girl killed one of them! He wasn't at all sure who, him or the American!

"Even for a Yankee, you're a clumsy bastard," he said conversationally, taunting the red-faced seaman who was advancing on him with murder in his eyes.

Lee danced backward to the edge of the pier, then waited until Phillips took another powerful swipe. At the last second, when the big man's momentum had carried him forward, Lee sidestepped and stuck out his booted foot to trip Phillips, catapulting him into the choppy cold water below the pier.

"I think we'd better collect your belongings and leave before he gets out of the water, or we'll both be in trouble," Lee said, rubbing the laceration on his arm gingerly. "The next time a man attempts to rescue you, have the good grace not to stab him or brain him, will you?" He reached down and picked up her trunk from the end of the gangplank, then strode toward town with her scurrying behind.

"Of all the ungrateful things to say! Phillips is twice your size. If I hadn't distracted him, he'd have killed you," she sputtered.

Lee cocked one eyebow at her. "I'd have managed, Miss Fleming," he replied stiffly.

The girl looked at him suspiciously with large gold-coin eyes, widened in confusion. "Why do you call me Miss Fleming? Our name is Flamenco."

"Not in Texas it isn't. Here the owner of Renacimiento calls himself Rafe Fleming, if he *is* your papa as you claim," Lee said.

"He certainly *is* my father, and he's expecting me," she replied in affront, fairly skipping to keep up with his longer stride.

"Then why isn't he here? A girl shouldn't be traveling alone," Lee replied, not slowing for fear the enraged brute swimming for the nearest piling might yet catch up with them.

"Well . . . I wasn't supposed to arrive until next Tuesday. But I just couldn't stay another week in New Orleans! Joline was supposed to come with me, but I had to escape without my stepfather Francois finding out, so I left her behind." Once the breathless confession began, she couldn't seem to stop herself.

Scanning the buildings stretched along the flat, open expanse of the beach, Lee chose what looked to be a good hotel and headed toward it. "I never knew Rafe Fleming had a daughter, but then I never knew Deborah Kensington had a husband either," he added with a chuckle. "What's your name?"

"Melanie Marie Fla-Fleming." Obviously the new name stuck on her tongue.

"You sound French. Was your mother a Creole?" For all her education and expensive clothing, something wasn't right about Melanie Fleming.

"My family is mostly of French descent. We've lived in New Orleans for generations, but I was raised by my *Grandmere* in St. Louis," the girl replied uneasily.

"Fleming scarcely seems old enough to have a daughter your age—how old *are* you?" Her features were delicate and cameo-perfect, her curves only budding, but definitely visible. A mysterious child-woman, indeed.

"I'll be thirteen in a few months," she said with bravado.

"How many months?" he shot back.

"Nine," she sighed, looking up at his chiseled, handsome face. "Are you a cowboy?" she asked, wanting to change the subject. "How do you know my father?"

"Yes, I'm a vaquero for the Slade ranch, Bluebonnet, outside of San Antonio. And I never met your father, exactly. But I know Deborah and Adam . . . you do know about them?" He looked at her in puzzlement. What a strange tangle this was becoming.

"I know of papa's Yankee wife and my half-brother, yes," she answered stiffly.

Again a ripple of unease washed over him, but he ignored it as they entered the hotel. The lobby was crowded and he prayed they could secure rooms.

Soaking in a hot tub of sudsy water, Lee reviewed the day's incredible events. Not even dinner time and I'm exhausted, he groaned to himself. Small wonder he was tired. After settling Melanie Fleming in a room, he'd located Morgan-Kollar Ltd. and found out the horses were expected on a ship due in from Mobile tomorrow morning. He could take them and leave but for the girl. Her father wasn't due in Galveston to collect her until Tuesday.

That wretched Phillips had stormed into the hotel like a Gulf hurricane later that afternoon demanding his money, which Lee had paid. Now if he were to recover it, he must wait for Rafe Fleming. That meant cooling his heels in Galveston for five days, during which time he couldn't even do the recreational things he'd planned earlier because he now had a twelve-year-old child hung like a millstone around his neck.

He groaned in frustration, damning his perverse luck and the spoiled, sullen adolescent who was even now probably waiting for him to squire her to dinner. Sighing, he crawled from the tub and began to towel off, then swore when her scissors' wound stung anew.

The elegantly clad young man dressed in black wool pants and short fitted jacket studded with silver, with a snowy linen shirt and blue silk waistband, presented quite a different picture to Melanie than he had in casual cowhands' clothing. How handsome he was!

Why did I decide at the last moment to dress so formally and pay the maid extra to press my good clothes? I'll send that child to bed early and then go to one of the places down on the waterfront. Lee answered his own question determinedly as he offered her his arm, wincing when she pressed on the wound she had inflicted.

Seeing him flinch, Melanie said, "Oh, does it hurt? I am terribly sorry about missing him and hitting you."

Lee grunted, then smiled at her piquant little face in spite of himself. "Just so I have your assurance you aren't carrying any more scissors, hatpins, or other lethal weapons."

A tiny bubble of laughter erupted from her lips as she shook her head. For the first time, Lee noticed the obvious care she had taken with her appearance. Her gleaming jet hair was piled in high, saucy curls atop her head, spilling down her back, a rather adult hairstyle for a twelve-year-old, but enchanting. Her dress, although girlishly modest with a high neckline and frilly ribbons down the front, was a soft rose color that set off her pale golden complexion to perfection. One day she would be a real beauty. But that day was years away.

Clearing his head of such distractions, Lee signaled a waiter as they approached the hotel dining room. The place was scarcely elegant, but it did afford a splendid view of the harbor, and the food smelled significantly better than it had at the hotel in Houston City.

By the end of the first course, it was obvious to Lee that he had made an error in dressing up to squire her to dinner. She was infatuated with him, chattering and giggling, attempting to flirt coyly as she gazed adoringly at him with those big golden eyes. She'd be a real Creole belle someday, and have a string of suitors swarming around like bees at a honey tree. He was certain with a man as formidable as Rafe Fleming for a father, she doubtless would be married by the time she was seventeen. Just thinking of that made him eat faster. Soon he would see her safely ensconced in her room. Then he could head for the waterfront and some real fun. With an inward sigh, he considered the next five days, warding off her girlish flirtations while keeping her out of harm's way at the same time. He was beginning to believe some of Charlee's penchant for disaster had rubbed off on him.

The next day, Lee was sure of it. After a late, exhausting and expensive night at the best brothel in Galveston, he slept in. After he cut himself twice shaving and buttoned his shirt wrong on the first try, he finally succeeded in getting dressed in spite of his pounding head. When he knocked on Melanie's door, a maid who was straightening the room opened it and informed him Miss Fleming had left hours earlier.

The waiter in the dining room verified that, assuring Lee that his young charge had gone for a walk down the beach after her breakfast. Alone! Unescorted! Finding out the direction she had taken, Lee stomped after her, stomach growling, head buzzing, disposition snarling. He found her sitting innocently on one of the small docks at the far end of the beach, talking to an old black fisherman mending nets.

"You can't just wander around without a chaperone, least of all on a public beach in a rough port city in Texas!" he hissed at her as he fairly dragged her toward the hotel.

"My chaperone is back in New Orleans, and I had no one to accompany me. You were indisposed, or so the clerk told me, from a very late night in town," she said in pouting accusation. "Oh, drat, I have sand in my slippers. They'll be ruined."

"You should have considered that before you set out to stroll down the beach," he replied over-sweetly, trying a new tack of reason as his headache abated in the clear salt air.

An afternoon of escorting a young lady with boundless energy quickly brought the headache back. That night he considered having her dinner sent to her room and going out by himself. The next evening he considered locking her in her room and going to sleep early himself. Would Tuesday never arrive?

Saturday he feared Sunday might never arrive, at least for the two of them, after a second brush with death. It all began innocently enough as Melanie was chattering about her *Grandmere* in St. Louis. They had just eaten a splendid lunch, and at her instigation were walking down the beach to view some of the shipwrecked boats that were now used as dwellings. She had worn more sensible shoes, but carried a most impractical lacy parasol.

"How did those big hulks get washed all the way up the beach?" Melanie questioned in awe as they looked at what had once been a large sloop, now converted into a cottage by an immigrant family.

Lee laughed. "I've heard about Texas winds back inland ever since I was a boy. Will Slade used to say it took one man to saddle a horse in Virginia, but two in Texas because of the wind. Here on the gulf they have terrible hurricane winds, Texas-sized for sure."

"Oh, pooh," she replied dismissively. "We have hurricanes in New Orleans, too, but I never saw a whole ship washed up into the market!"

"I suspect New Orleans is a bit farther inland and not situated on quite such a flat stretch of sand as Galveston Island," Lee explained with the condescension an eighteen-year-old reserves for children.

Just then their debate was cut short by some noise from down the beach. Four burly seamen in rough work clothes were gathered at the end of one pier. Wanting to get the child away before something dangerous befell her, Lee took her arm to steer her in the opposite direction.

Before he could do more than turn around, Melanie looked past his shoulder at the melee, seeing a lone figure push his way free of his captors and sprint toward them. He wore buckskin pants, a roughly cut calico shirt, moccasins on his feet, and large brass loops in his ears. His austere copper features and straight black hair further proclaimed him an Indian, although Melanie could not recognize what tribe.

Before the man got but a few yards, two of the younger toughs tackled him and brought him to ground. The other two quickly caught up. When the Indian was hauled up roughly, the biggest of the sailors hit him squarely in the midsection while his two companions held his arm immobile.

"Stop them, Lee! Oh, they'll kill the poor fellow!" Melanie cried, her small face red with fear and anger.

He barely managed to grab a fistful of shiny black curls and pull her back before she could take off brandishing her ridiculous parasol. "Be still, you little idiot! Whatever they do to that halfbreed Krank is none of our business. Now let's get out of here."

She squirmed furiously in his grip, slippery as a little eel. "Ooh, let me go! They're beating him to death. If you're a coward, I'm not!"

With that, she jammed the sharp point of the parasol into his knee with bone-splintering impact, then slipped free when the stabbing pain caused him to lose his grip on her for an instant. She was off like a shot up the beach and into the thick of the battle, screeching and stabbing with her weapon. The seamen dropped the now unconscious Karankawa in amazement when she lit into them.

Having a whole new respect for her weapon, Lee limped after her, thankful he had learned his lesson that first day on the waterfront. He never left the hotel without carrying a gun.

"Lookee here, an Injun lover. Honey, what you doin' tryin' to save a worthless Krank ... if he warn't a drunkard, he'd eat you fer breakfast," one of the sailors said as he grabbed her parasol while his friends subdued the flailing girl.

"Let me go! My father'll kill you," she shrieked.

"Her father's been detained, but I guess I'll have to kill you for him if you don't do like the little girl says," Lee said as he cocked his Wilkinson over-and-under at the apparent ringleader's belly.

Melanie quickly squirmed out of one malodorous man's grasp. "You do well to call this poor Indian a drunkard. You all reek of cheap whiskey!" she spat as she knelt by the prone body.

"Why you strangers butt'n in ta save a Krank, anyways?" one of the other sailors questioned peevishly.

Lee thought it a more than fair question. The tame Karankawa indeed had the appearance of a derelict who would doubtless cut a man's throat for the price of a shot of whiskey. "I'm just trying to get my friend's daughter out of harm's way. He's a real mean fellow and I've sort of been put in charge of her safekeeping until he arrives."

"Why did you beat him?" Melanie glared at the tallest fellow.

"Little lady, he's a Krank—oh, I can tell you're not Texian—a Karankawa, a cannibal. They eat little gals like you."

Melanie paled as she looked over to Lee.

He nodded in agreement. "Yep, the coastal tribes have been known to have a barbecue now and then."

"But he's dressed in white man's clothes. And he's alone and unarmed, an old man," she argued despite her repugnance at their accusations.

"He stole my watch, sneak thief Injun," the thinner of the two young sailors said. "Check his pockets. No tame Injun ever had a silver watch. It was my pappy's."

Lee walked up to the body, his gun never wavering from the four drunken sailors as he knelt and checked the inert form sprawled in the sand. Sure enough, he swore to himself, the Krank had a small silver watch in his right back pocket.

"This it?" he asked the sailor.

Melanie grabbed it out of his hand and opened it. "There's no engraving, nothing to prove it belongs to him rather than the Indian."

Lee gritted his teeth and swore. "You want to get us both killed?" he hissed beneath his breath. "No Krank begging drinks in waterfront bars ever owned a silver watch."

"That's still no reason to beat him to death for petty theft . . . if it *was* theft. We should take him to the police and let them settle it," she finished with a dare in her voice.

Lee shook the old Krank, who was beginning to stir. His eyes were bloodshot and his breath reeked of whiskey. "I'll be the arbiter in this game, since I'm the one holding the ace." He turned the gun so the afternoon sun glinted on its barrel. "You keep the watch, we take the Krank to the sheriff to sleep it off in the lock up. Agreed?"

At their shuffling, muttering agreement, Lee tossed the young sailor the watch and motioned for them to amble up the beach.

* * *

"Quit sulking, Melanie. Your supper is getting cold," Lee said impatiently as he cut into his thick steak.

"I'm not sulking. I just don't have an appetite. I'll bet that poor Karan-...."—she stumbled over the unfamiliar name—"that poor Indian isn't getting steak for supper!"

"He's not out slitting someone's throat for a pocket watch either," he snapped testily. "Damn lot of trouble over nothing. Those charming fellows on the beach could have brained us along with that stinking savage."

Melanie sat very still, her big golden eyes boring into his curly black head until he felt her stare and looked up to meet it. Her face was chalky and her voice vibrated with a child's righteous anger. "You don't like Indians, do you, Lee?" The gaze never wavered but her voice did.

"My ancestors colonized Texas a hundred and twenty-five years ago. *Tejanos* and Indians just naturally never got along. Yes, I hate the butchering, torturing fiends! There, does that satisfy you?" He threw down his napkin like a gauntlet, heartily sick of a child debating a situation she was so abysmally ignorant about.

"Yes. It does. You really shouldn't be sitting at the same table with one of us 'butchering, torturing fiends'—should you, then? I'm descended from Cherokee on my mother's side—oh, and that's not all—my mother's side also included Africans. You see, I'm Lily Duval's daughter! Deborah Fleming is my father's Yankee wife, and Adam is his legitimate son. I'm just a..." She summoned up her courage and went on, "mongrel bastard—that's what that awful man in New Orleans called me!" By this time the tears were overflowing her golden eyes. Wiping them away with her tiny balled-up fists, she leapt up and dashed headlong from the hotel dining room.

Lee sat stunned through her whole tense, painful speech, frozen to his chair. It took him a moment to collect himself sufficiently to drop some money on the table for the bill and chase after her.

He cursed himself for not having recognized sooner the truth of the situation. How stupid of him! He recalled Melanie's evasive answers about her mother, who had not been a wife to a very young Creole man but his quadroon mistress! He groaned. Why had the girl come to Texas? Did Deborah even know about the result of Fleming's illicit affair? Was Fleming really coming to Galveston to meet the child?

Visions of him explaining to Slade about how he came to have a vicious-tempered, disaster-prone twelve-year-old in tow flashed through his mind. He resolved he was not taking her back with him; he'd put her on a boat to New Orleans! Then another thought occurred to him. What if her mother was dead? Melanie had told him that her grandmother and aunt in St. Louis had been killed in an accident but had never talked about any family in New Orleans, except to mention the stepfather, Francois, whom she heartily detested.

By the next evening, they had worked out an armed truce. After she had locked herself in her room all day Sunday, Melanie's healthy young body was starved into submission. When Lee made a handsome apology, she reluctantly agreed to eat dinner with him that night. By the time they had finished dessert, her youthful curiosity got the better of her and she asked, "Do all the white people in Texas hate Indians like you?"

Feeling some things were simply too painful and private to discuss ever again, especially with a snippy, spoiled child, he evaded the question.

"Let's just say *Tejanos* and Texians have good reason to mistrust most Indians."

"As much as Texians mistrust *Tejanos*?" She remembered the sailor's slur against Lee's Hispanic ancestry.

At least he'd steered her away from talking about Indians. "It goes both ways. *Tejanos* have good reason to dislike Anglos, too. This land was settled by the Spanish long before the Americans reached the Mississippi," he said with more than a touch of arrogance.

Melanie sensed the pride in his ancestry that his every word and movement conveyed. Wanting desperately to take him down a notch, she searched for a way to do so, dredging up her tutor's sketchy lessons in recent history. "But the Anglos whipped the Mexicans, and now Texas is a republic modeled after the United States, isn't it?"

Ignoring her supercilious manner, Lee nodded and countered,

"Yes, the dictator Santa Anna was defeated by General Houston's army, which included a lot of *Tejanos*. Lorenzo Zavala was the first vice president of Texas. Juan Seguin was one of Houston's most trusted colonels. Jim Slade fought with Houston at San Jacinto, and he's a Sandoval on his mother's side. Anglos don't have a monopoly on opposing dictators, Melanie."

"Your boss was there but you weren't, were you?" Melanie hated to lose a good argument.

"Considering I was eleven years old at the time of the Revolution, Will Slade would have locked me in the horse barn if I'd tried to go with Jim," he said in dismissal.

Her little face puckered in sheer frustration. "Well, I'd have gone, even if I am a girl, and even if I was only eleven years old! I'm not afraid of anyone, Lee Velasquez!"

He let out a snort of disgust. "You sure don't have the sense to stay out of dangerous situations where a spoiled child can get a man killed, not to mention herself. When you grow up, Melanie, maybe you'll learn not to tilt at windmills." He looked at her skeptically. "Then again, probably not."

"What do windmills have to do with courage?" she blurted out before she saw the smug amusement in his expression. Without being able to recall anything specific, she knew she should have paid more attention to her tutors back in St. Louis. Just you wait, Leandro Angel Velasquez, just you wait. Someday . . .

He only laughed at the pugnacious set of her little chin.

chapter
<u>19</u>

All the way back to San Antonio, Lee alternately worried about the tense triangle between Jim, Sina, and Charlee,

and tried to put Rafe Fleming's sullen brat of a daughter
from his mind. Never had he been so overjoyed to see
anyone as when the dangerous-looking Creole had walked
purposefully across the hotel lobby to confront him.

Mercifully, he was able to explain the series of fiascoes
with Melanie while she was still upstairs pouting in her
room. After Rafe repaid Lee the money he'd put out to
ransom the worrisome chit from First Mate Phillips, he
collected his horses and left posthaste. Let her father make
my goodbyes, he had decided on the spot, fondly wishing
never to lay eyes on her again. Given the distance between
San Antonio and Renacimiento, he hoped for the best.

Of course, considering that Charlee and Deborah were
such close friends, there was the possibility Lee might run
afoul of Deborah's stepdaughter again. He winced and
turned his thoughts to Charlee and Jim. What would get
those two blind hardheads to see what he, Asa, and Weevils
knew was the only answer. But what were they to do with
Tomasina? Such a tangle! At least the brood mares were
beauties. Slade would have two females to be pleased with,
Lee thought wryly.

As he rode toward San Antonio, Lee thought of several
ideas for getting Jim and Charlee together.

Slade was considering that very same problem back in
San Antonio as he waited for Kennedy to arrive and claim
his gold. Tomasina was recuperating nicely, under house
arrest. Her health was much better than her disposition, he
mused wryly. Now free of his deadly ex-fiancée, Slade
focused on Charlee. He resolved to go to her boardinghouse
and tell her of his plans that very night. It wouldn't be *her*
boardinghouse much longer! Whistling, he swung into the
saddle and kicked Polvo into a brisk canter.

Jim walked up the steps of the boardinghouse and waved
good evening to Mr. Schwartz and Miss Clemson, who
were sedately sipping lemonade on the porch. Schwartz
puffed on his pipe and waved back. Miss Clemson smiled
sweetly at young Mr. Slade, with avid curiosity brightening
her eyes.

As he entered the front door, Slade heard Charlee's voice

down the hall informing Sadie that the new cook would be arriving in the morning.

"Sounds like you've got a regular going concern set up here. Too bad you're going to have to sell it so soon," he said innocently.

Charlee whirled around to face him, unconsciously wiping her wet hands on her apron front. She had just finished doing dishes and was hot and sweaty, dressed in her oldest work dress, a faded yellow print. Damn!

Narrowing her eyes, she asked belligerently, "Just what do you mean, I'm going to *have* to sell *my* boardinghouse?"

He looked down at her, noticing the way the sheer cotton dress hugged her small waist and curved around those delectable little breasts. She was all in yellow like a daffodil, with spitting green cat eyes and wisping tendrils of hair spilling onto the perspiring sheen of her forehead. "You know good and well what I mean," he said with a touch of arrogance, bemused, wanting to grab her right in the middle of the kitchen and make love to her. "You can't run a business here and live at Bluebonnet."

"And just why should I live at Bluebonnet?" She stood very still, daring him to deny that he was going to stay with Tomasina.

"We'll be going back to the ranch in a few days," he said impatiently, planning to whisk her off to Padre Juan for a quick wedding before any more mischief befell them.

"And wouldn't it get rather crowded," she shot back scathingly, "with me in the kitchen and your ladylove in the parlor!"

He clenched his fists in absolute fury, fighting down the urge to turn her over his knee and paddle those petite buttocks until they were good and pink. "Sina is not my ladylove and I am not taking her to the ranch. I meant—"

"Then what are you going to do with the murdering bitch?" she interrupted. "She killed my brother and her own husband. Markham deserved to die for it; so does she."

"Markham was a professional killer, a spy, and Comanchero, a foreigner. Sina is an Aguilar. Her family settled Texas two generations ago. They're people of honor. She can't be dragged out and hung like some common horsethief. I have plans to deal with her.'' He finished rather lamely, realizing he was caught between an old obligation to Simon Aguilar and a new one to Sam Houston, and he could not explain either to Charlee's satisfaction.

''I'll just bet you do! She's a real blueblood, too honorable to die, but what does that make my brother? He was expendable, I suppose, just a Missouri nobody without a family tree, without honor!'' She was screaming now, and Jim was reacting to her temper as he always did.

''Your brother was a skulking blackmailer,'' he shot back furiously, goaded into a corner because he could not explain to her what he must do. The minute the words escaped his lips he wanted to call them back. She stood stunned for a moment, then hauled back and struck him across his face with all the strength her tiny hand possessed.

''You arrogant, priggish bastard! If you're so worried about pure bloodlines, you sure can't get yourself involved with trash like me and my family, can you!'' She braced her hands on her hips. ''Get out of my house.'' Her voice was ice-cold now.

''Charlee, wait.'' He struggled to calm his own raging temper before he did something he knew he'd regret. ''I didn't mean it that way. I don't give a damn about your brother and what he did, only about you!''

''It's quite obvious you don't care about Richard Lee's murder, so you can't care about me. Please leave.'' She was proud of the control in her voice, now that she had regained her composure, at least superficially.

He looked into her glacial green eyes for a full moment. It seemed like an eternity; then he turned down the hall and walked out the front door. If the old folks sitting on the porch heard their shouting match, Slade was too preoccupied to notice. He leaped to Polvo's back and kicked the big buckskin into a hard gallop, churning up the thick dust in floury clouds.

Jim rode for several hours, until darkness finally forced him to return to town. He mulled the whole messy situation over and over in his mind, confused, angry, and wounded. ''I was damn well rid of Sina, now I'm damn well rid of Charlee McAllister,'' he muttered to Polvo as he dismounted in front of the Carver town house, thinking for the hundredth time in the past months how he preferred the simple, uncomplicated relationship he had shared with Rosalie Parker.

On sudden impulse he swung back into the saddle and took off for the edge of town. There was a small house on a quiet back street where he knew the women were significantly more accommodating than Charlee McAllister.

The object of Slade's ire spent a miserable night, pitching and rolling, until Hellfire hopped from the bed in disgust. He jumped on the windowsill and fixed his baleful gaze on the starry night sky.

"Even you desert me, huh," she snorted at the cat, who responded with a couple of jerky tics of his tail and the raising of one fringed ear. He did not deign to look at Charlee until she spoke again. "I know what you're think-ing, you tomcat. All you males stick together...I do not need Jim Slade to have a good night's sleep!" With that she swore spitefully again and rolled over with a resounding *thunk*. The cat only looked at her turned back through slitted eyes, which seemed to say, and I do not like butter or catfish, either...

After a thoroughly miserable week, during which she worked herself into exhaustion each day in an unsuccessful attempt to forget Jim's perfidy, Charlee went to Bainbridge's Mercantile with Chester to purchase what supplies were available since the Mexican Army had left. She had just jumped from the wagon seat in front of the store when she saw Hannah Wilcox's spoiled young daughter walk out the door. Suzannah's big brown eyes narrowed in jealousy as she watched Charlee's hair turn to bronze fire in the morn-ing sun.

Forcing a smile, she said, "Fancy seeing you out and about so early, Miss McAllister. What with your new business to run and all, I scarcely expect you have much time for anything but laundry and dishes."

Her catty, singsong voice grated on Charlee's ears, but she nodded, trying to be marginally polite.

Suzannah seized the opportunity to catch her old rival's arm as Charlee began to walk through the doorway into the store. "I just had the nicest chat with Paul, and he told me the naughtiest tidbit. If you're going to take Deborah Ken—I mean Fleming's place as a respectable member of our church group, I feel it my Christian obligation to tell you about that dreadful man you used to work for."

Charlee's eyes flashed but she said levelly, "I'm already aware he's been staying with Mrs. Carver at her house, Suzannah, but even a frightful satyr like Jim Slade could hardly commit an impropriety with a woman who's been critically shot. Now, if you'll excuse me—"

"Oh, I meant *besides* that rather gauche display. At least they *are* engaged, and it is his duty to care for her, I suppose. Oh no, it's his going to that place at the end of Soledad Street that Paul was so shocked at. You know, the place where those awful painted women ply their trade. He's been seen there every night! Why Paul says—"

Charlee cut in, "I can just imagine what Paul says! But tell me, Suzannah, if Paul doesn't visit those painted women himself, how did he happen to run into Jim Slade in the establishment—*every night*?"

All the buxom brunette could do at that point was roll her eyes and gasp, rather like a banked carp.

If Charlee appeared cool and composed when she faced the knowing, hateful smile of Paul Bainbridge in the store, she was aching inwardly. She quickly placed her order with the owner's son and then left Chester to load the wagon while she walked swiftly back to the boardinghouse.

Edith LeBeau looked at the lean, golden body of Jim Slade, asleep across her bed. "Make that passed out, not asleep," she amended beneath her breath. Sighing, she walked back to the bed from her position by the window. She had been watching the sunrise, hardly an ordinary occupational practice for a prostitute, but Edith did not consider herself ordinary at all. In the two brief months since she had arrived in San Antonio, Edith had become the highest-priced whore in the city, the favorite of all the wealthiest and most discriminating men. One or two had offered to set her up as a discreetly kept mistress. While she mulled that over, she had examined the rest of the potential customers in town.

Edith knew Jim Slade on sight; rich and handsome were marvelously compatible qualities, she had always thought. The gossip about his two-year liaison with a Houston City harlot whom he had kept at his fancy ranch house was still circulating months after Rosalie Parker's departure. He was a bachelor who could do as he pleased. Obviously he didn't give a damn if the whole city was scandalized or not. However, since he had not been a customer at her place of employment, she abandoned the idea of becoming Rosalie's successor, until a week ago, when Jim Slade had walked in the door and run an appraising glance over her sultry French beauty.

Edith was vain about her glossy raven hair and voluptuous body with its creamy white skin. One scorching look from her sloe eyes, a smile from her tantalizing carmine lips, and she was sure she had him hooked. If he seemed a trifle hurried and impatient, not fully appreciative of her coy games and artful poses, he was still a strikingly attractive man who had used her gently, if rather perfunctorily. As a professional whore since the age of fourteen, Edith expected no return of sexual satisfaction from her customers, but she did enjoy their appreciation of her superior style and beauty. When Slade had ignored the fact that he had paid for the best, his indifference had challenged her. She would take that Parker woman's place at Bluebonnet if it was the last thing she did. Both his Mexican fiancée and that Yankee girl she'd heard rumors about could cool their heels in town. Edith planned to be sitting pretty—in Jim Slade's bed.

But in the past week, although Slade had visited the bordello three times, he had not asked for her specifically. It had nearly cost her a terrible fight with Marge Waller to get him on his second visit. Last night he had entered the bar downstairs, grabbing her with one hand and a bottle of brandy with the other. Upstairs, he had taken her quickly, with no preliminaries. Then he proceeded to get filthy drunk. Things were not going according to plan.

Slade awoke to the smell of heavy perfume, not exactly cheap, but musky and far too generously applied. His head ached abominably, and his tongue was so thick and dry that his throat seemed closed off. Just as well, since his stomach began to make its roiling protest known when he rolled over.

"*Bonjour, cheri*. Did you sleep well?" Edith forced a tone of brightness that she did not feel. Perhaps he was upset over a woman and needed a shoulder to cry upon. That sometimes worked. "I will bring coffee and we can talk, *non*?"

While she bustled off, black silk robe swishing, Slade swung his long legs over the edge of the bed and sat with his head in his hands, held like fragile crystal. His skull felt as though it would shatter from the agonizing noise of her rustling departure.

"Why the hell do I keep coming back here? It isn't working," he said aloud to the garish red wallpaper. He had hoped the exotic and practiced-looking Frenchwoman would blot Charlee's wholesome innocence from his mind. Nothing could have missed the mark any wider. The more he brooded and drank, and the more times he performed— badly, he admitted—in Edith's bed, the more he was forced to confront the hold that Missouri hoyden had on him. Facing it was one thing, liking it quite another.

If only Kennedy would show up and he could write the ending to this whole miserable chapter in his life, things would be less complicated. First he should get shut of this scheming little tart, Edith. She was as unlike Rosie as Sina was unlike Charlee. Charlee. He cursed and got up, wobbling to an overstuffed chair, where he found his pants lying in a wrinkled heap. The day was off to a great start.

When Asa arrived at the boardinghouse that same morning, he found Charlee still feeling wounded and brooding over Slade's newest betrayal at the bordello on Soledad Street. Of course, she did not confide the exact reason for her depression to the old foreman, but he knew she grieved for Jim. He also knew that until Tomasina Carver's fate was decided, there was nothing to be done about the situation, so he tried another tack. He and Weevils would take

Charlee on a picnic to cheer her up. At least it would distract her from the rocky road of love.

The following hour Weevils stood in the boarding-house kitchen with the picnic basket while Sadie put some additional items into the burgeoning larder.

"If'n yew take radish root 'n polk greens 'n soak 'em in a quart o' bourbon whiskey, yew'll have yew th' cure fer thet rummytism," the fat old cook remonstrated to Sadie, who cherished the belief that her copper bracelet was the best way to ward off the crippling affliction.

She snorted, "If'n I throws away th' roots 'n greens 'n jes' drinks th' whiskey, I won't feel me no achin' in my joints, ner no place elst, neither!"

While they argued, a bemused Charlee changed clothes for the impromptu outing, and Asa saddled Patchwork and brought her from the livery stable. While he was leaving the stable, another figure was just arriving.

William Kennedy tossed the reins of a well-winded mount to the stable hand, indicating that he would be gone for about an hour. When he returned, he would require a fresh horse. He walked briskly to the Carver townhouse and announced himself to the maid, asking in fluent Spanish to see Jim Slade. When she informed him that Señor Slade was not there, he calculated a moment, then requested to see the lady of the house.

Tomasina was able to walk about with care. When Jim had visited her room the previous afternoon she had pretended to be far more frail than she was. But he had checked on her progress with the physician and knew better. All her best cards had been played, and she was decidedly down on points in this game. If only she had some means of escape.

Providentially, William Kennedy was announced by the maid as Tomasina considered her plight. She dressed in an enticing gray silk peignoir and arranged her hair in artful dishabille before admitting him to her sickroom.

Smiling wanly up at him, she allowed him to kiss her fingertips in perfunctory politeness. His shrewd gray eyes were as unnerving as ever. "I have been gravely injured, Mr. Kennedy, and now find myself a prisoner in my own home. Our army has gone, leaving me to the uncertain mercies of the Texian rabble. I fear for my life if you cannot help me.'' There, just the right touch of drama with tears and softly clinging hands that would not release their grip on his wrist.

"Save your theatricals for your fiancé, Mrs. Carver. He's the one to be your savior, not me. I've simply come for the gold. Where is it?'' He pulled free of her grasp and skewered her with his icy eyes.

She felt a sudden rush of fury, but she suppressed it immediately, realizing that he must have some dispensation from the government to come here so openly and demand the gold. "The gold has been confiscated by the Texians, Mr. Kennedy.''

"I know that, Mrs. Carver," he countered, noting the murderous look that she had quickly covered. Dangerous bitch.

"If you know they have it, why ever are you asking me about it then?'' If he could walk off with the gold, he could easily take her with him, away from Texas and the threat of retribution here.

"I have it on excellent authority,"—he paused for an ironic laugh—"that it is still here in this house, held by your Mr. Slade . . . or aren't you privy to his secrets any longer? I would hate to think you overplayed your hand when General Woll was here and now have lost such a good source of information as James Slade.''

Tomasina realized he knew nothing of what had transpired since he had left San Antonio a month ago; she planned to keep it that way. However, her plans were thwarted by the untimely arrival of her ex-fiancé.

Slade stood in the doorway, eyes bloodshot and clothing rumpled, looking decidedly cross and dangerous. "It's me you have to deal with, Kennedy, not the *lady*.''

The scathing way he referred to Tomasina made her redden in mortification. Forgetting all her good intentions, she clawed up a pillow from the huge pile on her bed and threw it at him. Then deciding that was not lethal enough, she heaved a heavy leather-bound book, followed by a china plate and teacup from her breakfast tray. She accompanied the barrage with an outburst of furious Spanish profanity and some rather graphic threats of violence intended for his privy parts.

Understanding the language full well, the Englishman paled and looked at Slade, who ducked flying crockery and ignored her actions as he might the tantrum of a spoiled three-year-old. Looking instead at Kennedy, Slade said coldly, "I'll get your blood money, but there is a price for it." He turned and walked out of the room, with the Englishman quickly following.

"Just what do you mean, old chap, a price for it? I do trust you've been instructed by your president that the money in question is to be released to me." The clipped accent held an edge, whether fear or impatience, Slade could not discern.

However, he was in no mood to quibble with Kennedy. He held all the aces in this Texas-style card game. He ushered his guest into the study. "Now I am going to explain and you are going to listen. I'll tell you precisely what you have to do in order to get the money in question. Pay close attention—I have a filthy headache and I don't feel like repeating myself. There is a convent of the Little Sisters of Mary Magdalene just outside New Orleans..." He closed the study door.

After a few hours of sleep, followed by a rejuvenating hot bath and shave, Slade felt almost human again. He dressed and walked out of the house, intent on his mission. Two problems down, one more to go, and the day would end with significantly more promise than it had begun. He headed toward the boardinghouse, lost in his private thoughts, staging and restaging the upcoming scenario with Charlee.

Edith LeBeau paused in mid-twirl of her jaunty parasol. Dressed in a chic pink batiste day gown, she was out for an afternoon stroll when she caught sight of Slade's pantherish stride. He was wearing an elegantly tailored cream linen planter's suit and flat-crowned hat. He looked almost like a New Orleans Creole gentleman, she thought, but for his tigerish golden coloring and the faintly menacing way he moved. He was cutting across the street toward the other

side of the plaza. If she hurried, she could accidentally run
into him at the far corner.

"James, *cheri*, what a surprise! And dressed so different-
ly from when you left me this morning." She winked
wickedly and hooked her hand around his arm before he
could ungallantly pull away from her clutches.

He groaned inwardly, then reassessed: Make that three
problems down before I take on Charlee.

"Afternoon, Edith," he said with a smile, pushing the hat
back on his head. "Mind if we take a little detour through
the park over there?"

He steered them into a small oasis of whispering cypress
trees, interspersed with lacy figs and pomegranates. A
sparkling public fountain gurgled in the midst of the grassy
haven, inviting the passersby to stop for a cooling drink.
Several *Tejano* women filled large earthen jars from the top
of the font. A small boy sat with his feet dangling in the
bottom of the sunken limestone pool.

"What a romantic spot," she said, eyeing a wrought iron
bench to one side. They ambled toward it, then sat down.
She still held his arm possessively. "How long until you
return to your ranch?"

"I plan to leave in a few days at most. First I have some
personal matters to take care of here in town," he answered
while carefully removing her offending hand from his arm.
"This past week I've had a lot on my mind, but after
tomorrow, life should get simpler," he said, smiling
mysteriously but elaborating no further. "I've had the chance
to think about the rest of my life and how I want to spend
it." He had her undivided attention now, if he hadn't had it
before! "I concluded this morning that I don't want to wake
up in any more strange beds after drinking myself to sleep
like I did last night."

"*Cheri*, if you mean you want a woman in your bed at
Bluebonnet, I would consider the offer."

She got no further before he shook his golden head, his
lips twisted in a wry smile. "Sorry, Edith, I guess I'm
giving you the wrong impression. The reason I asked you to
sit with me was so I could tell you I won't be seeing you

anymore, on Soledad Street or anywhere else. I'm going to marry Charlee McAllister and go straight.''

"But . . . but you were engaged to Tomasina Carver," she sputtered.

"Not anymore," he answered with a grin.

"You are staying in her house, sleeping under the same roof with her," she accused with rising temper now.

"Not anymore," he replied once again, this time with the grin widened to devilish proportions. "I wish I could have enjoyed our nights together more, but the timing wasn't right. Sorry, *Cheri*."

Earlier, while Slade had been sleeping, Charlee had been picnicking. The warm afternoon in the country was exactly what she needed, not, as she assured Weevils, any of the pigweed tonic that he had brought along to perk up her flagging spirits. They had gorged on fried chicken and cornbread, cheese, apples and grapes, all accompanied by liberal amounts of cool wine. The site was picturesque, an old mission now fallen in ruins; San Juan Capistrano was filled with grandeur even in decay.

She laughed and told them about her childhood, while Weevils and Asa kept up a bantering dialogue about home remedies. They were still at it on the return ride into San Antonio.

"Onliest way ta beat a cold is a tallow coat," the fat man averred. "Yew take yew a length o' flannel 'n cut it ta fit yore chest. Then soak it real good in beef tallow, turpentine, 'n garlic oil. Wrap it 'round yore chest 'n wear it fer th' winter. Don't niver take it off till spring. Keeps colds away fer shore."

Asa shuddered. "Yup. Colds 'n everthin' alive in a twenty-mile radius!"

Charlee laughed. "Remember the one about the chihuahua dog?" She looked over at Asa. "Seems you can take a Mexican hairless and put him at the foot of your bed each night. Whatever illness you have is transmitted to the dog in a week—anything from asthma to snakebite."

Knowing he was being teased, Weevils couldn't resist putting in half earnestly, "But yew got ta be careful if'n ya like th' dog, cause if yore ailment's real serious, it'll kill th' pore critter. 'Course, yew git cured.''

"Or, as Sadie told him, 'ya git fleas,' " Asa added, with a chuckle.

Charlee wiped a tear of laughter from her eye and thumped Weevils across his rounded shoulders affectionately. "What a wonderful day I've had! I can't remember when I laughed this much, and I promise on my honor, Weevils, if I start failing, I will drink your pigweed tonic. It's the least a body could do," she said with a wink at Asa.

Just then they rounded the corner on Commerce Street and passed one of the numerous small parks that added such verdant beauty to the city, courtesy of the underground springs that fed the San Antonio River. Charlee was sitting back on Patchwork, pushing a stray lock of hair from her forehead when she saw Jim and the beautiful brunette.

A full moment earlier, Edith had seen Charlee McAllister slowly riding her paint horse across the square. Slade stood up, with his back turned to Commerce Street, and bid Edith farewell. Off to the boardinghouse and his true love, was he? Not if Edith could throw a wrench into the works. Here was his skinny little *amour* coming to meet him, albeit quite unintentionally. Edith knew what to do.

In a flash she caught up to Slade and said with a sobbing catch in her voice, "Forgive me, *Cheri*. I know I will never see you again, but I want a good-bye favor. Is that too much to ask?" As she reached one hand toward his chest, she swung her parasol up, over her shoulder, effectively blocking his view of the street as she drew him into her embrace.

With a sardonic grin, he obliged her, thinking to himself that he was already such a subject of public scandal that one more provocation could scarcely matter. Anyway, if it got rid of her, he was well served by it. Trying in some subconscious way to soothe her vanity, he gave the kiss his full attention. That was his first mistake.

Feeling his response, she lowered the parasol just as Charlee and her friends rode past. Then she tightened both arms around him.

At first Charlee sat rooted to her saddle. Her two companions had not seen the torrid act being played out in the

park and were still laughing, until Asa caught sight of her
stricken face. He followed the path of her glazed green
eyes.

"Son of a bitch," he breathed.

"He sure is and then some!" she hissed. With that she
jumped from her little filly before Asa could stop her.
Landing on her feet, she hiked up her skirts and flew toward
the embracing pair.

"Not bad enough you let her get away with murder, now
you flaunt her right out in public, in front of the whole
city," she shrieked, grabbing a handful of Edith's black hair
and ripping it free of its pins. When Edith spun around with
sparks flying from her dark eyes, Charlee let her hand drop
and croaked in astonishment, "You're . . . you're not Tomasina
Carver! But from the back, you looked like her . . . your
hair . . ." She subsided into stunned silence, which Slade
quickly filled.

"If you'd taken a second to check the lady's wardrobe,
you might have noticed the cut of the clothing isn't exactly
Sina's style," he said sarcastically, turning his back on the
scorned Frenchwoman to face Charlee. That was his second
mistake.

"And just what is wrong with the cut of my clothes,
cheri? Or do you prefer me without any?" With a startlingly
imaginative French oath, she raised her parasol and jammed
it into his ribs, then stalked off with what dignity a destroyed
coiffure and bent umbrella would permit.

While Slade labored to get his breath, he considered
lunging after Edith and throttling her, but quickly dismissed
the idea and the woman as unworthy of further consideration. Instead he grabbed the seething girl standing by his
side and walked them both toward a secluded copse of
cottonwoods on the other side of the park. They were
attracting far too much attention out in the open. To get to
the refuge of the trees, he had to drag Charlee past the
fountain. That was his third mistake.

She moved unresistingly along with him for several paces.
"You've been a really busy boy, haven't you, *Don* Diego.
Tell me, does your fine ladylove know about her lookalike
from Soledad Street?"

When she prodded him in his aching ribs, he swore beneath his breath and gave her arm another yank. That was his last mistake.

She pulled back and then lurched forward, catapulting his much taller and heavier body over the low stone enclosure into the shallow water of the pool. He landed with a sickening *splat* as his backside connected ingloriously with the foot-deep water. It barely broke the impact of flesh and bone meeting limestone.

The spouting fountain bounced its spray down on his head, refashioning the wide hat brim with cold rivulets of water. He was soaked to the skin. He looked balefully through the waterfall at the smirking girl, who stood by the water's edge, elbows akimbo, one slim foot perched saucily on the stone rim. That was *her* first mistake.

Ignoring the screaming pain in his lower regions, Slade sat up and lunged forward in one continuous motion. A long arm connected forcefully with her ankle, hauling her off balance. She let out an oath and struggled to regain her footing by reaching for the rim of the pool with one hand. Once her wrist was in his range, he let go of her ankle and grabbed it, pulling her headforward into the water alongside him.

She cursed and thrashed as he subdued her. "Damn you, calm down before you drown us both in a foot of water! Do you realize you just ruined my best suit of clothes, woman? One I wore especially to propose to you in?"

She pulled one great mass of water-darkened bronze hair from her mouth and sputtered, "You have damn peculiar ways of coming courting! Or do you always make a detour through a public park to ravish a whore on your way to propose to a woman?"

He gritted his teeth. "I only encountered Edith by accident, and I told her I'd never see her again." A thought flittered across his mind—Charlee seemed to know Edith was the whore he'd been seeing on Soledad Street.

Before he could think that through, she snapped back, "Some farewell! But then you do have your original whore waiting for you in her town house. You must really like the Latin type, all that black hair and big tits. I'm surprised you ever had the faintest inclination to seduce me!'' With that parting sally, she wrenched free of his grasp and struggled to regain her footing, slipping and splashing furiously in the pool.

The two men on horseback had sat frozen in horror and incredulity during the entire exchange in the park. Asa was the first to emerge from slack-jawed shock and leap down to run the short distance to the fountain. He attempted to extricate the flailing, swearing girl from Slade's entangling limbs. Charlee was in such a rage that her small, slippery body was exceedingly difficult to grasp. After two tries, during which process he thoroughly drenched himself, the older man finally succeeded in helping her to stand up and step over the rim. It was miraculous there was any water left in the fountain.

Charlee looked for all the world like a half-drowned kitten, with green eyes spitting fire and great sodden masses of bronze hair spilling in a waterfall down her shoulders. The once crisp mustard silk shirt and brown linen skirt clung to her in wrinkled lumps. A small cluster of wild daisies she had fastened in her hair now trailed down her back, scattered through the tangled tresses like yellow confetti. While Asa helped her to keep her balance, she wrung most of the water from her seemingly thousand-pound skirts.

Slade, in the meantime, began to unfold himself from the cold limestone floor of the fountain, being very careful not to make any more precipitous moves. ''Half the bones in my body must be shattered,'' he complained, gingerly edging toward the rim of the basin.

''I'm sure you'll live,'' Charlee snarled, ''much to my sorrow and the joy of all the loose women in Texas!'' With that parting remark she whirled to stomp back toward Patchwork, only to have her skirts nearly knock her down once more as the force of their water-laden weight sent them flying in the opposite direction from her legs. Asa steadied her as she limped off with the shreds of her dignity trailing behind her in a series of puddles and flower petals.

Slade watched her, too bone-weary to be angry any longer, but too cold and sore to see any humor in the

situation. When he stood up and stepped onto the dry
pavement, his boots let out a loud, whistling *squish* as the
imprisoned water inside oozed between his toes. A muffled
giggle echoed from across the fountain. He looked straight
into the wide brown eyes of the small *Tejano* boy who had
sat solemnly still through the entire fiasco. Jim glared
fiercely for a moment. Then seeing the mirth struggling to
escape from the child's artfully immobile face, he let out a
long sigh and grinned at the lad, who returned the smile.

"*Buena suarte con su novia, señor,*" he called after Slade
as the hapless man squished up the street.

"*Gracias, niño.* I'll need all the luck I can get with her,
that's for sure," he replied grimly.

chapter
20

Charlee dismounted behind the boardinghouse, where she
was greeted by the returning Hellfire, who had mysteriously
vanished on one of his private expeditions that morning and
so had missed the picnic. Although his mistress had saved
him some meaty chicken bones and hunks of cheese, she
was in no mood to lavish the bounty on him in her present
infuriated state of mind.

He sniffed her sodden clothes and detoured around her
wet person with obvious distaste. "Just another one-way
male, off philandering like your friend. See if I feed you,
you moldy bag of orange fur," she snapped. With that, she
fled into the kitchen, while a subdued Weevils lugged the
picnic gear back into the house and Asa took the horses to
the livery stable for a rubdown.

Charlee spent the next several days awash in new humiliation. Word of her disastrous fiasco had not spread through
the Anglo community, only because the encounter had taken

place in a *Tejano* section of town; but even if the likes of Suzannah Wilcox or Paul Bainbridge didn't know of her degradation, Charlee knew. To have leaped on that harlot like some common woman of the streets herself—what would Deborah say! And then to get into a wrestling match with Slade in a public fountain. Her litany of woes was too long to admit hope of deliverance.

Only one thing heartened her in her lonely misery; her courses had come last week. At least Slade had not planted his seed in her. Charlee shuddered to think what such an unwanted pregnancy would have meant—leaving San Antonio and her boardinghouse. She was a respectable woman of property in this city, and she planned to stay here among her friends. No man, least of all a ruthless, womanizing bastard like James August Slade, was going to disrupt her life henceforth. Charlee made a solemn vow never to become a prisoner of her body or be tied to a man by his child as Deborah had been.

Tragic, brave Deborah, her friend and mentor. Thoughts about how she was faring at Rafe's ranch frequently crossed Charlee's mind in the following days. She hoped for a letter but realized the post was so uncertain she could not reasonably expect to hear for weeks, even if Deborah had the opportunity to write. If only Rafe Fleming loved her enough to make her happy as she deserved. Considering her present feelings toward the deceitful male of the species, Charlee had scant hope for her friend's well-being.

For several weeks she worked hard at the boardinghouse and immersed herself in a routine that allowed little time for social life. Since her one disastrous foray to a church service the past summer, she had avoided the Sunday morning prayer meetings held whenever Reverend McGuire or Preacher Morrill made a swing through San Antonio. However, Miss Clemson, who always attended the raucous spiritual entertainments, came home the second Sunday after Charlee's dunking debacle with Slade, bursting with the latest gossip.

"Tomasina Carver has simply up and vanished," the prim, plump old lady had said, her rheumy eyes alight. She had followed Charlee back into the kitchen before the midday meal, catching her in the midst of slicing a glazed ham. Swiping a sliver and quickly popping it into her mouth, she avidly licked her lips.

Charlee was not sure whether her guest relished the superb smoked meat or her succulent gossip more. But she was positive she did not want to hear about Jim Slade or his ladylove.

"I tell you, it's all over town. Jim Slade's gone back to his ranch, her house is all sealed up, and the servants were dismissed with a month's pay. Mrs. Wilcox told me one of the maids told her that her mistress ran off with some English nobleman or prince or something!"

"How sad for Mr. Slade, after he so nobly nursed her back to health," Charlee said without apparent interest, continuing to slice the juicy pink meat in neat, even slabs.

Miss Clemson sniffed. "Well, if you ask me he got exactly what he deserved after staying in the same house with her, unchaperoned and all. You're well rid of that wild young ruffian, mark my words, Miss McAllister."

Charlee almost cut her finger, then put the knife down in agitation. "I never had him to be rid of him, well or otherwise, Miss Clemson. I was merely his cook for a while." She turned and began to carry the tray to the dining room.

The rotund little spinster kept on her heels like a panting dachshund hot on the scent of a fresh bone. "Of course, my dear, I didn't mean to imply anything, but he has come here, and I did once hear him ask you to marry him . . . that is,"—she reddened at her gaffe—"Mr. Schwartz and I could hardly escape hearing your heated words right in that hall. I only assumed that you were upset over his shameful relationship with Mrs. Carver. After all, you never accept gentlemen callers anymore." She paused reflectively and then blurted out, "Say, you aren't secretly married like Mrs. Ken—Fleming was, are you?"

Charlee almost knocked a glass over as she placed the large platter in the center of the table. Sighing, she straightened up and said, "No, Miss Clemson, I assure you I have never been married. Nor do I ever intend to be," she added darkly under her breath.

So, his ladylove had flown the coop, she thought to herself

later that afternoon. She was alone in the ice cellar, storing some perishable foods from dinner, and had plenty of time to consider what Tomasina's disappearance meant. Prince or nobleman, indeed! Slade probably hired some trustworthy *Tejanos* to spirit her safely out of Texas before she was accused of murder and treason. He had protected her and kept her from facing her just punishment, even though doing so meant he must lose Tomasina forever.

"Well, let him pine for her or find a dozen replacements like that LeBeau hussy. I won't sit here and mold any longer!" Her voice echoed strongly in the high-ceilinged underground vault. The resolution in her own words surprised her. Charlee knew she must emerge from her shell and get on with her life. Miss Clemson's absurd speculation about her having a husband hidden in some closet had hit home. Why was she letting a foolish, hopelessly incompatible love ruin her life? Men had flocked to court her when she first came to Deborah's place. Why not again?

Not that she necessarily wanted the legal encumbrance of a husband. "If I ever do marry, it will be a man I choose, on my terms," she pronounced in finality.

"Tomorrow's the feast of San Juan of Capistrano. You going to San Antonio for the celebration?" Lee looked over at Slade as he unsaddled Liso. The feast was one of the city's biggest and most gala occasions, with a religious procession, the celebration of mass, dancing, and merry-making far into the night.

Slade, who had just walked down to the corral to look in on the new mares, had greeted Lee's return with little more enthusiasm than he'd shown for anyone since Charlee had returned to the boardinghouse. He grunted noncommittally in reply to the question. The day after the infamous encounter at the fountain, he had returned to the ranch, chastened and noncommunicative. He arose daily before sunrise and worked grueling hours in the saddle, giving himself and the men no respite.

Jim had always had a short fuse, but no one crossed the boss these days without treading a tightrope between life and death. Slade was continually preoccupied, and Lee

knew the reason was Charlee McAllister. But he also knew
better than to bring up her name in Jim's presence. Since
Tomasina Carver was gone, it had seemed natural that Slade
would go to Charlee and straighten things out. Yet when
Asa had brought up the subject, he was given a cold, steely
look that forbade any further pursuit of the topic. "I'll
handle it," was the glacial reply. Everyone walked on
eggshells and waited to see precisely how Jim planned to
"handle it."

Seeing the foreman had no luck in his absence, Lee took
matters into his hands and openly broached the subject of
the feast. Was Jim going to town to see Charlee? By asking,
he was risking the full fury of the Slade temper.

The chaotic revelry of the festival seemed a natural time
for the lovers to be thrown together, but only if Lee could
get his hardheaded boss to attend. On the long ride back to
Bluebonnet with the brood mares, he had worked out his
plan. Placing life and limb at risk, he remarked casually, "I
stopped in town on my way home to see how the prepara-
tions are going. Big fandango at the Johnson place."

"Lots of dances all over town on the feast of San Juan,"
Slade said, swinging his heavy stock saddle over the stall
bar and reaching for a currycomb to work on Polvo.

"Yeah, but Billy Wilcox's taking Charlee to the Johnsons'
place." Saying no more and avoiding the murderous glare of
Slade's cougar eyes, Lee walked out of the stable whistling.
Now let it work, he thought to himself.

Slade had found the waiting exceedingly difficult. But he
knew he must give Charlee time to cool down. Who knew,
he might even get lucky and find out she was pregnant.
Then the whole thing would be automatically settled. As a
respectable woman of property in San Antonio, she couldn't
slink off with her cat and vanish in the night, as she had
tried to do earlier. He had stayed close to the ranch, working
himself hard, falling into a good tired sleep each night,
trying to think as little as possible about the petite witch in
town who had turned his life upside down.

Perhaps it was time to take action. He had expected her to
pout and brood, lick her wounds, and eventually realize she
couldn't live without him. But from all reports, the per-

verse, fickle little creature was living it up, accepting a veritable horde of admiring bachelors as callers, green boys not dry behind the ears. She was fast becoming the belle of San Antonio once more. As if any of those slick-eared youths could handle a woman like Charlee McAllister. Still, perhaps that was what she wanted—some mewling young milksop she could lead around like a gelded horse.

Slade grinned wickedly and said to Polvo, "We'll just see about that, won't we, old boy."

Charlee eyed herself critically in the big mirror in Deborah's— no, *her* room, she corrected. "Oh, I do wish she were here," she wailed aloud, pulling on the waist, then the neckline of her new gown. It had just arrived from the dressmaker early this morning. She had only an hour or so to get ready for the big dance.

The dress was a vibrant deep bronze that highlighted her unusual changeable hair color and flattered her golden, tanned complexion. Yes, the color was right. Her cheeks glowed and her green cat's eyes were sparkling. But the cut was scandalous! Her dainty curves had never been so blatantly on display. Well, almost never, she amended to herself with a flush, running her hands down the sleek lines of the skirt. She had chosen satin for the gown. It was rich, lustrous, and very clinging, hugging her high, pert breasts, molding beneath them to accent her tiny waist, and then gently flaring to the tips of her matching high-heeled slippers. The sleeves were long and tapered at the wrists, emphasizing her fine bones and delicate hands. However, it was the shockingly low-cut neckline, dripping with delicate cream lace that was causing her to have second thoughts. The lace brushed the tips of her breasts, emphasizing the décolletage.

"Now if I was built like Tomasina Carver or Edith LeBeau, I'd be barking up the right tree...but I'm too little." She placed her fingers gingerly around her small upthrust breasts and measured.

Just then Lena came into the room. "*Dios*! What a picture you make," the maid said in awe, recalling the shy, awkward girl back at the ranch who had to work up her

courage just to put on a simple peasant's dress. Was that
only a few months ago? "You are perfect!"

"No," Charlee said petulantly. "I'm too flat-chested to
wear this. Try to sew some of the lace over the cleft here."

Lena laughed. "If you have a cleft there—and you
do—you have no reason to cover it up. A woman does not
have to be a great cow with bulging udders to look good in a
low-cut dress," she finished, inspecting the fit of the gown
with a critically appraising eye.

"But . . ."

"No buts," Lena remonstrated, playfully slapping her
hands away from the neckline. "You will be the most
beautiful woman in San Antonio. Now, let me help you
place the mantilla and combs properly."

As she artfully set two beautiful ivory combs in the piled
burnished masses of Charlee's hair, she chattered on. "Oh,
I saw Lupe in the market yesterday. She had just spent two
days at Bluebonnet cleaning for Don Diego." Feeling Charlee
stiffen, she hesitated a moment, then picked up the length of
matching cream lace that would go over Charlee's hair, and
began to attach it to the combs. "It seems," she paused for
effect, "*everyone* from the rancho will be in town today."

"I'll be glad to see Asa and Weevils. It's been weeks.
Lee just came back from some errand in Galveston yesterday," Charlee said, purposely omitting the one name they
were both thinking about.

"I am so glad you asked me to work for you, Señorita
Charlee," Lena burst out impulsively. "But I do so wish
you and the *patrón* would marry and stop all this foolishness. That *bruja* is gone now, and there is no reason—"

"There are lots of reasons, but I don't want to talk about
them, please, Lena." Charlee's tone was gentle but final.

Sighing, Lena stood back and admired her handiwork.
Well, if the *patrón* came to town and saw the little one
looking like this, how could he resist her?

All his friends had called Willis Elijah Wilcox Billy since
he was a boy. Now at twenty-one, he felt himself a man
grown and wished he could undo the nickname, but it stuck.
The only one who called him Willis was his mother, Hannah.

Thinking of her, he winced. She was furious that he had been courting Charlee McAllister.

Well, he just didn't care, that was all, he averred to himself. It was high time he asserted his independence from Mama and Suzannah. Taking a deep breath, he swallowed hard, and his Adam's apple scraped on his stiff shirt collar. Nervously he looked around the neat, cheerful parlor with its soft blue curtains and stout overstuffed chairs. Several tallow candles were lit, although the sun had not yet set. Walking over to the mirror, he slicked down his thatch of unruly russet hair for the hundredth time. A generous if rather weak mouth, wide-set blue eyes, and a prominent straight nose greeted his inspection. Yes, he was certainly presentable looking. His stocky frame was muscular and well proportioned. Then why was he so nervous every time he escorted Charlee anywhere?

It must be love! His absentminded mooning was interrupted when a low feminine voice called to him from the parlor door.

"I'm ready, Billy."

He turned and stood frozen in admiration, wide-eyed and enthralled, then let out a rush of breath and said hoarsely, "If you don't beat all. Charlee, you're so beautiful I can scarce believe my luck!"

She smiled as his bulging eyes raked her slim bronze figure, lingering on her cleavage. Then with a reddened blush, he met her eyes. When she offered her small hand, he kissed it gallantly and put it around his arm. They were off to the Johnsons' fandango.

Ernst and Sally Lou Johnson were relative newcomers to San Antonio. He was the owner of the second-largest mercantile in town and had just moved his family from Galveston to the dryer inland climate of San Antonio, where he was giving Simon Bainbridge sharp competition indeed. The Johnsons had built a large frame house with two stories, decorating it as if they were still residing in Georgia, from where Ernst had moved twenty years earlier. The grand ballroom would have done justice to many in Savannah, high-ceilinged and spacious with a polished plank floor and gleaming glass-paned windows.

If the decor was graciously southern, the entertainment was pure Texian raucous, loud and hearty. Out in the backyard a whole steer was turning on a spit, roasting to golden brown succulence, while the ever-favored pork was present as well, covered in a bed of the sizzling coals, steaming to mouth-watering tenderness. The pungent smells of chili pies and the sweet fragrance of crispy cornbread were added to the tantalizing aroma of the meat. Whiskey, sweet wines, and home-brewed beer flowed freely, while a brace of fiddlers warmed up their instruments with a fast reel.

Men and women dressed in their best finery danced, laughed, ate, and drank. Women with elaborate feathers in their hair and tightly cinched gowns sweated during the fast reels and waltzes, while men surreptitiously loosened stocks and shirt collars to breathe more freely between sets.

From the moment Charlee arrived on Billy's arm, she had been besieged with requests to dance. Men brought her refreshments, escorted her to the yard for fresh air, sought anything she desired. Several older men, one a bachelor from Goliad, the other a local widower, indicated an interest in seeing her again, but she decided the youthful adoration of inexperienced boys such as Billy was the safest choice. She would pick and choose her callers strictly for fun now. Time enough later—if ever—to think seriously about settling down. Then maybe a rich older man, but one who'd be indulgent . . .

"Deep thoughts to wrinkle a pretty brow, Cat Eyes." The rough gravel voice glided across the night air like a caress. Slade had been watching her reverie from behind a brace of poplars near the side veranda. When her current adoring young pup had left her side to fetch something for her, he quickly climbed up the stairs.

Caught in her rather mercenary fantasy, Charlee flushed and stared into Slade's glowing eyes. Lord, he looked splendid, the hard, chiseled planes and angles of his face lit in the torchlight from the yard. His firm, sensuous lips widened in a blinding white slash of a smile. He was dressed for the *Tejano* fiesta in the traditional Hispanic horseman's fanciest garb, tight black pants with flared legs and a short fitted bolero jacket that emphasized his broad shoulders and slim hips. The whole striking ensemble was trimmed with silver conchos and accented by the snowy white lawn shirt, opened to reveal a narrow expanse of golden chest hair. She had never seen him in black before. It made him seem exotic and foreign, hypnotically dangerous.

Charlee instinctively took a step back and said, "What are you doing here?" As she asked the question, she felt the heat of his eyes on her body, even noted the faint intake of breath as he took in her satiny curves at close range. A small, queer thrill began to tingle in widening ripples from somewhere deep inside her, radiating out to her fingertips.

"I came to celebrate the feast day, same as everyone else in San Antonio," he said, reaching out one warm, callused hand and cupping it possessively around her shoulder, turning her to face him. "You've danced with every man and boy here tonight. Dance with me. Please?" He waited a moment while she struggled to catch her breath. "Or are you afraid to be in my arms, Charlee, afraid of yourself."

The taunt was soft, caressing, but nonetheless, it steeled her nerves. "I scarcely need fear you, Jim Slade. Come, you'll have your dance." She turned briskly, freeing her shoulder from the warm pressure of his hand, but he quickly caught up to her and slipped her arm through his, leading her to the large, crowded ballroom.

Just as they entered, the raucous stomp that had been playing ended and a slow, sentimental balled wafted out on the warm night air. He held her much too closely, she knew, but she was powerless to stop him. They moved in perfect rhythm, their bodies seeming to melt into one another.

"People are staring," she breathed against his neck, trying halfheartedly to pull away.

"After our little bath in the fountain, I think we're souls of decorum now," he whispered, relishing his hold on her. She smelled like wild honey and sweet clover. "You look like a beautiful Castilian lady in that mantilla."

She stiffened in his arms. "But we both know I'm just

plain Charlee McAllister from Missouri, not Spanish, certainly not pedigreed.''

"Don't sell yourself short, Chastity Charlene. Quite a mouthful, that name, not plain at all.''

"You read Richard Lee's diary!"

"Lee brought it to me. It was evidence,'' he replied evenly. Noting the sharpness in her voice, he maneuvered them to the door and whisked her out onto the veranda, near the place where he had first accosted her.

At once she turned on him with green eyes spitting. "Yes, evidence, all right. Evidence Tomasina was guilty of murder. What did you do, burn the diary, then help her escape justice?''

Looking around at the people standing on the porch and leaning against the railing, he said in a gravelly whisper, "This isn't the time or place for me to explain about Sina.'' Guiding her away from the curious ears of the revelers, he tried to lead her down the back porch steps into a darkened portion of the yard.

But Charlee was having none of it. She stopped mulishly at the top of the steps and faced him. "There will never be a good time or place, will there, because nothing you could possibly say to me could make up for my brother's death going unpunished. I'm not a blueblooded criolla and I don't want to be. You're looking for red raspberries in the chokecherry patch, *Don* Diego.'' Looking him up and down and taking in his elegantly tailored Mexican clothes, she said, "Go back to your *Tejanos* and leave me alone.''

He caught one slim wrist as she turned to flee, pulling her into his embrace. He was standing on the first step but she was still on the porch floor, causing her to look eye to eye with him. She saw the burning, compelling hunger of the male predator written all across his features.

"No . . . no, I won't—''

Her protest was muffled by his mouth, hot and insistent, slashing across hers, brushing, bruising, opening her lips and probing with his tongue. He pressed her full length to his body, holding her small heart-shaped face with one hand clamped behind her slender neck, stilling her struggles.

She pulled at his thick golden sideburns and writhed to

get free for a moment. Then abandoning the efforts as futile, she dug her long nails into his thick hair and pressed her body tightly to his in surrender.

He could sense her quivering assent even before she gave it, but when her sweet little tongue darted into his mouth and those delicate little hip bones rocked against his belly, he was blinded by passion, lost, as he reached down to scoop her into his arms and carry her home to Bluebonnet.

"What the devil do you think you're doing, Slade!" Billy Wilcox's thin voice broke on the tall man's name, but he took a steadying breath and let his indignation build to give him courage. "Unhand this young lady. She's under my protection tonight."

Jim was pulled from the sweet promise of Charlee's yielding body to confront her quivering escort. He shook his head to clear his drugged senses as the piping voice of the Wilcox boy persisted.

Charlee struggled free, mortified, as she realized how her passionate abandon must have looked to the group that was gathering around Billy.

"It seems to me I'm always being pestered by the *boys* you have hanging on your skirts, Charlee." He released his grip on her, but stepped in front of her to challenge Wilcox. "You don't want to get hurt, Billy. Ask the little lady what happened to Paul Bainbridge a couple of months back. And he's a lot bigger than you."

Wilcox's face turned from florid red to chalk-white in the time it took Slade to step up on the porch and make his terse statement.

Before Billy could gather his scattered wits to reply, Charlee took matters into her own hands. Slipping from behind Jim, she reached for Billy's arm and began to turn him toward the door to the ballroom. "Mr. Wilcox is quite right to defend me, Mr. Slade. After all, I did arrive with him, and a lady should always leave a party with the gentleman who escorted her there." With that sally she led the befuddled Billy into the house.

"If that's the way you want to play it, you little witch, so be it," he called after her. Shrugging nonchalantly, he turned to amble down the stairs and vanish into the darkness.

It took only a few minutes to ride to the boardinghouse,
despite the revelers still abroad. He walked Polvo quietly to
the backyard and dropped his reins. Then Slade looked
carefully around. The kitchen was dark. Good. Noiselessly
he entered and let his eyes become accustomed to the dark.
Sadie was asleep, along with the elderly boarders. The rest
were out at various festivities in town—at least he hoped so
as he climbed the stairs at the end of the long hall. Charlee
was using the big bedroom Deborah had occupied. Knowing
that, he opened the first door at the top of the stairs and
stepped inside.

A pair of bright green eyes narrowed to lazy slits,
glowing through the darkness. The cat was reclined in the
center of the bed, eyeing Slade with the disdainful curiosity
felines reserve for their humans when the latter make feeble
attempts to be amusing.

"Hellfire, old boy, how'd you like to take a ride back to
Bluebonnet and visit your favorite mole hole?"

chapter
21

"I don't like it, Sadie, not one bit. He's been gone
for two whole days." Charlee sat on a kitchen stool,
scrubbing sweet potatoes, her face screwed in concentration
and worry.

"Dat critter be back when he got his catterwallin' done,"
the black woman replied with a snort of dismissal.

"But he's never taken off for more than one night. I'm
afraid something's happened to him, damn his worthless old
tomcat hide!" She threw the brush down and tossed the last
fat golden potato into a pan. "Here, rub these with butter
and I'll stick them in the oven when I come back." She

shoved the pot toward her helper and then paused. "Hellfire loved butter so . . . oh, drat!"

"Doan go takin' on lak he daid. Mark me, dat debbil cat smart. He be back." She nodded her head in finality.

Charlee felt little reassured, but she nodded and walked outside. She had felt so restless, confused, and unhappy since that terrible night at the dance. "Every time I set out to have fun he comes along and ruins it," she said aloud to the empty back porch.

Of course, that was not strictly true. Even without Jim Slade's arrogant interference, she would not have enjoyed the dance. Slobbering pawing by clumsy boys like Billy was becoming increasingly repellent to her, as was their banal conversation and puppylike adoration.

She was bored, bored, bored, not even considering the aching sexual frustration buried deep inside her awakened woman's body. She cried for satisfaction, a satisfaction and completion that would bind her irrevocably to the one man she feared most, who could crush her spirit and destroy her very soul.

Forcing herself from such dark ruminations, she considered her options. "Face it, there's no man you've met here in town who you'd even consider spending time with, much less marrying." However, she concluded with forced joviality that even without a man in her life, she could live damn well and provide for herself. She had her health, her brains, her business—*and her body*, a traitorous voice from deep within added spitefully.

She kicked petulantly at the solid wooden porch post and was rewarded with an aching toe; then she decided to head down toward the garden beyond the shed. Maybe there would be some beans ready to pick for the table tonight.

Lee caught sight of her solitary figure wending its lonely way to the vegetable patches as he pulled Liso up to the kitchen porch. Nervously he dismounted and rehearsed his speech for the hundredth time as he ran to catch up with her.

"Wait up, Charlee!" He watched her turn as that instant, winsome smile wreathed her lovely face. This had better work!

"Lee! You're early for supper but very welcome to stay. I

missed you at the fandango the other night. Do you have a
novia hidden somewhere you're not telling us about?'' she
teased.

Despite his swarthy complexion, he blushed but denied it.
That was the last thing on his mind at the moment. ''I only
came to tell you some important news, not to eat supper.
That dratted cat of yours has gone crazy, Charlee.''

''Hellfire's at Bluebonnet?'' She was incredulous at his
nod of agreement. ''But that's two hours' ride on a good
horse. How did that scamp get so far afield, and why?''

''I don't know, but he's raising hell all over the place. He
got into a fresh catch of fish and really chewed them up
yesterday afternoon, and last night he tangled with Mutt
again. Near clawed the poor old dog's right eye out.
Weevils is threatening to brain him with a skillet, and Asa's
threatening to shoot him. As if that wasn't bad enough, this
morning way before sunrise he set to caterwauling right in
the middle of the hall and woke the boss out of a sound
sleep. Jim hasn't been sleeping too well since the two of
you split up, Charlee. He was kind of cross.''

She smirked. ''I'll just bet he was! He ought to import
another lady of the evening to help him relax at night. Then
he'd sleep well enough,'' she added saucily. ''But why on
earth couldn't you just bring Hellfire back home to me?''

He shrugged. ''Like I said, he's acting crazy. No one can
get near him, not Weevils or Asa, not even Jim or me.
You'll just have to try your luck yourself.''

''Oh, get Patchwork from the stable for me, will you
please, while I change into a riding skirt. I'll bring that
rascal home tonight!'' She tripped off jauntily to the house
and Lee headed to get her filly.

They rode to Bluebonnet at a leisurely pace, enjoying the
warm, clear afternoon air. The closer they came to the ranch
house, the more nervous and restive Charlee felt. She could
sense her young friend's questioning eyes on her as they
rode.

Finally, he said, ''Something bothering you, *chica*?'' He
knew what her problem was even before he asked.

She squirmed on Patchwork's back for a moment and
then sighed in resignation. ''All right, I hate to confess

cowardice, but will Slade be at the house when we get there? I really don't want to have another run-in with him.''

Lee said guilelessly, "He's off to Houston City to talk to the president. Be gone a week."

"I thought President Houston was with the assembly in Washington-on-the-Brazos," she replied questioningly.

"Er... he must have been called home for some emergency or other, I guess," the youth improvised.

"Well, if you say so..."

When they rode up to the big house, Charlee scanned the yard and corral area nervously, looking for signs of Slade more than for signs of Hellfire. "Let me call him. Do you think he'd be around the kitchen or down by the barns?"

"Oh, he might as well be in the house. It's been warm the last few days, and Weevils has had the kitchen door open. He comes in all the time," Lee replied.

As soon as she jumped down from Patchwork, he took the reins, saying, "I'll just take her down to the watering trough for a little drink."

When Charlee entered the front door, that same old feeling hit her once more, part nostalgia for the bittersweet homecoming, part apprehension, for the essence of Jim Slade seemed to permeate the very air around her.

"Weevils?" She headed toward the kitchen, hearing no one stir. Of course, if Slade was gone, the cook might not be preparing a full dinner just for Asa and Lee. "Hellfire? Where are you, boy?"

Just then she caught sight of an orange blur heading lickety split up the hall stairs. "You devil! Sadie's right. Come back here." She picked up her skirt and dashed upstairs after the bobbing tail that whisked around the corner into Slade's bedroom.

Warily she slowed down, then got a grip on her faltering courage and took the last several steps into the room. The sight that greeted her caused Charlee to gasp in indignation.

Slade was negligently stretched across the bed with the cat sitting attentively alongside him while he fed the feline several bits of what looked to be raw beef. "He's disgustingly predictable when it comes to food," Jim said with a disarming grin slashing across his face. "Ouch!" The grin turned to a scowl when the cat's sharp incisors connected with his thumb in quest of the last meat scrap, which he had neglected to release quickly enough. "He's also disgustingly greedy."

Charlee smirked for a second, then felt a surge of anger rush through her. "Exactly how did he get here in the first place? And why are you here instead of in Houston? Did Lee know about this whole charade?"

Jim swung his long legs off the bed and stared at Charlee with a hypnotic golden gaze. "One question at a time, my little Cactus Flower. I sort of catnapped Hellfire, I guess. As to Lee, well he knew I wasn't in Houston. He's rubbing down the horses."

A ripple of apprehension coursed through her now, fear replacing anger. "I am not sleeping the night beneath your roof, Jim Slade." Why wasn't her voice steadier, dammit!

He stood up and slowly walked toward her in sinuous pantherish strides. "Not only will you stay beneath my roof, sweetheart, you'll sleep beneath my body."

"Like hell I—" She was cut short in her angry retort.

Jim's arms grasped her slender waist, virtually lifting her into his devouring kiss. His mouth met hers with violence and hunger, forcing her head to drop back, holding her lips prisoner until they opened beneath his onslaught of passion. He groaned then and ravaged inside, probing her tender palate, gliding across her small white teeth, twisting around her tongue.

Charlee concentrated on remaining limp, hanging like a rag doll in his arms, but her senses swam. She was hot; she was dizzy; she wanted so desperately to kiss him back. Her tongue moved against his, and her lips returned the bruising pressure of his. There was nothing she could do to withhold her response as her arms clutched at his waist and her pelvis writhed against his hard belly and thighs.

Gradually he gentled the caress, loosening his crushing grip on her arms, delicately tracing his hands and fingertips up and down her arched back. His kiss, too, became softer, nibbling, experimental. Then he left her mouth and the warm, soft pressure of his lips trailed along her jawline, across the sensitive column of her throat, feeling the wild hammering of her blood as it pulsed through the arteries in her neck.

Her heart felt as if it would burst from its pounding triphammer beat. When one of his hands softly insinuated itself around her side and upward to cup and stroke her breast, she felt the electricity shoot from him to her like shimmering waves of summer lightning. He bent down then and began to pick her up, intent on carrying her back to the bed. The sudden movement gave her reeling senses a tiny respite and she struggled to wrest free of his embrace.

"No, let me go." It was more a breathless plea than the firm command she wished it to be.

Futilely she pressed her small hands against his chest, but he ignored her protests and swept her onto the bed. When he reached his hand up to unbutton her blouse, she slapped it away and tried to roll across to the other side. However, he was sitting on her full riding skirt. Slade reached over and shoved her onto her back once more, then leaned over her, his face looming inches above hers.

"Don't fight me, Charlee. Just let it happen. You can't hide your feelings from me." He lowered his head to claim another of those kisses that robbed her of reason.

She turned her face, trying to avoid his erotic onslaught. "Why are you doing this?"

"That should be pretty obvious, for both of us." He breathed against her temple as he kissed her eyelids, cheek, jawline, nuzzling along her neck and trying to unfasten the blouse once more. This time he had more success, despite her twisting and bucking beneath him. When one large, warm hand slid beneath her sheer camisole and slipped a taut-nippled breast free, she gasped and arched. His hot mouth quickly followed his teasing fingers, fastening eagerly on the delicate pink bud.

Before she could stop him, he had the blouse and camisole both worked down to her waist and was dividing his attention between her breasts. And oh, how they ached for his suckling kisses and soft caresses.

Like some mindless thing she felt herself slipping, giving way to erotic need. Desperation coursed though her body as he murmured soft love words in Spanish and English, all the while continuing to undress her ever so slowly. She was at the end of her resistance, moaning feverishly, when he slid her riding skirt off in one swift, smooth roll. Then he ran his hands down her sleek little legs and pulled off one boot, then the other, then peeled off her pantalets. He kissed his way back up her body, stopping at her inner thighs. She reached her hands down and tangled her fingers in his thick, tawny hair.

His eyes were blazing like golden comets when he raised at last from her quivering, breathless body. She locked eyes with him for a moment. Then as he began to unbutton his shirt and peel it off, her green gaze was compelled to dip downward, feasting on the hard, lean contours of his chest and arms. When he stood up and quickly stripped off his pants, she watched the play of corded muscles ripple beneath the golden-furred skin of his belly and legs. He was splendid to look upon, and as he returned her ardent stare, she realized he felt the same way about her.

Jim devoured the delicately sculpted little body lying before him, open to welcome him in a drugged haze of passion. It would work; it would be all right. Quickly he dropped beside her and drew her full length to fuse their burning flesh together. As they rolled over in the welter of covers, his knee came up between her slim thighs, spreading her legs wide. Then he slid in, untested, but knowing by her writhing, arching movements she would be slick and ready to receive him. She was.

With a muffled sob of surrender, she closed her arms around his shoulders and clung to him, raising her face to kiss him blindly as he thrust deeply inside her. After a moment, he slowed their frantic movements, stroking in long, slow, languorous caresses. Sweat sheened their bodies, causing them to slip and slide like satin as they rubbed together in sensuous rhythms that left them both breathless.

When he felt her stiffen, he raised his head and watched her small, slender body redden and convulse in orgasm. Then he spilled his seed deeply within her in completion of the act and collapsed onto the bed, rolling her from beneath him but continuing to hold her fast.

Charlee slowly came back to earth, leaving the magic,

dizzying heights she had just visited. She felt Jim's warm protective body pressed comfortably against hers as he softly stroked her hair, pushing the perspiration dampened locks back from her forehead. She felt content and at peace until his words jarred her.

"Now, if you aren't already pregnant, a few more times like that ought to do the job," he murmured into her hair as he nibbled playfully on an earlobe.

She shot bolt upright in bed, with her hair flying like an iridescent curtain around her shoulders. "What do you mean, do the job," she shrieked in mortification. "I was so gratified last week for my deliverance, and now I'll have to wait and worry another month! Ooh, let me go, you . . . you womanizer, you!" She struggled to get free, swearing and spitting furiously like a cornered puma cub, but he rolled her easily back down onto the bed, laughing all the while.

"Look, my prickly Cactus Flower, get it into that pretty little head that you're not leaving here . . . ever." His golden eyes were no longer laughing now but glaring down into her green ones with possessive anger and impatience.

"And just how do you plan to keep me here? Lock me up like a prisoner? Make me into your cheap, live-in harlot? Isn't that more in Edith LeBeau's line of work? I'm sure she doesn't have to worry about getting pregnant!"

"In case you hadn't noticed, it wasn't very difficult to . . . ah . . . persuade you to stay a little while ago," he answered arrogantly as one hand trailed leisurely down her bare torso, lightly fingering the slowly fading splotches, clear evidence of her surrender and fulfillment. "Anyway, I'm not interested in Edith, only one small, green-eyed waif with changeable colored hair and a rotten temper. I plan to marry her, fool that I am."

"Even if you lock me up for a year, you can't make me marry you," she gasped back.

"I think I can," came his silky reply as his large, warm palm came to rest protectively over the concave hollow of her belly, "after you begin to swell with my child. Then you'll have to marry me, Charlee. Think of the scandal if you didn't." He shook his head in mock reproof.

"You're insane! This isn't a . . . a heathen seraglio in

Turkey. This is Texas and it's the nineteenth century. Why, Asa and Lee—''

"Work for me, and will do what they're told." He cut her off abruptly, finality evident in his tone of voice. "In case you haven't been listening to them and everyone else around here, they think I should have married you months ago. I plan to rectify that little mistake as soon as I can get you to listen to some sense."

He should have married her? He obviously felt morally obligated because of taking her virginity, and now that his precious Sina was gone, he was free to assume his responsibility to her. Charlee choked back aching tears, stubborn pride keeping them at bay while she glared mutinously back at him. "Do your damnedest. I'll never marry you!"

"Perverse, maddening female." Slade swore beneath his breath as he sat in Asa's cabin with his head in his hands. Across the table from him, the foreman was pouring two drinks. He shoved one shot toward his young boss, who took it in his hand and gulped it quickly.

Asa shook his head as he sipped his drink at a more reasonable rate. "It don't make sense, but then, women never do. 'Pears ta me if she'll let ya make love ta her, a girl like Charlee must love ya. You tell her?" His shrewd gaze fixed on Jim's slumped form.

"Tell her what?" he questioned in irritation.

"That ya love her, ya young jackass," Ketchum replied in exasperation.

Slade stopped to think, dumbstruck by the most obvious oversight. He sighed. "No, I don't recall that I ever did, for all the times I proposed to her. Dammit all, Asa, when a man asks a woman to marry him, she full well ought to have the sense to know he loves her! Anyway, she was always in such a temper, I was lucky to escape without broken bones, much less have time to explain my finer feelings to her."

The leonine head nodded dolefully. " 'Course, you never have a temper a'tall. Ya just charged in 'n grabbed her like she was a calf ta be thrown 'n branded. Ya courted Miz Sina real proper, Jim. I expect Charlee's worth the same kinda trouble, don't you?''

Charlee slept alone in her old room the next two nights. Slade had disappeared on some errand or other. Weevils brought her meals but turned a deaf ear to her pleas for help in getting back to town. Everything had been taken care of, he assured her. Gerta Raufing, her new German cook, was in charge of her boardinghouse while she was absent. Slade had notified everyone that they were getting married and going on a honeymoon to Galveston.

Realizing it would do no good to try to cajole Jim's friends, who steadfastly believed she should marry their boss, Charlee decided to use the few days while Slade was gone to plot her escape. Sleep was a long time in coming each night, filled with disturbing dreams of Slade when it did overtake her.

She woke the third day to feel the wet, cold nose of the cat snuzzling her affectionately. He had climbed silently into her bed sometime toward morning and finally decided they had slept long enough. Opening one eye, she glared at him. "If it weren't for you, I wouldn't be in this mess, you traitor. You were in on this . . . this conspiracy, weren't you?" she accused.

Hellfire looked at her calmly, as if to say, "I did it for your own good." Then he jumped down and stretched indolently. What a bother humans were.

By the time Charlee completed her morning toilette and came downstairs it was after the noon hour. She picked at the lunch Weevils had prepared for her and racked her brains for the means of escape from the old cook's watchful eye. Then she heard a team and wagon pulling up to the front door. It was Jim and Lee, returned from town with all her belongings. However, there were more items than she owned, she was certain.

"What are all these?" She eyed several large, fancy boxes suspiciously.

Slade smiled. "Just a few things I picked out for your trousseau, love. If you don't like them, we'll buy you more in Galveston." He walked briskly past her, carrying a stack of packages upstairs.

Lee followed with more packages. When everything was

deposited in her room, Jim came down to confront her. Lee and Weevils made themselves scarce.

"I have all the clothes I want, thank you, and I won't be needing a trousseau," she added emphatically.

"Be reasonable, Charlee. You can't go around indefinitely in those wrinkled riding clothes. At least look at what I selected and tell me if you hate them." His smile was guileless and sincere.

Charlee felt a sudden tightening in her throat as she looked at him. If only he loved her as she loved him. Staring deeply into those golden eyes, she felt for a moment that he did. When he reached out his hand, palm up to take her upstairs, she was unable to refuse. Woodenly she placed a small trembling hand in his and he pulled her gently toward the steps.

"I could only have a few things altered to fit you in two days time. All the rest will have to be sewn when Mrs. Mendoza gets here tomorrow." He handed her one box from the exclusive seamstress's shop, waiting for her to open it.

The forbidding Jim Slade seemed as eager and nervous as a schoolboy... or were her senses deceiving her? Gingerly she opened the box and gasped in delight as a delicate lawn dress lay before her. It was cut very simply, with a scooped neckline and puffed sleeves that ended at the elbow. The color was a soft, pale green, with a darker green sprigged pattern embroidered across the bodice and sleeves. She had been afraid he would try to make her over with the kind of elegant Hispanic clothing Tomasina wore, but this gown was a delightful surprise.

"Perfect for a picnic. Asa told me you had a good time on that picnic the other week. I'm sorry I sort of spoiled the end of that day for you, but I want to take you on a picnic today, to make it up." He waited, tentatively.

Thrown off balance by this sudden reversal in the demanding Jim Slade's personality, she pulled the dress from its box and held it up. She was certain it would fit. For the first time in weeks, she smiled at him and said, "The dress is lovely and the day seems perfect for a picnic. I'll go if you wish."

Slade was dazzled by the beauty radiating from that small

face but wary of her sudden acquiescence. "I'll see to packing a lunch. Look at the other things while I'm gone and wear the green dress, please?"

With that, he departed, leaving her to ponder her next move. If they took the wagon, she would be unable to escape. She needed access to Patchwork, and a head start. No help for that now, but she must keep her wits about her and await her chance. As she ruminated, she opened boxes, bemused by his sudden burst of generosity and the superb taste he showed in his selections. Most of the packages were filled with fabrics and accessories and the modiste's pattern drawings, which showed how the clothes would look once sewn. A riding skirt and two tailored shirts were already made up, as was the green dress and some delicate lawn undergarments. Everything was beautiful, but more important, selected with her in mind, in shades of bronze, red, green, aqua and brown. And the styles were simple, unpretentious, and very decidedly American. At least he had the good sense not to try to make her over into a *Tejano*'s lady. The last box held yards of diaphanous white silk and delicate white lace trim. It was obviously for a peignoir. Something to wear on her wedding night?

Resolutely she stuffed the silk back into the box. No, she couldn't do it, not knowing she was only a substitute for his real love, a guilty encumbrance he must make amends to by offering marriage. Oh, but how desperately she ached to go along with his high-handed plans, to become Mrs. James August Slade.

chapter
<u>22</u>

It was a lovely late fall afternoon, with the sun making its warm arch across the western sky in trailing golden

splendor. The breeze was redolent with the scent of pine and
sagebrush. The fragrance of cold roast pork, spicy German
potato salad, and sharp white cheese wafted invitingly from
an overflowing hamper sitting on the wagon floor.

Both Hellfire and Mutt had noses aquiver, edging nearer
the basket while warily eyeing one another.

"I still think it's a mistake to take both the dog and the
cat along," Jim said dubiously as he heard a faint growl
emanate indistinctly from one of their passengers.

Charlee laughed. "Hellfire goes wherever he pleases. I
don't *take* him along. And I feel guilty about poor Mutt.
Ever since I moved to town, no one's taken him hunting or
spent much time with him at all. I couldn't just ride off and
leave him sitting there, tail wagging."

He watched her sparkling, animated little face and felt a
sudden rush of tenderness. How could he ever have thought
to wed any other woman? "You're just too soft-hearted, at
least where animals are concerned, lady."

The warm, husky way he said lady made it sound like a
love word. Charlee swallowed and looked ahead, nervously,
concentrating on the scenery. They were nearing the old
mission ruins where he had promised they would picnic.
The five missions, beginning with the Alamo, were set at
roughly three-mile intervals south from the city, following
the meandering course of the San Antonio River. Their
destination was the third one, San Jose de Aguayo, thought
by many to be the loveliest.

"Oh, just think of how beautiful it once must have
been," Charlee breathed as she watched the bell tower and
dome of the basilica come into view. The limestone mortar
had crumbled, and the elaborate carved stone facade above
the doors gave only a sad hint of what had once been the
grandeur of imperial Spanish architecture, now a neglected
sentinel of bygone glory.

Slade pulled the wagon up in the shade of a copse of
willow trees beside the bubbling river's edge. A narrow
band of green meandered alongside the river, while the
surrounding open landscape was caught dusty and brown in
the dry hues of a rainless autumn.

Jim jumped from the wagon and reached up to help

Charlee down. Nervously she handed the heavy basket to him and watched him deposit it effortlessly on the ground with one hand. The cat pounced immediately after it, but Mutt had to remove his much larger and clumsier frame to the rear of the wagon to leap down. Slade stood patiently waiting for her to gather her full skirts and let him help her down. He could feel the tension in her tiny body as he swung her to the ground as easily as the lunch hamper.

She immediately swished free of the disquieting grip of his large hands, which spanned her waist so easily. Her own hands' touching of his shoulders was no less disturbing. Not wishing for any close physical contact, she quickly skipped off toward the grassy shade of one large willow.

"This is the perfect place for a picnic, I think," she pronounced while kneeling with her skirts spread in a graceful arc beside the river. She leaned over and ran one hand along the cool, sandy shallows of the water, splashing it playfully. "Full of fish, Hellfire, old boy," she teased. "Too bad you hate to get wet."

The cat ambled over and rubbed against her, while Mutt watched like a woebegone outcast from the sidelines. Jim sat the hamper down and then reached inside for the blanket folded on top. Spreading it out, he made a grand gesture for her to sit down.

"Milady, your repast awaits." His smile was so ingenuous and boyish, she found it irresistible.

Charlee sat on the blanket and opened the basket to remove the enormous feast. "Roast pork, fancy German potato salad, even an apple pie—Weevils didn't make this," she said, eyeing and sniffing the culinary perfection displayed before her.

Slade laughed. "We did want to eat the meal, didn't we? I brought it from town this morning. Your new cook, Mrs. Rauling, prepared it especially for me."

"You can charm women when it suits you," she said petulantly, irritated that her employee jumped to do his bidding so precipitously. He had taken charge of her boardinghouse just as easily as he had taken charge of her whole life!

He watched the shifting play of emotions cross her face as

she unpacked the food. Sitting down beside her, he was careful not to move too close to her. "We have to talk, Charlee," he said quietly.

She looked up. "I thought you wanted to enjoy the meal, not get indigestion right off."

He chuckled. "All right. Eat first, then talk." He placed a generous slab of the spicy roast on each plate, along with a dollop of the rich potatoes and some green beans in vinaigrette, then tore off two hunks of black bread and slathered them with butter. Hellfire waited patiently at his side until he finished with the butter, then put one tentative paw forward and stretched his neck to an incredible length, inhaling the irresistible fragrance. With a pat to the battered head, Slade laughed and offered him the remainder of the butter.

Charlee poured cool white wine into tumblers while she watched the interplay between the cat and the man. Was everything she thought her own to be usurped by this arrogant Texian? They exchanged a plate for a glass, and ate and drank in silence, broken only by the sound of the cat's rasping tongue as he attacked the butter noisily.

Mutt, eyeing the preoccupied cat, slowly eased near Charlee on the far side of the blanket, keeping the mistress between him and Hellfire's line of vision. Picking bits of pork from her plate, she fed him and talked to him while everyone ate. "You need Asa to take you out for a good long walk by the creek and bag a few squirrels, don't you, boy?"

Jim watched her, surrounded by her critters on two sides, like a princess holding court in the countryside.

"You ever miss going squirrel hunting yourself, Charlee? Baggy boys' clothes and all the freedom to roam that way?" He watched her consider her reply carefully.

"Sometimes. Not as much as at first. When I went to Deborah's and she made me dress like a lady and learn manners, I'd dream of running barefoot through the creek every night. But then after . . ." She paused and looked up at him uneasily, as if she were about to reveal too much.

"After what?"

He knew. She reddened in mortification, angry at his

presumption, afraid of his ability to read her. "You know I wanted you to notice me back then, to think of me as a woman, not just a . . . tomboy." She sighed. "But it never worked out the way I wanted."

"Oh, lady, I noticed you." He let out a long, low whistle and lay back on his elbows, stretched out on the blanket, looking up at her. "How I noticed you that day at the pool. My water sprite."

"There, you see, that's just what I mean! You were spying on me, watching me in the . . . the altogether," she stammered. "That's not the way you'd treat a lady. Telling me I danced out of step, manhandling me and embarrassing me and—"

Just then a furious hiss rent the air, followed by a ferocious growl. Slade had tossed the scraps from his plate into the grass beyond the tree while listening to Charlee's diatribe. Both Mutt and Hellfire took off after the treats, colliding over a particularly juicy pork bone. The cat stood arched with tail up straight, while the dog lowered his head and stuck out his neck while emitting a continuous low, warning growl.

Charlee clapped her hands sharply, breaking the stalemate. "You two calm down. There's plenty for each of you. See, here." She tossed a hunk of cheese to each of them, throwing wide so each had to turn and back off farther from the other to devour his prize.

Jim quickly retrieved the bone of contention and placed it in the hamper. Sitting down beside her again, he smiled and said, "You know, we've been just like those two from the day we met."

"Fighting like cats and dogs, you mean?" A wobbly smile appeared half unwillingly. "I remember how I looked in that mud wallow after I rescued my poor defenseless feline from that ferocious dog! If I had only known then how well he could defend himself, I could have saved myself a lot of grief!" She looked down at her hands, clenched tightly at her sides.

"So, you weren't always a model of decorum. You still aren't. I have bruises from that dunking in the fountain I'm sure to carry to my grave, but I love you anyway, Charlee. I don't want you to change ... just to marry me. I guess I went about it all wrong, luring you back here and trying to force you to say yes, but dammit, it seemed every time I tried to talk to you in town, some explosion or other occurred.'' He ran his fingers through his hair as he sat up, leaning forward in earnest entreaty.

She sat stiffly, staring out at the river, not daring to look at him. ''What you're saying, Jim, is that you'll do your duty and marry me now that Tomasina is out of your life.''

He took a deep breath while he frantically sought a way to compose his thoughts, and to repress the urge to pummel that mulish hard head of hers. ''Charlee, I never loved Sina. I only thought I did when I was a green boy. My family and hers had made an agreement. I felt honor-bound to go through with it. But when you came into my life, everything changed.''

''Not so I noticed! You seduced me, but you treated her with respect. She was a lady and I was a nobody,'' she spat, furious hurt tears gathering in her darkened green eyes. ''Even when you found out she was a traitor, in league with a murderer, you protected her! My God, even your fancy piece in town looked just like her. Consolation after *Sina* was gone, Jim?'' Her eyes were full of accusation.

''You mean Edith?'' he asked incredulously. ''You thought she looked like Sina? They both have black hair, for God's sake! That's all.''

She knelt now, hands on her hips, glaring at him furiously. ''You mean to sit there and tell me you didn't pick Edith because she looked amazingly like your lost ladylove?'' she railed.

He rolled back on his elbows again and laughed. ''Jesus, if you'd seen my other options at the bordello, you wouldn't be surprised I took Edith! It was either her or a horse-faced blonde, a chubby Indian girl, or a redhead wearing enough paint to coat a two-story house! It never crossed my mind that Edith resembled Sina. Anyway, she was just a conniving schemer, and I was getting rid of her that day by the fountain, no matter how it looked at the time. I don't want any more casual liaisons with whores. I want marriage with you." He knelt up and caught her hands before she could retreat from her awkward position and avoid him.

She forced herself to look in his eyes despite the pain it cost. "You let Tomasina go to save her from punishment, but it also cost you your first choice for a bride. I don't like being second choice, Jim." She tried to break free of his grip, but he held her small fists prisoner in his large hands.

"You are going to listen and listen good, Miss Know-It-All," he gritted furiously. "I didn't help Sina escape just so she could attach herself to another stupid rich old man and kill him off to inherit his fortune." At her look of startled incredulity, he went on. "I'm suffering under no illusions about what she's capable of. I only wanted to protect her family name. I owed that to her father and my own. Can you understand that, Charlee?"

She couldn't tear free of his hypnotic eyes. "Yes, I suppose so, but she's gone. How did she escape?"

"With an Englishman. I had to do the president a favor and let a British agent have something of value. We made a forced bargain of sorts." His eyes suddenly took on a devilish glint. "Tell me, Charlee, did you ever hear of an order of nuns called the Little Sisters of Mary Magdalene?"

Charlee thought for a moment. "Yes, they had a convent in St. Genevieve. A French order, very strict, total isolation from the outside world, vows of silence and complete self-sufficiency. Once a woman goes behind the barred walls, she never comes out again." A dawning understanding began to spread across her face. "You don't mean . . . you didn't!"

He nodded in mock gravity. "Of poverty, chastity, obedience, and silence, I expect the silence part will be hardest for Sina. You should have heard her shriek when I broke the news to her! You see, there's a convent of the good sisters outside New Orleans. Conveniently, my British adversary had orders to embark for home from that port city. If he ever expected to set foot in Texas again, he had to deliver an unwilling traveler to her new vocation behind those imposing barred walls."

"But surely she'd refuse," Charlee questioned, even as her eyes gleamed at the thought of Tomasina Carver outfitted in shapeless brown sackcloth.

"It was that or the district court in Houston. I sent a letter ahead of her with a sizable endowment to the order. They understood she was of unstable mind and required protective custody when Kennedy delivered her, probably bound and gagged. She won't get her hooks into another man, or kill anyone again, Charlee. It was the best compromise I could arrange." He held his breath while he waited for her reaction.

It began with a tiny giggle. He let a low chuckle of pure relief escape. She responded with a full-fledged laugh, rocking back on her heels to fall on the blanket, wiping tears of mirth from her eyes as he rolled down beside her.

They lay sprawled side by side, facing one another, and the laughter died. He reached a hand over to smooth a lock of wayward hair from her cheek. "I love you, Chastity Charlene McAllister, only you, always you. I've made a lot of mistakes, and I expect I'll make a lot more where you're concerned. But I want to marry you and no one else."

"Even if I don't always act like a lady? I have a rotten temper—"

"So do I. And I don't want a perfect, cool shell of a lady. I want a woman—a Texas woman, a woman as beautiful yet tough and resilient as a cactus flower. Will you be *my* Cactus Flower?"

"Life won't ever be dull, will it?" she ventured, her fingers trailing along his jawline.

"Asa asked me if I ever told you I loved you, and I realized I never had, until today. Of course," he said wryly, "you never gave me much of a chance."

"We have lots of time now," she said softly, waiting to hear the words once more.

"I love you, Charlee. I think I have ever since that day I saw you frolicking naked in the swimming hole, singing that bawdy song. God, I couldn't get the picture of you out of my mind, asleep or awake." He pulled her to him and began to rain soft nibbling kisses on her face.

Breathlessly she replied, "I loved you even before that— from the first time I ever saw you, towering over me so forbiddingly when I rescued a stray cat from Asa's dog. I never wanted to be a woman until that moment."

"Well, you certainly got your wish," he said fervently,

running his hands up and down her delicately curved body, pulling her protectively to him. "What do you say to a honeymoon night the day before the wedding?"

When she reached up to kiss him, it was impossible to tell if the purr of assent came from deep within her throat or that of the large orange cat watching intently from the lengthening shadows beneath the willow tree.

epilogue

Austin, Texas, February 6, 1846

The crowd gathering on the capitol grounds was boisterous and carefree, typical of Texians anytime. But this was not just any occasion. There was a sense of expectancy and impatience permeating the air.

"Some folks just want to git it done, I reckon," a grizzled veteran of San Jacinto said, spitting a wad of tobacco onto the clean carpet of grass.

Eyes shiny in excitement, a youth replied, "It's the greatest moment in our history!"

Dogs barked and babies cried. Tennessee twangs blended with Georgia drawls and harsh New England inflections. Spanish, French, and German were mixed in with the cacophony of English regional accents. All were Texians now and soon to be something more.

Charlee sat in the shade of a comfortable black buggy, leaning against the padded leather seat to rub her swollen abdomen. "Ouch, you rascal, that hurts," she groused.

Jim, standing next to the team and holding their two-year-old son Will, looked up at her with undisguised affection in his gold eyes. "All that kicking must mean it's a hellion of a daughter, just like her mama," he teased.

She wrinkled her nose at him and reached down to tousle young Will's thick yellow hair. "Or, it's another male Slade, all temper and cougar's eyes."

Just then there was a signal from the platform by the steps of the capitol building. "They're beginning, Jim. Do you think Lee will be here?" She looked uncertain.

Slade smiled and patted her hand. "If he can tear himself away from his beloved Dulcia, he'll be here . . . speak of the devil." He waved to the elegant figure striding across the grass toward them.

Lee Velasquez was taller and heavier now, a man grown, but still possessed of that irrepressible boyish charm that made his black eyes dance when he smiled. He reached up to give Charlee an affectionate hug, then shook hands with Jim and reached his arms out in invitation to young Will, who squirmed eagerly forward to be given a bird's-eye view of the festivities from his uncle's broad shoulders.

"I wasn't sure you'd be here in time," Charlee said uncertainly.

He grinned in understanding. "You mean you weren't sure if I *wanted* to see the festivities, *chica*, I know. It's all right. I understand our options, and this is the best of them. *Tejanos* and Texians will have to see it through together. Your husband fought at San Jacinto. He believes what's about to happen is for the better. So do I."

Jim gave his friend a gentle smile and said, "I'm a man with feet in both worlds, Lee. Maybe that makes it easier for me. I fought with Houston and I still follow him. This is his time above all."

The presentations had been going on for a while now. They fell silent to hear President Anson Jones give the last words of his valedictory address.

"The first act in the great drama is now performed. The Republic of Texas is no more!"

Before Governor James Pinkney Henderson gave his inaugural address, the flag of the Republic was lowered for the last time, and United States Senator Sam Houston knelt to gather its folds in his arms.

Shirl loves to hear from her readers.
You can write to her at
P.O. Box 72,
Adrian, Michigan, 49221